After  pected to was in a s

With a half-dressed man next to her. In a pair of shorts.

Right next to her. So close, she could feel the heat of his body, even though they were separated by a good buffer of space about the width of a pillow.

A pair of shorts.

Would it have been easier to turn off her racing mind if he'd been wearing, say, heavy jeans and a bulky sweater? If he hadn't stripped off his T-shirt in front of her . . . even though his back was turned?

If he'd left his hair pulled back in its tie instead of loosening it?

Sage swallowed and the sound was loud to her ears. Her insides tingled, her foot itched, she needed to move . . . but she was afraid she'd awaken him.

Or, worse, that he'd realize she wasn't sleeping.

And she couldn't put the image of his tanned, muscular shoulders out of her mind. She hadn't even known men had muscles in their back like that, rippling like gentle waves.

"Sage."

And then he touched her, brushing lightly against her arm with his fingers.

Romances by **Joss Ware**

EMBRACE THE NIGHT ETERNAL
BEYOND THE NIGHT

Forthcoming
ABANDON THE NIGHT

JOSS WARE

Joss Ware

Embrace the Night Eternal

AVON

An Imprint of HarperCollinsPublishers

This is a work of fiction. Names, characters, places, and incidents are products of the author's imagination or are used fictitiously and are not to be construed as real. Any resemblance to actual events, locales, organizations, or persons, living or dead, is entirely coincidental.

AVON BOOKS
An Imprint of HarperCollins*Publishers*
10 East 53rd Street
New York, New York 10022-5299

Copyright © 2010 by Joss Ware
ISBN 978-0-06-173402-1
www.avonromance.com

First Avon Books paperback printing: February 2010

Avon Trademark Reg. U.S. Pat. Off. and in Other Countries, Marca Registrada, Hecho en U.S.A.
HarperCollins® is a registered trademark of HarperCollins Publishers.

Printed in the U.S.A.

10 9 8 7 6 5 4 3 2 1

For my handsome boy, with much love

ACKNOWLEDGMENTS

There are so many people to thank for their support for this book and the series as a whole.

As always, thanks to my agent, Marcy Posner, and my editor, Erika Tsang, for believing in this series and helping me to get it off the ground. Also much appreciation to everyone at Avon and HarperCollins for everything from the zombie brains to the fabulous covers and the all-around support. Thank you all!

A big hug to Tim Gleason for his continued computer expertise. Here's hoping there aren't too many mistakes! (Which, of course, are all mine.)

Thanks to Kati Dancy for letting me steal the name of her blog—and for all her support on and off the Internet. Also, big thanks to Kate Garrabrant, the gals at RNTV, SciFi Guy, and all the other bloggers who've supported this series from the beginning.

Deep gratitude to Tammy Kearly and Holli Bertram for being my stalwart critique partners, and also to Jana DeLeon for being an early reader as well. As always, huge hugs to my mentor, Robyn Carr, for her unfailing support and advice.

The biggest hugs ever to Nalini Singh, Kathryn Smith,

ACKNOWLEDGMENTS

and Jeaniene Frost for the best endorsements a gal could
ask for, and for all your support and help.

And, finally, much love and many big, squishy hugs to
my husband and children—thank you for understanding
when the deadlines loom, and for all those plot-discussions
around the dinner table. I couldn't do it without you!

Embrace the Night Eternal

PROLOGUE

Sedona, Arizona
June 2010

Simon Japp was damned tired of running.

The cold, heavy weight of a Beretta's nose smashing against his forehead would be a relief. Or the barrel could be shoved into his mouth, damn the straight white teeth with which he'd been blessed, and the trigger pulled. Or firm, capable hands positioned around his skull, and the nasty, lethal twist. Quick.

Then the bliss of ignorance. Of escape.

Because, really, death was the only way to escape Mancusi.

The desert air was dry and cleaved into his raw lungs. Blinding sunlight burned gritty eyes and tightened his skin. But green clumps of brush and trees softened the arid landscape, and brilliant flowers sprang from their depths. Above and around him, the iconic red rock rose like stacked sandstone plates, all shades of flame, copper, and orange. Breathtaking from a distance, daunting from up close. No one could deny the beauty of this place.

He'd come here to Sedona, to hide. To try, anyway.

Florita, of the perky ass and multiple wrist bangles, had

rambled on about how beautiful it was in Sedona, rattling on about things like energy vortexes and crystals and shit like that. And then Rita got a little too friendly with her bodyguard, and Mancusi kicked her the hell out.

Simon had run here for no other reason than to get away from Mancusi, but he couldn't deny that he felt different here. He really did. Maybe it was just the fact that he was away from it all, even if it didn't last very long.

Nothing could erase what he'd done. Who he was.

Oh, God. He wanted to put it away, to crawl out of his skin. Out of this person.

Usually so surefooted, so sleek and feline in his movements, he stumbled. Grabbed with a shaking hand at a branch. A shadowy crevice yawned before him. Here, in the middle of nowhere, along shallow, rocky hills, small mountains, the opening of a cave.

Simon cast a glance over his shoulder. He hadn't seen Mancusi's *bolillos* for the last hour of wavering, stumbling flight, but that didn't mean they weren't hot on his heels.

Of course they were.

Of course they had found him, only a breath after he'd left East Los. Probably even before.

For his pursuers belonged to Mancusi. *El Mero Mero.*

As did he.

Dammit. *Goddammit.*

Inside, the narrow cave was cool—cooler than the air outside, anyway—and dark. Simon dragged the crushed water bottle he'd bought at the last party store and drank. The liquid instantly rebelled in his belly, and he coughed it up. It splashed over the dirt-packed floor and onto his dusty boots, just as clear as it had been going down.

Pushing back the long strands of hair clinging to his face, he swore, and then prayed as he knelt there, weak, shuddering, shaking, puking up nothing.

He hadn't done that for a long fucking time.

Prayed.

Did God care if he swore when he prayed?

Please. Aliviáname. Dammit, please.

He sagged to the ground, face into the dirt, unable to control the withdrawal shakes, the dry heaves, the incessant, paralyzing nausea. Simon inhaled sand and dust, the floor gritty beneath his cheek, dry and rough beneath his fingernails.

He closed his eyes and waited.

They'd find him here. And at last, in a spray of blood and minced bone and flesh, he'd find release.

Suddenly, the earth moved beneath him. Furious. Pained.

Deep.

Then again, harder and more violently, trembling, splitting . . . The rumbling grew louder and the ground cracked before him. Stones rained down from above, pummeling his shoulders and back.

With one last silent plea, Simon sunk into oblivion.

CHAPTER 1

City of Envy
Fifty years after

"So you do come up from out of your lair."

Sage Corrigan started, jolted from her contemplation of the sunset, and barely resisted the reflex to clap a hand to her leaping heart. She turned from the view of a roaring ball of red-orange bisected by the horizon, and saw the man . . . Simon was his name . . . standing there behind her.

A generous distance gapped between them, as if he took care not to get too close and spook her. As if she were a skittish cat.

Maybe that's what he thought. And maybe he wouldn't be too far off about that.

"Just because the only times you've seen me have been below doesn't mean that I never come outside," Sage replied, the words tripping sharply from her tongue. "I know I have pale skin, but I'm not some sort of vampire. Or . . . or . . . ghoul."

And, okay, she did spend a lot of time in the secret computer room two floors below ground level. Maybe too much time. But she was tired of being teased about it.

Even Theo Waxnicki, her closest friend, had made a few comments recently about her propensity to stay below, alone, working hard in secrecy.

That had ticked her off because Theo and his brother knew exactly why she spent so much time there. She was helping them in their secret war against the Strangers.

"Sorry. Bad joke," Simon replied. The inflection of his voice sounded different than anything she'd ever heard before—a slip of an accent, and a harsh, staccato rhythm, as if words were precious to him and therefore must be measured carefully.

"How did you find me up here, anyway?" she asked, gesturing to the rooftop area around them. The yellow glow of setting sun muted the sharpness and color of the space, and below was the City of Envy, already shadowed from the close, tall buildings.

Sage knew she sounded defensive, but it was hard to keep her voice measured when her heart was trammeling along at warp speed. She didn't know this man very well, and she had no idea what to say to him. Most of her conversations were about facts—things she found while doing her research. Easy things to talk about.

"Accidentally. I didn't follow you." He took a step back, as if to leave, his boots grinding quietly on the dingy rooftop.

Sage looked at him, suddenly feeling guilty. It wasn't his fault she couldn't carry on a conversation. "You don't have to go. It's not my view."

He paused. "You want to be alone. I understand."

"No. Wait. Really." Sage knew she sounded just as clipped as he did. She drew in a deep breath. "I don't mind."

In fact, now that she was over her initial startle, she burned with curiosity. She'd been curious about Simon

Japp and his four friends since they had arrived in Envy only a few weeks ago.

Sage was twenty-eight, born twenty-three years after what everyone called the Change—the deep-seated earthquakes, raging fires, and devastating weather that had destroyed twenty-first-century civilization and nearly all of the human race. For the last half a century, the survivors and their children and grandchildren had worked to rebuild some semblance of civilization. The result was this small pocket of a city—the largest settlement of humans—in what had once been the western United States.

Although they looked as if they were in their mid-thirties, Simon and his male friends had actually *lived* in that world fifty years ago.

And somehow, they'd been preserved, intact, for decades in a place called Sedona. They'd emerged unscathed and unchanged from a cave, half a century after the earth, and life as they'd known it, had been annihilated.

Simon was looking at her as if he wasn't sure whether to believe her implied invitation to stay—sort of sidewise—while half his attention appeared to be focused out over the city.

She was struck, as she had been every time she'd seen him, by how simply beautiful his face was. Lean and chiseled, with perfect angles at chin and jaw, cheeks and nose, his was the most handsome face she'd ever seen. He had dark, exotic eyes with slender, well-formed brows arching over them, and a mouth that looked as if it had been carved lovingly by some heavenly sculptor.

And yet, despite the startling beauty of his face, Simon had an aura of reservation about him. Reservation and . . . something else. Something she couldn't quite define.

It was in his eyes. Something haunting . . . something dark.

As always, his walnut-colored hair was pulled back in a low ponytail. It looked as if it would just brush his shoulders, but she'd never seen it loose, so she wasn't sure how long it was. He wore a crimson T-shirt that hugged his muscular upper arms and loose, comfortable pants with many pockets.

Curiosity gave her the words. "Had you been here . . . before?" She gestured to the city below, her hand spanning what had once been known as the Las Vegas Strip. She'd seen pictures of it, had heard about it from Lou and Theo Waxnicki, who had also been alive during the Change.

Now what was left of the city was known as New Vegas, or N.V.

Envy.

He stepped closer, coming nearer to the edge of the building, but not any closer to her. "Yes. Many times."

Silence descended and she followed his gaze, looking out over the landscape of buildings demolished by the furious earthquakes, of steel beams and jagged walls now sprouting trees, bushes, and grass. And beyond, to the ocean, glittering fire, bronze, and orange as the sun touched it. She knew that fifty years ago, the ocean had been nowhere near Las Vegas, and that more than half the cluster of tightly packed hotels and resorts had crumbled beneath the onslaught of the Change.

"What was it like?"

At first, she thought he might decline to answer. But then, he stepped way, *way* closer to the edge of the rooftop than she ever would, and drew in a deep breath.

"Vegas never stopped moving, or breathing. It was wall-to-wall people, lights, activity, sound. The sole purpose of the city was pleasure. Hedonism. Food, sex, money, entertainment." He looked at her, the words rolling out bitterly. "Superficial. Tawdry. Garish . . . yet, beautiful and exciting."

Sage had seen pictures, of course, but those were images, frozen in a moment. The way he spoke, with his short, sharp sentences, painted a more fluid image, albeit a tainted one.

"But now," he was saying, almost to himself, "all of that's gone. The hype. The desperation hidden beneath the lights and sounds. It's not a place for pleasure anymore. It's been reborn. There's greenery. And new life. And . . ." He seemed to catch himself, and she saw the way his jaw shifted when he closed his mouth as if to cut off the words.

"It must be horribly weird for you to see it now. After."

His reply was a derisive sound, as if to say, *Yeah, duh, of course it is.*

She gritted her teeth, mentally kicking herself for the inane comment. And she wanted to ask more, but a sound behind drew her attention. She turned. "Theo!" A rush of relief swept her, and became even stronger when she noted that he seemed to be walking on two legs and fully intact. "You're back."

He'd been gone on one of his missions for four days, working to extend the secret computer network he and his twin brother Lou were building. This particular task had been to install several network access points for what was going to be a communications and information system— a new, covert Internet—for those who joined them in the struggle against the Strangers. The NAPs were strategically located, hidden in the overgrowth of old structures or high in trees, and powered by solar energy. Neither the Strangers nor the zombie-like night monsters known as *gangas* would suspect their existence.

They hoped.

"I'm back, and in one piece. Of course." He smiled as he came toward her, smooth and easy. His tattoo of a writhing red dragon curled down from beneath the sleeve of his T-shirt to wrap around his wrist. Whenever he flexed his substantial muscles, Scarlett shimmied and curled along with them. "I knew I'd find you up here if you weren't in the computer room."

"Did you get them set up?" Sage asked. "All ten of them?"

His glance strayed behind her, obviously to Simon, who'd also turned from his contemplation of the view, and then back to Sage. It was still light enough to see the question in Theo's eyes, and something else that he quickly hooded. He stepped closer to her.

"Yes, all of them, in a fifty mile arc. As soon as you and Lou are ready, you can test their status." He paused for a moment, his eyes crinkling at the corners as he smiled. "I brought a bribe," he said, producing a small satchel he had slung behind his back, "in case you wanted to start right away."

When he produced three books from the depths of the bag, she snatched them up, then flung her arms around his neck in a big hug. *Books!* Unmildewed, unmoldered, unnibbled books.

"You know I don't need a bribe to work on the computers," she said, looking at them behind his shoulder, "but I'll take them anyway."

"I know that," he said. And his arms tightened around her just as she would have pulled away. "I'm glad I found something for you." Then she eased back, and she felt his arm loosen almost reluctantly.

"Thank you, Theo," she said, already flipping through them. He always seemed to pick novels she'd like . . . and never once had he brought back something she'd already read. And it wasn't as if there were many to choose from in the homes, stores, libraries . . . whatever . . . that he might encounter during his travels.

It was rather miraculous, really.

She glanced up from an Elizabeth Peters novel about a mummy case and found Theo looking down at her. There was an expression in his eyes that she'd never noticed before, and it made her feel hot and cold at the same time.

She glanced away, feeling a slow heat explode over her face, glad for the lowering sun and lengthening shadows to hide it . . . and noticed that Simon had gone.

Now why would the fact that she and Theo were alone suddenly make her heart start pounding? She wasn't afraid of him of course, but the way he was looking at her made her wonder how she *did* feel about him.

They'd known each other for more than fifteen years, ever since she'd come to live in Envy as a shy, withdrawn girl of twelve. Witnessing the murder of her mother tended to do that to a girl, no matter how confident she might have been before. Not that Sage had been. Confident.

Which was why her palms sprung dampness as she felt the weight of his gaze on her. Something was changing. And change always seemed to bring . . . unrest. Discomfort. Upheaval.

Theo'd always been older than Sage, but because of what had happened to him during the Change—of which he was one of the survivors—he'd stopped aging for a long time.

He looked as if he were no more than thirty, but he had been alive for seventy-seven years. Only in the last few years had his hair begun to start growing again, his beard and nails. And the few gray hairs he'd bragged about indicated that his body had begun to age at a normal rate.

"Sage," he said.

She looked up and his head bent . . . and the next thing she knew, his mouth descended and it brushed over hers. His hands had moved to the tops of her shoulders, and before she could quite assimilate the fact that Theo *had kissed her*, he did it again. Longer this time, the gentle fitting of lip to lip, barely touching, really . . . as if he, too, were afraid she was skittish as a cat.

When he lifted his face to look down at her, Sage couldn't read his expression, or what was in his eyes.

"I've wanted to do that for a long time," he said softly. Then he set her away from him, stepping back as if to give her space. As if he could tell she needed it, needed to contemplate and examine what had just happened.

Because that was what Sage did. She analyzed, dissected, weighed.

And she wasn't exactly sure how she felt about this . . . strange, crazy, unexpected event. She smiled up at Theo, not offended or put off by the fact that he'd kissed her. No woman in her right mind would be, really, once she thought about it.

But she wasn't certain how she felt about it.

He was handsome and strong, brilliant . . . and unique. Very special. And the kiss had been very tender. Warming. Unexpected. It had been a long time since she'd been kissed. She'd forgotten how nice it could be.

"It was nice," she told him, resting her hand gently against his chest where a strong heart pounded beneath her fingers.

"Nice," he said, and she could tell, even in the dusk of twilight, that he was smiling. "That's good."

She looked at him for a moment, feeling a little confused, and a little odd. She'd never really thought about him as more than a friend. What should she do now?

But Theo answered that question for her. "Are you hungry?"

"Yes," she said. "I told Lou I'd meet him for dinner."

"All right, then I can give both of you the update while we eat," Theo said, seeming to be in a particularly expansive mood. "And then you can get to work on testing out the network."

That was good. Work was something Sage understood very well.

"Finding Remington Truth isn't going to be easy," Lou Waxnicki was saying. He took a big sip of his wine and set the glass down carelessly enough to slop over its edges as Simon chose a seat next to him.

Since they were in one of Envy's communal restaurants, Lou kept his voice low and his head bent toward the others. The casino resort hotel rooms Envyites lived in didn't have kitchens, so most people took their meals in one of the three eateries and everyone took their turn with KP duty.

Although he was Theo's twin, Lou's appearance was nothing like that of his youthful-looking brother. The older man wore his silvery white hair in a ponytail at the back of his head. He also wore a pair of dark-framed, rectangular glasses that had been at the height of trend in 2010 and sported a neatly trimmed gray goatee.

"No bloody shite," replied Quent Fielding, with a bit of British in his voice. He was one of the men with whom Simon had emerged from the caves a little more than six months ago. Simon knew he'd lived some of his youth in England before moving to Boston. "It's going to be damned impossible."

"But we're going to try," Simon said, his attention drawn to the splash of cabernet on the table. It looked like a pool of shiny, dark blood. Soon it would roll to the edge and drip off. *Drip, drip, drip.*

Simon yanked his attention away, focusing on the conversation, ignoring the flash of memories. He couldn't do anything about his nightmares, but now, during the day, yes . . . it was easier to remind himself that the past was past—completely, miraculously erased. And that he would never allow himself to return to it.

"If the Strangers are so intent on finding Truth that they've been sending their *gangas* searching for him for years, he must be important," he said calmly, using a cloth napkin to wipe up the splash of wine.

Paper towels? Nonexistent in this post-manufactured society.

Lou nodded, oblivious to the mess he'd made and the ugly memories he'd churned up in Simon. "And if it's important to the Strangers, it's even more important to us. If we can find the man first . . ."

Simon knew the name Remington Truth. Most Americans who'd been alive in the early 2000s would, for Truth had been the head of National Security for the second Bush administration. Because of 9/11 and other terrorist attacks, you'd have to live under a rock not to know the name . . . and even though some of those years had been a dark blur to Simon, he hadn't been completely submerged in his misery.

Although there were times he wished he had been.

"But are we certain it's *the* Remington Truth we're looking for?" Simon asked. "And not some other symbol or object? After all, the *gangas* have been looking for him for fifty years. As dumb as they are, they should have found him by now."

"Since I'm pretty certain he was a member of the Cult of Atlantis, and we're damned sure that they were the

ones who caused the Change, I think it's a good assumption it's the actual Remington Truth," Quent replied, his
voice flat. "He and my wanked-off father, and a whole
bloody cult of rich and powerful people who decided to
annihilate the damned world. Even their own country-
men. And their goddamn families."

Loathing burned in Quent's blue eyes, and Simon
couldn't blame him. When Quent had seen a picture of
the Stranger leaders and recognized his father, Quentin
Parris Brummell Fielding, Jr., as one of them, the pieces
of the puzzle had fallen into place. In the photo, Fielding
had looked exactly the same as he had fifty years earlier.

The man had not aged, and he had somehow become
one of the immortal Strangers, who wore glowing crystals in their skin. Quent's recognition of his father had
been the confirmation of what the Waxnicki brothers had
suspected for half a century: the Change had been not
only man-made, but premeditated.

That was why they were intent on destroying the
Strangers.

If Simon had been unconvinced as to the Strangers'
threat to humans and chalked it up to Lou Waxnicki's
paranoia (as was the case with most Envyites), that hesitation had been put to rest two weeks ago, when he and
his friends had helped to free a group of teenagers from
the Strangers. They'd been abducted and would have been
sold into slavery.

Slavery. Beholden to, owned and abused by another.

Sometimes life could be worse than death.

"Building our network and identifying trusted contacts
will help," Lou said, taking another drink. "When Theo
gets back, we should have a fifty-mile circumference of
network points in place."

"He's back," Simon told him. "I just saw him awhile ago."

Lou looked surprised, and Simon could understand why. One would think that his brother, and partner, would be the first person he would see on his return . . . at least, if one didn't know he was in love with Sage and would, of course, seek her out first.

"Speak of the devil," Lou said, looking toward the door.

But Simon, who never sat without a view of all entrances and exits, and with his back protected by the wall, had already seen Sage and Theo walk in.

He hoped it didn't show in his face, the way his chest squeezed when he saw her, but Holy Mother of God, she was beautiful.

Simon, who had run with and met, and even slept with, a variety of gorgeous women in L.A.—the stock of starlet wannabes who would do anything to get ahead—could hardly breathe when he looked at Sage Corrigan.

Part of it was that what he saw was what God had given her. There was no plastic surgery, no makeup, no hair dye and highlights, no orthodontics in this world. So he knew that the impossible color of her long, curling hair—the color of a shiny new penny with a rosy tinge—was natural. And the unusual blue eyes, pale and vivid, weren't helped by tinted contacts. Ivory skin, fair and luminous as if she glowed from inside.

She wore her hair loosely tied back, with little tendrils curling around her face, and a casual off-white dress that fell in a single line from shoulder nearly to the floor. Sage carried the books Theo had given her, and as they walked across the room toward them, Simon noticed the way the other patrons turned, watching her.

Not men staring at her with lust or appreciation in their eyes, or women with envy or even admiration. Not curiously or with interest.

No. The room took on a sort of tension. Unease. Revulsion.

The sort of thing that would happen when Mancusi entered a place like Nobu or Sunset Tower. Though the other patrons and staff knew who and what he was, they dared not express their opinion of him . . . but the expression in the eyes, the physical distancing, the little hush of silence . . . told it all.

Sage noticed it too. Simon could see by the way she moved a bit closer to Theo, almost behind him. He didn't recognize fear or anger in her face. Yet, she kept her eyes focused straight ahead, toward Lou, resignation in her demeanor.

Simon's eyes narrowed, and he straightened, primed and ready for anything. His hand slid automatically to the shoulder holster under his jacket before he realized not only did he not wear a jacket, but he had long given up the holster and its weapon.

And the life it represented.

When Sage reached the table, which was tucked into a dim corner, she sat with her back to the room. Theo settled next to her. And Simon continued to observe the other diners, waiting to see what . . . if anything . . . would transpire.

Hell, if this was what happened when she ventured into public, no wonder she remained cloistered in that computer lab.

Simon's attention remained split between the conversation between Theo and Lou and the rest of the room, a simple habit for him to fall back into. After a moment, that odd tension eased a bit, likely because Sage was now out of sight of the others. Still, he continued to scan the room.

"I've already begun my search on Remington Truth,"

Sage announced, glancing at Quent. "Once you'd mentioned that he was a close friend of your father, and a member of the Cult of Atlantis, I dug deeper. And since the Strangers are looking for him too, I've been focusing on that." She shrugged and spread her hands. "There's a lot of data, and I'm not sure what to look for."

Simon remained silent. Not because he didn't have anything to contribute to the conversation—as a matter of fact, he did—but because he preferred to remain unnoticed, nonparticipatory, under the radar, so to speak. That was part of the reason Mancusi had called him a shadow. Silent, smooth . . . deadly.

He'd share his information after pursuing it himself, if there was anything worthwhile to share.

"But doesn't it seem odd that they've been looking for fifty years and haven't found him?" Sage asked, voicing Simon's own question from earlier. "And if he was a Stranger, wouldn't he be with them anyway?"

"How do we know they've been looking for him for that long?" asked Quent.

Lou adjusted his glasses and set down his *wineglass,* which was empty. "Because the *gangas* came on the scene about seven or eight months after the Change. From the first time we saw and heard them, we thought they were saying 'Ruth' over and over again."

"But when Jade was captured by Preston, she figured it out and realized they were saying 'Remington Truth,'" Sage added unnecessarily. Simon had noticed she liked to spout information whenever the chance arose. "She mentioned that he seemed almost afraid when she asked him about Truth."

Jade was a friend of Sage's, and a member of the Resistance. When the teenagers had been abducted, she'd also been captured by Preston—a Stranger who'd once enslaved her after murdering her husband.

"I made her write it down for me, exactly what he told her," Lou said, pulling a worn little notebook from his shirt pocket. "My memory's not as good as it used to be." He flipped through a few dog-eared pages, then read, "The only one who knows about everything is Remington Truth. And until we find him, Fielding has no power over me or anyone else."

"That's basically what he said," Theo agreed, resting his elbow on the table in a display of his muscular, dragon-tattooed arm. "Sounds like they're desperate to find him . . . maybe to put him out of commission or at least under their control."

"Well, if he's alive, he should look the same as he did before the Change," Sage said. "That's assuming, as a member of the Cult of Atlantis, that he has the same immortality as the rest of them and that he wears a crystal."

"Did you find a picture of him?" Simon asked. He knew she did her research through a sort of cobbled-together Internet that the Waxnicki brothers had been building for the last half-century.

The way they'd explained it, they'd been able to take cached information from any hard drives they were able to find from undamaged personal computers, as well as the big backup caches from local or national hosting and search engine companies like Google, Yahoo!, Comcast, and so on, to re-create a static picture of the Web. That meant that any link might lead to a website with missing pages or images, leaving them with lots of holes. But the more information they gathered, the more holes were plugged. Simon had found Internet research less than a barrel of laughs on its own, but in this case, the process must be ridiculously tedious.

Sage nodded. "I did find several pictures of him that were recent—or at least, recent in relation to the Change—so we know what he looks like. I have some printouts here," she said, half rising to dig into the pocket of her long, loose dress.

As she leaned forward, the vee-necked bodice gapped a little, offering a teasing peek of glowing, freckle-dusted skin and an enticing curve.

Simon dragged his eyes from her and focused them on the edge of the table. She probably figured the dress, which had some sort of curly feminine stuff along the edges and hem so it wasn't completely sacklike, enveloped her enough that no one would notice her curves. She would be wrong.

He'd walked onto the roof and found her standing there, the blazing ball that was the sun lighting a fiery nimbus around her amazing hair, making the ends burn and shimmer, settling a brilliant red glow over her figure, and, yeah, *through* the light, pale-colored material of her dress—he'd seen more than he should have . . . but less than he wanted to.

Simon would have walked away, leaving her to her solitude if she hadn't started talking to him. Since they'd exchanged maybe five words including introductions since their first meeting, he found himself intrigued that she meant to press the conversation. She showed no sign of apprehension or nervousness at his presence.

But then again, Sage Corrigan didn't know anything about him. How bloody his hands were, and how black his conscience was, how irredeemable and unholy he'd been.

Now, she tossed a thick fold of paper onto the table and settled back into her chair, the teasing bodice sliding into place.

"I made several copies," she said as Theo unfolded the papers and passed them out. "I suppose showing them to people might help us locate the man, if he still exists. There aren't many places he could be. But I—"

"Unless he's holed up somewhere alone," Theo said. "Which is where I'd fucking be if I knew all the Strangers and their *gangas* were after me."

"Looks like a bloody wanker to me," said Quent, who'd barely glanced at the picture. Bitterness flattened his aristocratic features.

"He was born in nineteen fifty-seven," Sage said as she shoved one of the papers across to Simon. "Grew up in Boston, went to Boston College for mathematics and joined the CIA. Stationed in Russia for a time, then Turkey, then came back to . . . where was it? Not Quantico. The other place. Anyway—"

"I'm sure you have it all written down, organized chronologically," Theo interrupted. "If I know you."

Simon glanced at him, surprised at the faintly dismissive tone in his voice. Not really dismissive, but . . . he couldn't put his finger on it. And when Theo reached over and squeezed Sage's delicate wrist, smiling at her as if she were a puppy who'd just done a new trick, it was all Simon could do not to shake his head.

Right, vato. *Treat her like a child.*

Sage settled back in her chair, smiling sweetly. The reserved curve of her lips had the effect of elongating her face a bit, making it look almost feline. "You're right. I can give it to you without rambling on about it. But at least you know what he looks like."

Well, at least Dragon Boy hadn't ruffled her feathers.

But the guy had sure been annoyed when he came upon Simon and Sage on the roof together earlier. Simon had met Theo's immediate questioning—then warning—gaze with a blunt one of his own: *message received, but don't fuck with me.*

The old Simon, the one from East Los who always carried and was tied to Mancusi, would have raised both his hackles and the blade he carried in his boot, and drawn a little blood on that overkill dragon tattoo to prove his point.

Whether he gave a shit about the woman or not.

But this Simon, the mellow one, the one who'd had the miracle of rebirth, had merely snorted to himself and walked away.

Now Simon reapplied himself to the crinkled paper in front of him and took a good look at Remington Truth. The face in the photo was familiar, but Simon had never had reason to study the man. He looked about mid-fifty, with startling dark blue eyes and silvery hair. His features were unremarkable except for the piercing gaze that displayed marked intelligence, and a strong, determined chin. From the picture, he appeared rather stocky but not unhealthily so.

"That's why the *gangas* take only blondes, and kill everyone else," Simon mused, half to himself. "They're looking for a man with silver hair."

"But they've been known to take light-headed women too," Quent said, smoothing his blond hair. He'd taken to wearing a bandanna whenever he might be out of Envy's protective walls at night.

"Yeah, but they're dumb as stumps," Theo said with a quick smile, "so they probably can't tell a woman from a man anyway. They just know they're looking for someone with hair that's not dark."

Simon realized that Sage had stood, and was now bending to give Lou a quick hug. "See you all later," she said with a smile as she straightened. "I've got stuff to do."

"Have fun," said Theo, his eyes lingering on her for a moment. "I'll stop by later to see how things are going." As Sage walked away, he returned to his companions, glancing at Simon as if to check whether he was watching his woman.

He wasn't.

He was watching the other patrons.

A few of them stared, giving snide looks as she passed by, and Simon recognized the same tautness as before . . . subtle, again, but noticeable if one were looking for it. Lou and Theo didn't seem to be aware of the unpleasant attention that Sage attracted, or if they were, they'd become used to it and dismissed it.

Sage, head high and appearing to ignore the looks, passed through the restaurant without any incident, but Simon felt uneasy nevertheless. He glanced at Theo again, who was in a lighthearted argument with his brother about who was more godlike—Donald Knuth or someone called the Woz.

"I'm going to head up," he said, standing abruptly, still eyeing the room.

"You're not eating?" Quent asked.

Simon shrugged. He'd noticed Sage hadn't eaten either and wondered why no one had commented. Either they didn't notice or didn't care, or she was so independent or that much of a recluse that she was left to her own devices. He wasn't certain if either instance would be considered flattering. "Not hungry. See you later."

"Well, I'm going to eat," said Lou, waving over one of the waitresses as Simon left. "Tonight's meatloaf night."

As Simon passed through the restaurant, he continued to scan the tables, noting with relief that none of them had emptied or changed since Sage's exit. That was good.

The restaurant had once been part of a cluster of eater-

ies and shops in the lobby of New York–New York Casino
and Resort that were made to look like street blocks in the
Big Apple. The area had been maintained as well as possible—which was to say, very well—since the Change, and
Simon found that much of the basic setup was intact. A
little shabby, not so obviously NYC-ish. The high ceiling
that had covered the lobby area now had some skylights
in it (likely holes that hadn't been able to be fixed and now
protected by screens or pieces of glass). Some living trees
and bushes grew as well, and someone had even taken the
time to plant a random cluster of flowers.

He left the restaurant and walked along in the path that
Sage likely would have taken if she were going back to
the secret computer lab. He listened carefully, passing
one of the ballrooms that had been turned into a movie
theater. Tonight's feature was *Pirates of the Caribbean,*
causing Simon to roll his eyes because, living in L.A. and
frequenting places like Chateau Marmot and Nobu, he'd
been mistaken more than once for the star of that film.

He hadn't seen the resemblance except for the long
dark hair, but what the hell.

At least he hadn't been mistaken for that lip-glossed
pretty boy *bolillo* Orlando Bloom who couldn't even
grow a full beard.

Simon strolled along the way, moving beyond what had
been the tourist area toward the administrative wing of
the casino.

He turned down a hall that led to the depths of the old
hotel, brushing past a warped wooden park bench flanked
by two bushes, and would have continued on his way if he
hadn't seen it out of the corner of his eye.

Open, pages bent, its soft cover crumpled at the corner,
just beneath the shadow of the bench: a book.

Vegas!

I'm staring out the window, looking down on the Strip. It's two in the morning and it's still incredible. The lights, the sounds, the people, all the activity—it's nonstop. They say that New York is the city that never sleeps, but I think it's truer for Vegas. And it's all contained in a much smaller area. Pleasure within walking distance. I love Vegas!!!!

Drew and I had our first dinner as a married couple (the reception yesterday didn't count—but it was great seeing all of you there!) at a great Italian place, and then lost $20 each playing slots. Tomorrow, we'll sleep in, have breakfast in bed, and then hit the Strip. Two more days of bliss!

But for now . . . Drew's giving me that look. Better close up the laptop and join him. This is, after all, the honeymoon suite. *wink*

—from Adventures in Juliedom:
The blog of Julie Davis Beecher

CHAPTER 2

It happened so quickly that Sage didn't have the chance to cry out.

Strong hands shoved her hard, whipping her against a wall. Her temple and shoulder slammed into it, and the books slipped from her fingers as she struggled to recover from the sudden assault. But by then, he'd yanked her around so quickly that she couldn't keep her balance, and his fingers closed over her mouth, pinching into her cheeks. Her head and shoulder throbbed but she tried to shake off the shock and fear, twisting beneath his grip as the man dragged her into a dimly lit area.

"This way, little Cor-Whore," he said, his voice low and steady.

A room. The door closed quietly behind them as he shoved her down hard. She crashed into a table, its edge banging into the back of her hips, and she cried out at the pain as much as to raise alarm. In the dim light, she could see little detail of her attacker, other than that he was a man of average size and height.

Fear threatened to clog her mind, paralyzing her, but Sage forced herself to push it away. To concentrate and pull from the dregs of her memory the moves Theo had taught her.

Use your legs. They're the strongest part of your body.

She collapsed on the floor, tumbling half under the table, her dress wrapping around her, but oh, thank God, she felt a wobbly metal leg.

"Now, let's take care of some business," he said, a hint of laughter in his voice. "Come on, now. Don't be shy."

As the man lunged toward her, Sage surged up from beneath the back of the table as she lifted it. The table tumbled forward and she scuttled back as it crashed onto his feet or arm or something—she didn't know and didn't care.

He grunted with rage and came after her again, but Sage knew she couldn't get past him to the door, so she'd remained on the floor with her legs half-bent as Theo had taught her, gasping for breath, trying to focus the pain away. As he lunged, she slammed her feet forward with all of her might, catching him in the gut and sending him off balance.

Scrambling to her feet, head and shoulder aching, hardly able to move from the pain in her lower back, she stumbled toward the faint outline of the door. But a hand lashed out and grabbed at her ankle, and with a hard yank, he dropped her to the tile, palm-flat, knee-hard.

Sage shrieked with rage and pain and tried to crawl away as he dragged her back toward him, her dress bunching and catching up around her hips. His fingers curled tightly into her right ankle and then his other hand pulled on her bare leg, and then as she came close enough, he backhanded her across the face.

Even in the dimness, she saw stars and a streak of light, then felt the wave of pain and grasping, clawing fingers tugging at her dress. "Now, that's more like it," he said as she struggled to breathe, to regain her focus, not to think about where his hands had moved . . .

She thought she was imagining it when the light seemed to grow brighter, but that galvanized her into hope. Sage twisted one hand away and, as he was tearing at her dress, buttons flying, she slammed her palm up and into his nose. *Aim for the septum.*

Something crunched beneath her hand, he cried out, and then suddenly, he was gone. Lifted, like a puppet . . . and then his silhouette was flying through the air. Sage heard the crash as he landed on some furniture, and then the unmistakable sounds of fists thudding into flesh and bone, and even over the man's groans and the slams and slaps, she discerned a nauseating crackling sound.

Sage pulled to her feet, knees weak and fingers trembling, just in time to see her attacker slammed down onto a table—ouch, no, it was the *edge* of the overturned table onto which he was shoved, bent backward over, by a powerful hand at his throat.

She recognized Simon with a little jolt of surprise, and then the surprise was replaced by awe. Unruffled, unmoved, he held the man's life in the palm of his hand, in the little vee of his thumb and forefinger jammed up against the attacker's neck. One twitch, one twist and she knew it would be all over.

"Wait," she said, pleased that her voice came out steady, if a bit husky from the dryness that barely allowed her to swallow. "Uh—Simon?"

He turned to look at her, casual in his movements, unquestionably certain of his control of the situation—as if she'd simply hailed him while walking into the room, not as if he'd just finished beating the bunk out of the guy. He wasn't even breathing heavily and his dark hair was still pulled back neatly in its low-riding tail.

Unlike hers, which straggled in her eyes.

Simon nodded, and Sage took that as invitation to

approach. He didn't talk much, but in this case, speech wasn't necessary.

She walked closer, steadying herself, feeling the rush of adrenaline still burning through her. Her fingers were shaking, and she would probably puke as soon as she was alone, but she refused to cower in front of this man who'd tried to violate her. She might be a curdled mess inside, but she wasn't about to show it.

"Someone you know?" he asked.

The door hung open, allowing plenty of light into the room for her to see details. Even through the shiny dark blood that dripped from the attacker's face, and the eye that was beginning to swell shut, she knew she'd never met him before. "No."

Then she looked at Simon, who'd not moved a muscle, except perhaps to tighten his fingers warningly over the man's throat—for he'd stopped struggling and simply rasped heavily. She noticed that Simon's tee was stained with what had to be blood, and that there was a streak along the shoulder of the unbuttoned shirt he wore over it, but there wasn't a cut or bruise on his face, nor was the tee even untucked from his many-pocketed pants. The light from the door poured in behind him, casting his beautiful, carved features half in shadow.

"Could you just . . . step aside a bit?" she asked.

Sage could have sworn she saw the white flash of a smile, but if she did, it was gone just as quickly. He moved to the side, still holding her assailant. She walked up to her attacker and, without hesitation, jammed her knee into his groin.

"Don't ever come near me again," she said as he squealed and choked beneath Simon's hand. An elegant hand, wide and dark with slender fingers that looked as if they couldn't be strong enough to hold a man at bay. He wore a strap around his tanned wrist, flat and smooth.

"You heard the lady," Simon added, then as nonchalantly as if he'd shaken the man's hand, he released him and turned to Sage. "What do you want me to do with him?"

"What do you mean?" Despite the casualness of his demeanor, now that they were facing each other, she could see the danger in his eyes. Cold and merciless. Was he asking if she wanted him to *kill* him? Or what? She felt a little tremor deep inside her belly and bit her lip. Ow. It was sore and puffy from when the guy'd hit her.

Simon shrugged, a subtle movement as if he were as spare with his gestures as he was with his words. "The cops? Jail?"

Sage glanced at the sorry excuse for a man, who looked as if he were about to expire on the spot. He wasn't going anywhere for a while. And she really didn't want to draw attention to herself.

As if reading her mind, Simon looked back down at the puddle of skin, bones, and sticky blood. There might have been a heartbeat in there, too, somewhere, and maybe a few working organs. But no brain to speak of.

"If I see you near her again—or hear about any other incident, I'll break both of your legs. Into four pieces each." He said it as if he were ordering a dish of ice cream. With caramel sauce. "And then I'll sic her on you to finish the job."

Sage felt the man shiver next to her leg and felt a grain of pity for him. Only a grain. Then it was gone. "Leave him here," she said, answering his original question. "He won't bother me again."

Simon gave a nod. He didn't say anything, but she felt his eyes score over her as if to ensure that she was all right. As he did that, Sage realized that the bodice of her dress hung open, torn to her waist, barely clinging to her shoulders.

"Here," he said, slipping off the shirt he wore over his tee.

She took it. The fabric was warm and well wòrn, and she slipped her arms through the sleeves, unable to ignore the scent that came with it. Nothing that she could identify, but it was subtle and masculine, and she liked it. She buttoned it and rolled up the sleeves even more than they'd already been rolled.

"You broke his nose," Simon commented, directing her toward the door.

"Did I?" Sage was more than willing to leave, as she felt the adrenaline beginning to subside. Her knees buckled as she took a step, but she caught herself before Simon noticed, and she swallowed back the nausea that threatened to bubble up from her suddenly churning stomach. She was glad he hadn't made any move to comfort her, to put his arms around her or to otherwise croon over her, pet her—do all the things people did when something awful happened.

She wasn't a child, needing to be held and petted, tears brushed away. She could handle this. The worst that had happened, thank God, was a few bruises and a torn dress. Jade hated that sundress anyway, so she'd be glad it was ruined. Even Flo wouldn't be able to fix it.

And besides, if Simon was going to touch her, she didn't want it to be because he felt pity for her.

Whoa.

She almost stopped walking, the thought had been so . . . unexpected. So non sequitur So . . . odd.

Her belly tingling, Sage resisted the strong urge to look up at him. "Thank you," she said, realizing suddenly that she'd been remiss in expressing her gratitude. She might have broken the guy's nose and fought back, but he'd been gaining the upper hand. If Simon hadn't arrived . . .

He shrugged again as he closed the door behind them. "Here," he said, and handed her one of the books.

"Oh, thank you," she said, taking it and clasping it to her chest. "I was afraid it had gotten lost or destroyed."

"Here's the other." He bent and retrieved it from under a low-growing bush.

"How did you find me? How did you know?"

"The book."

She shook her head. "I mean, you were eating—or going to eat. Why did you leave? And how did you know to come . . . this way?"

Now he looked uncomfortable, then all expression was wiped from his face. "I had a feeling." He shrugged again.

A feeling. Sage narrowed her eyes as if that would help her read his mind. It didn't. But then, before she could speak, she heard her name and turned to see Theo approaching.

He took one look at her, and even from the distance she could see his face turn shocked, then black with anger. She must look terrible if he could tell something was wrong that far away. Sage automatically brushed her hair back, refastening most of it in its band, and adjusted Simon's shirt over her torso.

"What happened?" Theo fairly ran up to them, glancing at her, and then turning to Simon. He bristled with ferocity. "What the hell happened?"

It took Sage a moment to realize that Theo wasn't accusing Simon—which had been her first thought after seeing his expression—and that not only was he asking *Simon* to explain what had happened to *her*, but he wasn't even acknowledging her, let alone asking how she felt.

But then Theo, her dear friend who'd *kissed* her earlier tonight (a consequence which still surprised her), curled an arm around her shoulders and tugged her up against his side. Hard and tight. Still not looking at her . . . but now she felt the rage and trembling beneath his skin.

"Why don't you ask Sage?" Simon replied coolly. Again, she noticed that flavor of an accent in his voice. "She broke the bastard's nose." He met Theo's eyes and she felt as if some sort of message passed between them that she didn't comprehend. Then, with the barest of nods in her direction, he turned and walked away. Casual, loose, easy.

And as he disappeared into the shadows, the last bit of her control slipped away. Her stomach swirled like a vortex. She looked up at Theo and said, "Get me out of here. I don't—"

But it was too late. She lunged for the bush and barely made it before her stomach rebelled.

He gently pulled the straggling hair back from her face as she bent and violently emptied her belly.

Theo. Lucky she had such a good friend that would stand by, holding her hair and wiping her face while she puked.

Simon told himself he should seize the opportunity.

He'd only been to the underground computer lab a few times since he and the others arrived in Envy and were brought into the inner circle of the Waxnickis' Resistance, but he knew the way. And now that Sage was with Theo, they'd be busy for a few minutes—hopefully longer, if Theo would hitch his *ganas* up and do something other than flex that ridiculous dragon *placa* and look at the woman with puppy-dog eyes when he thought no one was watching.

Chavala. *Take her back to her room, or* your *room or somewhere and tell her how it is.*

At the very least, Simon was glad to escape from what he recognized as a rapidly deteriorating situation. Sage was about to fall apart, and the last thing he needed was to be trying to comfort her. He didn't need to be getting anywhere near those delicate shoulders and slender hands and that long, thick, fascinating hair. He could fairly smell her innocence, all wrapped up in that smooth skin and intelligent blue eyes. Hell, her upper lip had a small freckle right on it, right at the fullest part, and every time he noticed it, the bottom dropped out of his stomach.

No. He needed to get far away from the breakdown on the horizon. Especially since he didn't want to deal with the complication of Theo coming upon such a scene.

Not to mention the fact that he'd just about gone over the edge—*back* over the edge—there in that room. He was right there, right on the fucking line. It would have been so easy . . . too easy . . . to finish the *gabacho* off. He'd killed for much less. Those dirty hands and greedy mouth manhandling Sage, tearing at her—

Simon blanked his mind. *No. Don't fucking go there.*

But it still nestled in his body, that cold rage, as he cruised quickly and silently through the hallways that led to the uninhabited part of the hotel.

He could have acted on that rage, and no one would have been the wiser. In fact, in this world, it was more than like the Old West—a man had to take the law into his own hands because there wasn't widespread authority.

There were a few small prisons cells in Envy, but not much of a legal system. Simple trial by jury . . . if anyone made it that far. No, most of the time, it was up to the individual to mete out the punishment if someone was caught in the act, which could include banishment.

But Simon had a more severe punishment in mind, and he found the thought more tempting than he fucking should.

He could even go back now and take care of the bastard. A heartbeat, a quick twist and a snap or a well-placed slice, and it would be over.

Simon strode faster, putting distance between himself and the temptation. Stepping over that line, even in this case, would be only the beginning of a very slippery slope.

Now he understood what Jesus felt like in the desert, when Satan had tempted him. The enticement was everywhere . . . and he had to fight it. Though he had the power, the strength, and the protection, he couldn't act on it.

At last he reached the split doors that led to the old elevator shaft. The area was dim and cluttered with debris and cobwebs in staged neglect. He found it short business to open the doors, and they slid apart silently and easily once he pushed the right combination of the buttons. *Down, up, up, up, down.*

Simon's mouth twisted in a reluctant smile. Obviously the Waxnicki brothers were not only computer and electronics geniuses, but also Bond fans. He stepped through the open doors onto the landing of a tight spiral staircase, and the doors rolled closed behind him, leaving the world dark.

But he knew the trick—step on the right side of the third stair—to activate a soft glow of light.

At the bottom of the spiral was a smaller room, another display of perpetual neglect, and Simon felt around for the latch that opened the door to the lab. Moments later, he slipped inside.

The room was warm and hummed with the whir of computers and soft buzz of monitors. He found the lights that illuminated the spare space, which was filled with nothing but tables lined with computers, monitors, and keyboards. He quickly situated himself at one of the stations Sage often used.

Fully aware of the limitations of the haphazard, patch-worked Internet, Simon didn't expect to find the information so easily. But it took only a few minutes using the Yahoogle search engine to pull up the news article he remembered seeing, and to scan through to confirm his memory. He'd been right.

Considering that he'd been functionally illiterate until he was fifteen, Simon still felt a little thrill of amazement that he could so effortlessly breeze through the printed word. Even though he'd been reading fluently for more than twenty years, the memory of his frustration, and then belligerence, when it came to understanding how the letters fit together to form words had not altogether left him.

He considered his education the single gift he'd received from Mancusi. The only thing that had made his years of hell worthwhile.

Just as he turned off the computer monitor, he heard a quiet *ding*.

Pinche. Someone had just opened the elevator doors above.

Simon moved quickly to turn off the lights in the lab just as he recognized the soft ringing of footsteps on the upper stairs. He drew in a deep breath and relaxed, imagining himself seeping into nothingness, becoming unnoticeable, invisible, as he'd done many times in his old life.

Back then, it was a matter of sliding into shadows, flattening himself against a wall, slipping silently from a room.

But now . . . it was real.

Simon heard the steps coming closer and recognized two pairs of feet. Just fucking great. Sage and Theo.

Coming down here.

Nice place for a seduction, *vato*. The computer lab.

Simon remained focused, for it was still new to him— this ability to become nothing. To shimmer into invisibility. It was so new, in fact, that he hadn't told anyone about it yet—even Elliott and Quent, who also had discovered supernatural powers since coming out of the cave. He was still trying to figure it out himself.

Simon had to think about it, concentrate, and breathe carefully. And he'd only seen himself do it once, after they'd arrived in Envy and he had privacy and a mirror with which to practice.

Shimmering into nothing was pretty much how he'd describe it. One minute he was there, the next . . . he sort of evaporated after turning transparent and wavered away.

Sage and Theo had reached the bottom steps. She brushed past him, close enough that he felt her warmth. And smelled the fresh, pure scent that seemed to accompany her every move.

His concentration wavered, and Simon closed his eyes. *Focus.*

It wasn't that he wasn't allowed down here. It was simply that he didn't want to have to explain his purpose for being there. His lead would either pan out or it wouldn't and why waste anyone else's time or energy if it didn't?

Now they were talking quietly, and Simon felt in control enough to look over as Sage took her regular seat at a bank of five computer keyboards and monitors. Theo stood behind her, and Simon watched as the other man slowly lifted his hand, pausing over her head, as if to settle it on top of her bright, warm hair.

Simon turned away and slipped silently, unnoticed, from the lab.

Thank God he had the power of invisibility—otherwise he might be forced to watch Dragon Boy try his hand at seduction.

That would be excruciating.

In more ways than one.

Sage dragged her dry eyes open, delighted that the sun had begun to peep over the eastern horizon. Now she had no more reason to stay in bed and try to sleep.

As she surged up from beneath her covers, Sage glanced at the empty bed in the hotel room she'd shared with Jade, who now shared a room—and bed—with Simon's friend Dr. Elliott Drake. She yawned, not because she'd just awakened, but because she hadn't slept much. Weariness curled through her body, but her mind was bright-eyed and bushy-tailed. She hated when that happened.

She slid out of bed and padded to the bathroom, afraid to even look at the rat's nest of her hair.

The nightmares she might have expected after her attack had been tempered by other convoluted things. Yes, there'd been some dark moments twisting in her dreams—the suffocating feel of heavy hands and a dominating weight, but thankfully, those images had slid away to be replaced by other, more intriguing, ones.

Memories of Theo's kiss on the rooftop . . . that soft, hesitant brush of lips. The "I'll take it" response and his sober, hopeful eyes after she told him it was nice.

The way Simon Japp had appeared moments before,

standing at the very edge of the roof, *much* too close to the edge—as if he flirted with danger. The red sun blazed in front of him, swathing him in fire. He stood tall and lean and controlled . . . yet lonely.

And then, a very different Simon, dangerous and hard, violence rolling from him as he held her attacker's life in his hands. The drawn expression, the elegant hand, the spare, swift movements. The very thought of him made her belly tingle.

Theo's gentle fingers brushing the hair from her face as she vomited in the bush, offering his shirt to wipe her mouth, then taking her to get some water so she could freshen up and rinse out her mouth. But then he tried to insist that she go back to her room to rest, as if she were a fragile child, and her insistence that she had work to do.

Didn't he understand? She needed to do something to get her mind off the attack.

For some reason, when she and Theo had come into the computer lab, Sage had felt certain she'd find Simon there. She swore she sensed him, maybe smelled his scent . . . but that was absurd. He had no reason to be there, and if he'd been, he'd had no reason to hide. And she probably just smelled his shirt that she still wore.

And what made her so psychic all of a sudden? He wasn't there, she and Theo were—and they'd ended up getting into a rare argument.

Sage felt a lump in her throat as she turned on the shower. Theo was her best friend. She'd known him and Lou for fifteen years. And if it was odd that she hung around with seventy-seven-year-old twins—even though only one of them looked it—well, so be it. She was, after all, a Corrigan. A Cor-Whore, as they were labeled. Or a Falker . . . said a certain way, it sounded like a nastier word. But she'd heard worse.

As the warm blast of water sprayed down on her, washing away her weariness and the ugly thoughts, Sage raised her face and let her hair become saturated, trying to remember how she and Theo had come to argue.

She'd still been upset from tossing her cookies, still a little shaky and weak-kneed yet more than a little defiant. She had, after all, kept her head during the attack, remembered what Theo had taught her, and inflicted her own damage. That satisfying crunch beneath her palm, just before Simon dragged the man away . . . that feeling would stay with her a long time.

When Sage informed Theo of this, she felt him stiffen from where he'd been standing behind her at the computer table.

"How can you be so nonchalant about it?" he said. His hand brushed the top of her head, lighter than the wings of a butterfly, then fell away. "You were *attacked*."

"You call horking in the bushes nonchalant?" Sage retorted, turning to look up at him. "I'm far from nonchalant, Theo," she said reasonably. "See this?" She raised her hand, which trembled noticeably. "I'll probably have nightmares. And be nervous about going anywhere by myself for a while—"

"Damn straight you're not going anywhere by yourself for a while," he snapped, folding his arms over his chest. Scarlett writhed on his rippling arm, her catlike golden eye glaring at Sage from the back of Theo's hand.

"—but I'm not going to hide away."

"Isn't that what you've been doing for the last five years?" Theo returned. "Cloistering yourself down here, tapping away at the computer?"

"I've not been *hiding*!" Fury blasted through her—righteousness tinged with a bit of shame. Maybe she had. A little. "I've been working to help you and Lou and Jade."

"Look," Theo said, stepping back as if to gather his thoughts. He ran a hand through his shiny jet-black hair. "Sage. It's not your fault you attract attention. I understand why you like to stay out of sight."

"So you're saying it's my fault I was attacked?" She realized she was nearly shrieking, something that, despite her red hair, she rarely did. "Because I decided to come up from the dungeon?"

"Sage—"

"Because I walked somewhere by myself? Because of the color of my hair and eyes and skin?"

"No, it's not your fault. But you need to be more *careful*," he said. "Pay attention to what's going on around you." His voice was shaking.

She opened her mouth to shout something back at him, and realized her fingers were shaking. Tears stung her eyes and her nose was running.

"Sage," he said, now hard and clipped as if fighting for control. "I don't want anything to happen to you. I couldn't handle it."

She looked up at him, recognizing fury in his eyes. At her? He was furious with *her*?

"I know it's hard for you to think of me as—as a friend, when I'm so much older than you," he began.

Sage snorted an angry, crying, derisive laugh. Yeah, he was a *lot* older than she. He'd been around during the Change, and because of a fluke accident, his body had stopped aging for almost fifty years. Only in the last two had he begun to show signs of aging.

"I mean, you were, what . . . twelve when you came here from Falling Creek? And I was . . ." His voice trailed off as he spread his broad hands as if to say *and I was like this.*

Like this.

He looked no more than thirty, and he'd changed hardly at all in the last fifteen years.

"You look exactly the same as you did when we first met," Sage said. And probably exactly the same as he had on June 6, 2010, when everything had changed. Close-cropped ink-black hair with longish sideburns and a slightly prominent nose. He was a handsome man with dark, Asian eyes and a strong, square chin, and despite his hours hunched over a computer or digging around in an electrical box, he had long, lean muscles. Not to mention the fact that he had the ability to force a power surge from his body at will.

Suddenly, her heart was beating faster than it should have been. There was something in his eyes, something had changed. With heat swarming her cheeks, Sage remembered the kiss, the way he'd stepped closer to her suddenly, and then brushed his lips over hers.

Confused, she whirled to turn back to the computer, her heart pounding. Her palms felt damp and she began to type rapidly into the Yahoogle search box. *Remington Tr—*

"Sage," Theo said, his voice still tight. "Look. I want you to promise me that you won't go anywhere by yourself, at least for a while."

"I don't want to promise that," she said, knowing her voice was muffled. She stared at the white computer screen and saw that a list of options had dropped down below the search engine box; search strings she'd used earlier.

Remington Truth Cult of Atlantis
Remington Truth Parris Fielding
Remington Truth June 2010
Remington Truth Las Vegas condo
Las Vegas? Condo?
Now, in the steaming shower, Sage remembered the

surprise when she registered that search string. She hadn't used that phrase when searching. Huh.

This was her computer station; Theo and Lou used their own.

She'd clicked on it and pressed *GO*, feeling the weight of Theo's stare on the back of her head.

"At least I remembered the things you taught me," she said stiffly. "Simon said I broke the guy's nose."

"What's up with Simon?" Theo asked. Very casually.

She turned toward him without looking at the results on the screen. "What do you mean?"

"Is he hitting on you? Do I need to check him out, like I did for Owen?" Theo said, one side of his mouth lifting in a sort of grimacy-smile.

"*No,* he's not hitting on me," Sage said. "He's hardly said two words to me. He's . . . quiet." Well, that wasn't quite true. He'd said more than a few sentences when he talked about his memories of Las Vegas.

"Well, I wondered if I was interrupting something when I found you two on the roof today." Theo gave a little laugh.

"Nope. He was probably glad you came, because he definitely wanted an excuse to leave."

Yeah, Simon had definitely wanted to hightail it out of there. And he couldn't wait to take off tonight after he'd beat up her assailant. And that was just as well with Sage. She didn't exactly want to be seen puking her guts out. By him, anyway.

"Okay." Theo looked at her oddly for a moment, then, shoulders bunching, he turned away.

She spun slowly on her chair, back to the keyboard, feeling as if he'd meant to say something else, something more. And for some reason, the back of her neck prickled

. . . like she wasn't sure if she *wanted* to hear what he was going to say.

"Sage." He said her name suddenly, with an odd note. A sort of resolve, maybe.

The next thing she knew, he'd spun her chair back around to face him, and he lunged forward and down, hands planting on the arms of her chair.

And he kissed her.

Not at all like he'd done earlier today.

He wasn't tentative, as he fit his lips to hers, gently tucking his mouth around her top lip, then shifting as she softened against him. Sage kissed him back, slowly, examining and tasting, aware of the tenderness from the cut on her mouth. She enjoyed the way they fit together and remembered how long it had been since she'd experienced this pleasure. Years.

Then, before his hands moved, or their mouths opened, or even before her eyes closed, she heard the soft *ding* that announced an arrival.

Sage and Theo pulled away at the same moment, and he looked down at her, unmoving despite the sound of footsteps on the stairs. "Just tell me," he said quietly, a bit unsteadily, "if that was like kissing an old man."

Her eyes widened and her cheeks warmed. "No," she replied. "It was nice." She smiled, realizing that things really were changing . . . and she hoped it would be all right, whatever happened. Was he having some sort of midlife crisis? "I don't think of you as an old man, Theo. Not at all."

And just as he smiled back, his eyes settling on her in a way they never had before, the door opened and Lou appeared, saying something random about meatloaf.

Now, as Sage stepped out of the shower, tucking a

towel around her hair and another around her body, she touched her lips, remembering how full and lush they'd felt afterward. Or maybe that was just because her mouth was already swollen from being hit. She glanced toward the steamy mirror, able to see only the muted image of herself, so she swiped the fog away, leaning toward the streaky glass.

Yikes!

She stared at her face, seeing for the first time the puffiness around her eye and the darkening bruise on her cheek. Horrified, she angled closer to the mirror and observed all of the damage. A little cut on her lower lip, just below the freckle that dotted her upper one—the freckle she hated. She'd tried more than once to cover it with Flo's experimental lip color or gloss. Ugh.

At least the cut below detracted from that annoying blob on her lip.

Funny. She hadn't felt more than a twinge when Theo kissed her last night.

Theo kissed her for a second time. And for some reason, she wasn't anticipating a third time. He was nice and all, he didn't turn her off or anything, but, well, even when she'd kissed Owen, she remembered there being more of a spark. With Theo it was just . . . merely nice.

Would that change? Could one get used to kissing someone?

Sage allowed the towel to fall from her hair, and the mass of curls—now smelling of lavender and rose from Flo's shampoo and conditioner—tumbled over her pale shoulders. Even though it was wet, her hair still shone with red and orange glints, though not nearly as brightly as when it was dry.

Most of the time, she didn't mind having the Corrigan coloring—the hair, the distinctive blue eyes, the fair, fair skin that had too many freckles. But that was because she kept to herself, out of the way, out of sight for the most part. She could almost forget what it meant.

Sage touched her lips again with light fingertips and looked at herself.

Owen had done more than kiss her before they'd gone their separate ways. She felt her traitorously fair skin heat even in the steamy bathroom, remembering his hand slipping up under her T-shirt, working her bra loose and then curling up around her bare breast.

But that had been years ago. Five, six, maybe even seven. She'd lost track. Hadn't really cared to keep track.

She'd always stopped Owen's hand before it went too far south, partly because she wanted to make it clear she wasn't a Cor-Whore, and partly because she wasn't ready for that. And, frankly, after having grown up in Falling Creek and barely making it out of the settlement without being married off at fifteen, she wasn't sure when she'd ever be ready for sex.

Annoyed with her woolgathering, Sage glared at herself in the mirror and winced when she felt a pang at her sore eye. "Better quit wasting time," she lectured her reflection. "You've got things to do."

Indeed she did, for after Lou had arrived last night and fractured whatever tension had been growing between her and Theo, she'd returned to the computer screen and the search-engine results that someone had previously generated while Theo explained about the attack.

By now, the sunlight had spilled over the eastern horizon, filtering into the hotel room in which she'd made her home with Jade for the last five years. Sage worked her thick, wet hair into a braid and twisted it into a low coil on the back of her neck, then pulled on a lightweight sweater that also boasted a hood.

With her hair wet (and thus darker) and tucked away, she wouldn't be as noticeable, especially if she pulled the hood forward to partially obscure her face and wore dark sunglasses. Aside from that, it was early enough that few people would be up and about to notice her.

As she'd told Theo last night, Sage was not about to keep herself locked away, hiding from the world. His comment had hit a little too close to home for her, and that had been part of the reason she'd slept little.

Not that she was foolish. Sage slipped a knife into the pocket of her hoodie, just in case, and planned to keep specially alert.

Finally, her belly fluttering with nerves and excitement, she left her room and headed out, surprisingly glad to be up and about.

It was about time she allowed herself to live again.

Oh my God. Oh ym GOD!!!!!!!

Whats happenning???

The earthqaukes. They started this afternoon and went onfor hoiurs. Or maybe it's aftershjocks. People screamng. Ive never heard the noise of buildings falling. of crashes like this. It's terrible. It's lioke a war.

There's no one else arund! No ambulnaces or pokice. No one. Justscreams.

I onlysee dead people, inujred people everywhere I look. DRew and I have some cuts and bruises. We'te safe but we'te scareed. When will it end? WE can hasdly see thru the smoke and dust.

Outside the STrip is fillled with more screams and falling debris. Most of the lights have gone out, but there are a few left. We seefires allover, and elexctric sparks flying. It's getting darker. The ground lkeeps moving!!!!!

I wWANTt to get out ofhere, but there's mnowhere to go.

Drew is freazked, yellng at me for writign on my laptop, but it's the onyl way I can handle this. Through I casn hardly typed,, I have to qwrite it down. EVen if I can't upload it, I'll wqrite it.

> *—from Adventures in Juliedom, the blog of Julie Davis Beecher*

CHAPTER 3

Sage knew that Las Vegas had originally boasted a desert climate, but since the Change, its weather had turned damp, and almost tropical.

Lou Waxnicki believed that the appearance of a new land area in the Pacific Ocean—along with the other devastating tectonic plate movements of the massive earthquakes—had caused an adjustment of continental mass. The result, he theorized, was that the earth's axis had shifted, changing not only climate, but weather, geography, flora and fauna.

With California, Oregon, and part of Washington under the ocean, and the shoreline intruding on what had been the Strip, the land surrounding Envy now grew green and lush.

Sage had seen pictures of Las Vegas in its heyday, and as she walked from a rear entrance of New York–New York, she found herself looking about with new eyes. After hearing Simon's surprisingly poetic description the night before, she was more curious about the city and what it had been like when it was so alive. She'd never known Envy to be anything but a half-ravaged mecca of civilization in a world that reminded her of the Old West—at least, as portrayed in movies and books.

But today, she looked up at the buildings that loomed over her. New York–New York still rose fairly intact, but the ragged rooftops of other structures that hadn't fared so well caught her attention. She tried to imagine what it would have been like with pristine walls and lights and sounds and color everywhere, instead of the trees, bushes, vines, and even grasses sprouting from broken windows, ledges, crevices, and wherever their tenacious roots could delve.

Although the thoroughfare near the inhabited section of Envy was maintained and kept free of extraneous growth, the street signs were long gone—destroyed or otherwise removed. Years after the devastated area had been looted and scavenged for anything worthwhile, Envyites had no reason to venture into that area, for the disabled structures were uninhabitable and potentially dangerous.

Sage slipped the knife from her pocket as she traveled farther from the familiar part of the city toward the northeast, and let her hood fall back a bit to gain better peripheral vision. The buildings that hadn't been reduced to rubble during or after the Change clustered together, tall and dark and close, and overgrown enough that she felt as if she were approaching a dark forest. Windows broken, rusted signs and cars, jagged concrete that sprouted bushes or patches of grass . . . and silence.

What few street signs remained were often bent, crooked, or otherwise mangled—offering little in the way of direction. But Sage had scrutinized a map of the city as it had been, and, having spent enough time on the rooftop overlooking the new terrain, felt confident that she could find the building—or at least its location and remains—that had once housed a condo owned by Remington Truth.

She'd had to look up the word "condo," not being exactly sure what it meant, and had come away with the understanding that, at least in this case, it was likely some sort of penthouse or apartment.

Although she wasn't exactly sure what she thought she might find, Sage felt compelled to be doing *something* other than remaining cooped up in the computer lab. Theo had been right about that. She had hidden herself away after arriving in Envy—partly because she was a Corrigan from Falling Creek, and partly because she found it easier to spend time on the computer than to actually *talk* to people. Especially ones that treated her like a Corrigan from Falling Creek.

The structure she sought had apparently been the newest, most grand of its kind in Vegas, in an attempt to outdo the Wynn . . . and, if her calculations were correct, while the Wynn was now under the ocean, the Beretta was not. So at least in one way, the Beretta won the longevity competition.

From the images she'd been able to find, she'd also identified the building on the jagged skyline of Envy. Originally intended to be as black and sleek as the weapon for which it was named, the cluster of narrow cylinders no longer appeared as lethal as it had in the photos. Instead, many of the windows were broken, showing steel girders and the overgrown interiors of the seven cylinders of varied heights. Though it wasn't under the Pacific, the building hadn't been able to completely withstand the force of the earthquakes and storm-force gales that had followed, and a portion of the structure had caved in, crumbling away over the years.

Sage's information indicated that Remington Truth's condo had not, fortunately, been a penthouse at the topmost level but on the top of one of the shorter cylinders. That gave her hope that it might still be intact.

After nearly an hour of walking through dark, over-grown and littered streets, Sage reached the base of the building and found herself facing a twenty-foot barrier. The wall, made of hundreds of cars piled four or five atop each other, created a fence around the structure. And as she drew nearer, peering through the moldering and broken windows of the smashed vehicles, she smelled it.

The stench of *gangas*.

Her mouth dried and her heart pounded faster as she whipped around to look behind her, as if they were about to appear. Sage had only seen *gangas* from a distance, but she recognized their smell—that of death, of rotting flesh and decaying bone.

Or so she was told.

Heart pounding, listening for their *Ruuu-uuuth, ruuthhhh* moans, Sage scanned the area not only for the creatures, but also for a place to clamber up and away from them if necessary. But the sun had risen higher, casting a gentle yellow glow over the patches of ground it could reach and the sides of buildings where it could not, and she knew that the *gangas* couldn't move about in the sunlight. She was safe out here, at least.

Thus reassured, she eased up to one of the vehicles and attempted to look at the building through the jagged window, but found that other cars piled on and next to it blocked her view.

It was obvious that the fence meant to protect the building that had once housed Remington Truth—or to keep intruders out.

And more than possible that the *gangas* she smelled guarded the place.

Or was she crazy?

Sage listened, sniffed again, looked around and even paced along the fence's perimeter. But the more she thought about it, the more she believed she was right. Why else would someone build such a barrier? And there were no *gangas* in Envy—an even higher, deeper wall kept them out and the humans safe.

But apparently, someone had brought *gangas* in, secreting them here in this area separated and distant from the rest of the city.

Standing in the largest area of sunlight she could find, Sage considered her options.

Gangas were slow and clumsy. They couldn't climb. But they were bigger than a man and a half, and strong, and they ate human flesh . . . after tearing it into bite-sized pieces.

Sage didn't want to come face-to-face with one. But she also wanted to get inside that building, now certain more than ever that there was a reason to do so. Someone—the Strangers?—was protecting something.

And she wanted to find out more.

She could go back and find Theo, get him to come with her. It would be the smartest thing to do. He was superhumanly strong and he'd fought *gangas* many times before. He might be annoyed with her for coming out here on her own, but he'd want to investigate.

Then she frowned. He'd want to investigate, and he'd insist that she stay safely back home.

Sage glanced at the building again, this time peering up at the jagged shape that looked as if some gigantic scythe had hacked off its top. She had to shade her eyes to see, for the sun had risen even farther behind it, and though it was still near the horizon, it blazed hot and bright.

She froze. Had it been a trick of her eyes, or had she seen something—some*one*—moving? A shadowy figure, shifting in front of a shattered window. Too tall to be an animal, too definite to be a tree branch or vine. Too sleek and quick to be a *ganga*.

Someone was up there.

Sage swallowed. Her heart raced faster as her mind clicked through the possibilities. A Stranger, here to protect the area. Some other Envyite—a hermit who lived with the *gangas*?

Maybe even Remington Truth.

Had whoever it was seen her?

The thought sent her ducking down into the shadows of the vehicle-fence, pressing close against the cold metal, a sharp stone digging through denim into her knees. Crouching thus, she duck-walked as quickly as she could halfway around the perimeter of the barrier, stopping occasionally to peek through the spaces between the smashed cars, hoping that whoever might have seen her from the building had lost track of her presence.

She listened, sniffed, and after a bit of a panic, assured herself that no one was about. The *ganga* scent lingered, but it hadn't grown stronger, and she saw and heard nothing to announce the presence of anyone but herself. And a few bold rodents. And—

Her heart shot up into her throat. From the shadows between two close buildings she saw the lean shape of an animal. A wolf or wild dog, with pointed ears arched forward and a long dark snout. Crouching, eyes glinting in the shade, the canine fixated on her as she attempted to push closer to the car . . . as if she could become absorbed by the rusted metal.

Still watching the canine, she reached for the knife right there in her boot, sliding it free. The creature hadn't moved, but now its teeth showed, and over her pounding heart and raspy breathing, she heard its low growling breath. Without

moving her head, Sage slid her eyes away for a moment—
was there room for her to slip under the car?

But no, it was wheelless, and sat directly on the ground.
Nowhere for her to go. Nowhere but . . . *in.*

Her eyes moved back to the wolf and she felt the vibra-
tion of its tension as it gathered itself up, ready to bound
forth from the shadows. He'd be on her in a moment . . .

She gripped the knife, keeping the blade at an aggres-
sive angle—a position she'd seen on an old website about
self-defense—and felt around for the car's door handle.
Slender and cool, the handle materialized under her fingers as she eyed the wolf.

He slinked from the shadows, a gaunt creature looking
desperate and angry. Hunger and fear shone in his eyes.
He wasn't about to let this prey escape, but he was also
slightly cowed.

She half turned away, yanking desperately at what was
surely a rusted door that only a miracle would open. A
glance back told her that the wolf's hunger had won out
over his fear, and, teeth bared, he was bearing down on
her. She turned to the car, gripping her weapon, and with
a shriek of frustration, smashed the butt of the knife at the
window just above her shoulder.

The glass shattered and Sage swept the remnants out
of the way as she launched up and into the vehicle just as
the wolf leapt.

He slammed against the car, and she felt the whole
thing jolt as she tumbled into an overgrown, moldy car
seat covered with glass. Shards sliced into her palm and
upper arm, and cut through her jeans and above her knees,
but she was in, knife in hand. Scrambling around to face
him, her head bumping the half-caved roof, Sage readied
herself.

The wolf snarled and leapt at the car, but she could

fight him off with the blade now as he tried to get at her through the small opening. Blood flew, splattering her, the mildewed glass that remained at the edges, and the wolf's gleaming black nose. Fury lit its eyes as it lunged again, and she stabbed out with the knife, sending the wolf squealing and writhing away, his snout and face cut deeply.

He cried and howled, then came back once again, but Sage was ready, gripping the knife now slippery with their blood. With a grunt of exertion, she angled her weapon to the left and, when he lunged, she shoved it into the wolf's neck.

The animal froze, its body snapping and seizing . . . then suddenly went limp, sliding off the blade and slumping to the ground.

Sage sagged back into the car, bloody, trembling, queasy . . . and triumphant.

Not that she ever wanted to repeat such an event, but . . . she'd done it.

Saved herself.

Stomach still roiling, she pulled herself up from the seat of the vehicle. The heavy scent of blood tinged the air, partly from her wounds, but mostly from the dead wolf. Her belly pitched and swayed, and the rush of adrenaline had washed into weakness.

Where had he come from anyway? Envy was supposed to be safe—from *gangas* and wolves and the lions and tigers that lived beyond the walls. He'd obviously been starved and desperate.

Sage looked out from the car window, in the direction from which she'd come, back toward the civilized part of Envy, and then she turned and looked on the other side. Her knees were weak and her hands shook, but she still wanted to investigate the building.

But maybe that wasn't such a good idea. At least, not alone.

Still nauseated, she managed to get the rusted door to open by kicking at it while lifting the latch. And, for the first time in her life, Sage stepped out of a car.

The wolf lay in a bloody heap in front of her, a dark pool seeping into the dirt and grass beneath it. That was all she needed. Her stomach rebelled, and she held on to the side of the car while everything came up. Just like last night.

Wiping her mouth with the back of her hand, she took a deep breath. Then Sage cast one last, long look at the sleek Beretta building, and turned to go.

And suddenly, Simon Japp was standing there. Right in front of her. Lean, and humming with tension. His expression was more than a little frightening.

"Are you hurt?" he asked.

Sage had to blink a few times to make certain she wasn't hallucinating—and after what she'd been through, who'd blame her? Though why she should conjure up Simon Japp, in a tight black T-shirt and faded jeans, she couldn't imagine.

"Sage?" he asked, and she felt his attention swipe over her. Then linger.

"I've got a few cuts. But nothing really bad." She realized suddenly that the cut above her knee was really hurting, and that her jeans were sticking to its drying blood.

"You did that?" He gestured to the dead wolf.

Sage nodded and straightened her shoulders, showing him her knife. "I did."

"*Buena.*" Then he gestured to the blade, a sharp, short movement of annoyance. "But now you've got to clean it."

She nodded again, trying not to notice how fast her heart was pounding, and that her hands were unsteady.

Of course, anyone's heart would be racing if they'd just beaten off a wild canine, puked their second meal within twelve hours . . . and were suddenly being lectured on cleaning their knife. By a handsome, secretive man with steady, dark eyes . . . who'd appeared from nowhere.

"Did you follow me?" she asked suddenly.

"No." He shifted and she noticed how the sun filtered over him from one side, fringing his long lashes and smooth, tied-back hair, and all along a sharp cheekbone and chiseled jawline. Her mouth felt even drier.

"Are you sure?" Sage demanded, all at once annoyed at the thought of him watching her creep around the fence, and then as she desperately fought off the wolf. And, oh yeah, horking up her breakfast. Just wixy great.

It wouldn't be the first time he'd come upon her unexpectedly. He'd shown up on the roof last night. And then in the nick of time after she left the restaurant. Her heart began to pound again . . . and she wasn't sure why. Was Simon following her? Was Theo right . . . was something going on with him?

"I'm sure," Simon said, those dark eyes hard. "If I'd followed you, I'd have made sure *that* didn't happen." He shoved the wolf with his booted toe. "What the hell do you take me for?"

Sage recognized that he was truly irked and decided to believe him. And the realization followed. "You were here. In there," she amended, pointing to the Beretta building. "Weren't you?"

He hesitated a mere moment before giving a short nod.

"You saw me? How did you get past the *gangas*? There are *gangas* in there, aren't there?" she demanded. Damn it. He'd figured it out before she had, and he'd already gone in and found whatever there was to find. "Did you learn anything?"

"How did you know to come here?" he asked.

"I found your search results—it was you, wasn't it? On my computer? Searching for 'Remington Truth Las Vegas condo'?"

His mouth twitched in a sudden flicker and Sage noticed. Yes, she definitely noticed . . . they were beautiful lips. Just perfect, with sharp angles and the right amount of fullness for a man—

"And you figured it out from that?"

Sage felt her telltale fair skin warm as she realized she'd been staring, distracted. "That's what I *do*. I figure things out. Did you get in there, Simon? Really?" She tried to hide the wistfulness in her voice, the hint of petulance. "Is his place still there?"

"I think so. I didn't get all the way in . . . I left." He held his hand out. "Give that to me before the damned thing's ruined."

She realized he meant the knife, and she obeyed. The dried blood on her hand itched, and she tried to wipe it away as Simon cleaned off her blade, swiping it expertly over the side of his jeans. He handled it so easily, comfortably, and she felt a little shiver, imagining him putting it to use. The image came readily, and seemed to fit all too well with the underlying violence she sensed.

Without speaking, he gave her back the knife and she slipped it into her boot. She realized that he must have cut his exploration inside short when he noticed her from the building, and had either come to her rescue . . . or simply came to rush her off, back to Envy.

Looking up at him, Sage said, "Great. So, why don't you show me the way inside and we can finish checking things out? Obviously, you know a way in past the *gangas*."

He looked at her for a long moment, *"absolutely no*

way" all over his face and stance. Then at last, he said, "Because if I don't take you in now, you'll come back on your own."

She grinned at him. "Right you are." She didn't mention that she'd probably bring Theo with her. Why give him an excuse to change his mind?

"Better be careful with that," he said, turning away, fingers tucked into the front pockets of his jeans as he sauntered a few steps off.

"The knife?" she said, glancing at the hilt sticking up from her boot as she started to follow him.

He cast a quick look over his shoulder, fast, liquid, and dark. Her belly dropped. "Not the knife. That smile." Simon slowed so she caught up with him, but he was staring at the Beretta building in front of them.

The rush of embarrassment heated her face and Sage didn't know what to say. But it didn't matter, because he continued, "You try that out on Theo Waxnicki, and he'll do anything you want."

What about you?

Sage stumbled on a rock and reached for Simon, who easily caught her arm and steadied her. Now her face blazed hot and red, as if she sat directly in front of a roaring fire. *Where did that come from? I didn't say that out loud, did I?*

"As you've already realized, there are *gangas* in there," he said. His long, deceptively easy strides had taken them around the perimeter of the barricade once again, nearly to the hundred-eighty-degree mark from where she'd first approached. "They appear to be living on the lowest level—what's left of it."

"And feeding off wolves?"

Again he gave her that quick flash of a look. "Right. Wolves, and I'm guessing any humans who might venture into their area." Simon bent forward and opened the sagging door of a large wheelless vehicle. "Follow me."

For the second time that day, Sage crawled into an automobile. But at least this time, she wasn't running for her life. This auto was larger than the one she'd tumbled into, and though the roof was smashed into a deep vee, leaving the door unable to close properly and little head room, she still had plenty of space to crawl through.

Despite the ache in her thigh and the hand that had been cut, Sage moved quickly and saw that the other side of the car was missing its door. Someone had already created a passageway through, and following Simon, she made her way up, down, left and right through a tunnel-like maze of the ruined cars.

Mildew and mold grew beneath her hands, and their musty scent filled her nostrils. She noticed items left by the occupants of the cars a half-century earlier—rotting shoes, nibbled-upon bags, cans, and bottles. Some of them even had strings and ornaments dangling from a little mirror in the front of the car. Leaves and other debris crunched beneath her, and flaking rust and curling plastic caught at her hands and knees. Just as she reached the other side of the fifth vehicle, she felt a tug on her jeans.

Startled, Sage turned to look behind her, certain that someone had reached up and grabbed her. She was proud of herself for not gasping, especially when she saw that she'd somehow just gotten hooked on a knob in the car.

"I'm caught," she said, twisting in the space to free herself. But she couldn't undo whatever had gotten hold of her, and Simon had to help.

"Hold still," he said, sliding back past her, reaching around to free her belt loop from whatever had caught it. She hadn't realized how tight it would be until his shoulder brushed against her waist, and his warm body nudged her. Then he was there, shoulder bumping her shoulder, so close she could hardly breathe . . . and when she did, over all the mustiness in the air, she smelled the clean, sharp scent that clung to his dark hair.

Sage closed her eyes for a moment, then opened them, but dared not look over. He'd be too close . . . their faces only centimeters apart. Her breathing felt heavy and slow . . . and why were her hands suddenly damp on the palms?

"Okay?" he said, right next to her ear. She was again aware of that subtle flavor of an accent, just enough to be intriguing . . . but not enough to obscure the syllables.

"Yeah," she said, and he eased back ahead of her again, his bare arm brushing against hers once more. Taut from holding himself up, his shoulder and biceps rounded hard and smooth beneath the sleeve of his black T-shirt, showing the bottom edge of a tattoo. His shirt had come loose from his jeans, and as he moved ahead of her, she saw the shadowy hint of a bare, smooth hip as he reached up to the roof of the car.

Suddenly she was thirsty again. Really thirsty, and warm.

He reached above and shifted something on the roof. There was a dull clunk and an opening appeared above them. Simon pulled himself up and through the top of the vehicle and moments later, a strong tanned arm reappeared to help pull her up and through.

Instead of being in an open area in front of the Beretta building, as she'd expected, Sage found that they were in a shadowy area between two tall trucklike vehicles.

"Stay here while I check on things," he said. "Don't move. Okay?"

"I'm not stupid," she said, thrusting her chin out at him.

Simon looked at her in that way that made her belly

flip. "No, you're not." And then he slipped away, leaving her alone in a silent, unfamiliar world.

Simon had found only one way into the building, and it took him right through the darkened lobby—where the *gangas* lived.

He hadn't mentioned to Sage that there were just as many canine bones as human bones littering what had once been a highly polished black and yellow marble floor. Nor had he told her that there were about two dozen of the creatures trapped in there—obviously set to guard the place from inquisitive people like the two of them. He wondered how often someone came to provide the *gangas* with food—in the form of feral canines or unlucky humans. Or could the monsters subsist for months without food?

During the day, the *gangas* must stay in the building, but at night they were free to roam within the perimeter of the vehicular barrier. The wolf that had attacked Sage must have somehow escaped from the corral. Fortunately, it hadn't gone as far as the inhabited part of Envy, or something worse than a few cuts and scratches might have occurred.

Simon mulled these thoughts as he moved out of Sage's sight, forcing himself to keep his mind away from . . . other things.

If he weren't such a *chavala*, he'd have taken her back to the city and been done with it. But he'd seen the enthusiasm and determination in her eyes, and knew it wouldn't be long before she was back here.

Of course, he could have taken her back and turned her over to Theo Waxnicki, who could probably have kept an eye on her if he knew she'd try and come back. That would have been the smart thing to do.

But no. He'd let a killer body and one soul-shattering smile override that sensible solution, and now he had to find a different way to get into the building so that she could come with him.

Simon paused and listened. Silence.

With a deep breath, he stilled, focused, and drew deep down inside himself, wavered . . . and disappeared.

Now he could move quickly, walking across the empty corral toward the Beretta building. He remembered when it had been built, for Mancusi had been interested in one of the condos in what would be Vegas's premier residential property.

At least until the next hot development came along.

The *gangas* might smell him, but they couldn't see him, and Simon walked boldly through the entrance of the lobby. It had once been decorated with colorful blown glass that put the Bellagio's famed glass flower ceiling to shame, but of course, there was nothing left of that but a few swaths of dirty, broken waves. Some of the *gangas* milled about, but most of them were sleeping or lying comatose—or whatever the fuck they did. The ever-present moaning *ruuu-uuth* came out in the form of snores and exhales from the prone monsters.

He counted four that were up and about, and from the way they stiffened and looked in his direction, Simon knew they scented him.

Ignoring the creatures, easily evading their clumsy feet and loglike arms, he hurried through the room, wondering how long Sage would stay put.

I'm not stupid.

Fuck no. And that was a big problem.

Not that a woman like Sage would want anything to do with Simon anyway. Nor could he imagine even touching her with his corrupted hands.

He saw a door in the corner and realized it would be the stairs. And that there might be a building exit in the stairwell.

Moments later, Simon found just what he was looking for. The exit had been locked and barricaded from the inside, which was why he'd not been able to access it when he originally searched for the entrance. But it took him little effort to clear it away and open the door, thanks to the super strength he seemed to have acquired in that Sedona cave.

When he returned to Sage, fully visible again, he found her sitting in nearly the same position in which he'd left her. "Ready?"

She looked up at him, her lovely face dirt- and blood-streaked, her blue eyes accusing. "I thought you might have gone in without me."

Simon shrugged. Why should she trust him? She didn't know him, and after all, she probably sensed he was exactly who he was: Simon Japp. Bodyguard, goon, right-hand man to Leonide Mancusi. He might have had a chance to start over, but his sins, his choices, his corruption, still clung to him like a bad odor.

There was no sense in defending himself. "Come on."

Sage pulled to her feet, and he heard the faint groan of pain as she did so. The cut above her knee had bled into a large dark stain, and he noticed the way it stuck to her skin. That was going to hurt when she undressed— *don't think about that.* And the cuts and scrapes on her hands . . . she was lucky they weren't any worse. Maybe he should check on them before they went any farther.

No. Dragon Boy will make sure she's all patched up. And then some.

They crossed the corral-like space between the vehicle barrier and the building, running the twenty yards quickly and silently to the door Simon had left open. It was unlikely that the *gangas* would see them from inside the building, and if they did, they'd never figure out where they went or how to find them. Nor could they venture into the sunlight.

Simon was confident they were safe.

"Lots of flights to go," he said once they were inside the dim stairwell. There was only a window every three or four floors, so the light was iffy. "Twenty-three floors."

"No problem," she told him, flashing a quicker, less potent version of the smile that had fairly dropped him to his knees earlier. "I always take the stairs to my room. On the fourteenth floor."

Simon nodded. It was obvious she got her exercise despite the hours sitting at a computer table. She had a sweet ass and slender, delicate body with curves exactly where they should be.

And she was going to be climbing twenty-three flights of stairs in front of him.

"I'll go first," he said, slipping past her. "One flight at a time, then you follow."

She nodded, surprising him when he was prepared to have to argue and explain the logic of allowing his heavier weight to confirm that the old steps were stable. "Right behind you."

Simon turned and jogged up the first few flights. The steps were metal and the railings completely intact, except for peeling paint, even after fifty years. He'd gone up a different stairwell awhile earlier, and was confident that they would hold. But it was a good excuse to not have to torture himself.

Twenty minutes later, they reached the top floor of the tower where Remington Truth had a penthouse. Birds fluttered and took flight as Simon and Sage walked across what would have been the threshold to the condo's entrance. Something rustled in a pile of leaves caught up in the corner.

The apartment's expansive French doors sagged in place. On the next wall, a stream of light came through a wedge of broken window, while the rest of the plate glass shone grimy and gray. A lush patch of green grew on the floor in an elongated vee where the pure sun would shine and rain would enter, though a bit of tenacious growth attempted to spread beyond the triangular patch.

"I can't believe it's still intact," commented Sage.

Simon raised a finger to his lips and gestured for her to hold back. He didn't think anyone was here, but he wasn't about to assume anything. On feet silent over the dried leaves and branches, he moved to the doors and carefully peered into the room beyond.

The place was in shambles, as one would expect. Shadowy furnishings melded with strips and patches of sunlight, and vines and bushes sprouted everywhere. Nothing moved. No sign of life.

Easing the door open, he slipped through and crooked his finger for Sage to follow.

She raised her brows as if to ask permission to speak—why did women always have to talk?—and he nodded, shifting away so that he wouldn't brush against her shoulder.

"If he was one of the Strangers, one of the people that caused the Change, do you think he meant to live here After?" she asked, looking around the room. "I mean, it might not be an accident that his home wasn't destroyed. Do you think?"

Good point. Simon shrugged. "You might be right. But he's not here now."

"And he hasn't been here for decades. Or they wouldn't

be looking for him. I mean, if you found out about this place so easily . . ." She'd moved along the perimeter of the room, trailing her hand over leather sofas and along a long sleek table, kicking up dust and disturbing birds, mice, and God knew what else. It didn't seem to bother her, though.

Not squeamish. Smart and practical. And the most beautiful woman he'd ever seen.

Pinche.

Simon turned away and cruised along the other side of the room, then down a dark hall. Something slithered over his foot and he kicked it away, then felt something else bump into his heel as it scurried for safety. No, Remington Truth hadn't lived here for a long time.

He wasn't certain exactly what to look for anyway. Surely anything of interest would have been destroyed or found long before now.

What had been the master bedroom opened before him, complete with a waterbed long since drained and a jetted tub large enough for half a dozen people. The skylight over the tub was broken, and tall slender plants grew in the circle of light, spindly and greedy for sun. They looked like skinny bamboo plants, with their random, delicate leaves near the top.

Maybe Truth had some good-luck feng shui bamboo that had sprouted. Simon grimaced as he was reminded that, along with her myriad of crystals, Florita had grown a few stalks of curling green bamboo in a glass vase. She'd lectured Simon on how important their position and placement was for good fortune.

That was early on, when he'd been assigned as her bodyguard, and he'd had no choice but to listen to her prattle on. And on. And on. But then she'd tried to get too friendly with Simon, Mancusi found out . . . and he'd shipped Florita and her fake tits off with her crystals and bamboo and red candles. But not long after, in true fuck-you spirit, she'd made it huge on the big screen.

And back in East Los, Simon had been promoted, so to speak, because of his loyalty and prudence. And cuffed even more tightly to Mancusi.

"Simon!"

He turned from the bamboo growth in the Jacuzzi tub, making his way quickly toward her voice.

"I found something!"

No fucking way.

When he came into the room, which appeared to have been an office, Sage was standing in the center of a pool of sun. She was holding a small black item. "Look!"

"A jump drive?"

She nodded, her aqua blue eyes shining. "It was wedged inside that desk drawer there, and it's so small, it would have been easy to miss. Besides, I'm sure they took any computers or files he might have had."

Simon examined the small black flash disk drive and came to the conclusion that it might just have survived fifty years exposed to the elements. The USB plug slid in and out, and the whole thing was cased in soft, protective plastic that appeared intact. "Well, I'll be damned." He looked up and gave her a little smile. "It might have something interesting on it. Or it might just have a bunch of old Neil Diamond songs."

"Who?"

He smiled before he caught himself. "Look him up. Isn't that what you do?" Simon turned away before the bantering could go any further. Bantering led to camaraderie, and camaraderie led to flirtation, and flirtation could only lead to fucking trouble.

He wandered close to a massive opening in the wall, a

window broken completely away, and looked out over the ruins of Las Vegas.

The ocean—the damned Pacific Ocean, here in Vegas!—sparkled blue and green to the west and north, and between this structure and the water were a variety of buildings and ruins. Brick, glass, curling steel beams, all fringed with green and other organic trim.

"Do you have to stand so close to the edge?"

He cast a look over his shoulder. "You afraid of heights?"

Sage shook her head. "No. But I don't see why you have to stand so close to the edge."

Simon shrugged, fighting a grin, and turned to look back out over—and froze. "What the . . ." he muttered, moving closer to the side of the window where he wouldn't be seen. Curling his fingers around the edge, he carefully leaned forward for a better look. Space loomed before and below him, and a little breeze skimmed his cheeks.

"What is it?" Then, she must have seen how near the edge he was, because she added, "Simon! Be careful! You're going to fall."

He swallowed a chuckle. If she only knew how close he'd come to death so many times. "Looks like a boat of some sort, on the shore . . ." Some type of watercraft had definitely been pulled up on the rough beach. Out of sight of Envy, here on the northwest side of the deserted area . . . That didn't bode well.

He scanned the area between the shoreline and the building, the hair on the back of his arm lifting and prickling like it did when he knew something bad was about to happen. It was like a sixth sense.

The ruined buildings and their rubble-strewn footprints hid much of the ground, but then he saw them. Three men, walking . . . pushing a large, enclosed wagonlike object making their way toward the Beretta building. Much too close; in fact, they were just about to the vehicle barrier.

Pinche.

But how were they going to get that big cage through the barrier? He watched a moment longer, and then saw the ramp. The men had pulled it from a pile of debris and were putting it into place.

Damn. "They're coming," he said turning to Sage, adrenaline pumping through him and clearing his thoughts. "We've got to go *now.*" Before they get over the barrier and into the corral.

"*Gangas*?" she said, following him toward the door without hesitation.

"Strangers. Or bounty hunters. But whoever they are, they're not coming from Envy. They came from the west. From the ocean." And they were either bringing something for the *gangas* . . . or more *gangas* . . . or planning to take something away.

Then he heard it . . . faint on the air. Howls.

Definitely *ganga* feeding time. *Fuck.*

He should have expected it. The wolf remains below in the *gangas'* lobby were old and dried . . . not recent. If the Strangers, or whoever set the zombies to guard the building, visited regularly to check on and feed them, it had been a while since they'd come. And why wouldn't they come today, when he and Sage were there poking around?

It just about figured.

As they hurried through the ravaged condo toward the French doors, Simon kept his ears attuned for any sounds from below. But he didn't need to listen to know that the ramp would soon be in place and those wolves would be released into the corral.

The *gangas* would be happy—distracted, probably—

but that would make it all the more impossible for him and Sage to cross back over.

If the Strangers didn't come into the corral, maybe they could wait it out.

Sage stumbled and he grabbed her arm. Smart, not squeamish . . . but a bit of a klutz.

"Ow," she gasped and more of her weight tipped against him.

"You okay?" he asked.

"Yeah," she said. But when she tried to pull away, she sagged again. "I might have pulled something."

"Or twisted it." He saw that she couldn't put her full weight on her left foot. "Okay, come on." He steadied her by linking his arm around hers and she hobbled along with him across the threshold to the stairwell.

This was definitely going to be a long trip down.

"Hold on. Stay here a sec."

Simon settled her inside the stairwell and dashed back into the condo to look out the window at the Strangers' progress. *Pinche*. He could already see the pack of wolves down in the corral, and the three men standing about with some sort of weapon—guns? Tazers maybe?—to keep the feral animals away from them as they herded them into the lobby.

He watched a few moments longer, waiting to see if the Strangers were going to come into the building or if they were going to leave. When he saw them walk closer to the building, he swore again under his breath. They looked like they were going to go in.

Simon stilled for a moment and thought. Yes, he'd closed the door that he and Sage had come through. And the one from the ganga lobby to the stairwell. There would be no sign of any—*oh, fuck*. The dead wolf. The sliced up, fresh dead wolf . . . next to a car with the door open. On the other side of the barrier . . .

Sonofabitch.

Back in the stairwell, he explained the situation to Sage. "It's unlikely they'll come up through this stairwell," he said, hardly able to see her face in the dim light. "So I suggest we go a few flights down and wait for a bit."

"Sounds good." Though her eyes were serious, she didn't appear frightened or apprehensive. Either she was taking the danger in stride, or she was trusting him to keep her safe. Simon wasn't sure that was such a good idea.

He helped her down four flights of stairs and then settled her against the wall. "How's the ankle?"

"It's fine. I can walk on it if I need to."

"No reason to f— mess it up anymore if you don't need to," he said.

Her lips twitched in a moment of humor as she looked up at him in the wash of light. "Do you think I've never heard the f-word before? It's Lou and Theo's favorite word. Sometimes I think they compete to see who can use it more creatively. Once I think Theo said it five times in one sentence."

Simon blinked and pulled his attention away from that intriguing freckle on her lip and refocused. "I'll remember that. Stay here—okay? I'm going to go a few flights down and see if I can find out anything."

Sage nodded, then grabbed his arm. "Be safe."

He slipped away, then turned himself invisible. He found it easier and easier to concentrate himself into nothingness—almost like flicking a switch. He'd gone only a few flights down when he heard the unmistakable sound of advancing voices. *Fu-uck.*

Was he just super unlucky, or did God simply have it in for him?

Still invisible, he hurried back up to Sage. Finger to lips, he turned back to normal just before coming into view. "They're coming. Up. Here," he said softly, gesturing so that she understood he meant *in this stairwell*.

Her eyes widened. "What do we do?" she mouthed, then pointed upward, then downward, then toward the door.

Simon didn't answer, but tried the door instead. It might open, but it might make a really loud sound . . . Did he dare chance it? Rusted metal scraping or creaking?

The knob didn't turn. The voices were coming closer. And Simon and Sage were on a level with a window directly above, leaving no shadows or possibility of hiding.

Simon looked at Sage and made his decision. He pointed down and raised two fingers so she'd know he meant for them to go two levels. At least it would be dark there. And . . . maybe the door would open.

Sage didn't wait for his steadying arm, she had already started down the flights. Simon followed, both of them silent and doing their best to avoid stepping on crunching leaves. He moved so he was right next to her in case she lost the strength in her injured ankle. At the second level down, the voices were louder, coming closer, and sounded urgent.

Pinche.

They were definitely suspicious. Simon reached for the doorknob and prayed . . . but it didn't turn easily, and the Strangers were too close to chance making the noise.

Though the space in the stairwell was dark and shadowy, it probably wasn't enough to obscure them. *Fu-u-uck.*

He'd have to try it.

In the dimness, he saw Sage's eyes wide, and a little frightened now, and he nodded calmly. Then he turned her gently to face the wall, in the corner, and even as the voices came closer and he felt the pumping of his heart speed up, his palms dampen, he remained calm. "Close your eyes," he mouthed into her ear. "Don't open them, don't move, till I say."

Simon drew in a deep breath, steeled his thoughts, and prayed.

And then he wrapped his arms around Sage from behind, enclosing her with his body, feeling her warm, bare arms under his hands . . . and, drawing upon all his strength and concentration, flicked his internal switch.

Yep, God definitely had it in for him.

Is this the end of the world? A terrorist attack? What's happening?

I can't get cell phone or Internet to find out anything. The power's out. Everywhere I look there are dead people and piles of broken buildings, holes in the street. It's horrifying.

I think it's a day after everything started. I don't know. I can't tell what time it is or whether it's day or night, it's so dark. All I know is it's been hell. I'm so scared.

Drew is with me. Thank God.

The earthquakes are over but there are aftershocks. And big storms, strong and angry, like the earth is furious. The sounds . . . I can't tell if they're people screaming or the wind.

There's been no sign of help. Nothing from the outside. No planes, no helicopters. Nothing.

What's happening?????

—from Adventures in Juliedom, the blog of Julie Davis Beecher

CHAPTER 4

Sage could hardly breathe.

Not because Simon was hurting her, but because . . . he was so close, so big and powerful and warm and so *near*. All around her.

She couldn't have opened her eyes if she'd tried.

So she kept them tightly closed, and strained to listen for the sounds of approaching Strangers . . . because she didn't know what else to do.

Her world was dark and warm and solid and safe . . . and she felt a sort of shimmery feeling sweep over her. She rested her forehead against the old crumbling wall and Simon's taut muscles eased the slightest bit. The biceps that curled around her belly and the forearm that crossed up and between her breasts loosened, and the warm breath against the back of her head slowed.

The Strangers pounded closer and she buried herself in the darkness of her closed eyes and the corner of the dark stairwell, felt Simon pushing her deeper into the corner, tightening his grip. Her mouth was too dry to swallow. Was it shadowy enough that the Strangers wouldn't see them?

She didn't move, she barely breathed. Her heart

slammed in her chest and she wasn't sure if it was because of the proximity of danger . . . or the proximity of the raw maleness surrounding her.

The odd shimmery feeling continued to sprinkle over her, leaving a pleasant sort of humming deep inside her body. Simon's scent, fresh and masculine, enveloped her . . . just as his shirt had last night. Her ankle throbbed a little, her forehead scraped against rough wall.

Oh God. Here they come.

The steps were louder now, the voices *right there.* She could discern three different ones. Sage held her breath, felt Simon doing the same, squeezed her eyes shut, felt him close in even tighter around her . . . and prayed.

And then she felt the swish of air as the men rushed by, on their way up the stairs, clearly on a mission.

They'd passed them. *They'd gone by.*

Sage still didn't release her breath, sure that at any moment, they'd stop and shout and come rushing back.

But they didn't.

The Strangers had been in a hurry, and it had been dark enough. The shadows had hidden them. A miracle.

After a moment, Simon released her, pulling silently away, taking the warmth, the comfort and power, even the soft tingling. They needed no words, and she turned and started down the flight of stairs.

Ignoring the pain in each step, aware that Simon was there, waiting to grab her if her ankle should fail her, she descended as quickly as she could. Which was pretty quick, considering her knees were shaking.

As they descended, she heard the horrible sounds of squeals, and the cries of animals in distress growing more distinct. The *gangas* were tearing the wolves apart. Perhaps even fighting each other for their meals. They'd have to be inside the building, for the sunlight was too destructive. But Simon knew where they were going. And she trusted him.

At the bottom, Sage saw that a door that must lead into the other part of the building was ajar—it had to be the way the Strangers came in—but the exterior door was still closed.

Everything was a blur after that. Simon didn't stop and give her explanations as he'd done earlier; he simply slung an arm around her waist. Lifting her against his hip, face dark with tension, he dashed from the exterior door into the corral area around the building.

Out into the open.

The expanse of ground—at least in this corner—was empty and clear of danger. The rusty vehicular fence rose in front of them, and Simon reached it almost before Sage could comprehend it.

The terrible sounds faded behind them, and as they approached, Simon thrust her, none-too-gently, on top of the nearest car. He leapt up next to her and fairly dragged her over and across the pile of cars. It was like climbing a steep hill of jagged steel—tough, slow, and painful—but he was surefooted and quick. And very strong.

On the other side, he pulled her down to the ground, picked her up again, and ran toward the walls of Envy.

They were safe.

•

The flash drive actually worked.

Sage plugged it into a USB port and waited impatiently for the list of files to come up, listening to the comforting hum of the computer and ignoring the throbbing pain in various places on her body. Denim was still encrusted to the cuts on her thigh and her sliced palms ached and stung when she rested them on the computer keyboard. But she didn't care.

She was just about to scan through the list of files when a soft *ding* sounded, alerting her to a new arrival.

Her heartbeat skipped and she looked up.

"Simon said you had a few cuts that should be looked at." Dr. Elliott Drake, for some reason known as Dred to his friends, stood at the bottom of the spiral staircase.

Sage tucked away the wedge of disappointment. "That was nice of him to send you."

"Mind if I take a look?" His blue eyes held warmth and compassion—pleasant, but quite a different expression than the hot, intense one when he was looking at Jade.

Of course, the feeling between the two was quite mutual, and Sage had never seen her friend happier now that she'd met Elliott. Since they'd resolved some initial problems, they'd been inseparable.

Always so calm and empathetic, with an easy sense of humor, he did seem as wonderful as Jade said he was— just the kind of guy she deserved after her experiences with the Strangers. And, as it turned out, not only had he been frozen in the Sedona cave with Simon, Quent, and the others—Wyatt and Fence—but he'd also come out of it with extraordinary abilities. As a medical doctor trained before the Change, Elliott brought not only experience and knowledge that had been lost since the catastrophic events, but also an extra element: he could diagnose, and sometimes heal, with the touch of his hands.

At least, that was what Sage understood . . . but from what Jade had indicated, there were also some sort of complications to his skills that were not so pleasant. So he didn't use them all that often.

Sage frowned, wondering once again why Elliott and

Quent seemed to be the only ones who'd acquired special abilities after coming out of the cave. All of them were extraordinarily strong, but no one else had changed in the way those two had. Was it some random thing? Or had they simply not discovered their abilities yet?

She realized Elliott was waiting for an answer and was just about to respond when she was interrupted by the sound of footsteps hurrying down. Those light, fast clicks she recognized—Jade's, of course.

"Are you all right?" her friend asked even before she came fully into view. At the bottom of the stairs, touching Elliott casually as she passed by, Jade hurried over, her dark auburn hair flying. "Sage, what happened? Good grief, look at your face! And your hands!"

Automatically, Sage's hands went up to her cheeks, smoothing over her hair and back down, feeling the blood crusted on her skin. *Oh. Yikes.* She hadn't given her appearance a thought since returning with the flash drive.

"Just a few cuts," Sage said.

"Elliott," Jade said impatiently. "Aren't you going to look at her? She's been bleeding. A lot, it looks like."

"If she wants me to," the doctor replied mildly, giving Jade a bemused smile.

"Well, of course she does. And I'll get Flo over here too. No, wait, we'll go to her place—she's got everything we could possibly need. She fixed up my face when I fell off the horse, and no one even noticed all those bruises." Jade, as was her way, was firmly in charge. Taking control.

"I don't really—"

"She'll have you all fixed up for tonight. You are going to wear that rosy-tangerine dress, aren't you?"

Sage blinked. "Tonight?" *Rosy-tangerine?*

Elliott had moved toward her and stood, waiting, still

watching Jade with that combination of amusement and deep affection.

"Don't tell me you forgot about the Thanksgiving Festival!"

"I forgot about the Thanksgiving Festival." *It looked more peach-colored to me.*

"See, this is what happens when I move out. You spend all your time down here in the computer lab and you forget everything else that's going on."

"Gee, maybe you ought to move back in," Sage teased.

"No," replied Elliott firmly. Jade glanced at him and the look that passed between them was enough to singe her fingertips. Then he turned back to Sage. "Now, why don't you let me take a look? I don't know what you cut yourself on, but I don't want to see any infections starting up. It's not like I can prescribe antibiotics."

She sat obediently and closed her eyes as Elliott examined the cuts on her face, then on her palms. *Crap.* She'd totally forgotten that today was Friday, the day of the annual festival.

Like the Pilgrims of long ago, survivors of the Change had marked the end of their first year of endurance with a celebration. It had become an annual event in Envy, with music, feasting, and other festivities. People from other settlements often came and joined in the revelries as well.

But Sage, cloistered in her subterranean lab, hadn't noticed the recent influx of people into Envy, nor the excitement going on around her. If she hadn't left so early this morning to investigate Remington Truth's condo, she might have seen the preparations in full swing . . . but going out the back way and into the deserted area had taken her away from all of that.

"Sage!"

Theo's urgent voice pierced her thoughts, and she looked up as he rushed down the spiral stairs. "Hi, Theo," she said.

"Another attack?" he said. His expression was stark.

"*Another* attack?" asked Jade, looking sharply at Sage. "What?"

Sage glared at Theo and shrugged as Elliott began to smooth his hands over her body in a sort of scanning process. She guessed that was part of his paranormal abilities. "I'm not hurt."

"*Another* attack?" Jade repeated.

Sage explained about last night as Elliott paused, his hands settling over her sliced, throbbing thigh. She felt a little tingle of energy flush through her body, warm and comforting, almost like that shimmery feeling she'd had earlier when encompassed by Simon.

"So that explains the guy we found in one of the halls, beaten to a pulp," Elliott said as he stepped away. "Hmm." He looked down at his hands and then glanced at Jade. "I patched him up a bit earlier. But I think I'll go check on him again."

"You might even want to squeeze his hand," Jade replied, her voice taut. "The scrub."

Elliott looked at Sage. "How do you feel now?"

"Better," she replied. Then realized, "Wow! I'm completely healed. No scars, no pain . . . how did you do that?"

She reached for him and Elliott, smiling, stepped away before she could grab his hand for a shake. "No thanks necessary," he said. "Except, maybe a dance tonight. I hear the band is really good. Especially the lead singer." Considering the fact that his lover was the front woman, he was safe to say that. With a glance at Jade, he added,

"I'm off to go check on my other . . . patient. See you at the festival." And off he went.

"Are you sure you're all right?" Theo demanded. "I ran into Simon and he mentioned that I should come and find you."

"I'm fine," Sage said. *Nice of Simon to let you and Jade and Elliott know. And to send you all down to interrupt my work.*

She was suddenly doubly glad she hadn't come back to retrieve Theo to accompany her to Remington Truth's condo—by the way he was looking at her, he wouldn't have allowed her to come with him.

And that part really bunked her off. *Allowed.* As if he were her parent or boss or something. But she knew from his expression that she was right. He somehow felt as though he had control over her. Or was responsible for her.

"Now that you're all better, we've got to get you ready for tonight," Jade said. Her brilliant green eyes glinted with determination.

Sage looked at her friend—beautiful, confident, outgoing, and a bit neurotic. And a horrible control freak. There were times when she'd wanted to be more like her. Not the control freak part, but the strong, confident part. Not only that, but knowing exactly what Jade had been through at the hands of the Strangers, and seeing how strong and capable she was now that she went on secret missions for the Resistance, Sage admired her even more.

And, if she was really honest, she also envied her, just a bit, the relationship she'd found with Elliott. That she'd found someone who *understood* her, accepted her for who she was . . .and who made her glow the way Elliott did.

Some noise or movement pulled Sage from her contemplation, and she realized Theo was standing there, looking at her. Giving her a funny look, as if he was trying to tell her something without actually speaking. His eyes shifted to the left, toward Jade, and then to the right—oh. He wanted her to get rid of Jade.

Her heart started thumping a little harder. *No, I don't think I'm wanting a lecture from you right now, Theo.*

Then she glanced at Jade, who looked ready to lecture her as well. *Crap.*

If Simon were there, she'd cheerfully murder him for having her sanctuary invaded . . . while he was off doing who knew what.

And then . . . no way. Yes, the sound of more footsteps—heavier ones, multiple pairs—followed the little chime that portended an arrival. Now who?

"Heard you might have found something about Remington Truth," said Quent before he even reached the bottom of the stairs. Behind him followed his friend Wyatt, a rude man with lots of messy dark hair, and a bald black guy called Fence—all of whom had been in the Sedona caves together with Elliott and Simon.

"I might have," she said, accepting the fact that with the whole crew of them in here, not only wasn't she going to get much work done, but she was also going to escape her lectures.

"Simon said you found a flash drive," Quent continued.

Gee, nice of Simon to spread the word . . . but neglect to come down here himself and see how I'm doing. Or how things are going.

A fine-featured blond man with a British accent, Quent'd recently begun to look more strained and tense than when he and his friends had first come to Envy, nearly a month ago. That likely had to do with the fact that he'd recently learned that his own father—by all accounts, a hateful, arrogant man—was one of the Strangers and had helped to cause the Change. "Right, then. Shall I take a look?"

Sage had already pulled it out of the computer. "Good idea. You should be able to tell us if it really belonged to him or not."

Quent took the slender black object hesitantly, and Sage watched his face as he closed elegant fingers around it. He wore a simple gold signet ring on the middle finger of his right hand, and held a pair of gloves in his other.

Like Elliott, who seemed to have acquired extraordinary abilities while in the cave, Quent too had emerged with his own paranormal skill: that of psychometry. The power to "read" the history of inanimate objects.

Sage couldn't imagine that it would be a pleasant talent to have. If every time she touched something, she was also assaulted with the images and possibly sounds, feelings, and so on, of its history . . . she shivered. What would the walls of this hotel, or even the computer keyboards that she typed on every day, tell her? How awful would that be?

No wonder he'd taken to wearing gloves.

And from the expressions flitting across Quent's handsome face, she could tell her concerns were justified. When he opened his eyes, at first they were cloudy and dull. His face had taken on a light sheen of perspiration, and she could see that his heart rate and breathing had both kicked up. Lines on either side of his mouth etched deeper and longer.

"Quent." Wyatt, showing the first bit of compassion Sage had noticed, rested his hand on his friend's shoulder. He seemed truly concerned, and only when the other man seemed to pull out of some deep dreamlike state and looked up at him with clear blue eyes did he relax. At least, his stance relaxed. The same underlying anger and bad humor remained in Wyatt's face.

"It's his." Quent handed the jump drive back to Sage with icy fingers. His face appeared a little clammy, but he sat straight and determined. "Have you looked at it yet?"

Sage knew that at least part of his interest was in finding out as much about Fielding as possible. Horrified and devastated by the knowledge that his father had been involved in the Change, Quent had vowed to find him and kill him. The only thing holding him back was not knowing where or how to find him, or even being certain that he *could* kill him.

After all, the Strangers were immortal, made so by the special crystals they wore embedded in their flesh.

"I haven't had a chance, I've had so many interruptions." Sage didn't care that she sounded annoyed. They were interrupting her work and she knew she wasn't going to get out of attending the festival tonight, so she only had a little time. "If everyone would clear out of here," she added pointedly.

No one moved. She sighed and stuck the drive back into the USB port. A few moments later, she had the list of files up on her screen.

"They're . . ." She stared at the list of gibberish and flapped her hand at it angrily.

Theo was at her side in a minute, and, hand resting lightly on her shoulder, leaned forward to look. "Ah. They're encrypted." The relish in his voice tugged a smile from beneath her annoyance, and she looked up at him. "Of course I can get in," he told her with a smile. "It'll take some time, but no problem." He was fairly slathering at the idea of sitting down and getting to it, apparently his need to lecture her gone in the excitement.

Sage rose from her seat and he slid into place. She would have stood to watch, but Jade came forward and curled no-nonsense fingers around her arm. "Good. It'll take him some time to do that, which means we can go do something with your hair and get you ready for the festival."

One glance at her friend told her there would be no escape, so she bowed to the inevitable and, with one last woeful glance, left the computer sanctuary.

Hours later, back in the hotel room that had become his since their arrival in Envy, beneath the hot shower that pounded the shite out of his shoulders, Quent was almost able to forget where he really was. In hell.

As the water rained down on him there in the fancy marble bathroom, he was back home, fifty years ago, in another fancy bath (a bit larger, of course, with windows overlooking the Atlantic and dual showerheads).

And Bonia Telluscrede, whom *Vogue* had called the next Gisele Bundchen, was waiting for him in the master bedroom, dressed in that red silk thing she'd worn in Paris.

Or . . . he spun his memories a different way. Perhaps Lissa Mackley, who'd just won an Oscar and had brought it into the Jacuzzi with them. She had the poutiest lips he'd ever had the pleasure to have around him, though she couldn't carry on an unscripted conversation to save her life.

And his Piper would be waiting, ready to fly them from Boston to Naples for the weekend . . .

Maybe it was Marley Huvane, the socialite with whom he'd hooked up at more than one of his family's elite gatherings. Even when he'd brought a date.

Marley could actually put sentences together in an interesting way. And she understood what it was like to grow up with more than a silver spoon.

They might have had a chance.

But when the water from the single shower head turned cold much too soon than it would have back home, and Quent stepped back out into reality and a too-small Astroturf towel, the truth settled on him once again like the weight of the world on Atlas.

Everyone was gone.

Every*thing* was gone.

Thanks to his goddamned wanker father.

A mass murderer. A *global* mass-murderer.

He whipped another towel from the rack, the snap loud over the last remnants of dripping water. The mirror was too steamy to see anything but a muted shadow, and he wrapped the towel around his waist wondering, as he did, why bother?

As he stepped out of the steaming bathroom, Quent automatically scanned the room.

She wasn't there.

Of course she bloody well wasn't there. But that didn't stop him from looking every time he came in.

Wet hair dripping rivulets down his shoulders, Quent toweled it dry furiously.

Zoë Kapoor was a bad-tempered and demanding prat, and had nonexistent social skills. God knew where she came from and where she lived and what she did besides hunt *gangas* and snipe at people. She could shoot an arrow as well as Robin Hood, but that was about all she was good for.

Well, that wasn't precisely accurate, he had to admit. Certainly without her help a few weeks ago, they wouldn't have been able to save the teenagers who'd been abducted. And the mayor of Envy, Vaughn Rogan, might have died from a lion attack.

And Quent would still be wondering if his dick worked properly after fifty years of hibernation.

But other than that intense, tear-your-clothes-off-and-slam-against-the-wall fuck that he still woke dreaming about, hard and hot and damp, there wasn't any reason to think about Zoë.

Although he did have that fantasy of her in thigh-high leather boots . . . and nothing else.

In one of his weaker moments, he'd even gone so far as to wonder how he might find a pair . . . or have them made. Soft, supple leather that laced up the back . . .

That was, before he realized he had no way to pay for them. And no skills to barter. A rude awakening for a bloke who'd always had it all.

Now he had nothing. Nothing but the legacy of his murdering father.

Quent flung the damp towel over a chair and stalked over to his bed. He'd expected her before now, to be honest. She'd made such a big deal about those bloody arrows, following him back to Envy to retrieve the ones he'd found after she shot a few *gangas* the first time they'd met.

And yeah, she'd bloody well got them back after that destroy-the-sheets episode, sneaking off with them while he slept in the afterglow . . . but then Quent had acquired two more of her special arrows after she'd shot a lion and saved the mayor's life. She'd know he had them.

Yes. He'd expected her before now. If for no other reason than to retrieve—or steal back—her precious arrows.

With a grunt of annoyance, he lifted the mattress and looked down at the box spring.

"Bloody fucking *hell*," he breathed, staring in disbelief. They were gone. The arrows he'd hidden there were gone.

Quent dropped the mattress back in place and resisted the urge to throw something.

It was bad enough that she'd somehow, sometime in the last five or six hours, sneaked in and taken them . . . but that she hadn't stuck around for Round Two of let-me-thank-you-for-keeping-my-arrows-safe-by-balling-the-shite-out-of-you was a real slap in the face.

Angered by his rush of emotion, Quent turned away from the empty, lonely bed and stalked to the window. The sun had lowered in the west, but his view faced east and he could see only the faint glow of its last vestiges rising from over the roof above. The sky ahead had darkened, and the glow of Envy lights burned below.

Loosening his jaw, Quent realized he was being a bloody knob-end. There were other women, several of whom had made their interest very clear since he'd arrived in Envy. He and his companions were heroes for saving the teens, and as such had attracted more than their fair share of attention.

Besides, he liked variety. It was the spice of life. And variety meant no complications. No expectations.

And tonight the pints and wine would be flowing freely. Everyone would be in a celebratory mood. He'd have no trouble finding a soft, warm companion.

He never had before.

Simon ran.

It was different from when he ran before—on the streets of L.A. or Hollywood, on a track, round and round and round, on a treadmill.

This was wide-open infinity, overgrown and natural. Ghost towns. Wilderness.

He realized he could keep going, leave the dark, awkward walls of Envy behind him forever. He could no longer be found by anyone or any*thing* if he didn't want to be found. A miracle.

Too bad it hadn't been this way when he worked for Mancusi. How many times had he wanted to sink into the shadows, dissolve into nothing? Become transparent.

Escape.

Freedom.

He ran and ran, keeping his mind empty, pushing his body for hours. The sun rose to its zenith, then began to descend. He ran till he puked, and half choked on it when he remembered the irony of Sage doing the same. Then he puked some more.

And ran hard again. For hours.

In the end, he returned to Envy, shaky and weak, just as unnoticed as when he had left. And not just because it was pushing dusk.

He still had to think about it, concentrate, to turn himself invisible. He couldn't hold the transparency for very long—five minutes maybe. Although it was getting easier.

And thank the Holy Mother of God, because apparently, *apparently*, he could turn someone else invisible. As long as he was touching them.

Curled around them. Enveloping them.

Her.

Simon scrubbed away the grime and sweat and kept his mind from temptation by counting the tiles on the shower walls—three hundred sixty-seven. Twelve were cracked. Three had chipped corners.

Then he checked to see if he needed to shave.

Not yet. Still no stubble sprouting on his chin, though Fence's baldness wasn't as smooth as it had been. And Wyatt and Elliott had each shaved once.

The Waxnickis were sure it would come in time, and

since something similar had happened to Theo, Simon didn't doubt them.

He delayed as long as he could, but in the end his empty belly won out and Simon left his room. At that moment, Quent came down the hall, walking quickly, exuding determination . . . and something else. Something a little wild in his eyes.

"Any news about the flash drive?" Simon asked when they fell into step toward the elevator.

"It's Truth's for certain. But the files are encrypted. Theo and Lou are competing to see who can get in first."

So Dragon Boy was going to miss the big celebration? Didn't that just sound like a computer geek.

Though it pissed him off to ask, he had to. "Sage working on it with them?"

"No."

"Heard Dred was gonna take a look at her."

"Right. He healed her."

So she probably was going to be at the festival. And Theo wouldn't.

"Did you see anyone in the hall?" Quent asked suddenly. "Just now? Or recently?"

"Like who?"

"A woman. Messy dark hair, tall. Darkish skin . . . Hot."

Simon glanced sidewise at him. So that explained the underlying tension. "You expecting someone?"

"No."

When they got to the elevator, Quent gestured at the buttons. "Right, then. Do you mind?"

Simon pushed the down button so his friend didn't have to be invaded by the images and memories held by the wall. Sometimes he wore gloves, but apparently tonight he'd decided not to.

As they stepped into the elevator, Simon thought about the fact that he'd chosen to hide his unique ability while Quent and Dred had not. Of course, the fact that Quent could hardly touch anything without being bombarded had something to do with it—sometimes it was enough to knock him on his ass. And it was sort of obvious when Dred healed someone—or at least diagnosed them.

It was a lot easier to hide invisibility than those other talents.

But for the first time, Simon wondered about his reticence. If he should keep it a secret.

The elevator doors opened and Simon followed Quent out. The sounds of partying in full swing reached his ears and already he wanted to turn around and head back to his sanctuary.

But he didn't.

Instead, he and Quent found Elliott, Fence, and Wyatt in the Pub, already jovial and loose from a healthy number of draft beers.

"Man, if I ever seen two men on the hunt, I'm seein' 'em now." Fence rumbled a low, knowing laugh as they sat. He was a big fucking guy, linebacker size, with a ready smile and a mind that was always in the gutter. Yet, charm rolled off him in waves and the women seemed to gravitate to him like flies on shit. Fence shoved an empty glass at Quent and filled it with dark beer from a pitcher without asking.

Simon held up a hand to forestall any movement in his direction and instead beckoned for one of the servers. When she came over—a cute blonde named Dayna— he ordered his single whiskey, neat, and broiled snapper, fresh from the Pacific right down the street.

They sat for a while, shooting the shit—at least, Fence

and Elliott were. Wyatt slouched, quiet and brooding, making his way steadily through the beer in front of him. Simon knew that Wyatt, Quent, and Elliott were longtime friends. They'd been on a caving expedition led by a hired guide, Fence, when the Change occurred—which made Simon the outsider.

Maybe that was why he'd kept his strange new ability to himself.

Yet, they'd accepted Simon as one of them, no questions asked. And the four of them, even the brutally honest, harsh Wyatt, had become his friends.

Something Simon hadn't ever truly experienced before.

Music from the stage beyond drew Simon's attention, and he was glad to have something to focus on, other than the lowball that sat, untouched, in front of him . . . and the entrance to the Pub.

Beneath the lights, Jade sang deep and throaty about being almost blue, and Simon allowed himself one sip from the hot, burning whiskey.

After a while, Quent got up. The next thing Simon knew, the Brit had his hands on the hips of a fine-looking woman, slow dancing at the dark end of the crowded room. She was blond and tiny. Definitely not the woman Quent had been looking for in the hall, but apparently a worthy substitute.

Wyatt had disappeared with his arm around a brunette. Silently approving, Simon took another sip of whiskey.

At that moment, Elliott brushed against his arm, nonchalantly leaning closer. "Heads up. See the guy in the dark green shirt, unbuttoned, by the bar?"

Simon slid his gaze in that direction. Guy about their age stood there, holding a drink, watching the stage. Dark blond hair, cropped short. Slavic sort of appearance with high cheekbones and a strong, square chin. If he didn't know it was impossible, Simon would peg the guy as a cop or Fed.

Or someone like himself.

"That's Ian Marck."

Simon met Elliott's eyes without moving the rest of his body, and understood the disquiet there. Ian Marck was the son of Raul Marck, the bounty hunter who'd taken Jade and brought her back to the Strangers. Elliott and Theo had rescued her, and although there was no longer a threat to her safety, that didn't mean the Marcks didn't have some other plans in mind.

"You got unfinished business?"

"I don't know." Elliott's mouth was a flat line and his eyes had turned hard. "I thought we were square. But I don't like it."

"Stay with Jade. I'll take care of it." Simon pushed his chair back and stood, bringing the drink with him. He walked casually around the perimeter of the Pub, adrenaline beginning to surge.

A sense of déjà vu filtered over him as he made his roundabout way to Marck.

I'll take care of him.

How many times had he said those words, and then proceeded to do just that? His stomach soured for a moment and he almost took another drink to settle it. Then decided not to.

Then he came around the corner, glancing automatically beyond the Pub entrance into the shadows beyond, and saw them. Simon faltered.

He shouldn't be surprised. He'd expected it. Known it was going to happen.

Hell, he'd practically initiated it by telling Dragon Boy

that Sage had been injured and letting him know, without so many words, that he'd better step up.

Apparently he had, if the way they were kissing was any indication.

Simon pulled his eyes away and allowed himself another sip. And he walked on past, angling through the crowded Pub, to stand next to Ian Marck.

"I hope you're not planning to make any trouble," Simon said without even looking at the man.

Marck didn't move. Just took his time, raised his glass of clear iced liquid, and took a sip. "Friend of the doctor's?"

Simon nodded once.

Jade finished her song, accepted the applause, and started into another.

"Doctor did me a favor, I did him one back. That's it."

"You planning to renege on the balance, you're going to find yourself more than a little uncomfortable."

Marck still didn't look at him, but his lips moved in a sort of half-smile. "Point taken. You can assure the doctor that Jade is of no interest to me."

"And your father?" Simon relished the feel of balled-up energy waiting beneath the surface of his calm exterior.

"My father is . . . no longer interested as well."

Despite the overlay of music, Simon caught the odd inflection in the other man's voice. "Is he dead?" He remembered Elliott saying that Marck's father had hung his son out to dry, and that Ian had planned to "take care of him."

Marck didn't respond except to turn and order another vodka.

Simon remained silent for a long moment. Then, following a little urge from his gut, he said, "Remington Truth. Know anything about him?"

This got Marck's attention and he glanced briefly at Simon. "You know about Truth?"

Simon shrugged. "I know the Strangers are desperate to find him."

"They're not the only ones." Marck turned back to watch Jade, who was now singing something from an old eighties movie Simon couldn't remember.

"If not for Jade, then why are you here?" he asked the other man.

"Same as you. Celebrating. Relaxing. Looking for a good lay." Ian Marck turned to look fully at him at last. He had cold blue eyes. "So fuck off."

Simon didn't bother to reply. He believed the man, but he was going to stick around him for a bit.

He didn't want to go back to the table quite yet, for Sage and Theo had just appeared and settled next to Elliott.

It looked a little too crowded.

Quent had his hands full of lush curves and his nose buried in sleek hair. The music and Jade's bedroom voice, combined with the pints he'd knocked back, left him feeling easy and sultry. Ready.

Very ready.

Nadine had caught his eye the other day when he'd been at dinner, and tonight she'd made her interest very clear. And Quent, a bit buggered by it all, had seen no reason to be reticent. Beautiful, tiny, blond . . . curvaceous. He had no complaints, and apparently neither did she.

She pressed herself against him just enough to let him know she was interested. Though he wasn't a fan of overt displays, he slid his hands to pat her ass and bent to taste her mouth.

As he was kissing Nadine, Quent looked up . . . and that was when he saw her.

Leaning arrogantly against the wall, she was mostly in shadow but for a swatch of light over her face. Arms crossed over her belly, beneath small, tight, high breasts. Perfect, warm handfuls.

She wasn't looking in his direction. Thank God.

Quent retrieved his tongue smoothly, aware that his heart was racing and it had nothing to do with the willing woman in his arms.

And then Zoë was looking at him, and he realized with a sudden body-wide heatwave that she *had* been watching. He looked straight back at her, feeling her eyes burn into him, dark and hot as their gazes met across a room filled with hundreds of other people.

He couldn't look away. Blood rushed through him, everywhere.

This was the first time he'd seen her, really seen her, in full light.

And bloody hell, she was stunning. Exotic, with her Bollywood actress coloring—stylelessly chopped blue-black hair, cinnamon skin, almond eyes, and lush, wide lips. A small pointed chin. A long, lean, athletic body, honed from what must be years of climbing through buildings and hunting *gangas*.

She wasn't in those thigh-high boots he'd pictured— that fantasy came roaring back to the front of his mind— but in low-riding many-pocketed pants and a skinny tank top. She wore a fisherman's vest open over it, but he knew very well what lay beneath.

Quent hadn't stopped dancing, nor did he release Nadine. Yet, even as he swayed and held another woman, he looked at Zoë. And told her exactly what he wanted.

She stared back, lifting her nose regally in a clear reference to his compromised position. He glared back, blatantly communicating his displeasure at her sneaking into his room and stealing the arrows.

Her mouth curled in haughty annoyance, then slid into a provocative smile.

Quent's belly dropped, his palms went damp, and he stepped on Nadine's tiny foot in an effort to keep from turning and breaking eye contact with Zoë. His partner gasped and looked up at him, drawing his attention from Zoë as the dance continued and they shifted away.

When he looked back, Zoë was gone.

Quent finished the dance and deposited Nadine back at the table with her friends. He didn't rush it, but he didn't waste time either. He wasn't about to go running off just because Zoë appeared and crooked her little finger.

The cute blonde seemed confused by his sudden change of heart, and he extricated himself from that awkward position carefully, leaving himself a back door. He was an expert at that, after all—hadn't he been found with Marley Huvane the same night he'd escorted Frankie Delaney to an event? Despite that, he'd taken Frankie home, spent the night, and escaped early the next morning.

Besides, he and Zoë didn't have any sort of arrangement. He owed nothing to her, nor she to him—which she'd made very clear.

But right now, she was what he wanted. And he knew just where to find her.

Trying not to think about how much of a Pavlov's dog he was being, Quent forced himself to saunter through the hotel and up to his room on the fifteenth floor.

He paused when he got to the door, and needed to take a deep breath before he opened it. The knob felt cold under his palms, and he settled a cool, amused smile on his face as he pushed the door and went in.

She wasn't there.

He checked the bathroom, then settled on the bed to wait.

But after twenty minutes, Zoë still hadn't arrived.

She was gone.

Drew's dead.
> — *from Adventures in Juliedom, the*
> *blog of Julie Davis Beecher*

CHAPTER 5

Simon would have kept his distance if Lou hadn't come into the Pub and, catching sight of him, gestured him over to the table.

Something must have happened, and although Simon could have found an excuse to stay by Ian Marck, he found himself unable to resist the pull. Curiosity.

Maybe a little bit of masochism too.

He sat down at the table next to Elliott, positioning himself so Sage and Theo were on the other end of the U-shape configuration and Lou was in the center next to Fence. Quent had disappeared after dancing with the blonde, and hopefully, Wyatt was getting laid.

"Anything?" Elliott asked, his voice muted by the music and low roar of voice around them.

"Marck claims he's here for social purposes," Simon replied. "I believe him, for now. He said his father's no longer interested in Jade. And that the two of you are square."

"I don't trust him."

"I don't either. And he wouldn't confirm whether Raul is dead or not. But I really don't think he's here to cause trouble."

Elliott gave a short nod, and settled back in his chair as he shot Simon a glance. "I have a feeling you'd know."

Simon took that for what it was worth—a subtle acknowledgment that his background might be unsavory, but that he wasn't going to be asked for details. "If he is . . ."

"If he is," Elliott said, "I'll take care of him." For a guy who was a doctor and had lived a fairly uneventful life—compared to Simon—he looked fully capable of doing so. Simon had seen that look on his own face, recognized it in many others.

"You won't be alone," he promised Elliott.

Then he turned his attention to Lou.

"You found something?" Theo was saying to his twin. He seemed relaxed and jovial, and a bit of smugness lurked in his eyes.

Simon thought he looked assy from a smear of lipstick near his mouth.

Did they even have lipstick now?

He supposed if they'd had makeup in Egyptian times, they could have it in post-cataclysmic eras too.

"Broke the code, of course," Lou said. "Three hours and nine minutes."

"That's 'cause I loosened it for you, bro," Theo replied. Sage laughed, and the sound rose above the sounds of revelry, catching Simon's attention before he could stop it.

Even in the bar light, her hair glowed like rich, curling flames. Someone had piled it so loosely on her head that little curls escaped, brushing her ears and cheeks and the nape of her neck. Either that, or it had been neat and formal till the Geek Squad got his hands on her. The dress plunged, but not indecently, nor was it the loose sack she'd been wearing the other night. But Simon was only too aware of the shape beneath the pinkish orange dress. And, by now, he figured Dragon Boy was too.

Despite the fiery color of her clothing and matching

hair, Sage's eyes held an impression of innocence and even a bit of absentmindedness. Simon suspected that if he were able to crawl inside her mind, he'd find that instead of knowing how much attention she was garnering tonight, dressed to kill, Sage would be mentally filing through her latest research. And wishing she could be back in the lab.

As his attention split between Lou and Theo's bantering, his normal scan of the crowded room, and the woman at the other end of the table, he noticed that her fingers were moving. And he realized she was typing.

Simon's mouth twitched in a surprised grin and he entertained himself with the possibility that the movements of her hands at the back of Theo's neck had been air-typing instead of a reaction to what was going on.

He tuned back into the conversation, which included a review of the files Lou had found on the flash drive. They huddled together to keep the conversation close, although the noise around them would act as a buffer.

"A list of contacts. Could be members of the Cult of Atlantis, or just his personal contacts," Lou was saying. "Quent will want to see it, but I already glanced through. His father is on there. Also, Truth's calendar. Might be interesting to look at." He shrugged. "Not sure if there's anything else that will help us."

Simon wanted to see it too. Mancusi didn't run in the mega-leagues like Parris Fielding or Remington Truth, but he needed to make sure.

"But the more we know about him—through his calendar and contacts, the better we'll understand him. And anything could help us determine where he might be, or how he disappeared. Names, addresses . . ." Sage said. Her fingers were still, settled on the table as she leaned forward to talk to Lou. Simon caught a glimpse of her blue eyes, now sparkling with intent instead of clouded with thought.

"I'm not sure that addresses will help us with anything anymore," Theo said with a little laugh. His arm rested around her waist and Simon could see the awkward stretch of her silky dress from its weight.

"It was an address that brought us to his place here in Envy," Sage replied, arching her fine red brow. "Otherwise, we wouldn't even have his flash drive."

"True," Theo replied. He looked down at her and tapped her pert little nose with a finger. *Vato.*

Sage rolled her eyes but she didn't appear offended. "Those documents will require a lot of study and analysis. Who knows what we'll find." She stood then, a bit clumsily. She must have tripped on Geek Squad's boat feet. "I'll be right back," she said, smoothing her hands down the front and sides of her dress and looking everywhere but at Simon.

"Where are you going?" Theo asked. As well he should, after what had happened last night.

"Restroom. Back in a sec."

Simon did not watch her toddle away on heels that she was obviously not used to. Instead, he made certain he was focused on the stage where Jade seemed to be wrapping up her set—in the opposite direction. A quick glance toward the bar told him that Ian Marck was still there, nursing a vodka. He turned back to the conversation.

"So you and Sage, huh?" Fence said as soon as she was out of earshot. His wide grin seemed even brighter because of his dark skin. "Nice job, brother. How long has this been going on?"

"I wondered the same thing myself," Lou added, peering at his brother above his glasses. He wore an expression that was somewhere between awkwardness and appreciation.

Theo rubbed his chin and had the grace to look a little bashful. "It's . . . in its early stages," he said, shifting in his seat.

Bueno. Simon nodded mentally, congratulating the *vato* for playing it cool. Maybe he wasn't as much of an idiot as he thought.

Despite Fence's inclination to probe for further details, Theo played the gentleman and changed the subject to the Internet-like network they were building of access points, filling in more details for those who weren't involved. "The next stage would be to expand it to the north and west," he said. "And then expand concentrically where we've already got a network."

"How many people or locations are involved in the Resistance and the current network?" Simon asked.

"We have twenty NAPs set up, covering a geographic area of forty square miles, with Envy in the northwesternmost segment. At this time, they're secret and we only have three members of the Resistance actually online with their own computers. They're working to recruit more members and eventually we'll set them up with their own computers," Theo explained.

"But we have to be careful, keep it under wraps. After what happened with Charlie Venter, it's imperative that we know who to trust," Lou added.

"Charlie Venter?" asked Simon. "A snitch?"

Lou shook his head. "No, one of our technology experts. His wife was killed by a pack of *gangas* while a Stranger watched, and he came to Envy afterward. He lived here for four years, then about six months ago offered to be a satellite agent in Bracewood—to the southeast. He asked too many questions, and someone must have said something to a bounty hunter or a Stranger. His computers were taken and he disappeared. The assumption is that he's dead."

"Good guy," Theo said soberly. "Smart as hell, but he hated the Strangers so much, it was hard for him to hide it. We've got to be even more careful now."

"Especially you." Lou looked at his brother. "You, Jade, and Elliott are now recognizable by Raul Marck, his son, and anyone else Preston communicated with during Jade's rescue. As well, any information that might have been on Venter's computer could identify you. You're going to have to stay beneath the radar."

Theo nodded. "More careful, but I'm not going to stop now. We need that network to grow a lot faster than it has been."

"Word."

"So, obviously expanding the network could help to find Remington Truth," Simon commented. "If you could send out a broadcast of his picture and name, someone might recognize him." He noticed that Ian Marck had disappeared, and that little warning prickle started over his shoulders.

Jade was off the stage. Marck was gone.

And so was Sage.

Simon nudged Elliott and nodded toward the bar.

As the other man stood abruptly, obviously to check on Jade, Simon looked toward the entrance of the Pub. That uneasy feeling crawled over him, and he nearly stood to go check things out in person. But then he saw Sage.

She was talking to someone just out of sight of the doorway, but at least he could see her and know that she wasn't being dragged off into a dark corner. Her body language was one of awkwardness, but that didn't surprise him—she was fairly shy, and not at all gregarious like her friend Jade.

Theo had slipped into a familiar argument with his brother about something geek related, and once plunged into that topic—which included terms such as bigtable and redundant storage—seemed to forget about everything around him.

Damn good thing Simon was there. Watching out for his girl.

Of course, that was what he was trained to do. Watch out for the other guy's girl.

Sage shifted, and her hands fluttered in stiff animation. And then she moved again, and Simon saw whom she was talking to.

Ian Marck.

He was out of his seat in an instant. Striding through the Pub, he knew he appeared calm and casual, not a hair out of place . . . but inside, his muscles bunched and black violence stirred. He didn't make the mistake of reaching for that nonexistent holster this time, but instead he felt for the knife that he'd tucked into the back of his belt, beneath a tattered jean jacket.

Marck saw him coming. To his credit, he didn't flicker an eyelash. But their eyes met, understanding flashed between them, and then, when Simon was just out of earshot, Ian looked back at Sage. Said one more thing, leaned in much too closely and touched her arm, then turned and walked away.

Fuck-you was stamped all over his swagger as the bounty hunter melded into the crowd.

Sage turned and started back toward the Pub. Simon would have let her walk past and gone after Marck, but she noticed him and halted.

"Following me again?" she said. Chill brushed her voice.

"Do you know him?"

"No. He caught me as I was coming back." She seemed to rethink her coolness. "Do you?"

"That was Ian Marck." He knew she'd be aware of the name, but wasn't surprised she'd never seen a picture of him. The days of cell phone pics and Facebook were long gone.

Her eyes grew wide. "The bounty hunter?"

"What did he want?" But Marck'd already told him: *Same as you. Celebrating. Relaxing. Looking for a good lay.*

Fucking coño.

She started to speak, then stopped. "I think I'd better tell everyone at once."

Sage led the way back to the table, fully aware of Simon trailing behind her. She needed to put some space between them. He seemed ready to . . . do something.

Why was her heart slamming so hard in her chest?

Probably because he'd just appeared, suddenly, as he'd done twice now. No, three times. But it was the expression on his face, the set, black expression, that affected her. How could such a beautiful countenance turn so dark and frightening? Was it simply because he hated Ian Marck for kidnapping Jade?

Back at the table, Sage had no choice but to sit next to Theo again, despite the fact that she felt acutely uncomfortable with his arm around her. In front of everyone—Lou, Fence, Elliott . . . and Simon.

Especially Lou.

And most especially Simon.

And now that Jade was approaching, the goggling surprise in her friend's eyes was just too much. Sage felt her cheeks heat and she shifted slightly away from Theo, under the guise of adjusting the stupid heels Jade had insisted she wear.

Theo had sort of backed her into a corner outside the pub, and the look in his eyes had been so . . . intense. When he started to kiss her, Sage hadn't pulled away. Even when she felt things get a little . . . intense.

Yes, that was the only way to describe the manner in which Theo had begun to act around her. Intense.

Obviously interested in more than just a few kisses. *Obviously.* Her cheeks heated even more and she realized her heart was thumping faster. The things he'd murmured into her ear, the way his hands settled around her waist, and the lingering way he looked at her. All of a sudden, things had changed.

Sage hadn't realized he thought of her so . . . intensely. That made her a little nervous because she wasn't feeling the same way. And she was curious, although she tried to keep things from getting too heavy. This was new. Why not? She'd be careful. Take things slow. This was a different Theo, and this . . . *thing* . . . with him felt a lot different than it had with Owen. Not overwhelming, but . . . nice. Not frightening.

Maybe she was ready to have a relationship now. And Theo was . . . well, her best friend. And he obviously— *obviously*—felt something for her. And he was handsome and very special, and—

Sage realized everyone was staring at her. Now her face was burning up and she quickly tried to corner her shattered thoughts. "Um . . . Ian Marck intercepted me on my way back from the restroom," she said.

Apparently, they already knew this, because the expressions in the faces around the table didn't change. "I didn't know who he was until Simon told me," she explained, gaining control of her scattered brain and focusing on the story. "And he didn't pretend to know me, but he did ask me if I was a Corrigan from Falling Creek."

"What did he say? Exactly?" Theo's voice was hard, and she saw the same sort of darkness in his eyes that Simon's had held. She felt the tautness of his body next to hers.

"He wasn't rude, if that's what you mean. He just asked me." She caught Jade's concerned gaze and suspected that her friend was thinking about the last time she'd come face-to-face with Ian Marck and his father. That was when she'd been brought back to Preston, the Stranger who'd imprisoned her for three years as his mistress.

"What else did he say?" Lou asked, his voice calm, his bespectacled eyes steady. Lots of people in Envy—in fact, most of them—thought he was more than a little crazy, with his conspiracy theories about the Strangers. But Sage knew how brilliant and razor-sharp he was, and how perceptive. Now he sat, waiting for her story without making assumptions or inserting his own opinions.

"He said, 'You might want to let your friends know there's information in Falling Creek.'" Sage remembered how serious his eyes had been, those intense blue ones. If she'd known he was Ian Marck, she might have been apprehensive, but the man she talked to hadn't given her any reason to be concerned.

"I asked him what he meant, and he said, 'Remington Truth. They might find something there.' Then he sort of looked at me funny. 'They're looking for him. Trying to beat the Strangers, right?'"

"Opportunity there . . ." Lou murmured. Sage knew his mind was working because his wrinkled, veined hands drummed on the table. " 'Your friends.' He obviously knows who we are. After what happened with Jade, he knows we aren't supportive of the Strangers."

"Raul hung his ass out to dry, practically turned him over to Preston," Elliott said. "I doubt Ian's hanging around his father anymore. If Raul's even still alive."

"Nice thing to do to a son," said a clipped voice.

Sage realized Quent had been standing behind her for a while. The blond man didn't look happy at all. His hair, which was usually neatly combed away from his forehead and temples, straggled around his face, which looked haggard.

No one responded to his comment, which hung there for a moment. Then, with exaggerated, precise movements, Quent pulled a chair over and sat down.

"Anyway," Sage said, once again picking up the thread of the story, "I got the impression that he was trying to tell me something."

"Obviously," Theo said. He looked at Lou, and Sage could almost hear the sizzle in the air as their thoughts raced, connected, and swirled together. The fact that they were twins left them often following the same train of thought, usually ending up at the same location and conclusion.

"If there's a clue to Remington Truth in Falling Creek, we should check it out," said Lou.

"He's a bounty hunter," Theo added. "He kidnapped Jade and was working with Preston. Why would he want to help us find Truth?"

Elliott shrugged his broad shoulders and Sage saw him exchange glances with Jade. "He cared about a girl called Allie enough to risk bringing me there against the will of the Strangers," Elliott said. "Maybe now that he and Raul have parted ways, he's rethought his position."

"Or maybe it's a trick," Theo said.

"Maybe it is. But we should check it out anyway. And besides," Lou said, "Falling Creek would be a good place for an NAP . . . and a member of the Resistance."

"We can't just show up in Falling Creek," Theo said. "They're fu—" He stopped and glanced down at Sage.

"You can say it," she said, leaning forward on the table. The others who didn't know about FC were watching with interest. "They're strange. And weird. And very closed. Which is why it makes perfect sense for me to go." She smiled, looking around at everyone. *At last . . . something to do outside of the computer lab.*

"I'll go with you," Theo said immediately. "You're right—we can't just show up and expect them to allow us to join them. But they'll let you in. Hell, they'll welcome you back. The prodigal daughter returning home." He looked immensely pleased with himself. "And you definitely can't go alone."

She definitely agreed with that. There was no way she was going alone.

"I think we do need to check it out," Lou said. "And Sage is the obvious choice. You still have family there, and they'll remember you. And aside from that, you know exactly what we've been doing with the NAPs and the network. You could set one up yourself."

She nodded, her pulse faster and her mind racing. "I'll tell them I've just decided to return home, that I've come to agree with their . . . philosophy."

"Philosophy of what?" Elliott asked.

"The residents of Falling Creek live there in a sort of . . . well, commune. Compound. And they believe that the most important thing we need to do is to repopulate the human race," Sage explained. Remembering growing up there sent a little nervous shiver through her, but she reminded herself she was older now. In control of herself and she knew what life was like beyond the walls of FC.

"So all they do is have orgies? I'm so there," Fence said, then grinned as he took a big drink of beer.

Sage didn't take offense. She'd heard worse, much worse. "I was only twelve when I left, so I don't know all of the details," she said. Although that was a little misleading, because she knew more than she'd let on. Or cared to think about. And the proper term was escaped, not left.

After all, she was being prepped for her own wedding. To a man thirty years her elder. Who already had five wives and twenty kids. Yes. He'd been doing his part to procreate.

No, she was definitely not going alone. In fact, she was going to go as a married woman.

"You can't go, Theo," Jade said.

Sage felt him tense next to her again and swivel to face Jade. He opened his mouth to speak, but Lou beat him to it. "She's right, bro. You can't. You're too recognizable. It's not safe."

"I'll be fine," Theo said, stubbornness . . . and maybe a little desperation rolling off him. "Sage can't go alone."

"No, she can't go alone, but you can't go with her. It's too risky. Nor can Jade or Elliott. Or me," Lou added firmly. "It's got to be someone else."

"Theo," Sage said, putting her hand on his. "I don't want anything to happen to you. Don't risk it."

He squeezed her hand, hard enough that it almost hurt. "Maybe it's too dangerous for you too."

Sage shook her head. No, he wasn't going to win that battle. "Theo."

"I'll go," Fence said, sitting upright in his seat. His eyes were full of good humor.

Then Sage looked down the table at Simon, who'd said absolutely nothing since they sat back down. He was watching her, and as their eyes caught, a wave of trepidation . . . and something else . . . washed over his face. Then it settled into an expression of bald reluctance.

Before she realized it, Sage was speaking. "Simon's going to go with me."

"You going to fill me in on our plan for getting into Falling Creek?" Simon asked.

Sage looked over at him, her glorious hair caught up in a ponytail that rested as low on her neck as his own did. He exhaled slowly. He was in such deep shit.

She had to shade her eyes against the bright sun in order to look over and up at him. "I will. And I never did thank you for agreeing to go with me," she said as they hiked.

"You didn't leave me much choice."

She smiled. "I know. That's why I'm thanking you."

She might be thanking him, but Theo Waxnicki was definitely not.

No, the Geek Squad had *not* been pleased when he realized how it was going down.

Simon felt some sympathy for the *vato*, so he'd drawn Dragon Boy aside for a little man to man. "You're gonna have to trust that I know how to keep her safe. I will. I'll bring her back in one piece."

He'd met the other man's furious eyes and bored into them with his own steady ones. He made them cold and hard, and full of warning, and hoped Theo would get the message that he was not to be messed with, and what he was capable of. No one would hurt Sage on his watch.

Simon could also have told Theo that he had absolutely no interest in Sage, that his own unbreakable personal code included never, ever poaching on a friend's—or boss's—woman, and that he'd been in even more tenuous situations in the past . . . but he didn't. He thought it would be best not to even put the thought in the other guy's mind.

Let Geek Squad simply worry about her safety, not also about her affections. In either case, she was in no danger.

In order to expedite the trip, Theo had driven Sage and Simon most of the way to Falling Creek in an old humvee. He and Elliott had stolen the truck from the Strangers a few weeks ago, and it had become the Resistance's first official vehicle—kept hidden from prying eyes and used only when necessary. In this world, no one but Strangers had access to automobiles or fuel so they kept it under wraps so as not to draw attention to themselves.

Not that it made much difference, because what was left of the roads were fucked up so badly it was almost better to not to drive at all.

Jade preferred horseback, but she had a way with the wild mustangs and could capture them almost every time she needed one. Hiking was still the most common mode of transportation, since people didn't travel around all that much. Danger from the *gangas*, decrepit buildings, and wild animals kept everyone cloistered in their settlements or small villages.

Which was why the communications network the Waxnickis were building was so important to tie the human race together.

The trip in the humvee had been horrendously bumpy and jarring—due partly to the speed at which Theo drove—and Simon was sure that Sage was going to puke at any given moment. She hadn't, but she'd looked pretty pasty for most of it.

Driving through the overgrown, destroyed streets, towns, highways, and suburbs was still a surreal experience for Simon. Reminders of twenty-first-century America were everywhere—overgrown and cracked mall and theater parking lots, random letters of now-playing movies still hanging onto their signs like tenacious claws. But they were so few that he couldn't figure out the crossword puzzle of the titles, except one that said IR N M N 2.

Iron Man 2, a movie he'd actually seen, having slipped into a theater during his flight from Mancusi and East Los in an attempt to shake off his pursuers. A half-century ago, and not the best of choices considering its loud violence.

He had enough of that in real life.

After driving them more than forty miles, Theo had stopped in a large, thick forest that might once have been a park with neat pathways, bike trails, resting benches, swings and slides and a skateboard park. An old garbage can sat, rusted and covered with moss, next to a row of equally rusted cars and minivans. Picnic tables and decrepit outhouses sat amid tall grass and eager trees.

Simon and Sage would walk the rest of the way—about four miles—and approach FC on foot so as not to garner any added attention. Simon had turned and walked away while Theo was saying good-bye to Sage, trying not to think about the fact that he was going to be responsible for her—which meant constantly in her proximity—for at least a week.

Pinche.

But, hell, if he could resist the beautiful, insistent Florita's bold attentions—even after she ordered him to help her with her dress (getting out of it, on more than one occasion), and when she slid into his bed one night after he'd had too many whiskeys—Simon knew he'd have no problem keeping his distance from the unassuming Sage.

He was on a job, and it wasn't as if Sage was going to be sliding into his bed or even giving him languishing looks like Florita had. Yes, she was gorgeous. Yes, her smile made his heart go berserk. And, yes, she had a brain to go along with a killer body that was just the slightest bit klutzy . . . But she'd never look twice at the likes of him.

Especially when she had buff, brilliant, *nice* Dragon Boy waiting for her.

Especially if she ever learned who he really was.

Simon looked at her, realizing she'd never answered his question. "So. Falling Creek. What do I need to know that I don't already?"

She nodded and tucked a wisp of hair behind her ear. She'd gone for almost a mile without tripping. If she were Florita, she'd trip on purpose, just so she could brush up against him, maybe grab a handful of ass. "After the Change, there was a big argument about how to reinstate humanity, that we needed to repopulate the earth with humans. After all, the race had nearly been wiped out."

"Not just from the earthquakes and storms," Simon said, scanning the area of ghost-towned, overgrown subdivisions. Listening. "But some sort of disease or epidemic?"

"No one's sure what caused it. Lou and Theo were there when it happened, so what I know comes from them. They said that about three days after the Change, people just started dying for no apparent reason. Either something was in the air, some sort of poison or gas was released during the Change or something . . . but whatever it was, some people who survived the cataclysmic events didn't make it."

"Obviously a few did."

"But not many. They think more people died from the poison than the actual Change," Sage told him. "Anyway, in Envy, there were two brothers, Robert and Kevin Corrigan. They were friends with a guy named Marck—Raul Marck's father, I think. They survived the Change and believed that nothing was more important than to procreate and repopulate. I guess they were afraid another epidemic might happen and wipe out the rest of them. Everyone agreed, but most people didn't subscribe to their ideas of breeding schedules and actually regimenting the process. Some people were more interested in making sure we had food and shelter."

"Sort of like the opposite of the Chinese single-child mandate," Simon said.

"There were lots of arguments about it, and Marck ran for mayor of Envy. He didn't win, and when, afterward, he tried to force the council into supporting his ideas, he and the Corrigans were run out of town."

"So they took their ideas and started their own settlement in Falling Creek."

"Right. The basic tenets of the Falling Creek commune is that everyone marries as soon as they reach puberty, and they have as many babies as possible. If someone isn't able or willing, they're expected to leave."

"Sounds like the potential for a lot of in-breeding."

She shook her head. "No, they're actually very careful about that. Records are kept so they can manage the genetic mixing. And they bring in new blood whenever they can."

Simon looked over at her. "So . . . what's the big deal with being a Corrigan?"

She pressed her lips together. "The Corrigan brothers were redheaded, pale skinned, and had these awful blue eyes—and they were also very, very fertile. Between the two of them, they fathered more than eighty children in a single generation at Falling Creek. There are *lots* of Corrigans."

Eighty children?

"And most of them had red hair and blue eyes?"

"Strong genes," she replied. "Kevin had six wives, and Robert had eight, until one of them died. In childbirth. Marck had five wives of his own, and fathered twenty children."

Holy Mother of God.

A cult. FC sounded like a damned cult. No wonder Theo had been concerned.

No wonder people stared at her, and made assumptions.

As if reading his mind, she continued in a matter-of-fact voice. "That's why outsiders think the worst of Corrigans—especially the Corrigan women. Their philosophy implies that the simple, singular purpose of women is to breed and bear children."

Which of course meant sex. Regularly. For a single purpose. So if a person was obviously a Corrigan, she was obviously a brood mare. Meant for sex.

No, Simon didn't need Sage to fill in the blanks. It wasn't any different from the old prejudice of black or Hispanic women being easy. Or Asian women being good in bed. The thought made him sick.

"You said they bring in new blood," he said after a while, when he could trust his voice to be cool. "People actually agree to live like that?"

"Yes. Well, as I recall, it's more men than women who are attracted to the idea of polygamy," Sage said, giving him a sidewise smile that nearly made *him* stumble.

Yeah. "If you'd have mentioned that part, I might have had to fight Fence to go with you." *Holy fuck, what the hell are you* saying*? Shut your mouth, Japp.*

But Sage was already looking at him with those amazing blue eyes—ones that he'd swear were tinted contacts if he didn't know better. "Would you have?" she asked.

"Sure," he said lightly. "After all, he'd be more interested in the extracurricular activities than helping you set up a NAP." Not that she'd know what he meant by the term extracurricular . . .

"Ah," Sage replied. "So, that brings me to another thing I should tell you."

Trepidation seized him, but he wasn't sure why. "What's that?"

"Well, considering the fact that when I left FC fifteen years ago, I was already slated to get married, the first thing they'll do when I come back is try to find me a husband. Especially since my cover—is that the word?—is that I've decided to embrace their philosophies. So we're going to have to pretend to be married."

"Right. That makes sense. But maybe we could just be engaged?" Simon managed to say calmly.

She looked at him a little shyly, as if gathering up all of her courage. "That won't be good enough. They don't believe in engagements. I mean, the whole point is to have babies. Procreate. Anything that stands in the way of that is considered inappropriate, even impermissible. And if I'm not actually married, they might try and find a way to get around that."

Of course.

"So we're going to have to pretend to be married. I don't want to give them any hint of suspicion. Any excuses . . . okay?"

"Sure." *Caught. Completely trapped. Even Florita would have been impressed.*

Sage's shoulders fell with relief. "Good. Thanks." She looked up at him from under her lashes. "I owe you one."

Oh yeah, God definitely had it in for Simon.

June 30, about three weeks after the day all hell broke loose

Drew's dead. I still can't accept it, but I have to.

Life, somehow, has gone on. If you can call what we're doing here living.

I've lost some of the numbness over Drew's death, but considering the fact that nearly the entire city has been destroyed, and there's been nothing from the outside world, I'm terrified that what we've lost is much greater than what we at first thought.

Earthquakes and storms were only the beginning. Three days—we think it was three days, most people agree it was, but we lost our sense of time during those early days.

And then people just started dying. Falling to the ground for no apparent reason. For no apparent reason!!!

That's what happened to Drew. He was standing right next to me, healthy and strong, helping me look for some food on the shelf in a CVS . . . and he collapsed. He was holding a can of beef vegetable soup.

And that was it. He was gone.

I'll never eat beef vegetable soup again.

Hundreds of people did the same. There were more dead bodies after that, and it sent those of us who miraculously did survive back into hiding for days.

There were so few of us after that. There are so few of us.

Looking over my blog entries, I know they'll never be posted of course, but I'm compelled to finish writing them. Maybe someday someone will want to read what happened from an eye witness. Even if not, I still have to express myself. Get it on paper, so I can get on with life.

> *— from Adventures in Juliedom, the blog of Julie Davis Beecher*

CHAPTER 6

To Sage's surprise, Falling Creek looked the same as she recalled. At the entrance was a massive iron gate, the only opening in a stone fence that surrounded the settlement. The fence had been damaged during the Change, but Sage had heard stories of how the two Corrigan brothers and Thaddeus Marck had worked to rebuild it. They'd used parts of buildings that had been destroyed—rubble, massive metal doors, slabs of concrete from driveways—to fortify the barrier, intent on keeping the *gangas* and wild animals out of their sanctuary.

Sage was certain their plan had also been to keep other humans out as well, for their departure from Envy had been a violent one.

The same scrolling iron letters that spelled out the name of the settlement—*Falling Creek*, and then beneath it, in smaller letters, *Estates and Country Club*—still decorated brick pillars on both sides of the gates, gates that had been opened to them immediately upon her identification. She was stunned when Simon told her that each of the large brick structures had been single-family homes.

Having grown up in one of the intact buildings with her mother, brothers, half-siblings, and her father's three other wives—a total of twenty-three people—Sage simply couldn't imagine families of only three, four, or five living there. She wondered how many of her extended family was still here in Falling Creek. And how well they'd remember her.

"What did they need all that space for?" she asked as they followed one of the guards down a curving pathway. Flowers grew in organized clumps along the way and children played in the distance. "How did they use it?"

Simon had looked at her, the expression on his face sober and a little sad. "Sometimes it was a matter of status—having a large house. And sometimes it was for privacy or simply comfort. Americans were big on comfort."

"Did you grow up in a big house like that?" she asked curiously.

He gave a short laugh. "Not even close."

She waited for him to say more, but he simply transferred his attention to the area around them, effectively ending the conversation.

The original subdivision, as Simon called it, had contained twenty mansions clustered in a large circular configuration. When Marck and the Corrigans founded the settlement fifty years ago, only four of the buildings were habitable, although they hadn't been without some damage. By the time Sage grew up, twelve of them were being utilized for living space, although in some cases, the buildings weren't completely intact. Now, according to the guard, who turned out to be Bennie, one of her brothers, fourteen of the buildings were used in some capacity.

She was a little surprised that he recognized her immediately, and even more so when he acted pleased to see her, as if she hadn't disappeared years ago. "Glad you've returned," Bennie told her, glancing at Simon with interest.

This was her first instance of introducing him as her husband, and she managed to do so smoothly, adding, "I told Simon what a comfortable and welcoming place Falling Creek is," she said. "And since our home was destroyed in a *ganga* attack, we decided to start our life over here."

"They'll welcome you with open arms," Bennie promised. "Father's dead, but the rest of us who are still here—you know, the family—will be glad to see you again. And we're always looking for people who embrace our philosophy. In fact, Lark's working in the Community House and she'll get you all set up."

Lark had been their oldest half-sibling, and she would be close to forty by now. Sage learned from Bennie that one of their full brothers had left FC about four years ago, and that the other was responsible for managing the cotton farming this year. Five of their half sisters had run away or disappeared over the years—not an uncommon occurrence. But the rest of their fourteen half-siblings were also still in Falling Creek, married and having babies and doing their part for the community.

"Sharon will be surprised to see you," Bennie added as they left, mentioning the half sister that was closest to Sage in age. "She works in the southeast garden, fourth quadrant."

"I'll look for her," Sage replied, wondering how it would feel to see Sharon again. Which of them had changed more?

As she and Simon walked along the sweeping street to the east, Sage was mentally ticking off memories. The swings where she'd fallen off and skinned her knee on a pile of wood chips, the little cluster of almond bushes where she'd first discovered Buttons, her kitten; even the small pond where she and her friends had penned in turtles and frogs. Those were happy times, even the skinned knee.

But as she'd grown older—gotten breasts and begun to menstruate, an event that was publicly celebrated in Falling Creek—things had changed. The memories weren't as pleasant.

She noticed the willow tree where one of the candidates to be her husband had cornered her for a conversation about his hope that he'd be selected. This was in between his hawking and spitting, and scratching his sparsely haired, concave chest. She'd had to breathe through her mouth so she didn't have to smell his nasty breath.

In the end, he hadn't been the one chosen to be her husband. Instead, a man nearly thirty years her senior had convinced her father that he'd be the better candidate. Sage refused to look at the little chapel that had been used for all weddings—those that had been voluntary or not. She well remembered Sharon's dismay when she'd been wed to her husband, a rude man ten years her senior.

At the east end of the settlement was the Community House, where all of the community's administration and management took place. Sage well remembered this sprawling building, with its vaulted ceilings and cold marble floors, for this was where the records were kept, birthing and breeding plans were made, and the settlement's government met and functioned. It had seemed austere to her when she was a child, for they were always being hushed and shushed so they wouldn't interrupt "important meetings."

As she got older, and was assigned to work in the kitchen for a year, the building lost some of its formality, for it was filled with the muffled giggles of teenaged girls and muttered gossip in the corners. The large kitchen was still intact, but the floor-to-ceiling windows that had lined

the wall of its dining room had been destroyed during
the earthquakes. Now, although some of them had been
bricked over, others remained open to the mild elements.
It never got cold enough in Falling Creek for it to be uncomfortable.

Beyond the former line of glass windows lay acres of
rolling meadows. At one time, she understood that it had
been a golf course, also enclosed by the stone wall, but
now the fields were farmland where they grew cotton and
corn, as well as pastures for cattle, cows, and sheep.

The only thing Sage knew about golf was from the old
DVD *Caddyshack*. Theo and Lou had found the movie
unaccountably hilarious, and had made her watch it more
than a dozen times even though she didn't understand any
of the humor. That and another film called *Animal House*
were their favorites—and her reaction to both movies was
the same: complete confusion laced with horrified fascination.

Looming like a gray-blue beast on the northwest edge
of Falling Creek was Hell's Wall, the ragged, angry-look-
ing mountain that acted as backdrop for the settlement.
Its sharp clifflike top and sparse greenery gave it a forbidding appearance, and its sheer wall rose like an iron-
colored curtain beyond the stone wall.

"Jesus. Don't they worry about rockslides?" Simon
muttered, looking up at the monster.

Sage nodded. "It's always been a concern. But they've
been very careful, and have protection in place."

Before she could explain further, they had arrived at
the Community House and once inside, Sage and Simon
had fallen into their agreed-upon roles and story.

"Sage? Is it really you?" Lark rose from her desk to
show a large, pregnant belly as Sage introduced herself.
"I can't believe you've returned!"

They embraced, a bit awkwardly due to the desk and belly, and Sage looked over her half sister. "You look very healthy and happy," she said. They had a few moments of Lark filling her in on where she could find some of their other family members, and then Sage explained why she and Simon were there.

"So you wish to return to Falling Creek? As a full member of the community?" asked Lark, who was now Mrs. Lark Tannigan, as she settled back behind her desk. A boxy gray computer that chugged along as if it were on its last legs sat at one side of the table, and a stack of papers rested on the opposite. "It's been a long time, hasn't it? And I must say, it's not often that someone returns to FC after leaving. But now you have returned, and we'll welcome you back for certain."

"Thank you." Her response had been soft and mild, not because she was nervous or cowed, but because that was the role she played.

"Sage and I believe it's our responsibility to do our part to rebuild the human race," Simon said. He spoke in a more formal tone than she'd ever heard him, smooth and almost stilted.

"Indeed it is." Lark looked at him, avid curiosity as well as admiration clear on her face. "How long have you been married?" she asked, clicking industriously on the computer keyboard.

"Three months," Simon responded.

"Where did you meet? And where were you married?"

"In Turnedy Court," he replied. "We met and married there."

She looked up. "Is that the settlement that was destroyed by a river flood?"

"It was a flood as well as an attack by the *gangas*,"

Simon replied. They'd agreed to use that as their back story so that they would have a legitimate reason to move to a new settlement. "My family was killed in the event."

"I'm so sorry," Lark Tannigan said. She seemed sincere, and Sage remembered her oldest sibling as always being very motherly and kind. Then she asked, "No pregnancies yet?"

"No."

"But you have been attempting it, of course. Regularly? Are you familiar with your cycle? There are no health problems?"

Sage's face burned and she dared not look at Simon. She'd expected this sort of interrogation, but not so quickly. And not with him present. *How embarrassing.* "Yes, we have been . . . active."

When Lark paused, waiting for more answers, Simon responded. "No health problems." His voice sounded clipped.

Lark pursed her lips and delicate little lines that looked like stitches radiated from her mouth. "And you, Mr. . . . what was your last name?"

"Japp."

"Mr. Japp. Do you or have you ever had any other wives?"

"No."

Lark nodded, clicking another note, then looked up with a smile. The little lines smoothed out. "Well, we can certainly help you with that. We're always interested in more male residents in our little community here. For obvious reasons."

"Is that a real computer?" Sage asked, sounding breathless with amazement. She thought it prudent to change the subject. And maybe even to learn something that might come in handy, like how many computers they had.

"Why, yes it is," Lark replied proudly. "Only in the last five years have we been able to computerize everything. You can imagine how much easier it makes it to keep track of the family tree, so to speak." She laughed.

Yeah, it would probably work even better if you had a computer that actually ran. Sage guessed that the Council Leader, probably a son of one of the Corrigans, had a computer that worked much better than Lark Tannigan's. Something more along the lines of Lou's or Theo's.

She wondered if there was a way for her to look at it . . . and whatever secrets it might hold. It was too much to hope that Remington Truth had been a resident here, but there might be something else of interest. She tucked that possibility away for future contemplation.

She and Simon had already discussed and agreed upon their plan: to find a place to set up the NAP, and while doing so, to try to steer the conversation with FC residents toward Remington Truth whenever possible. It was unlikely anyone there would know the meaning of the name Remington Truth, so they weren't concerned about raising suspicions. Still. They had to be delicate about it just in case.

"Well, then," Lark continued after Sage had time to properly admire her desktop workhorse. "I'll bring your information to the board, and they'll make a decision about where you'll live. Sage, honey, I'm so glad you're back. Clearly you belong here, and we'll all be pleased to welcome you home. And . . . oh, yes, I neglected to ask about your trade or skills, Mr. Japp. We'll need to know what you can bring to the community besides your sperm." Lark beamed as if she'd just offered them a plate of cookies. "Not that we aren't glad to get that regardless!"

Simon answered smoothly, "I cook. And I'm an excellent hunter. A very good shot."

"Wonderful. We can always use another chef. And we do send out hunting parties weekly." Lark rested her fingers on the keyboard and looked at him. "Well, now, let's get you settled in a temporary residence. It's nearly time for dinner." Then she turned to Sage. "While your husband gets settled in your room, we'll get your medical exam started. Need to get the chart and vitals going. I'm sure you remember your mother doing all that, don't you? And of course, I'm an old hand too—this is my fifth." She patted her round stomach. "We can get your Mr. Japp's vitals later. Yours are much more important at this time."

Sage was whisked away for a variety of tests to determine whether she was healthy and where she was in her reproductive cycle. She didn't want to think about Simon's reaction when he learned he'd have to have his sperm count checked.

She had a feeling he wasn't going to be very pleased.

Things had moved rapidly after that. Her medical exam took some time, and by the time she'd been directed to the small room she and Simon would be sharing, he was gone. Their room was located in the Community House as a temporary accommodation, and Sage's first thought was how very small it was.

And how much smaller it would be with both of them in there. Dampness sprang onto her palms.

One large bed dominated the space. It probably would have appeared inviting to a woman sharing the room with a man who was actually her husband. A menagerie of red pillows had been arranged at its head, and although the air was warm, a thick pink comforter covered the bed.

The rest of the area was much less elaborate: A cushioned armchair sat in one corner with a small lamp and table. For reading, she thought. A bureau rested against the wall near a window. And, thank God, a door led to their own bathroom, complete with shower.

Now, hours later, Sage reflected on just how much the room had shrunk when she and Simon returned to it alone, at last. He'd been quiet and almost short with her, unwilling to converse about anything, despite the fact that she, for once, needed to talk.

"I'm tired," was all he'd said, cutting her off when she tried to converse.

Despite his sharp, abrupt tone, instead of being hurt, she'd brushed off his rudeness. After all, he was there because she'd forced him into it. He didn't have to be pleased about it.

And she couldn't blame him—it had been a long, difficult day.

Half the day had been filled with horribly nauseating travel—she'd nearly horked out of the humvee's window, but she absolutely did not want to puke in front of Theo or Simon again. Then she'd battled nerves and apprehension about their reception in Falling Creek, followed by the intrusion of an extensive medical exam, a dinner filled with veiled inquisition and blatant curiosity by other FC residents, and then they'd been taken on a walking tour of the entire settlement. But the most difficult of moments had occurred when she and Simon were informed publicly, during dinner as they sat next to Sharon and one of her co-wives, that they should refrain from intercourse that night because she was approaching ovulation, and he needed to save his sperm.

Sage thought she might dive under the table, and she definitely felt the muscles stiffening in Simon's thigh next to hers. But since no one else even flickered an eyelash at such a personal topic, her discomfort soon faded into pragmatism. Of course. This entire settlement lived, breathed, and existed solely for human procreation. Talking about it was like talking about the weather, or what was for dinner.

So, after a day like hers had been, Sage hadn't really expected to fall asleep easily. Especially since she was in a strange bed.

With a half-dressed man next to her.

Right next to her. So close, she could feel the heat of his body, even though they were separated by a good buffer of space about the width of a pillow.

But she didn't have to be *so* awake. Did she? It had to be well past midnight, likely cruising toward dawn. She'd have an assignment in the morning and plenty of work to do to contribute to the community.

Lying stiff, still, listening to the sounds of her new environment, Sage tried to ignore the most unfamiliar one of all: the low rush of Simon's easy, gentle breathing.

As quiet as it was, the sound seemed to fill her ears, expanding into the whole room and taking over her consciousness. She dared not move, and every time she took a breath, she held it, waiting to see if his rhythm changed.

It didn't. Unlike Sage, he slept soundly.

She didn't know that much about him, of course, but it had become obvious that he adapted easily, and was even used to adventure and danger. Change and unfamiliar environments didn't throw him off balance like they did her. She supposed that shouldn't be a surprise, after what he'd been through in the last seven months.

But it wasn't as if she was crippled or paralyzed by being here in Falling Creek. She just had so much to think about, to analyze and evaluate, to turn off her mind and sleep.

Especially with Simon in the room, sleeping soundly in a pair of shorts.

A pair of shorts.

Would it have been easier to turn off her racing mind if he'd been wearing, say, heavy jeans and a bulky sweater? If he hadn't stripped off his T-shirt in front of her . . . even though his back was turned?

If he'd left his hair pulled back in its tie instead of loosening it?

Sage swallowed and the sound was loud to her ears. Her insides tingled, her foot itched, she needed to move . . . but she was afraid she'd awaken him.

Or, worse, that he'd realize she wasn't sleeping.

Anyone would feel odd, sharing a room with a strange man, wouldn't they? Not that Simon was strange, but he was, really, a strang*er*. Invading her personal space, her privacy—out of necessity of course, but still. It was odd. Unsettling.

And she couldn't put the image of his tanned, muscular shoulders out of her mind. She hadn't even known men had muscles in their back like that, rippling like gentle waves.

Oh God. Now she really needed to move, to shake off that squiggly feeling in her belly.

She was going to be a *ganga* in the morning, and have heavy black circles under her eyes that would likely provoke comment. The people of Falling Creek were excessively concerned with one's health and well-being—especially the women. The precious vessels of humanity.

Some women liked that status. The protection, the caring, the reverence. Even the structure, the luxury of not having to make decisions or to worry. Her mother had.

And look what it had done to her.

Even at the young age of twelve, Sage had resisted the principles and rules, the blueprint for her life.

"Sage."

For a moment, she thought she'd dreamt it. The sound was so quiet, almost like a breath in the air.

She froze, on her back and staring at the ceiling, holding her breath. Then she felt movement next to her, slow, unrushed. As if he were merely shifting in his sleep. The bed dipped slightly.

And then he touched her, brushing lightly against her arm with his fingers.

For some reason, she could picture his hand perfectly, as if she were looking at it. He had an elegant, capable one. That was why she'd noticed it—with long fingers and a solid wrist loosely encircled by a slender leather band. Broad and smooth, with very little hair on the knuckles. Just enough to indicate it belonged to a man.

She began to breathe again—she wouldn't have been able to hold her breath any longer if she wanted to—then froze as his fingers brushed over her a second time, sliding along her arm, and then curling gently around her wrist.

"Shh," he said, on little more than a breath.

Sage realized he'd turned to face her. Heart pounding, palms dampening, and belly fluttering, she held still, wondering if he was going to touch her again. Roll closer, and bring his warm, muscled body next to hers . . .

Her heart thumped so hard she thought it must be jolting the bed, and she moistened her lips, realizing simultaneously that her mouth was dry . . . and that she wouldn't at all mind him coming close to her. *Oh God*. Her stomach flipped and she felt a rush of heat wash over her.

But he didn't move again. She felt the warmth of his breath, faint and distant against her cheek; he'd definitely shifted closer.

"The room," he said, very slowly and so softly she could barely hear him, "is being watched."

Great. How was she going to get dressed and undressed, knowing she was being spied on?

Simon's grip gently tightened around her, as if to ask if she'd heard him. She curled her fingers into a fist. The tendons of her wrist shifted beneath his hand. "Okay," she breathed.

"Be careful," he added, low and barely discernable, "what we say here." So that explained why he'd cut her off earlier.

She tightened her fist again in response, and, after a quick squeeze he released her, sliding his warm hand away.

Sage bit her lip. Silence. A million questions raced through her mind. No, she was definitely not going to get any sleep tonight.

She carefully rolled to her side, facing him. In the gray light, she could see the rise of his bare shoulder, squared off, sleek with muscle, and brushed with the same bit of moonlight that glossed his cheekbone. His eyes were dark, in shadow, and she couldn't tell if they were open or closed. She couldn't see anything but the silhouette of his facial bones and shoulder, and the wash of dark strands of hair on the side of his face.

Silence reigned for a moment, and she wondered if he'd gone back to sleep. He didn't move, and his breathing shifted the air, regular and easy.

How did he do that?

Theo could do the same thing—drop off to sleep at a moment's notice. She'd seen him do it—come to think of it, she'd shared a room with him once before too. Platonically, of course, sleeping in separate beds, when her room had to be redone. That hadn't been any big deal.

Sage pursed her lips and, telling herself this was no

big deal either, she reached out, sliding her hand beneath the covers.

Her fingers didn't go far before they connected, flat and solid, with warm, smooth skin. Not a gently haired arm, but solid and broad. His chest.

Oops. And . . . *holy crap. Solid.*

Sage pulled her fingers back, but she was suddenly very warm. Really warm. "Uh, sorry. Uh, Simon?"

"Yes?"

Her fingers were *tingling.* Good grief. "How do you know?"

Beneath the covers, she felt even hotter—as if heat rolled off her, settling in the sheet-covered hollow between them as they lay facing each other. She didn't need to touch him . . . she could already feel his heat.

"I did some checking." Again, his voice was so soft, she could barely hear it. "I don't know if they have audio," he added, and she smelled the faint mint of his mouthwash. "But they have a camera."

"Why?"

The bed moved as he shrugged slightly. "I'll try to find out. But . . . they want to see if we can be trusted. Probably anyone new is watched."

She thought about reaching to touch him again. She wanted to, and had an image of her hand, pale and slender, spread over his dark chest . . .

"Are you all right?" he asked a moment later, still so very softly. "Any problems today?"

"I'm fine. It's strange to be back."

"Bad memories?"

That stopped her for a minute. She had memories of her first twelve years . . . but were they bad? Or just . . . memories? Seeing her mother die was horrible, but other than that . . . she remembered playing, running in the fields, swimming, climbing on old tires that had been stacked and secured, even an elaborate tree house. There'd always been lots of kids to play with, of course. "Some."

"I'm sorry I snapped at you. Earlier."

"It didn't bother me."

"It didn't?"

"No. We all get stressed. I thought you were just . . . tense. All the stuff going on."

He made a little sound, not really a laugh, not a snort. Just a little choked guff of air. "Yeah."

All she had to do was move her hand into the space between them, slide it closer, and she'd touch him again. "Simon," she said, steeling herself . . . for something. She opened her hand, safely, silently, under the covers, her fingers reaching out into the pocket of heat between them.

"I promised Theo I'd keep you safe," he said suddenly. A little louder and more distinctly than he'd been speaking.

She nodded, her head rustling softly against the pillow. "I know you will."

"He was annoyed that he had to stay behind."

Yes, she knew that. Sage curled her fingers back into her palm. Theo. It could be Theo lying in this bed, facing her as if they were two lovers indulging in some pillow talk. Blind to each other in the dark, but close enough to hear, and feel, and even smell the other.

But it wasn't Theo. It was Simon. And the very thought made her belly tingle all the way down . . . low. And intimate. And she realized that she was glad it wasn't Theo here next to her. That it was Simon.

"I know," she replied. "He tried to talk me out of going, but I needed to come."

His head moved against the pillow as if nodding. "We have to be careful. I don't . . . trust them."

"Okay. Do you mean . . . we need to act differently? More . . . in love?" Her mouth went dry. What if she had to kiss Simon? Her heart thumped harder, and she thought about those beautiful lips . . . just a breath away from her right now. She'd kissed Theo, and Owen . . . would it be any different kissing Simon? Suddenly, she wanted to know.

Really. Wanted. To know. She licked her lips, once again glad for the darkness.

"Love has nothing to do with what goes on here," he replied in a low, flat voice. "It's a cold, organized human breeding factory. No emotion, no attachment." Silence settled over the darkness for a moment. His breathing sounded steady and easy, and she thought he'd fallen asleep. Then, "Good night, Sage."

Right. As if she were going to get any sleep.

"Good night."

Simon wasn't sure when Sage finally fell asleep, but it definitely wasn't until after the sky had begun to lighten in the east. She'd stopped pretending and her breathing slipped into a natural rhythm instead of the one she'd tried to force it into.

That meant he could finally relax a bit and try to mentally talk down his splitting hard-on. Although with Sage sleeping, there was the added danger of her accidentally rolling toward him, unconsciously moving her hand or legs and possibly connecting with some part of him. Any part of him.

A hasty exit was probably the best option.

He made sure she was asleep before he slipped from the bed, careful not to look toward the camera hidden behind a painting. A dog's eye had been cut out and the camera lens installed behind it, which he'd found in afternoon after turning himself invisible and taking the opportunity to investigate. He didn't know if it ran all the time, recording everything that happened, or if it was a live-cam that was only monitored at certain times.

Regardless, Simon had no doubt that some dirty old men used the room-cam as their version of post-apocalyptic porn. And probably other cameras in other rooms as well.

Falling Creek gave him a dirty feeling that worsened the more he learned about it. Not that there was anything wrong with making babies, but Holy Mother of God . . . the whole regimented setup sickened him, including the very public admonishment that they couldn't have sex last night because he had to save his sperm.

What the fuck? Was that what they were watching on the cameras? Checking to make sure he didn't waste his fucking *sperm*?

He hadn't been embarrassed at all. Enraged was more the emotion that swept over him.

The sooner he and Sage left here, the better—on more than one account.

Simon glanced toward the bed where a rounded shoulder rose from beneath the covers, richly golden from a wash of freckles. Her glorious hair tumbled over the pillows . . . including the one on which he'd just rested his head. He knew it smelled of some floral scent, and that the tips of her curls were soft and springy.

He spun and went into the bathroom, hoping they didn't have a camera posted in the shower. Because he was definitely going to be wasting some sperm.

By the time he finished his shower and came back into the room, dressed prudently in a pair of jeans, Sage was awake. She sat up in bed, the sheets down around her waist, exposing the little pink tank top she wore. She might just as well have been topless for all the good it did.

She was reading a book and looked up as he walked in. "Are you done in there?" Sage asked. She tried to hide the fact that she was staring at his chest.

"It's all yours," he replied, finger-combing his damp hair into its ponytail, aware that he had to lift his arms and that his biceps would flex as he did so. And that her cheeks were tinting pink, but she wasn't looking away.

"Good," she said, and slipped out of bed, scooting quickly into the bathroom. He caught a glimpse of slender white thighs, pretty feet, and the distracting bounce of her breasts before she disappeared.

He pulled on a shirt and it occurred to him that an unscrupulous guy who could turn invisible could pretend to leave, but stay here and spy if he wanted. A guy who was as warped and perverted as whoever was on the other side of those cameras, which definitely did not include him. It was a revolting thought.

But what the fuck. He was a man for God's sake, he was made to have thoughts like that . . . and being around her, in these close quarters, was making him mother-fucking crazy. What the fuck had he been thinking to agree to come with her—*come* being the *non*-operative word?

If she wasn't involved with Theo, things might be different. *Might* be different. But the fact was, Theo was waiting for her to be returned back, in one piece and unseduced.

By anyone.

A little chill washed over Simon. Was that something he had to worry about here in FC, where the sex flowed like money had in Vegas? Sage being . . . approached . . . by another man? Approached or otherwise manhandled into a potential *situation*?

Probably not. Adultery would just screw up their birthing plans.

But Simon wasn't going to take the chance. They needed to find out if there was anyone who knew anything about Remington Truth, set up the NAP, and get the hell out of here.

Especially, please God, before Sage fucking . . . good God . . . *ovulated*. What the hell was going to happen then?

Simon heard the toilet flush and then the shower running, and he began to straighten up the room. He made the bed and set Sage's book on the table. *The Count of Monte Cristo*. A thick one that might have once been terrifying to someone who didn't learn to read until he was fifteen . . . but that now was highly appealing. Something to take his mind off things too.

The door to the bathroom opened when he was on page twenty-two, and Simon looked up to see Sage poking her head around. Her face was flushed pink and her hair wrapped in a towel, and steam escaped from the crack of the door around her bare shoulder. "I forgot to grab some clothes, Simon. Would you?"

Rummaging through a woman's underwear drawer wasn't high on his list of desirable things to do, although Florita had slyly insisted he "pick out something Mancusi would like" more than once . . . but since Sage didn't actually have an underwear drawer but a duffel bag, he wasn't going to argue. Not only that, but picking out her clothes enabled him to select the loosest, most conservative attire she had, even though the task had the drawback of him having to decide between black bikini panties or red string bikinis.

God was really making His displeasure with Simon clear.

"Enjoying the book?" she asked, coming out of the bathroom, fully dressed. Her hair coiled in dark, damp curls around her shoulders, leaving little wet spots on the shoulders of her shirt.

"So far," he said.

Then, to his surprise, she came over to where he was sitting in the corner chair and settled on the arm next to him. Her ass was nearly brushing his upper arm and the fresh, clean scent of her washed hair filled his nose. "I want to show you one of the best parts," she said, and, leaning over, began to flip through the book.

Simon didn't move. He just concentrated on keeping his hands still and his breathing regular.

"Here," she said at last, near the end of the 1,200-page book. "This is one of my favorite scenes."

"You've already read it?" he managed to ask.

She just looked at him, her blue eyes so very close. Very steady. He forgot to breathe.

"It's a great book. Worth reading over and over again," she replied. "Edmond Dantès is a wonderful character. He's betrayed by three of his so-called friends and imprisoned for thirteen years. Then he comes back and seeks revenge on them as the Count of Monte Cristo."

He looked down at the book and saw . . . ah. So clever. He glanced at her with a brief smile of admiration and comprehension, and began to read.

She got up and walked away while he perused through the pages that she had inserted into the book at the very end. It was a list of names. His smiled widened. The documents, or at least some of them, from Remington Truth's jump drive.

Brilliant.

This was his chance to see if Mancusi was on the list of likely Cult of Atlantis members, and he quickly found the *M*'s. No Leonide Mancusi or Mancusi, Leonide. Or anything remotely like that. He hadn't really expected to see him in this sort of company, but Simon never assumed.

He flipped through a few more pages, uninterested in the rest of the list, although he did see Quent's father, Parris Fielding, on there, and closed the book. There would be more time to study the list and the other documents later.

"You were right," he said, putting it on the table. "Great scene. I think I'm really going to enjoy this book."

"I've hardly been able to put it down," she said. "We might have to fight over who gets to read it when. But don't lose my bookmark."

"Let's go," he said, standing. The sooner they got their mission accomplished, the sooner they could get the hell back to Envy.

The first real sign of trouble was when Simon and Sage approached the main gate. Unsure of their welcome, they'd left the supplies for the NAP, and Sage's little computer, hidden in an old car trunk a few miles beyond the city walls.

Now they meant to retrieve them, under the guise of taking a walk.

"Can't let you through," said the guards. "It's too dangerous."

"What?" Sage asked. "What's dangerous?"

Simon didn't bother. He knew they weren't going back through those gates now that they'd come in. For him, of course, it wasn't a problem.

"There's *gangas* out there, and lions and other feral animals," was the reply. This guard was not the friendly Bennie Corrigan from yesterday. But she remembered him as being a shy, pimply teen who liked to throw rocks at trees. Apparently, authority had gone to his head.

"*Gangas* don't come out during the day," Sage replied.

"And we didn't see any sign of wild animals on our way here."

"Sorry, ma'am. No one's going through the gates today."

"But—"

"Sage! There you are."

They turned to see a slender woman hurrying toward them. "That's Penny," Sage told Simon, leaning close enough to brush against him. "She's the one who— Hi, Penny," she said.

"We need to get your temp taken right away. It's supposed to be the first thing you do every morning," she chided. Penny was a grim-faced woman with iron gray hair streaked with white. Her hands were skeletal in their thinness. "And then breakfast. I know you haven't eaten breakfast, but it's imperative that you do. That's when you get your vitamins too."

"Go get yourself taken care of," Simon said, conscious of being watched. He knew it was only a matter of time before someone came looking for him. They'd probably want to check his sperm count or something obscene like that.

Sage looked at Simon, a flash of helplessness in her eyes that was quickly masked, then turned meekly to follow the other woman.

As soon as Sage was gone, Simon sauntered off toward the Community House himself. The moment he was alone, he shimmered into invisibility.

The first thing he wanted to do was find a place where he and Sage could meet and talk without being overheard or seen. After that, he'd leave the compound and retrieve their electronics and other items and bring them back through the gate while invisible. He wasn't sure how far his capabilities would extend when carrying items, but he thought that since his clothing disappeared on command, anything he might be able to slip under his coat or shirt might also become transparent. If not, he'd find another way to get them in . . . or to get Sage out.

In fact, as he walked around the perimeter of the stone barrier, Simon knew there had to be another way in and out of the compound. He just didn't know if he should waste his time looking for it when he had other ways.

What had once been an obviously extremely affluent neighborhood still maintained its air of pretension. The houses were massive—eight thousand or more square feet, made of brick and stucco, with single-acre yards that allowed a clear view into the neighbor's living room. Or bedroom.

Most of them appeared to be inhabited, and cloaked in his invisibility, Simon passed hordes of children in the yards, playing the games that children played. At least, children who didn't grow up on narrow streets and dark alleys, in hot, smelly one-bedroom apartments that housed fifteen people at a time. And who didn't have to watch for cars and drive-by shootings in their neighborhoods.

Those other children played with guns and knives and didn't know what an MP3 player or Xbox was until they were stealing them or making enough money dealing to buy their own.

As Simon observed the residents of Falling Creek, he noticed that certain mothers or older daughters were supervising the children. Others were obviously on garden duty, for they worked in small patches where vegetables grew. Still others were likely inside, cooking, cleaning, sewing, whatever.

Where were all the men?

He walked farther, realizing that his ability to remain transparent waned and weakened the longer he held it. So he allowed himself to fade in and out instead of trying to hold it for too long. He was still learning his new power's quirks and limitations, but one thing he had to be grateful for was that his gamble with Sage in the stairwell at the Beretta had paid off. He hadn't known if it would work to make her invisible too, and it had been a big risk.

And apparently, she still didn't realize what happened. He should probably tell her. Maybe.

By now, Simon had reached the far west side of the settlement. The sounds of children playing had faded, and he could tell that this was the section that hadn't been maintained like the other areas . . . which of course made him suspicious and curious.

A large house with broken windows and a sagging door sat amid piles of debris. It appeared that this was the place unwanted remains were dumped. Old cars—many of them Hummers, Beamers, Mercedes, and SUVs—sat in what had been perfectly manicured, landscaped yards. Grass grew between them, invading flagstone pathways. Untrimmed bushes had long overtaken the flower beds, merging into large, long clumps of growth.

But the sense of abandonment only intrigued Simon even more. And when he heard a faint sound . . . a human sound . . . he knew he was right.

Remaining visible, saving his energy for when he needed it, he slinked around the outside of the nearest of the decrepit mansions. It was also, he noticed, the closest building to the protective wall that encircled the settlement, on the opposite side of the former golf course and current farmland. A large pile of more junk and waste sat beyond, on the north side of the wall.

From the front, it appeared dark and forbidding. Simon was certain the children and women were told to stay away because it was dangerous and uninhabitable. He got closer, using the abundance of overgrowth as his shield, and made his way around to the back.

The grasses were tall enough to brush his waist in places, and even at the rear, it was unkempt. But Simon could see where someone or something had passed through—the grass was flattened in places, leading to the rear door.

A patio had once stood there, probably equipped with a built-in stone grill—but now, he saw little but rubble and the broken away half-wall enclosure. Simon drew closer, listening, knowing there was someone in the house. What was the best way in?

Then he heard voices. Simon ducked automatically behind a bush. Two men appeared, and he realized that they were guards, patrolling the area. They looked around, and as soon as they passed by, Simon went over to the sliding door that had led to the patio from inside. It wouldn't slide, so he moved on.

At last he found a small side door that opened with a minimum of fuss. Hidden behind a massively overgrown rhododendron, the door would have been easily over-looked. But from the way the backside branches of the bush were bent, and a few imprints in the dirt, he knew this was the regular entrance.

Inside the house, Simon found that it was not at all as decrepit as it appeared from the exterior—which was no surprise to him. At first glance, it seemed merely empty and uncluttered, but he saw that there was little dust and no stray plants or growth like he was used to seeing in ghost-town homes. A few small rodent and bird nests dec-orated the corners—likely to give the sense of abandon-ment realism, but the space was definitely not unused.

It was also where many of the men seemed to gather.

Loud, jovial voices arose from below, all of them masculine.

Simon remained in his normal condition since he was certain no one was around to see him. They were all below. His fingers trembled a bit and his body was damp with sweat from the effort of not only turning himself invisible, but also maintaining that state while moving, and for long periods of time. It was a little like holding his breath. He could still move about, but after a while, it became more difficult to maintain—especially while moving—and it took practice to hold it for an extended time.

Learning that he had such a skill had been an accident, a surreal experience, and Simon couldn't help but wonder what the drawback was, the *gotcha!* part of being able to turn unseen. He still hadn't figured it out yet, but he knew . . . there was no free lunch. Thus he didn't take it for granted and tried to be prudent about its use.

Using my powers for good.

Rah, rah, and all that.

He found the door to what must be the basement and was able to open it silently. Fully aware of the Waxnickis' tricky staircase, where one tripped an alarm rather than a soft chime if one didn't know better, he turned himself invisible and descended while stepping on the edges of the steps.

Even if he did step on a stair that set off an alarm, they wouldn't find him.

Confident in his obscurity, Simon moved rapidly down without incident and found himself in what must pass for a post-apocalyptic man's sanctuary.

Although what they needed to escape from, Simon wasn't sure. Any man who lived in Falling Creek had to subscribe to the multiple-wife theory and sex on cue.

As he moved silently, completely unnoticed into the room furnished with sofas and armchairs likely scavenged from the other houses, he counted heads. Maybe twenty or two dozen men aged mid-thirties to fifty or sixty sat around in various places. A lot of Corrigan-hued hair, but some others as well. Large screens were on the walls, and on low tables with chairs or other seats clustered around them.

Some of the men pored over papers on a large desk. They looked as though they were reviewing plans, or paperwork of some sort.

Others played cards. Ate. Watched movies or football. Football?

Yeah, it looked as though they were watching old football games. Simon didn't allow himself much thought about that, as anachronistic as it seemed. Somehow they had tapes or DVDs of football. It didn't matter how or why.

There were others in a corner of the room that seemed to be working on some sort of electronic project. Wires, metal pieces, tools were scattered over the table.

Beyond them, a room with computers, most of them old desktops . . .

. . . and, oh yes.

Simon had been fucking dead-on.

These assholes had live cams not only in his and Sage's room, but in a variety of other places.

Fucking coños.

As he sneaked up behind the two men who were obviously monitoring the computers, Simon saw that there were a variety of screens that flipped through feeds of not only his room, but other bedrooms, dining areas, as well as various locations in the settlement.

A garden abundant with vegetables where five women weeded and harvested. The children's play area. A schoolroom? What appeared to be a nursery, complete with a slew of rocking chairs, cribs, eight nursing mothers, tables for changing diapers. The Community House, with a camera aimed at Lark Tannigan's desk. And so on. Even what appeared to be the medical examination room.

Big Brother was definitely watching.

Sickened and yet disturbingly fascinated by the arrangement, Simon scrutinized not the screens but the men watching them. Why did they keep such close tabs? Was it simply for control, out of boredom, or for some other reason?

One thing was certain. He didn't want to stay here any longer than they needed to.

July 30.
Almost two months after.

Finally have electricity again, so this is the first chance I've been able to write since my laptop battery was dead. They've repaired a bunch of generators and have them working, at least for awhile. There's talk about sending a group to check out the Hoover Dam to see if it's still generating power.

I'm living in a hotel room on the second level of MGM. Across the street is New York-New York, which is still fairly intact. We've all been assigned to task groups (on things like water, food, clothing, shelter, power, waste disposal and I guess what you'd call community) since about the first two weeks.

There've been no sounds of vehicles, aircraft, or anything like civilization since the day it happened. No Internet connection, no radio. Everything's just . . . silent.

People I've only known for two months are people that I've bonded with and shared parts of myself like I never have before. Not a bit surprising, I'm sure.

I'm on the food task team,which is more involved than it sounds. Not only have we been searching as much through the city—every hotel room fridge, every kitchen, every store shelf, cooler, trunk, etc, that we can get into and salvage, but we're also trying to find and save plants and seeds from stores, nurseries, even gardens. In case things have been destroyed.

Because who knows what's left beyond our little circle of civilization.

All of the bodies have been taken to what's left of an airport hangar outside the city. That's another task group. Body disposal, I guess you'd call it.

There are thousands, too many to even imagine. At first, it looked like that scene in *Gone With the Wind*, where all the dead soldiers are lying there after the battle, as far as the eye can see. Except here, they're not lined up so neatly. They're just sprawled where they collapsed.

No one's really sure if we're the lucky ones, or if they were.

> —from *Adventures in Juliedom*, the blog of Julie Davis Beecher

CHAPTER 7

Sage didn't know how she was going to tell Simon.

She paced the bedroom nervously, wondering where he was. People had been looking for him, but he seemed to have disappeared—at least, according to the frantic man who'd burst into the examining room while she was being given the results she didn't want to hear.

That had been well over two hours ago, and the sun was high in the sky. Sage was expected to report for her daily duty—which today was working the rows of corn in the vegetable garden—in less than thirty minutes.

As she wandered the room, she alternated between annoyance with him for abandoning her, and hope that his disappearance meant he'd been able to accomplish something . . . like smuggling their other belongings into the compound. How he'd do that, she wasn't certain, but Sage had the sense that if anyone could, Simon was the guy.

She looked nervously at herself in the mirror, smoothing her hair up and into a twist that would be practical for weeding chores. How was she going to tell him?

And how was he going to react?

Then, at last, the door to their room opened and he came in. Limping.

"What happened to you?" she asked, rushing to his side.

Simon held up a hand when she would have embraced him, and that simple gesture of distance made her even more nervous. "I hurt my leg," he said, starting toward the bathroom.

"Badly?" she asked, watching him go.

"I just need to have it cleaned up. I'm fine." He didn't seem to be in pain, other than the limp. In fact, his eyes, dark and compelling, watched her steadily as he paused at the bathroom door. "They offered to patch me up, but I told them I'd rather have my wife do it."

Sage's breath stopped, and for a moment, she felt as if she wouldn't be able to get her lungs to move again. He was so beautiful, it was difficult to look at him without feeling unsteady.

Her breath came out in a soft *whoosh* as her cheeks warmed. "Uh, all right," she said when he jerked his head slightly, gesturing for her to follow him.

In the bathroom, he turned on the shower, then he closed the door partway and sat on the commode, making no move to take off his clothing except to roll up one of his pant legs. "Here," he said. "Will you get a cloth and clean me up?"

She turned to go look for a washcloth, but he grabbed her arm and stopped her, turning her to look at him. As she half bent, their faces came close and for a moment, her thoughts scattered. He was right there, so near, his expression so intense . . .

"I have some things to tell you," he said in a much lower voice.

Oh. The light dawned. He'd put the shower on to muffle their voices, brought her into the bathroom where they could have some privacy. Sage snapped out of the cloudiness and settled against the edge of the sink next to him.

"First tell me if you're hurt," she said, glancing down

at his bare leg. A very nice bare leg in fact, muscular and tanned and covered with the right amount of dark hair. Her breathing threatened to stop again, and she firmly brought herself under control. *Down to business. That's why you're here.*

"I had to have an excuse for not being able to be found today," he told her, still low-voiced, but not quite as close. "So when I was done, I pulled a heavy piece of old sheet-rock on top of me until someone discovered me, and I pretended I'd been there for hours. I also raised a little hell that one of the children could have easily been injured, and much more severely."

She nodded. Smart guy. "But you aren't really hurt."

"No. A little sore from the weight pressing into my thigh, but that's all."

That was why he wanted his "wife" to clean him up instead of the medical people at the Community House. "What did you find out?"

"There's a camera in the bedroom, aimed at the bed and it can see most of the room. So unless we're standing right beneath that picture of the dog, they can see us. I don't think there's audio, but I wasn't able to confirm that, so assume there is. I didn't see a camera feed in here," he told her, gesturing around the small bathroom.

"But it's better to be careful," she said.

Despite the partially open door, the steam from the shower was beginning to fill the small room, making her skin feel even more warm and damp. The spray of the water muted every word and she found herself leaning closer, placing her hand on the back of the toilet tank to brace herself.

"There is an uninhabited house on the northwest side of the settlement. Do you remember it?"

Sage thought for a moment. "I remember there being

an area they told us to stay away from. They said it was dangerous, with old buildings that could collapse on us. I guess it might have been in that area. Northwest? Maybe. What did you find there?"

"The house is where a lot of the men hang out. And where the camera feeds go." Simon's face had taken on a sharpness that made his handsome angles look brittle and waxy.

Sage waited for him to explain, but a nervous tingling had started up her spine. She knew it wasn't going to be happy news.

"They're definitely filming or at least watching everything," Simon said. "*Everything.* So we have to be very careful. I don't think they'd be very happy to know that we're not who we say we are."

"Did you find anything about Remington Truth?" she asked.

"No, I didn't talk to anyone. Anything on your end?"

"I've sort of mentioned the name a few times, just to see if anyone recognized it."

"That's probably not a good idea," he said. "Letting people know we're looking for him."

Sage shook her head. "Well, it's not common knowledge that the Strangers and *gangas* are looking for him. I've never heard the name before you and Quent showed up, and if the Waxnickis didn't know, with all the work they've done, I don't think the name would mean anything to anyone else. So I don't think that it should be a red flag to anyone. And no one seems to recognize it, anyway."

Simon nodded. "Okay. I trust your judgment on that." Then he looked up at her, sort of sidewise, and their eyes met. Sage's belly flipped. "But be careful about it, all right?"

Oh God, oh God, I can't breathe.

She almost did it, almost moved forward—it would only take a bit—but she held back. "Okay," she managed to say.

"We have to be very careful not to arouse suspicion. Act like a couple who really embraces this way of life," he said. "That's why I needed to make sure I had a reason for disappearing."

Crapola. I have to tell him.

With the door closed and the hot water blasting, the room was getting warmer and steamier, the walls and shower curtain all merging into muted colors and texture. She could hardly see the shower or the floor, or even the wall near her. But she could see Simon's face clearly through the murkiness.

"Is there anything else?" she asked, dragging in a hot, moist breath. Delaying the bomb she had to drop. "That you found out?"

"I think the roof or top floor of one of those abandoned houses would be a good place for the NAP. I don't think it would be stumbled upon there."

"How are we going to get the stuff inside the settlement?"

"I can do that." He stilled, as if contemplating something, then looked at her. "I should probably tell you something." He shifted his jaw and his cheeks became more hollow.

"I have to tell you something too," she said in a rush before she lost her courage.

He became very still. "What." He wasn't asking a question. It was almost as if he already knew.

Just then, there was a little sizzle and a *pop* . . . and the light suddenly dimmed. Sage nearly jumped, her heart slamming, before she realized it was just a lightbulb burning out. Another one remained lit, but it gave off only a sickly yellow glow.

An ugly yellow glow, foggy and muted, but enough that she could easily see the very set, very blank expression on Simon's face. Too bad the lights hadn't gone out all together—it would have been a lot easier to tell him. She might even have gotten up the courage to see what it was like to kiss him.

Maybe. If it were dark.

"I'm ovulating," she said, rushing through the words, feeling her face burn red. "We're going to have to—"

"No." He actually pulled back. He couldn't look anymore repelled if he held his arms up to block her as if she were a demon. "No, we're not going to do that."

Do that. *Geesh*. He made it sound like the most abhorrent activity. *Gee, thanks.* "You just got done saying we had to act—"

"We'll fake it," he said in a less strained voice. "No problem."

"Okay." She looked at him. "But . . . uh . . . how?"

"What, you want a fucking play by play?" He stood abruptly and opened the door. A waft of cooler air invaded, dissipating the steam. "Under the sheets, they won't see what's happening," he said, turning back to her. Then he turned and whipped the shower curtain open and slammed his palm a bit more forcefully than necessary against the faucet to turn off the water. "Okay?"

Sage nodded. But she had one more thing to tell him. She stood, moving close enough that they nearly touched so that she could speak low. Somehow her hand ended up on his arm. "I've never . . . I'm a virgin."

He looked startled, then his face returned to its blank expression. "I assumed you and Theo—"

"Just because he was kissing me at the festival?"

"Or someone else . . . maybe," Simon said quickly, not quite as softly as he should have. But they were still in the bathroom and the water was dripping loudly from the showerhead. "In the past, that you . . . knew. I mean . . . you're . . ." His voice trailed off and he seemed very clearly stuck with how to proceed.

Sage didn't say anything. She couldn't have if she knew what to say, but she didn't. *I'm . . . what? What?*

"Sage, I need to . . ."

"It was never the right time," she said. "Or the right person."

"Theo will be glad to know that. Very glad." And then he pushed past her, leaving Sage in a steamy bathroom with her heart pounding and an odd feeling settling over her.

Would being in Falling Creek take away her chance to decide on the right person, at the right time?

Or would it help her find him?

Simon left the guest room, his mind scrambling. He was not about to let himself think about the conversation that had just happened in the bathroom. Instead, he found other things to occupy his thoughts.

Such as . . . how was he going to account for the time he needed to spend going to retrieve their electronics? He could only use the excuse of being dumb enough to get trapped for "hours" under a piece of drywall one time. If he disappeared—literally or figuratively—and it was noticed, that would cast suspicion on them.

He wasn't worried about himself of course, but for Sage.

And the problem was, if the FCers were watching the camera feed for their room, they'd know when he left and when he returned. Unless they saw him go into the bathroom, where he was pretty sure there wasn't a camera . . . and didn't see him come out until later.

That could work.

Simon knew the crazies at the Community House were waiting for him to get patched up by Sage, and then for him to come back and meet with the cook to talk about his abilities and kitchen-patrol duties. He was just going to have to be too tired and sore to leave the room for a while.

Hm. Maybe he could be too tired and sore to fuck his wife tonight. Who was *ovulating*.

Even the thought, in such cold, brutal, inaccurate terms made Simon's palms go a little damp. And what was up with that? His palms never went damp. Even the time he'd come face-to-face with Tré Han, Mancusi's hated enemy . . .

All right.

He turned around and went back to the room just as Sage came out. He quickly explained his plan, giving only a vague explanation for exactly how he intended to pass through the guarded gate, and asked her to make his excuses at the Community House.

"They're going to think you're a complete wuss," she said as they stood in the doorway, speaking low. So low that he had to lean much too close to her. To the woman who was fucking *ovulating*.

Pinche.

"Good," he said.

"Anything I can do to help with that, I will," she said. And she gave him this sort of funny, evil smile that was just as potent as her one of pure delight. "I can make you sound like a total scrub."

"Ah, that's good," he said when he found his voice.

Then, loud enough for the camera to pick it up, he started complaining about being in pain and tired, and making a general ass out of himself.

Sage slammed the door in her wake as if to punctuate her own disgust with him, and Simon limped heavily to the bathroom, giving the camera a good show. Water still beaded the mirror and shower walls, but it was no longer as hot and steamy as it had been when he and Sage had been in there. He waited a few minutes, then turned himself invisible and slipped out from the half-open door, then pushed it nearly closed behind him as if he were drawing it closed from inside the bathroom.

Moments later, he was out of the room, and sneaking his way to the gate entrance. Once he got out of sight of the Community House or anyone who might be looking for him, he came back to his normal state to save his strength.

Getting through the gate and beyond caused him no trouble at all, and running—ahh, the freedom again—the three miles to where they'd hidden the electronics, even less. Out of sight of the settlement, he tested out his theory of disappearing anything that was against his body and confirmed that as long as his bare skin held or touched it, the item disappeared along with him.

Which worked well for bringing the two backpacks in.

Once he was back inside the gates with the packs of electronics, Simon hid them inside the room he shared with Sage, and then visibly emerged from the bathroom— making sure he limped heavily.

All told, he'd been gone little more than an hour.

The sun had dipped to a forty-five-degree angle, portending the approach of the evening meal . . . and, after, what he'd come to think of as his own personal torture.

Simon eyed the bed.

No problem. Just slide under the sheets and keep your shorts on. Move a few times, groan, and it's over.

He broke out in a cold sweat.

Simon couldn't fault the FCers on their food.

After returning from his smuggling trip, he had reported to the kitchen in the Community House and been given a brief tour, discussed his cooking abilities—which he'd not exaggerated: he'd actually done a little sous chef work for a bit. It had felt good to have a nonviolent knife in his hand again, and to hear the comfortable rhythm of it chopping against the wooden block.

Mundane. Simple. Mind-clearing. He ignored the curious looks from men and women alike—apparently the kitchen was not segregated by gender—and chopped.

The evening meal was excellent—filled with fresh vegetables and fruits grown in small patches near the houses, and tended to by a multitude of wives as well as young, strong men who hadn't been married yet and obviously didn't need to save their damned strength—and *sperm*.

While the food itself was tasty—roasted chicken, warm cornbread, slender green beans, roasted potatoes, fresh tomatoes, and strawberries—and served family-style, the rest of the meal's environment was awkward as hell. At least, for him.

Simon sat across from Sage, which was a torture all its own. At least when he sat next to her, yeah, he had to contend with maybe brushing against her arm or feeling the warmth of her skin, but at least he didn't have to struggle to keep from looking at her. Tonight her face was lightly flushed from spending time in the sun and her hair had been twisted up in a loose knot at the back of her head, leaving her long, slender neck bare and tempting. And then there was that distracting little freckle on her upper lip.

"I hope your leg is feeling better," she said from across the table. Despite the modulation in her voice, he recognized the subtle tease there and wondered where the hell that had come from. *I'll make everyone think you're a real wuss.*

Wuss was not a word anyone had ever used to describe him. Except, maybe, when he was three. But probably not even then.

"It's better," Simon replied. "But a little sore yet," he added in an effort to keep up a potential excuse for future disappearances. Then, unwilling to have to look up at her again or to carry on any conversation, he applied himself to his meal, keeping his attention trained on the chatter around them.

The dark, forbidding cliff face of Hell's Wall rose to the north, looking even more threatening as the sun lowered. Simon wondered how the FCers could live with such an imposing reminder that . . . any moment . . . their world could be wiped away. Again.

It seemed odd that men who'd lived through the Change, which had been rife with earthquakes, tornadoes, and other natural disasters, would have chosen to rebuild their lives—and the human race—in the shadow of such a monstrosity. If it had been Simon, he'd have found a place in the middle of a lot of flat land.

As he ate, partly to keep up his body's strength, and partly because the food really was good, Simon reflected on the people around him . . . and tried to keep his thoughts away from the woman across the table. Sage's half sister Sharon had made sure they sat at her table, along with some of her older children and another of her husband's wives. They were all chattering about children and babies and other feminine things that made him distinctly uncomfortable, considering the fact that he was supposed to be doing all of those things with Sage.

Rather than sitting in family units, like one might do when attending a banquet or restaurant, the children sat together at separate tables of counterparts their own ages. The adults sat in clusters—men together, women together, but not necessarily segregated by gender or table. Just, in clusters.

Sharon and the others seemed happy, or at least, content. None of the women seemed downtrodden or abused, despite the fact that they shared their husband with other women.

That caused him to think about partnerships and marriage, and what he—albeit from a distance, because of course he had no personal experience on that front—would expect from one, and how this cult turned those expectations on its head.

Was there any affection between the men and women, the husbands and wives? Or was their relationship really no more than the mechanics of breeding?

The last thing Simon had ever imagined for himself, in his life, was the sort of Hollywood marriage many people seemed to strive for—a partnership built on respect and trust and deep love. Yet, here, in this fucked-up world into which he'd been reborn, perhaps something like that might be possible even for him.

Because, here, there was no Mancusi. There were no "projects" or "deletions" or "taking care" of things.

There was no gun to his head—literal or figurative—and there were no longer those golden handcuffs of forced loyalty, fear, and obligation.

But, yet . . . Simon found it unimaginable.

Just then, he noticed a sort of ripple of interest flutter over the large room. Conversations slowed and attention shifted as some sort of message seemed to filter through pockets of people.

"Tomorrow?" Sage repeated, leaning close to Sharon, who, in turn, was leaning toward the table behind them. "They're coming here?"

"It's been nearly a year," Simon heard someone say. Excitement, and perhaps a little trepidation, laced the comment.

As he scanned the room, he noticed the diners' attentions seemed to gravitate toward that massive cliff—glances and stares, then animated discussions.

He caught Sage's eye from across the table and raised a brow in inquiry.

"The Strangers are coming tomorrow night," she said. "The ones who protect the settlement from Hell's Wall."

A variety of questions exploded in his brain, but Simon withheld them. He merely shrugged, met Sage's eye in a "we'll talk later" glance, and continued eating.

But now Simon sharpened his attention even further and listened more closely to the conversations around him. To his disappointment, the talk eased into mundane topics about children, the crops, some problems with repairing a refrigerator, a recent birthing, and, of course, who was ovulating and who wasn't. For fuck's sake.

When Simon glanced up from his second piece of corn-bread—complete with fresh butter—he saw Sage looking at him with what could only be described as a smirk. That lovely little freckle danced on the top of her lip and the twitch at the corner of her mouth curled enticingly.

He raised his brows coolly, even though his breath had caught. "Something amusing?"

Sage leaned forward—not a great move, because then he could see down the vee of her T-shirt, and how could he not look when it was right there?—and said, "I think someone's got their eye on you." And then she sort of lifted her chin and gestured with her eyes toward the right.

Simon glanced over and saw a group of young women— hell, no, they were teenagers. No older than fifteen or sixteen. They were all watching him, overtly, *very* overtly.

He looked back at Sage, who had an expression on her face that looked as if she were about to burst. Her eyes danced with humor—something he'd never seen before today—and those damn lips twitched.

"See," she said, her voice still low, her body still leaning forward, her words only for him, "since we're married, I'm already all set. But you, Simon, you're fair game."

Yeah, right.

Simon stopped himself from rolling his eyes. As if he'd be even slightly tempted to touch one of those schoolgirls. The very thought nauseated him. He looked over, but Sharon had turned in her seat and was talking to someone else behind her.

"According to Sharon and Dawn, you're a good prospect," Sage continued, the vee of her shirt still gapping, which gave him pretty much nowhere safe to look. Not at her mouth, not at her eyes—what might she see in his?— and definitely not down into the depths of that shadowy vee. He already knew what was down there. No need to remind himself.

"You're young," she continued, "and wixy hot, and you're new here. Fresh blood, so to speak. Even though you're a bit of a wuss, they won't care." Now the laughter was in her voice, low and intimate.

He shot her a dark look and wondered where this

sudden burst of humor and teasing had come from. What had happened to quiet, thoughtful Sage? And he was *wixy hot*? What the fuck did that mean?

Nor did he have anything to say in response. His brain seemed to have imploded. "I'm not . . . in any hurry," he said finally, aware that although the people around them were in their own conversations, they could still be overheard.

"To paraphrase Jane Austen," Sage said, settling back into her seat with a little boob-jounce, "it is a truth acknowledged here in FC that a man in possession of one wife must be in want of a dozen more. So you are, indeed, fair game."

And as if to punctuate her statement, she folded her arms over her middle just as a cluster of the girls—hell, some of them looked like they were thirteen!—came wandering over. Ostensibly to sit next to Sage and talk with her, but very clearly to really eyeball Simon.

They were all so young! Which of course made sense, because their older counterparts would have been married off by now. And many of them had bright red hair, like Sage's . . . but not. Not quite as gloriously coppery-pinkish, not as thick and long and curling. And those blue eyes, stamped in face after face . . . it was like looking at Sage surrounded by a gaggle of wannabe Sages. But none of them were . . . Sage.

Simon was so totally fucked.

Before he could figure out how to extricate himself from the meal, one of the men whom he'd met in the kitchen approached. "How're you at poker, Japp?" he asked.

"Not bad," Simon replied, leaping internally at the excuse, but remaining cool on the exterior. "Got a game going?"

"This way," said the man. Keith was his name, and he

looked as if he were about Simon's age. He had the Corrigan eyes, but not the bright red hair, and was married to one of Sage's half sisters . . . Simon couldn't remember which one. There were too damn many of them and they all looked alike.

If Simon had hoped his escape would also include an introduction to the "deserted" houses where the men watched the camera feeds and reruns of old football games, he was disappointed. As it was, by the time he got settled at a table with six other guys, he realized the poker game was a poker game . . . but also something more.

Turned out most of the men were fathers of marriageable daughters—marriageable-aged daughters to FCers, not to Simon. And not only did they want to see how he played poker, but more importantly, to determine whether he was worthy of any daughter.

Fresh blood. That was what Sage had called him.

Simon felt like he was on *The Bachelor*—on steroids.

Along with the cards, they had beer and some weaklooking malt whiskey. Simon had a single dollop of the golden liquid and barely tasted it, despite the fact that, as the poker hands went on and the sun lowered, he felt as though he were getting closer and closer to his own doomsday.

Which really was ridiculous.

Sage was just a woman and he'd certainly had his hands on plenty of them in many different ways. He didn't even have to do anything.

"*There* you are," came the words he'd somehow been expecting to hear. "We've been looking *all over* for you."

Simon looked up and saw Sage standing there, and with her was the bitchy looking nurse who'd scolded Sage about not eating breakfast that morning. "I can't believe you haven't taken *advantage* of her *situation*," the crazy

Nurse Ratchett said to him, her voice sharp and pitched high. "When she hit the target temperature *this morning*, you should have been having *intercourse* immediately."

Kee-rist.

Simon tossed his cards on the table. "Fold." And stood. *Get me the fuck out of here.* He glanced at his whiskey, but, much as he wanted . . . oh, God, he *wanted* . . . to reach for it, he didn't.

"There's no further time to *delay*. Your window of opportunity is *closing*," lectured the nurse, as if he weren't moving fast enough. Well, actually, Simon was taking his time. She might say jump and he might pretend to do so, but he sure as fuck wasn't going to ask how high.

"Come on darling," Sage said. "Let me help you. I'm sure your leg is still hurting."

Before he could react to that subtle teasing, and the little smirk that seemed to have become a permanent part of her expression, she scooted over and put an arm around his waist. As if he needed her help to walk.

But her arm was warm and delicate against him, and her leg brushed against his hip and thigh and Holy Mother of God, he was taking her back to pretend to screw her. On camera.

Maybe he really should slam that whiskey.

September 16
About three months after.

*Our number of survivors right now is about
750. Many of us were here in Vegas when it
happened, but over the last few months, the
lights here have attracted other survivors.
They tell a story similar to ours—the earthquakes and great shaking, then the horrifying storms, and then the sudden mass deaths
three or four days later.*

*Something odd has happened. The bodies
have begun to disappear. Ones that were lying on the street or in the corner of a
building one day, are gone the next.*

*The task force on shelter has been work-
ing on building a wall to protect the livable
part of the city, to keep out the wild animals that try to come in and scavenge.*

*So there's also talk about creating a gov-
erning body, which makes sense. Some sort of
city council and mayor.*

*Last night when we were gathered for what
they call Community Night (sounds so weird,
doesn't it?)—a movie on the big screen in
one of the hotel theaters—we heard a strange
noise . . . sounded like someone calling
for Ruth. I wasn't going to go out and investigate, and neither was anyone else. Too
creepy.*

*And I've met a man who seems nice. He's a
little older than me, and his name is Kevin
Corrigan. He's got the reddest hair I've ever*

seen and an identical twin brother. They were both here for a builders' convention when everything happened. He's got some good ideas about how to rebuild our world—literally the buildings, but also society. He's very passionate about reinventing the human race. He doesn't remind me at all of Drew.

　　Which is good.

　　　　　　—from Adventures in Juliedom, the blog of Julie Davis Beecher

CHAPTER 8

Sage opened the door to their room, and Simon, who'd pulled away from her teasing support as soon as they were out of sight of the iron-haired nurse, stepped back until she walked through.

As she heard the door close behind, all vestiges of humor and lightheartedness evaporated, leaving Sage feeling nervous. She bumped into a corner of the low table that sat beneath the dog picture/hidden camera and, rubbing her hip, moved across the room before Simon could notice her klutziness.

"Well," she said, "I guess she told us." Sage tried to smile, but found even that effort dying on her lips. Instead, she felt her heart pounding and realized that the room had suddenly shrunk.

"Get in bed," he said. Not unkindly or angrily, or even as a command. He didn't look at her as he limped over to the bathroom. The door closed behind him with a deliberate click.

Sage stripped off her cargo pants, then hesitated. After a brief contemplation, she dug in her duffel bag, grabbed what she needed, and pulled off her shirt and bra. With her back turned to the camera, of course. Bundling up the items she'd dragged out of the duffel, she slipped under the blankets and pulled on a pink skinny-strapped camisole that Jade had found in an old store on one of her missions. She hoped that it wouldn't show up on the camera. And then, for good measure, she flung the extra pair of panties she'd grabbed so that they soared across the room—in front of the camera—and landed by the bathroom door.

She swallowed. Simon was going to come through that door and climb into bed with her. He would be close and big and warm, and her heart was pounding like crazy, and her palms had gone damp, and she wanted . . . really *wanted* . . . to know what it would be like to touch him.

Maybe even more.

The door to the bathroom opened and Simon came out, still fully clothed. He froze when he saw her lingerie on the floor and the expression on his face went even more blank. "Sage," was all he said.

"It's all right," she told him. Her heart ratcheted up again, and she swore the bed was jolting with each pulse.

He sat on the edge of the mattress, back to her, and shucked off his jeans. He flicked off the lamp next to the bed, leaving the room lit only by a glow from the bathroom light. Then, he turned and started to slide under with her.

But Sage sat up, keeping the blankets up over her supposed-to-be-bare breasts. "Aren't you going to take off your shirt?"

He paused and she saw his jaw move. "No," he said. Very low, so that it wouldn't be picked up by the audio. If there was audio.

"You did last night," she reminded him. Also very softly. "It would be weird if you didn't tonight." To punctuate her words, she reached out and touched his warm arm. "Do it."

Turning away once more, he stripped off the clinging

T-shirt and she watched as his broad shoulders shifted, and those sleek muscles rippled over his back. Sage's mouth went dry and she felt her cheeks flush.

Once again, Simon lifted the blankets and slid under them, next to her. She turned to face him, and he lay there for a moment half reclining on a pillow, arm tucked behind his head, looking at the ceiling.

"You should take your hair down too," she said. "You did last night."

"Sage," he said. "This is . . . not very easy."

"Don't worry about me," she told him. "I'm fine."

"Why did you take off your clothes for fuck's sake?" Though the words came out super low, on the waft of a breath, they were tight and sharp behind his teeth.

"I didn't. I faked them out. For the camera."

She felt him relax next to her. Literally, felt the bed-clothes shift as the tension eased from him. "Ahh. *Buena.*" A glance told her that his mouth had also eased a bit in something like a smile. Not quite, but almost. Then, "Sorry."

"Simon, we're supposed to be married. It's probably not a good idea for you to lie there like you can't stand the thought of touching me."

He gave a little snort, but then the bed moved and the next thing she knew, he was there. Over her.

A gust of cool air slipped beneath the hot sheets when he raised himself up on his elbows, poised as he drew himself to straddle her hips. Warmth rushed over her face and down her throat as his figure half-blocked the spill of light from the bathroom, casting him in shadow.

Unsure what to do, Sage looked up, hoping for direction in his expression. But his face was turned away, lowered onto the pillow next to her. She felt the slide of his long hair—he'd released it from its tie after all—against her cheek as it pooled on the pillow, and the weight of his hands pressing into the mattress on either side of her shoulders. But nothing else.

He rose above her, warmth emanating from his proximity—from the nearness of his bare chest—but no other part of him touched her . . . except the brush of her feet against his calves.

Simon rocked rhythmically in his half-lifted position, and the bed jolted and creaked, and Sage lay there, arms crossed over her breasts, feeling at once absurd and bereft. She wasn't sure whether to giggle or to roll her eyes.

Shouldn't she move or moan or something?

Shouldn't he at least *kiss* her?

Sage shifted, uncomfortable and curious, needing something to do, and before she quite knew it, her hands had moved, all on their own . . . onto his shoulders. Lightly at first. Then settled there, fingers gently curling over, splaying wide to brush his neck.

His skin . . . warm and fluid and taut.

His shoulders . . . broad and squared.

He muttered something unintelligible, his rhythm hitching a bit.

"Simon," she murmured back, smoothing her hands from the curve of his neck to the edges of his shoulders. Down over the tops of his flexing biceps. So warm. So strong.

Heat rushed through her and Sage realized her body felt damp and tight all over. She wanted to brush her hands over the front of his chest, to feel the slide of his pecs as he moved over her, to determine whether he had hair growing there or whether it was smooth, along with being so warm and solid.

Simon gave a sudden hard jerk that jolted the bed, followed by a deep groan, and then he rolled away, dragging the sheets haphazardly with him.

So. That was it. They were done.

Sage lay there, listening to Simon's breathing as he collapsed onto the pillow next to her. Surely he wasn't breathing so quickly because he'd worked all that hard. Because, really, he hadn't.

She dared not move, not even to turn and look at him. But her hands tingled with the memory of his warm, damp skin and her stomach squirmed as it had last night, wanting . . . something more.

"You didn't even kiss me," she said at last. Low. "Don't husbands kiss their wives when they make love?"

The rough breathing next to her stopped, then started up again on a sort of gasp-snort-curse. "It's not necessary to the act," he said at last. "Believe me."

She lay there silently, tense, edgy, and warm.

After a long moment, he moved again and Sage tensed in expectation. But he shifted the other way and slipped from the bed. She caught a glimpse of his long, sleek back and tight—holy crap, *bare*—buttocks before he disappeared into the bathroom. Still limping.

Still in character. The man never missed a trick.

And when the heck had he taken off his undies?

Sage felt her face burn hot in the dark as she realized he'd been under the covers with her, completely naked.

The door had closed, shutting off the last bit of illumination from the bathroom. She heard clunking and movements from the other room, and then the spray of the shower, and she lay there, still and stiff. Waiting.

In the absent light, she glowered at the shape of the dog picture across from the bed and silently cursed at the men on the other side of the screen. If only there were a way to "accidentally" block the camera, to cover it up or move the picture . . .

And then she had an idea.

The thought settled over her, followed by a combination of thrill and fear. It might work. And . . . and . . . she could assuage some of her curiosity at the same time.

Innocently.

Heat rushed her face and she suddenly found it hard to swallow. But did she dare?

Just then, the shower turned off.

Sage knew she had to decide before Simon came out of the bathroom, or the chance to take him by surprise would be lost. So she flung the covers up and slipped from the bed, hoping that the darkness hid the fact that she was still wearing panties. Heart pounding, she hurried over to the low table that sat just in front of the dog picture and hoisted herself up on it.

Just as the bathroom door opened, light spilling into the room.

Simon stood there, glistening with droplets from the shower. His hair, though combed back from his face, was plastered against his head, neck, and the sides of his jaw.

And, no, he didn't have a big patch of hair on his chest. Just a slender little trail that ran down his belly to the towel he'd slung about his hips. Sage could hardly breathe. Holy . . . *crap*. The rest of him was just as beautiful as his face. Like, the pictures she'd seen of Michelangelo's *David* were nothing compared to this guy. Not that she could see *everything*, like in the statue, but . . .

At first Simon didn't see her perched on the table, but then he must have noticed that the bed was empty and he turned to look.

"What's going on?" he asked, his voice mild. But

she watched the tension settle back over him. What was wrong with the guy, to always be so darn uptight?

He came into the bedroom, eyeing her warily, clutching the towel, and began to rummage in his backpack. When he seemed unable to find what he was looking for, he snatched up the pack and took it into the bathroom without waiting for her response.

He reemerged a few moments later, dressed in a T-shirt and shorts, and dumped the pack on the floor.

"Sage, what's up?" he asked again.

"Come here," she said, hardly able to get the words out. There was one problem with her idea. If he resisted, it would look really bad. "I need you to come here."

Simon came closer. "Are you all right?" Now he sounded concerned, and he moved without hesitation, coming to stand right next to her.

Sage sat on the hip-high table and she'd positioned herself so that one leg was folded up under her, half-lotus position, and the other dangled. She looked up at him. Their eyes met and she hoped he could read the expression in hers that said, *Go with it.*

And then . . . she chickened out. "I . . . think I have something in my eye," she said in a rush of breath. "Can you take a look?"

He paused, looking at her. "There's better light in the bathroom."

"Right here is fine."

Simon made a little sound, but when she widened her eyes and gave him a meaningful frown, he seemed to relax. She tilted her head back, resting it against the picture behind her, and, as she reached up to pull away her lower eyelid she told him, "In my right eye."

"Uh, that's your left eye," he said, his voice mild with

. . . a bit of humor? But then he bent closer as if to look.

Sage moved her head against the picture and, reaching up behind her, shoved at the bottom of its frame with her hand. "Oops," she said loudly. "Be careful, Simon!" The picture moved behind her as she bumped it with her shoulder, making it sure it went totally out of whack.

By that time, Simon had stepped back and when she looked up at him, she saw that he was grinning. Actually grinning. And . . . *wow*. The bottom of her belly dropped a bit.

"Better now?" he asked.

"Much." A little shaky—from what?—she slid off the table and saw that the picture was now hanging crookedly enough to block the camera's view.

"Nice going," he said under his breath.

She looked up at him and realized they were both standing there—she dressed in that skimpy little tank top and a pair of black panties; he still wet-haired and in clothing that had damp patches from his showered skin. "Thanks."

The moment stretched, long and quiet, and Sage realized her breath had become weighted and slow. Then suddenly Simon, his voice low and rumbly, said, "Theo would be proud. That was clever."

Theo.

Right.

Sage opened her mouth to say . . . something . . . but then closed it.

But why was her heart slamming so hard?

And why did the mention of Theo, whom she cared for, and loved, and had kissed . . . feel like nothing but an annoying mosquito? Like something she wanted to brush off?

Simon moved away and Sage started toward the bed.

But she was surprised when he reached under and pulled out two packs from beneath it. She recognized them right away, and their eyes met.

He nodded, but, still leery of potential audio recording, Sage didn't ask the obvious questions.

"Ready for bed?" he said quietly.

"Yes. I'm exhausted. You wore me out, injured leg or not," she said, walking over to look at the packs.

His lips twitched in a bit of a smile—*another* one?—and as she leaned closer he said on a low breath, "I'm going out. Come with me?"

She looked at him in surprise. Then nodded, knowing that her eyes were wide with delight. She'd assumed it would have been a battle getting him to allow her to help do anything.

With Theo, it would have been.

"Good night," he said in a louder voice.

"Night, Simon," she replied, watching as he quickly changed from shorts into a pair of cargo pants.

She realized she'd better do the same, and turned to don her own protective pants and tank top.

Moments later, they were out the door, silent as shadows.

Simon carried the two packs over one shoulder and gripped her hand with his strong fingers. She tried not to think about the feel of his smooth fingers enclosing hers, how steady and solid his hand was, silently directing her to follow, turn, pause, start as they made their way out of the Community House.

There was a half moon obstructed by fast-moving clouds, which gave the odd effect of a low light coming on then fading as the wisps of heavy gray moved across it. Storm clouds, perhaps, Sage thought, glancing up at them.

Simon synchronized their movements with the ebb and flow of light, staying to the shadows when the moon was exposed, and urging her across expanses of grounds when the half-orb went dark. The night whisked its silence about them, broken only by the distant howl of a wolf and the closer chirp of crickets. Not one sound of human origin reached her ears.

It didn't take Sage long to confirm her suspicion that he was taking her to the supposedly abandoned house. He probably intended for them to try and set up the NAP, as he'd suggested earlier today. Excitement and, yeah, a little apprehension and nervousness, shot through her body, but she kept up with him and when they approached the buildings, she was gratified to find that they were dark.

Apparently, the men who "hung out" at these houses were in bed for the night. That made sense to Sage—the men were all home trying to impregnate their wives. Or should be, anyway.

Simon looked at her, meeting her eyes, as they waited in shadow near the mansion. He made a motion for her to stay and then disappeared into the darkness.

Sage huddled into the corner of a chimney jutting from the house's rough wall, feeling the cool damp of decades-old brick pressing against her bare arm. The structure loomed above her, tall and broad and dark. She still found it mind-blowing that single families had lived in such large spaces.

It must be well after midnight, and she wondered how much time they might have to move about safely, without running into an early riser—or did they have guards that patrolled the area? The thought sent her pushing even more deeply into the darkness, straining her ears to listen . . . for the approach of a guard, or for the return of Simon.

The minutes ticked by and the night remained calm

and quiet, the air shifting with a gentle breeze over her bare arms and throat. During the day, the sun made the temperature uncomfortably warm and humid. Especially when working in the garden. She was going to have to wear a hat tomorrow if she didn't want to burn her skin. But now, at night, the air was more comfortable.

A distant howl broke the silence, and Sage's gaze wandered over the dark blobs that were trees, bushes, and distant buildings. Where was Simon? Surely he'd been gone for more than fifteen minutes. Twenty? Thirty?

And then suddenly, he was there, appearing as if from nowhere, silent and sudden. She nearly gasped when he stepped toward her, melding into her insulating shadow from seemingly nothing.

"All clear," he said, and reached for her hand, tugging her gently from the cover of darkness along the edge of the house toward its rear. She noticed right away that he no longer had the packs on his back. Following his footsteps, trying to remain as noiseless as Simon, she paid careful attention to anything she might trip over or bump into. They made their way to a side door that opened easily under Simon's clever fingers.

Inside, Sage hung back as he paused, listening, and then started up again, pointing to a staircase that rose in a grand sweeping curve. It reminded her of the one in that movie with Scarlett and Rhett, where he caught her up in that dark red dress and carried her up the stairs.

And for a moment, Sage remembered that catlike smile on Scarlett's face the morning after what had surely been a most passionate night.

Sage paused when she heard the low rumble of voices from below, looking up into Simon's face. He nodded and pointed for her to go up. "They won't hear us," he said, breathing warmly into her ear.

She started up the steps. The little brush of a rodent scampered over her foot, but she barely hesitated. Two, three, five, eight steps up . . . and then it happened. She stepped on something that moved, lost her balance when she tried to compensate, and fell against the wooden railing. Managing to muffle a scream, Sage felt Simon move quickly to yank her back, but the aged railing had splintered under the force of her fall.

As he pulled her away, a whole portion of the rail tumbled over to the floor below, landing with the loud clatter of wooden pieces against old tile.

"Oh my God," Sage mouthed at Simon, her eyes wide. "I'm sorry!"

But he'd already moved, grabbing her by the hand and hurrying up to the top of the flight of stairs. The sounds of urgent voices came from below, along with the pounding of feet from the basement.

Oh shit, oh shit, oh shit.

Simon squeezed her hand and pulled her silently into a shadowy room. Sage saw a large desk against one wall and bookshelves lining another, and the next thing she knew, Simon was pushing her toward a dark corner. He followed her and, as the voices and foot pounding drew closer, they huddled into the shadows.

"Don't move," he said in her ear.

Sage's heart pounded with fear and apprehension. She heard the shouts as the men got to the top of the stairs; of course they'd seen the broken railing in a pile in the middle of the foyer. They'd have to know someone was there!

Simon sat, warm and solid next to her, but they were in plain sight of the half-open door! Even though they were in shadow, they were in plain sight if the door opened. All they had to do—

Oh, God, they have a light!

Sage's breath caught when she saw the beam of lights flashing around. She grabbed Simon's arm, knowing her eyes were wide and fearful. He looked at her steadily, then said into her ear, "It's all right. Don't move. Okay?"

And then, as the light came closer, he shifted nearer, gathering her onto on his lap. His bare arms came around her, his skin strong and warm, and Sage gaped at the ajar door where the light shone around. Shouts followed. The door began to open.

She felt Simon draw in a deep breath, felt a sort of warmth rush over her, followed by that same odd shimmery feeling she'd felt before . . . and all of a sudden, he . . . *disappeared*.

And so did she.

Quent had been over and over and over the list of contact names found in Remington Truth's flash drive.

The more he looked at them, this list of A-listers—politicians, movers and shakers, big-money, horribly powerful men and women, the more he felt sick to his stomach. Like bludgeoning something.

The list contained a variety of the privileged elite of the twenty-first century, many of whom Quent himself had met. Everyone from Tatiana, the famous rags-to-riches actress who'd brought Hollywood and the rest of the world to its feet, to the U.S. ambassador to France, to Liam Hegelsen, Danish CEO of the hottest electronics and computer company since Apple . . . even to Brandon Huvane, the British publishing mogul.

Of course, there was no proof that everyone on Truth's contact list were members of the Cult of Atlantis. But by the looks of the names and the amount of money, knowledge, and power these people had, each in their own right—but together, it would have been formidable—they were all candidates for the Cult.

The group of people who had brought down the world. For what?

For *what*?

For the one thing they couldn't buy or create. Immortality.

Quent had known, and loathed, his father. He understood the man's ego and desire for power. What greater power than to live forever?

Who gave a flying cock if he had to destroy the world to do it.

The very thoughts haunted him, nauseated him. Kept him from sleeping. Eating. The only thing he did much of was drink.

And now that Zoë had stolen back her arrows, and, other than the brief appearance two nights ago, had made herself scarce, Quent felt as though he were on the verge of exploding.

Why she, this woman of shadow and night, should make a difference was moot. He didn't spend any time analyzing it. He knew she was a hot, hard, fast fuck. That was what he needed.

That was the only thing that might ease some of his tension. Clear his mind.

So he could figure out how to find his father. And kill him.

Something Quent should have done—he'd had the chance to do—long ago.

If he'd done it then, when he'd had the chance, the reason, if he'd fought back then, harder, instead of just taking the beating, the pummeling that nearly killed him . . . would it have stopped the Change?

Quent tipped back the last of his pint and slammed

the glass onto the table. The Pub's noise drowned out the sound, and when he stood, a bit unsteadily, Wyatt looked up at him. "You all right, man?"

Quent nodded. "As right as I can be. Which isn't to say much."

"You heading up? Want company?"

He shook his head. "Naw." He glanced at the petite brunette sitting next to Wyatt. Good for him. "See you later."

He'd leave the Pub and, despite the fact that it made him feel like a bloody wanker, Quent would slip outside into the fresh, night air. He'd walk along what passed for a street, but was really little more than a glorified pathway, heading to the darker areas of the city. Not too far, but away from the people, because he knew if there was any chance . . .

Quent resisted the sudden urge to slam his fist into the wall. Maybe his father's violent tendencies had taken a hold on him, because for fuck's sake, that's all he'd felt like doing for the last few weeks.

He walked out of the bar and felt a stir of new air, coming in from the open skylights above in what had once been the ceiling of the New York–New York lobby. Even that bit of freshness was welcome. At least there wasn't any smoking anymore either. Apparently the need and desire for cigarettes had gone away with the rest of the world. Or maybe tobacco had simply become extinct.

Walking along as he was, his head in his ass as he stewed over his failures and loathing, he nearly bloody missed her.

"Hey."

Quent stopped, his mouth bone dry. He looked over and saw her, standing there. Not where he'd expected her—not outside, hovering on a rooftop. Nor sneaking into his room.

But . . . here. Beside one of the ridiculous trees that somehow grew in this parody of a New York street.

At first, he couldn't find the words. A rush of heat and pleasure and, yes, he'd be lying if he didn't admit to a blast of anger—at himself, at her, at whatever—washed over him.

"Took you long enough," he said at last, calming his racing heart. And then he ruined it by saying her name. Softly. As if he cared. "Zoë."

"Long enough for what?" she said, in her flat, sharp way.

"To come back." His own words surprised him. Then, to cover it up, he added in a stronger voice, "I don't have anymore of your arrows." The unspoken words laced his voice: *So you must be here for something else.*

Zoë lifted her chin at that, but not before he saw a flash of . . . something in her eyes. Something . . . soft? *Nah, you wank.* A trick of the low light.

"What makes you think I'm here for you?" she countered.

"You know you are." Now he'd regained control of himself, and moved toward her.

She put out a hand as if to stop him from coming closer, and he stepped into it. The feel of her fingers and palm against him made his chest tighten. "You look ill," she said. But she made no move to shift her hand, to push him away . . . or allow him to come closer.

"I'm not." *Not with anything you can't cure, baby.* At least for a while. "Not anymore."

Her fingers pressed into him and Quent lifted his hand to close it around her wrist. Slender. Warm. "Zoë. Do you want to come upstairs with me?" She drew herself up to reply—probably obstinately—but he continued, "Or do you want me to drag you outside, slam you against the wall, and do you under the moon?"

That did it. He felt her breath catch, shimmering all through her arm, and their eyes met, clashed, burned.

"That is why you came, isn't it?" he whispered. And moved in.

Her fingers curled into his shirt, tugging him, and she lifted her face to meet his. Despite the heated words between them, the kiss was . . . it was hot, but slow and deep and long. She tasted like cinnamon, and sex, her full lips soft and lush beneath his.

Quent pressed himself up against her, driving her into the wall behind, shadowing them with the tree and its trunk. His hands curved around her waist, pulling her close, the whole, long, lean length of her, up against him. And kissed her as though he didn't need to breathe.

When he pulled away at last, to look down at her tousled mess of a haircut and into her heavy-lidded eyes, she was breathing just as heavily as he.

"If that's your follow-through on that eye-fuck from the party," she murmured, low and dusky and out of breath, "it's a damn good start."

"Trust me," he replied, sliding his arm around her waist. There was no fucking way he was letting her slip away again. "That was only the beginning."

December 25
About six and a half months after

This was not how I'd imagined spending Christmas 2010, after marrying Drew.

A difficult day for many of us.

I helped cook a special meal with turkey, goose, duck and a variety of other wild fowl to feed the 800+ of us.

We're doing pretty well with food. Surprisingly well. As the canned and preserved items begin to wear out, we're replacing it with freshly grown or raised vegetables.

This is Vegas, or, as it's been renamed, New Vegas, but the weather seems to have changed with everything else. It's not like a desert anymore, but almost tropical. That's probably because the ocean is now where the Venetian and Bellagio used to be. Very surreal.

We're having elections for a mayor in a few weeks, and Thad Marck, a good friend of Kevin's and his twin brother, is running against a guy named Greg Rowe. Thad's a bit of a live wire, pretty intense, but he's funny as heck. And I sure could use a laugh or two. Kevin likes him and I trust Kevin. He's been good to me.

But there's no replacement for Drew, with his funny smile and warped sense of humor. Oh, that man could make me laugh.

God, I miss him.

   —from *Adventures in Juliedom,* the
    blog of Julie Davis Beecher

CHAPTER 9

It was one of the hardest . . . and yet, easiest . . . things Simon had ever had to do: gathering that lovely, soft bundle of Sage into his arms.

But he did, and forced himself to concentrate not on the curve of her waist and the fresh, sun-kissed smell of her hair, but the danger they would be in if he couldn't hold himself invisible. And so he focused on the shimmery feeling, the ebb and flow of his person, even as the blast of light shone in the room, shone *through* them . . . instead of on the woman in his arms.

He knew the moment she realized what had happened, because, although of course he couldn't see her any longer, she had been looking up at him, fear and remorse in her eyes as they both sidled into nothingness. And he could still feel her, dammit. Felt the tension of disbelief in her arms and shoulders and the catch of her breath.

Breathe. Concentrate.

He waited as the beam of light shone over and through the room, as three men pounded in, examining every corner. Brushing close enough to them that he could feel the shift in the air, even the touch of a pant leg. Sage felt it, too, and she tightened even closer in his arms. But she didn't make a sound. He breathed, focused, kept his mind steady.

And then the searchers were gone, moving on to the other rooms, other possible hiding places. Their light faded and the only illumination was the cast of that fickle moon, twining in the clouds beyond as it filtered through a northerly window.

But the light was enough that Simon could see the expression on Sage's face as he released his hold and they shimmered back into opacity. Her eyes were circles of astonishment, and her lips parted in shock and wordlessness.

He shook his head to keep her from speaking, for it wasn't yet safe. The men were still searching the upper floors of the house, and might yet return. Simon hoped that they would come to the conclusion that the railing had splintered and fallen simply due to age, but even if they didn't, they wouldn't find him and Sage. He'd make sure of that.

But now, the worst of the moment yawned darkly before him. He dare not release her in case they came back, and he had nowhere to look . . . or to concentrate . . . except on the face, the heart-stopping face, the lips he'd tried so hard to avoid.

In the bluish light of the moon, she looked more ethereal and beautiful than ever. And she was so damned close. Simon felt the rush of his breath threaten to take over his consciousness, and he struggled to contain it. For God's sake, he'd been in tighter situations than this, more dangerous, more threatening . . . and he'd kept himself under control.

But now . . .

She reached up, pulling out her arm that had been crushed between them, and touched his cheek. Lightly, but it had the same effect as if she'd shoved her hand down his pants.

"How did you do that?" she breathed. So softly that even Simon couldn't fault her. The men's voices were distant, on the floor above them. *Damn.*

He shrugged, feeling the heavy . . . yet light . . . touch of her palm, warm, on his cheek. Was this the first time someone had touched him since . . . since coming out of those caves? "I just did."

"You did it before," she added now, her eyes wider. "Didn't you?"

He nodded and she withdrew her hand. Thank God. But then it settled between them, and her fingers sort of curled up amid her chest and his. Could she feel the stampede of his heart? He knew she couldn't feel the rush of heat that swarmed him, and the faint sheen of sweat breaking out over his skin. At least, he hoped not.

"Simon."

He drew back a bit. "Hush." He did not want to hear what she was going to say, did not want to look into those eyes anymore. It would only take one little hint, one breath, and it would be all over.

Fuck Theo.

No, no, no.

But, *pinche*, she was looking up at him, and she was so damned close, and what woman wouldn't be starry-eyed around a guy who could turn her invisible?

"Can you do it again?" she asked.

Okay. Sure. This he could do. Then he wouldn't have to look at her, at least.

Simon drew in his breath, concentrated, and felt that now-familiar feeling sprinkle over him. Sage's face wavered, close . . . so close . . . then gently disappeared.

Just as it happened, she moved . . . in his arms, surged into him . . . and planted her lips against his.

Simon's concentration shattered. He lost it all—his mind, his place, his breath—and felt the whoosh of solidity return as the pleasure, something electric, jolted him. Soft, gentle, tentative, the brush of mouth to mouth . . . and then a soft groan from the back of his throat as he could no longer restrain himself.

His arms tightened around her, drawing her up and into his chest, and he found her lips again. They were ready, lifted and parted, and when he fitted his mouth to hers, she opened, pressing closer as if she too were as eager to taste him. And taste he did. Oh, indeed, and he was well and truly fucked.

Simon became lost in the wave of pleasure trammeling through him, the sleek, warm slide of tongue and busy mouths, moving, shaping and nibbling. Of Sage and her thick, heavy hair, of delicate shoulders under his palms, the soft little sounds she made, the smooth skin beneath his fingers.

But even in the back of his mind, he dared not move . . . dared not take it any further. Despite the searing need, he kept it easy, froze his hands in place, and tried to keep from devouring her, from sliding beneath that shirt and touching more of that warm, soft skin.

And when she tugged back a bit, her breath soft and fast against him, he instantly released her, his own lungs working overtime, his heart slamming and his jeans *way* uncomfortably tight. *Focus on that instead of dragging her back for more.*

"My God. Simon," she whispered. Her eyes were still circles of shock and awe, but now her lips were full and puffy and glistening and he had to draw himself back to keep from lunging back toward her again. Her body moved against him, her breasts rising and falling as she caught her breath. And she smiled. Up into his eyes.

Holy God in Heaven.

Simon felt the world tip and tilt and he realized his fingers had curled into what was left of an area rug beneath them. He pushed them deeper to stabilize himself. To fucking hold on.

And then, praise God, he heard the voices again, closer, and brought a finger to his lips. But Sage had heard them too and she closed her mouth, looking apprehensively toward the door.

Hard to believe it had only been a few moments since the searchers had been there, shining their lights around in the room . . . because to Simon, it had been a whole world of change. Eons. His own personal apocalyptic event.

And this time, when the light came back and the men clomped down onto their floor, out and around in the hallway, persistent, and Simon had to pull Sage closer, and focus his energy . . . it was all that much more difficult. She fairly cuddled into him, like a kitten—no longer skittish—and he felt her relax, trusting, and he closed his eyes for a moment.

Just a moment. Just . . .

The men arrived, pushing at the door again, and once more, Simon gathered his power and strength. Like holding his breath, he settled, concentrated, and, just as the light blasted into the room, he and Sage faded into nothing.

Only this time, Sage had her face buried in his neck, the press of her lips gentle against his warm, damp skin, the brush of her eyelashes under his ear.

Quent couldn't get her clothes off fast enough. Inside the door of his room, they stumbled into each other, half fall-

ing against the wall as he jammed his hands down inside
Zoë's pants, down over her smooth, lean hips, tearing at
denim and panties as she, just as ferociously, yanked at
his. A slice of moon cut through the open curtains, bath-
ing the room in bluish-white, showcasing the neatly made
bed and mounds of pillows.

Zoë gave a little laugh against his mouth as she caught
herself against a dresser, then pulled him with her as they
staggered toward the bed. They fell on it with a hard jolt
and it slammed into the wall from the force. Mouths,
hands, legs twined, clothes flew, skin slid against skin,
damp and hot and frantic.

Oh God, oh yes, Zoë . . .

He flipped on his back and brought her with him, and
as if reading his mind, she rose up over him, long and
slender and dusky, straddling his hips as he settled his
hands at her waist. "Zoë," he said urgently when she
ground herself into his belly, but made no move to shift to
where he bloody needed her.

She smiled then, fast and wicked, her white teeth flashing and her exotic eyes narrowing in delight. A stripe of
moon angled across her torso, like the sash of a beauty
queen. But Zoë looked more like some erotic dancer as
she stripped off her little tank top and flung it to the floor.
She wore no bra—she didn't need to, for her breasts were
tight and high and the perfect size for his hands. Lifting her arms, she tousled her hair, raising her upthrusting
breasts even higher, tormenting him as she circled herself
into his belly.

Quent met her eyes. "Now, dammit," he muttered, and
lifted her hips. She helped, her eyes dark and avid, and
when he settled her down on top of him in a deep, perfect
slide, he nearly went through the roof.

Everything disintegrated after that—his thoughts, his

concentration, his sense of place and time—and funneled into a whirl of pleasure and need, hard and hot and slick. Cinnamon and musk and silky, warm skin. Zoë.

As he moved inside her, feeling his body coil with readiness, watching her face settle and stretch with desire as she shuddered in the slam of a release, he almost let it go. Almost gave in, almost ignored what he knew . . . but at the last minute, the very last possible second, as the build became almost too intense to think, his conscience won. Quent rolled from beneath her, twisting them into an awkward heap as his world exploded.

When at last they lay, panting, sprawled, toes curled and bodies sticky, he reached over and touched her. Closed his fingers around her wrist, gently. Intimately.

Their fingers curled into each other, hers, slender and rough, his large and enveloping. And they slept in a slice of moonlight.

"Why the hell do you always do that?"

The low, annoyed voice dragged Quent from the first real rest he'd had in weeks.

"Huh?" he muttered, scrambling to clear his mind of dead sleep laced with afterglow. But when Zoë moved, pulling away, his brain sharpened enough to send the signal for him to *hold on*. He tightened his fingers around her wrist.

She stopped. Then, with a quick movement, jerked her arm away.

That caught Quent's full attention and he rose quickly. She was not going to sneak out on him again.

Zoë sat there, naked and seemingly unconcerned about that fact, if the position of her body was any indication. Completely bloody distracting, the way she was sitting, with one leg bent so her knee was straight up and her other leg bent with her ankle tucked near her inner thigh. The room had begun to take on a lighter glow with dawn easing the distance, and Quent could hardly keep his breath steady, looking at her.

"What were you saying?" he asked.

"Why the hell do you always fucking do that? It sort of blows the moment, doesn't it?"

Always? Do what? They'd been together . . . twice. They'd met, what, four times—the first time she'd saved him from the *gangas* with her arrows, then there was the wild and crazy session in this very room . . . then at the festival where they did nothing but eye each other . . . and then this. What *always* was she talking about?

"Pull away. At the last freaking minute."

Right then. Pull *out*, she meant. Yeah. That sucked.

And since birth control was practically illegal—or it would be if there were lawyers anymore—and certainly nonexistent in this post-Change world anyway, Quent supposed she was probably not aware of it. "I don't want to get you pregnant."

"Pregnant. Oh." She eased back a little, as if the thought hadn't really occurred to her. It probably hadn't. After all, in some ways this world was more than a little backward. Women were sort of expected to be pregnant as much as possible—not regimented like they were in Falling Creek, but it was a good thing to procreate. To add to the human race. And pregnant women were well cared for, pampered, and lauded by everyone.

Plus, there were no such thing as STDs anymore. According to Lou and Theo, anyway.

"I never pay any attention the other times," she said with a shrug.

The other times.

For some reason, those blasé words stopped him cold.

Not a good image, Zoë and her "other times." Not at all.

Quent steadied himself. He didn't know anything about this woman, other than her Robin Hood-like skill with a bow and arrow. Nothing but the way she made him feel. The way she touched him. From the first, it had been the way she touched him. And the way that, when their eyes met, he felt as if bloody rockets were shooting off all over his body.

For all he knew . . . she could be married. She could have a partner. She could have other guys with rooms that she sneaked into, stole back arrows from, visually undressed in bars and made promises to with those sloe eyes, whatever . . . all over Envy, all over this buggered up world.

He opened his mouth to say something. To ask. To demand. Then closed it. He closed his eyes. This wasn't him. Quent Fielding didn't care beyond the moment.

"Yo."

He opened them and found her watching him, even more clearly illuminated now as the half moon aligned itself better to the window. "You okay?"

"Zoë. This . . . is really good." He spread his hand around to encompass the bed, the room, her and him.

She gave another wicked flash of smile that sent a streak of heat down to his belly. "Damn straight it is."

"Why don't you . . . stay. Awhile." *Bollocks, Fielding. Could you sound more like a knobhead?*

She drew back, stiffened. Even adjusted her position, sliding both legs so that her feet were on the floor. Ready for takeoff. "No fucking way. And don't even try to make me."

Quent eased back, settling into a reclining arrangement, hoping to alleviate her skittishness. "Okay. Just thought I'd ask."

She seemed to relax, and he breathed easier.

"The other night, when we saw each other in the Pub
. . . why did you leave?"

She smirked at him . . . but he saw a glint of bravado in
her eyes. Arrogance, almost. Or . . . maybe . . . some sort
of shield. "You looked like you had your hands full."

"Uh." The truth was . . . and he'd never admit it . . . he'd
completely lost interest in Nadine the minute he saw Zoë.
And hadn't thought about following up on that moment
on the dance floor since then.

"Kind of ballsy of you, eye-fucking me while you got
your hands all over some other woman's ass," she said
with an unmistakable edge to her voice. "Besides, I saw
someone I needed to talk to."

"Who?"

Her eyes narrowed. "Someone."

"A man?" As if he'd know the guy. But, he'd gotten the
impression that Zoë didn't come to Envy often. He knew
she didn't live here. So how would she know anyone?
Unless she had another booty call besides him lined up.

"Yeah." She lifted her chin as if to challenge anything
he might say.

And what the hell could he say? After all, the last time
she'd seen him, he'd—as she'd put it—had his hands all
over another woman's ass. Aside of the fact that they were
nothing to each other but a quick, easy lay.

Right?

Right.

Right.

"Someone who lives here?" Christ, why couldn't he
shut the fuck up? Or, better yet, grab her and slam her
back onto the mattress and put all thoughts of everything
out of her mind but him and what he could do to her sleek,
cinnamony body.

Zoë was eyeing him speculatively. "No. Someone who might be able to help me. I've been looking for someone for a long time."

Quent stilled and the prick of annoyance eased. Just a bit. "Remington Truth?" he breathed. Just . . . just as a wild guess.

Her eyes widened in shock. "No. I'm not looking for that. But . . . how did you know about it?"

"That? You mean Remington Truth?"

She nodded. "The *gangas* have been searching for Remington's Truth for years, for the Strangers. As long as anyone can remember. The Strangers are terrified that someone else might get it first. Do you know what it is?"

"It? Remington Truth is a man," Quent told her. "A man who lived before the Change, and, most likely helped to cause it. As far as we can tell."

"A *man*?" She seemed to turn that over in her mind. "Hot damn. That makes total fucking sense. He's a *man*."

He reached over to the table next to the bed and scooped up a printout of Truth's picture. "This is what he looks like. Ever see him?"

She took the photo. "No."

"Why is it so important for them to find him?" It occurred to Quent that he didn't know something very important about Zoë—like, which side she was on. For all he knew, she could be booty-calling Strangers till their crystals glowed. She could be on the wrong side of this equation . . . but probably not. After all, she hunted *gangas* with her bow and arrows.

"The Strangers are afraid of it—him. *Him*." She was nodding, and he saw intelligence light her eyes. The moon had shifted to shine even more boldly now, and the room had taken on a light gray coloring that disclosed more nuances of her face and its expression. Her features settled in thought, and as if it were possible, it made her appear even more attractive. Softer.

Quent swallowed. His heart was pounding and his fingers itched to touch her. But he held back. For the moment. "Do you have any idea where he might be?"

She shook her head. "But finding him would be a good thing. Before the Strangers do. Although if they haven't found him after fifty years with an ass-crap army of *ganga*-zombies, how the damn hell is anyone else going to? I've only heard bits of conversation, from a distance . . . but they're desperate. Remington Truth must hold some hella big-ass secret that would damage them. Or help them."

Quent nodded. This was exactly what the Waxnickis had suspected, and why they were working so hard to find the man. Before the Strangers did. And Zoë had just confirmed their suspicions. "Want to help us find him? You could stay."

Her eyes flashed to him, then zigzagged away. "I told you, I'm not fucking staying." Then, her demeanor changed and her eyes took on a sly, smoldering look. "But I'd *stay* for another fuck."

Quent's belly dropped as she tossed away the picture of Remington Truth and leaned toward him. *Is that all I am? A good fuck?*

But he didn't say it. After all, that's all she was to him.

He closed his eyes and drew her close . . . lost himself in the pleasure.

Because he hadn't anything else.

At last, the searchers seemed to give up on their quest and accepted the fact that whatever had caused the railing to fall, it entailed no threat to them or their activities.

Sage allowed Simon to pull her to her feet, and she was

careful not to bump into anything again. All they needed was to alert the men below again. But, wow.

She was completely weak-kneed. And even a little dizzy.

That kiss . . . wow. Wuh-*how*. Those beautiful lips . . .

She'd waited till Simon's face disappeared before leaning forward, taking the chance. She'd figured she'd be assuaging her curiosity, and wanted the cover of invisibility in case he wasn't . . . interested. Or was even revolted.

Because, after all, he'd made a point of absolutely not touching her since they'd left Envy, except to guide her tonight.

But once she fell into the kiss, Sage had forgotten everything. Literally everything.

The men could have stormed into the room, guns blazing, she wasn't certain she'd have noticed.

She swallowed. He'd kissed her back. Oh, indeed. He'd kissed her back. Even now, as they slipped out into the hallway, his hand, as always, tight around hers—impersonal, guiding. Steady and strong. Just like the man himself. Even now, her belly fluttered and her breath caught. *He'd kissed her back.* And it had been so much more than . . . *nice.*

At the top of the stairs, Simon gestured her to another flight. This one was not quite so grand and winding, and it led to a fourth floor, accessed through narrow steps beyond a small door. Some of the treads made soft creaks, and Sage froze, her heart in her throat every time she stepped on one. But Simon urged her on, and she realized that distance masked them from the other occupants of the house, which had returned to the basement.

By the time they reached the top, Sage felt her nose itch with dust and the grind of grit beneath her fingers from the stair's railing. Obviously, this part of the house was never used and, as Simon had suggested earlier, would be a good place to install one of the Network Access Points that would allow Lou and Theo to extend their secret communications system.

The room into which Simon brought her was clearly an attic of some sort, and the half moon poured light through an octagonal window that had long been broken. Although not cluttered with trunks and wardrobes like the fascinating attics of fiction and film, the room did contain some furnishings. Light pooled onto a dusty wooden floor scattered with piles of debris and a few straggling plants.

"Do you need light?" he asked in a quiet voice, and gestured to the shadowy shapes of the two packs on the floor.

"Would it be all right?" she asked. "It'd be faster. I've only done this twice."

Simon pulled the packs over and they settled on the floor together, then he turned on a small flashlight powered by a hand crank. Keeping the illumination low would hide the light from the windows.

Sage set to work as Simon angled the light for her.

"This will run on solar power," she told him, showing him the box that would capture the network signals. "So we have to find a place where it will soak up the sun for a good portion of the day, but also be somewhat protected from the elements. Even though Lou designed it to be waterproof, we want to protect it as much as possible."

"Right there," Simon said, pointing toward the octagonal window nestled in a small, jutting dormer. "Outside there's an overhang that will protect it from rain, but it's a southeasterly window, so it will still capture a lot of rays. Unless you want to put it out on the roof itself."

Sage nodded, pleased, and said, "All right. Let's try it out, and hope that it still has some power."

He took the box over to the little alcove beneath the window and positioned it on a table. The long antennas veed out like two long tails and Sage clambered to her feet to check it out. A little flip of the switch and the un-obtrusive lights, designed for the bottom of the unit so as not to draw attention, illuminated. "We have power," she said with satisfaction. "Now let's hope it connects to the rest of the network."

Pulling out the small computer Theo had built for her, she sat down and powered it on. This would be the first time she'd had the chance to send a message back to Envy since they'd arrived two days ago. Unfortunately, they didn't have much news to report back other than the hope-fully successful installation of the NAP.

Simon sat down in the small space as well, folding his legs to fit, angling his knees up. One thin strand of glossy dark hair had escaped from his neat tail, making Sage wonder if it had happened during their kiss.

He leaned against the wall facing her and she felt his eyes on her as she bent to the keyboard. A little shiver sprinkled over her shoulders when she thought about the fact that they would soon be back in their room . . . shar-ing a bed.

She had to retype her password three times before her clumsy fingers got it right, and then she settled back against her side of the dormer space. "Now we have to wait and see if the network connects."

"Tell me about these Strangers coming tomorrow night," he said without preamble. He must have been waiting since dinner to ask.

"When we first got here to Envy, I started to tell you about Hell's Wall," she said.

"Yeah. I wondered why anyone who survived the

Change would build a settlement beneath something that looked as if an avalanche could destroy it at any time. You mentioned something about protection."

She nodded. "I don't really know all the details, but I've known since I was a kid—and everyone here understands—that the Corrigan brothers made some sort of arrangement with the Strangers—well, three of them. Three of the Strangers have created a crystal-powered guard, like a fence, to protect the city if there should be an avalanche or rockslide."

Simon watched her, disbelief and question in his face. "Why would they do that? Why would they care? A crystal-powered guard?"

"My understanding is that the Strangers get some of our—Falling Creek's, I mean—yield, a portion of the crops and food and cattle. In return, they protect us from the cliff. And . . . if you look very closely at Hell's Wall at night, you can see the faint glow of blue crystal light. Very faint, but very powerful. I guess it's like a shield that would stop anything from falling onto the city."

"So they protect the settlement in exchange for food that you raise?" Simon's brows knit together. "Very medieval."

She nodded. "Classic feudal system. There's nothing wrong with that, is there?"

He shrugged. "I guess if it's been working for fifty years, there's nothing wrong with it. It seems like a fair exchange." Then he looked at her steadily. "Unless the Strangers require other commodities as part of their compensation. Like . . . people."

Sage blinked. "Like . . . slaves?" The thought hadn't ever crossed her mind. Not when she was living here before. But now, years later, after seeing what she'd seen, and hearing from Jade about her experiences and observations in regards to the Strangers . . . "Oh my God. Simon, that could be true." All of a sudden, her stomach felt like a ball of lead had settled in it.

"Do you ever remember people disappearing?"

That leaden ball sat heavy and hard in her belly. "Yes," she whispered. "Once a year . . . usually about the time the Strangers came to visit. Oh, Simon." Her gaze flew to his. "They come once a year like this and I remember when I was eleven, three girls ran away shortly after."

"Ran away? Or were taken away?" Simon asked. But he didn't really need to, because she read comprehension in his eyes. The same understanding that was rising in her own gaze.

"One of them was my half sister Gina. I remember being so upset with her for leaving. Running away, I thought. And never saying good-bye. And Bennie said five of our other sisters ran away over the years." Sage's belly churned. "And . . . the following year after Gina disappeared, when I was twelve . . . my mother . . ." Her voice trailed off.

The arguments. The shouts and crying and pleading from behind closed doors. The desperation in her mother's face—desperation that Sage believed was weakness. Desperation that had caused her death.

Was it possible? Or was she jumping to conclusions?

"What is it?"

"I think . . . I think she might have been trying to keep them from taking me." Sage's mouth felt tight and worn. She could hardly say the words, could barely comprehend the possibility. "I was her only daughter. She made me wake up in the middle of the night, the night before the Strangers were supposed to come. We were trying to leave the compound and I thought *she* was trying to escape, but really, she was helping *me*. Maybe. They ran her down and the *gangas* came swarming in."

Her heart was pounding hard and sickeningly in her chest. It was possible her mother had been trying to get her out of Falling Creek. And Sage, as an adolescent, had been focused on herself and her desire to see the Strangers—not what her mother wanted.

"I'm sorry." Simon's voice held a stronger hint of that accent, that intriguing inflection she noticed. "Losing a parent is hard, but to see it happen . . . that makes it worse." He sounded as if he spoke from experience.

"I don't know for sure . . . but I do know she died. And that when the Strangers came, I was effectively out of sight because I was grieving for her. So I never saw them."

"And they never saw you."

Sage shook her head. "No."

"Any idea how they pick the girls they want to take?"

The nausea still heavy in her middle, she refocused her thoughts. "I don't know. It could be random or it could be some negotiation with the Strangers. Or maybe the Strangers came and scoped out the girls they wanted and then they were later delivered."

Glancing at the computer, she saw that there were status bars showing a good connection—which made sense, since the network access point was right next to the computer. She clicked on the message client that Lou and Theo had created—called WaxNotes—and waited to see if anything downloaded.

"How did you get out of Falling Creek, then? You must have left shortly after."

"They wanted to marry me to a man who was fifty. He already had three other wives, and his hands . . ." She shuddered at the memory. "They were large and really hairy, with lots of black hair, and he looked at me funny and I knew I didn't want to marry him. I didn't want him to touch me."

"And?" His voice was very low. Barely a breath.

"I hid in a crate that belonged to a traveling scavenger— someone who brought goods from other settlements and traded here anything he might find on the way, or anywhere else. Clothes, DVDs, books, anything he found that was usable. I was lucky he was a nice man, or I could have found myself in a much worse situation. And I was too dumb to know that at the time. Turned out he was married to Flo, from Envy, and when he found me huddled in there—you have to understand, I was still in shock from losing my mother, and I was a Corrigan, you know . . . but he took me back and let Flo mother me."

"Lucky for you Flo was the mothering type." Simon's voice carried that accent, and a deeper inflection. Maybe regret?

"I never realized how lucky—at least for a long time."

"And then you got to know Lou and Theo and Jade."

She nodded, and looked down to check the computer screen. "Lou and Theo at first. Jade didn't come to Envy until she escaped from Preston, almost four years ago. But Flo took her under her wing too."

"And you've been friends with Lou . . . and Theo . . . ever since."

Sage looked up and found his eyes heavy on her. "Yes." Then looked back down, uncertain why that heavy ball in her belly had settled deeper. "We're in," she said, seeing the messages on her screen. "We're connected!"

Simon settled back, extending his long legs and crossing them at the ankles as she skimmed through the messages. Several from Lou and Theo checking in with her, adding last-minute instructions for setting up the access point (although how they thought she'd be able to access them if she couldn't get the NAP to work, she wasn't sure), and then a final email from Theo sent earlier today. This last one had no subject header—an oddity that, for some reason, made her chest tighten. She waited to open it.

"No real news," she said, glancing up at Simon. She thought she felt him looking at her, but when she lifted her face, he was staring in the opposite direction. "The only thing Lou said is that they hacked into some more documents on Truth's flash drive, and they seem to have found a set of geographic coordinates. At least, that's what they think they are. A list of ten."

She skimmed the email from Lou. "But now that the earth's axis has shifted because of the new landmass in the Pacific Ocean, he's not sure how to plot the points any longer. Huh. Interesting."

During the Change, a large landmass about the size of Colorado had appeared in the Pacific. The Waxnicki brothers had surmised that if it had risen from the bottom of the ocean—which they suspected—it had caused or at least contributed to the devastating earthquakes, tsunamis, and other weather-related catastrophes, and also had the effect of shifting the axis of the globe, due to the shift in weight.

No one knew for certain what had happened, but it was their best theory.

"What does Theo say?" Simon asked quietly.

Sage glanced at him. How did he know she had a last message from him? That she'd been saving because there was no subject header. Because she had a funny feeling about it. Simon was watching her closely now, and she clicked open the email hesitantly.

Sage. Pls tell me ur all right. Am very worried not to hear frm u. Pls write back asap.

Okay, no big deal. Whatever apprehension or trepidation she felt ebbed. What the heck was wrong with her? She clicked to respond, and just then, another email popped into her box.

Also from Theo. Also with no subject.

Huh. What was he doing up so late?

She clicked on it.

I love you.

That was all it said. But the effect of those three words was like a douse of cold water. And a vortex of shock and confusion. Theo loved her? *Loved* her, loved her? Her palms sprang damp and her belly swished. *No, no, no . . .*

Something of her reaction must have been on her face. "What is it?" Simon asked.

And before she could reply, he was up and over and next to her, looking over her shoulder. Before she could close the message and hide it from him.

"I promised I would get you back to him, safe and whole," Simon said. Low and deep in her ear, and much too close. "And I will."

And from the look in his eyes, one that she recognized even in the face of jinky moonlight, she saw the message there: flat, distant. Removed and full of warning.

Off limits.

When Quent woke, the dawn streaming hot and heavy through his window, he found that he was alone. Again.

His body was loose and sated, but he felt cold and bereft.

She'd told him she wouldn't stay.

How long till she came back?

February 13
About eight months after.

*Thad Marck lost the election for mayor, and
Kevin and Robert Corrigan aren't happy about
it. Neither, of course, is Thad. He seems to
have lost his sense of humor lately, getting a sort of scary-intense gleam in his
eyes when he talks about his vision for the
future. He doesn't listen to any opposing
ideas, he just spouts his own. Loudly and
vociferously.*

*To me, he sounds like the CEO I used to
work for, talking about mission statements
and expansion plans and implementation pro-
cedures. Apparently enough people didn't buy
into his ideas and didn't elect him.*

*Something else creepy happened a few days
ago. A big black humvee drove up into town
and these people got out. People here from
N.V. swarmed them immediately, thinking that
help had finally arrived . . . but there was
something off about them. Something freaky
and odd.*

*They didn't offer any help at all, and just
stayed for a while, talking, asking a lot of
questions, and from what I heard, they didn't
answer any themselves. No one knows who they
are or where they came from and people have
been calling them the Strangers. Which, as
unimaginative of a name as it is, it's pretty
accurate. So it will probably stick.*

And speaking of weird names. Those sounds

at night, someone calling for Ruth . . .
well, they're monsters. Orange eyes, horrible
stink. They move like Frankenstein's monster, sort of jerky and awkwardly—at least,
from what I can tell from very far away.
People were calling them zombies and some
other people said they looked like a jiang
shi—which I guess is the Chinese name for
zombie or vampire or something.

Anyway, so now people are calling them
jiangas or ganga because they don't want
the kids to hear the word "zombie" and get
scared after watching horror movies.

Seriously . . . we're already living in a
horror movie.

> — from Adventures in Juliedom, the
>   blog of Julie Davis Beecher

CHAPTER 10

Dawn streamed through the room Simon shared with the woman who'd kissed him into a puddle of melted brains. He'd watched the pale sunlight start as the faintest of illumination, then as it spread into a wide swath over the bed, because he'd not closed his eyes once since returning from their midnight activities.

Was he afraid she might reach for him, roll into him with that soft, curvy body, brush against him as she slept? Yep.

But he was even more afraid of what he might do of his own volition. Now that he'd had a sample.

Theo. Remember Theo, who'd known her, wanted her, loved her for longer than Simon had.

And aside from that, even if Theo weren't looming over the whole damn picture, with his flashy dragon tattoo and his electronic brilliance . . . Simon had nothing to offer a woman like Sage. Really.

Yes, he'd reformed. Yes, he'd wanted to, needed to . . . even prayed for it. But that didn't change the violence of his past and the sins he left behind. Would a woman like Sage ever suffer such bloodied hands on her? Knowing the evils they'd committed?

What woman would love or even want a murderer?

He supposed—when he realized what a bittersweet, backward gift the Change had been for him, the elusive escape from Mancusi's golden handcuffs—he could picture himself as a lone do-gooder. A drifting Good Samaritan. One who showed up when needed, and left when done.

No relationships. No back story. No ties and certainly no responsibilities. And with the additional abilities he'd acquired, he really had no excuse for not living like some hermit-ish superman.

Which was what he was going to do as soon as he got Sage safely back to Envy. And now that they'd set up the NAP and they'd found no clues to Remington Truth's location, he figured it was about time to go.

The sooner the better.

When he slid from the bed, Sage murmured and shifted, as if fully aware that he'd left. Even though he'd made certain not even the heat of their bodies connected beneath the sheets, she seemed to sense the loss of his presence.

But he looked away and stole into the bathroom, where he took another shower and dressed for the day. They were going to leave as soon as she woke up.

Even if they had to barrel their way through the gates.

When he came back out into the bedroom, he found her sitting up in bed, looking at a full-sized laptop computer—definitely not the one she'd had last night. The one that had downloaded Theo's love letter.

"Good morning," she said, looking up at him through a tangle of hair that didn't seem to bother her. It bothered the hell out of him, though, because it looked like she'd just been well-loved. Her blue eyes skimmed over his chest, covered but a little damp beneath the T-shirt because he'd been in a hurry. A hurry to get the fuck out of here.

"Where did you get that?" he asked.

She glanced beyond him at the picture, as if to point out that it was still crooked and covering the camera, and replied very softly, "Last night. When you went to check to make sure we could leave safely. I put it in my backpack."

On their way back out of the house, he'd left her for a few minutes in the same room where they'd kissed so that he could check below to make sure no one was about. Apparently, she hadn't been content with sitting quietly and waiting.

"I found this and grabbed a few books too," she added. And smiled. "I saw them when we were in there . . . before." Her cheeks tinted pink and she looked back down at the keyboard. "It's an old computer. I just thought . . . well, Lou and Theo like to keep parts on hand."

"Oh. Well, look," he said, coming close enough so she could hear his low voice. "I think we can leave now that the NAP is up and running. Get back to Envy by tonight."

Now she looked up again, her face filled with surprise. "You mean today?"

He nodded, wincing at her louder tone. Why was she so shocked? "There's no reason to stay."

"But. . . ." She lowered her voice. "We can't leave. We haven't found Remington Truth yet, and besides, if the Strangers are coming tonight, it's possible they're taking people with them. We have to stop them. Don't we?"

Simon opened his mouth to argue.

"*You* can do it," she added, looking at him fiercely. Before he could react, she closed her fingers around his wrist and tightened them meaningfully. "You have the ability to do anything with your power," she whispered.

Aw, fuck.

He extricated himself carefully, but the feel of her fingers still remained. "We don't know for certain," he began, but at the mutinous look on her face—*pinche*, could he deny her anything?—he continued, "all right. One more night. We'll poke around and see if we can find anything more about Truth, and we'll see if there's anyone to be rescued from the Strangers. But I don't know how to figure that out."

She smiled. Again. And his heart dropped. Again.

Damn it to hell.

"You will. We will," she said.

And then he realized he'd just agreed to spend another night with her . . . with Sage, who was definitely still ovulating.

Who kissed like a goddess and had no idea what that little freckle on her lip . . . not to mention her quick mind and endearing clumsiness . . . did to him.

"Yeah," was all he could say. And he fled the room.

Sage's face didn't return to its normal temperature for several minutes after Simon left, and that was only because she forced herself to concentrate on navigating through the old computer she'd found.

It had been a moment of whimsy—or maybe just a way to relieve some of her underlying tension—that caused her to get up and investigate the dusty desk next to where she crouched. Or perhaps it was simply that she needed *not* to be sitting, crouched, in the place where she'd kissed Simon.

Regardless—heck, she could make up reasons all day—Sage had grabbed the computer and a few paperbacks and stuffed them in the small backpack she wore. And now she'd managed to boot up the old, cranky computer where she found a document called "Juliedom."

She opened the file and began to read through it . . . and with a wave of surrealism, realized two things. First, that it was a sort of diary of a woman who'd lived through the Change. And secondly, and most importantly and amazingly, that it belonged to Julie Beecher Davis Corrigan.

Her paternal grandmother.

The realization was enough to send rampant prickles down her spine.

What were the chances?

Of course, the electronic diary captured her attention and the next thing Sage knew, a knock at the door roused her from her reading. *Crap.* Late for her morning breakfast, prenatal vitamin acquisition, and temperature reading. The Falling Creek ladies were going to be horrified.

"Oh, dear," she called. "I'll be right there!"

She stuffed the laptop beneath the dresser and reluctantly left the room to begin her day. Later, she'd be able to read the heartbreaking, fascinating account of her grandmother's survival and new life.

When she left the room, Sage had the picture of Remington Truth tucked into her pocket. On the previous days, she'd simply attempted to drop the name into conversation to see if anyone recognized it, but today she would try a different tactic.

Hurrying off to the medical area of the Community House under the watchful eye of her nurse, Sage tried not to think about where Simon was and what he was doing.

And she certainly didn't want to think about Theo's email. Every time she did, her belly felt like it was cramping up.

And yet, she couldn't quite keep her mind off the great revelation.

I love you.

In the movies she watched, books she read, and even in real-life observances, that declaration was tantamount to a new beginning. Fireworks! Passion! Look at Jade and Elliott. She'd never seen her friend happier. And Flo and dear Ferguson, who'd passed away four years ago. There'd been such love and affection between the two of them . . . partnership and respect. Something she'd never really experienced before or since leaving Falling Creek.

So why did Theo's message make her sick to her stomach?

And how was she going to face him again?

One thing was certain. Until she had a better idea of how to react, Sage did *not* want to go back to Envy. Even if it meant staying here and pretending to make love to Simon every night.

"Ouch," she said, snapping back to awareness at the prick of a needle. "What was that for?" She hadn't even realized they were drawing blood.

"Just checking your hormone levels," the nurse said with relish. Sage was pretty sure she was a distant aunt or directly related to her father. The tip of her hook nose was tinged red with what Sage presumed was enjoyment. "To see if you're pregnant."

"What?" *What?*

"Hormone levels can shift as early as twenty-four hours after fertilization," lectured the nurse. "If we can verify fertilization, then you and your husband can cease having relations and he can save his semen for another wife."

Wow. These people are really jinky about this. "He doesn't have another wife."

"Well, perhaps not today. But it won't be long. My own Gretchen has already been expressing her interest in joining Mr. Japp's family, and she's not the only one."

Is that so? Sage recalled the teasing she'd given Simon last night about being the center of attention, and all of a sudden it didn't seem so funny anymore.

The nurse pulled the needle from her arm and removed the rubber tourniquet a little more roughly than necessary. *Sheesh.* Sage must have been deep in thought not to have noticed getting that tied around her arm.

"Now sit here," the nurse said. "I'll have your results in about thirty minutes. On second thought, you can go and help clear the dishes in the community dining room. Since you overslept this morning." She raised a dark brow and cast a disapproving glance at Sage.

"All right." Sage was delighted to flee the examining room. She didn't have any need to wait for her blood work results, and this would give her the opportunity to flash the picture of Remington Truth around. She'd thought about showing Nurse Ratchett, but decided at the last minute not to.

She just didn't seem very helpful.

In the community dining room, the fresh breeze from outside wafted in and the space was filled with the clang of glass and the clatter of flatware. Sage cleared dishes, making her way from table to table. She approached the women—most of whom were younger than she; a few might have been her nieces—and managed to show the picture.

"You know I used to live here when I was young," she'd say. "And I remember this man who was so nice. He was like a grandfather to me. But I was too young to know his name . . . and I can't remember anything about him. Here's what he looked like. Do you know if he's still here?"

The resounding response from the busy, gossiping—even singing—girls was negative. No one thought the distinguished man with silver hair and startling blue eyes looked familiar.

It wasn't until Sage was ready to report back to the medical examining room that she tried her tactic out on one of the other ladies in the kitchen. A skinny, ropy lady with thinning dark hair who looked as if she'd been washing dishes for a decade. She looked familiar, and after a moment, Sage realized she'd been married to her father.

The woman, whose name was Treva, remembered her after a memory jog, and Sage tried her story out on her, hoping the woman wouldn't ask too many questions about the fabricated "grandfather."

But Treva merely lifted her chapped hands from the hot soapy water to take the picture. Gingerly, at the corner, but she got it a bit wet nevertheless. "Shew. Maybe I have seen this picture somewhere," she said. "But I can't think where. Let me mull on it while I'm washing up here. The water soothes me. Clears my mind."

By the looks of her hands, Treva must be very soothed and relaxed.

"Well, if you remember, let me know," Sage told her. But she didn't hold out much hope.

After all, seeing a *picture* of Remington Truth wasn't going to be much help, and wouldn't be all that unusual. From what she'd learned from her Yahoogle searching, Truth had been a well-known face and could have appeared in any magazine or newspaper that Treva might have seen.

She was just leaving the dining room when she heard someone calling. "Uh, Sage? You there!"

Sage turned and saw Treva, busily drying her hands with a white towel. "Did you remember something?"

"I did indeed. I know exactly where I saw't. I've got a break now. If you come with me, I'll show you."

Sage followed her, glancing quickly down the hall toward the medical wing. No one was in sight, including

Nurse Ratchett. And it had been more than thirty minutes, for sure. Oh well. She already knew what the results would be.

To her surprise, Treva took her to a different area of the Community House. "The library?" Sage said, her eyes wide and her heart leaping with excitement. She hadn't been here since arriving, and had almost forgotten it existed. *Books!*

Books upon books lined the walls, and free-standing shelves laden with more of them crisscrossed throughout the room. Treva stood in the center of the space, obviously thinking, perhaps trying to recall which book she was searching for, and Sage kept her thoughts to herself. A picture of Remington Truth in a book was going to be no help whatsoever.

At least she'd been reintroduced to the space. And it begged the question: what else had Sage forgotten—or blocked from her memory—from her time here at Falling Creek? Was her suspicion about the reason for her mother's death possibly true? Could she have mentally erased certain memories and images to protect herself?

"Here!" crowed Treva, and she pulled out a thick hardcover volume from the wall.

Sage took the book. *The Count of Monte Cristo.*

Wow. That was weird. But what did that have to do with Remington Truth? She looked at Treva, who took the book back and began to flip through it.

"Ah, here it is. I was afraid someone had taken it out . . . shew, I think I'm the only one who's ever read this book." She looked at Sage. "Most people would rather watch the movie—even though it doesn't follow the book. But the book's so much better. Dantès is the greatest hero." She smiled. "I've read this one about ten times. Have you ever?"

"Funny you ask," Sage admitted. "But I'm reading it right now. And really enjoying it." And so was Simon, if the moving position of his bookmark was any indication.

"What did you find?"

"Oh." Treva plucked something from the pages of the book and handed it to her. "This. Is this the man?"

Sage took the object. It was . . . a picture of Remington Truth. And . . . holy cow, it even had his name printed on it. *Remington L. Truth.* It wasn't a photograph, like she was used to seeing. It was . . . thin. Plastic. About the size of her palm. Hard, but a little flexible. With a small slit cut in the top. And a sort of seal or symbol behind the picture, on the plastic, with the letters NSA.

What on earth was it? Little clear plastic curled up at the rounded corners as if it were peeling off.

She looked up at Treva. "Where did this come from? Do you know? Can I keep it? As a sort of keepsake?" she added.

Treva shrugged. "I don't see why not. I use it for a bookmark when I read the book, but like I said, no one else ever wants to tackle a book with more than a thousand pages, so no one else will miss it. Shew, and I can find another bookmark." She rubbed her red hands together and Sage winced, thinking about how much they must hurt.

"I can tell you exactly where it came from, now that I think about it. Musta been about four years ago. There was a man, and he had a young woman with him, and they stopped here wanting shelter one night. She was reading the book, and using that to keep her place. I know because I saw her—you never see anyone reading big tomes like that, you see. I notice stuff like that. I like to read, you know."

"I do too," Sage said encouragingly. "So, she was reading the book . . . ?"

"And, well, they stayed here one night, but she was gone the next day. And the man was dead."

"Dead?" Sage was horrified.

"Not murdered or anything. The doctors agreed on that. Something about eating peanuts—you know we grow our own here. His throat closed up and he suffocated."

"But the woman was gone? What did she look like?"

"I don't know. She had dark hair and she was really pretty. Maybe about mid-twenties—and let me tell you, they were already looking at setting her up with a husband after only one night. No wonder she got out of here," added Treva under her breath, glancing over her shoulder. "If I didn't have my own children, I'd be doing the same. Anyway, the book and some of her other stuff was still here. Like she left in a hurry."

"Any idea where she was going?" Had the woman needed to escape?

"Well, shew. They had to stop here that night and I got to talking to her—we were talking about books, of course, and I hadn't ever read *Monte Cristo* at that time. Anyway, she was asking me if I'd ever heard of a place called Redlow. I got the feelin' she wanted to go there." Treva shrugged. "I don't know for sure, and I never said anything when she disappeared the next day—figured if she wanted to get out of here I had no reason to mess up her plan. I never really heard of that place anyway."

Redlow. Excitement churned through Sage, though she wasn't certain why. Just because this man and woman had been in possession of a picture of Truth . . . but it was an unusual picture. It had to mean something.

Her next step was to figure out how to get a message to Theo and see if he'd ever heard of the place. And she could also check Truth's contact list and see if there was anything on there that mentioned Redlow.

Sage realized with a start that Treva had asked her a question and was waiting for her response. "I'm sorry, what was that? I was caught up in the memories for a minute."

"I said I never seen the man, and I don't know if it was much help," she said. "But I knew I recognized the face."

"Thanks," Sage said. "It's been more help than you know."

"Guess my break is over. I better get back," Treva said. She started to go, then turned and came back. "I think I'll take the book. It's about time for me to read it again." She smiled, her worn face showing a myriad of fine lines.

Sage handed her *The Count of Monte Cristo*, but kept the plastic picture of Remington Truth. And just as they emerged from the library, Nurse Ratchett appeared, her nose redder than ever.

"There you are," she shrilled. "I have been looking all over for you. You and your husband need to get back to work, because your hormone levels haven't shifted a bit. And your temperature is still elevated, which means you're still in ovulation."

Sage nodded, glad for the excuse. "Then I should go find him and we should . . . go back to our room and . . . er—"

"Yes, yes, of course. That's what I've been trying to tell you. No more time to waste! You only have forty-eight to seventy-two hours of fertile time, and you've been wasting it this morning." Ratchett glared at her, then muttered, "Twenty-eight years old and not one pregnancy to show for it. Time's wasting, Mrs. Japp. You go back and I'll have him sent to you. No need for you to wander around and get lost, lollygagging and wasting time."

Sage scooted away, tucking the new picture of Truth into her pocket and hurrying back to their room.

Once inside, she glanced automatically at the picture of the dog and realized that someone had come in while they were gone and readjusted it. They hadn't wasted any time, for she and Simon had been gone for little more than a couple hours.

Now she had to figure out another way to obscure the camera again. But first, she wanted to send an email to Theo and Lou and tell them what she'd found. She dragged her pack and settled herself against the wall flush with the camera, out of sight, and dug out her little computer.

She should be able to connect to the network now, and communicate from here in this room. And moments later, she had done so, quickly and easily.

There were two new emails, both from Lou, one in response to the one she'd sent last night, expressing relief that she and Simon were safe and had set up the NAP. The other was a quick update regarding the number strings from Truth's documents that appeared to be geographic plotting points, and asking her to try and take some measurements of the sun and moon while she and Simon were in Falling Creek, so they could attempt to adjust from the original aspects of the earth.

He'd given simple, clean directions, and Sage wrote back and agreed to do her best to note the time and position of the sun and moon according to his plan. She also explained what she'd learned from Treva and asked if they could find anything out about Redlow. Maybe she and Simon would go there when they left Falling Creek.

There was, however, no email from Theo, and that fact sat heavily on Sage's mind.

The message she'd sent to Lou and Theo, letting them know her update, had been sent only moments after Theo's declaration email had arrived. This meant, she hoped, that he thought she hadn't received it before closing down for the night. She hoped.

But now, the silence yawned and the decision . . . how to respond? She had to acknowledge it. But what to say?

Ah, Theo . . .

She hesitated, fingers still poised, and called up an empty message. *Theo, thank you for your note.*

Er. No.

Theo. I got your message and I confess I am both flattered and surprised. I had no idea you felt this way. I . . .

No. Oh, good grief!

Sage closed the computer and decided to take a shower. Maybe the spray of water would clear her brain. She remembered reading something once about the molecules of water and how they affect the mind and its creativity. Maybe it would help her think of something creative to write back to Theo.

The shower felt good: hot and cleansing, and the nature of the beast—washing her naked body—gave her other things to think about. Like the fact that Simon was going to be back in the room as soon as the FCers could find him and get him there . . . and they were going to have to start all over again with the fake-sex thing.

This time, though . . . Sage thought it might be a little more difficult.

In fact, from the way her stomach was swishing and fluttering, she thought it might be a *lot* more difficult.

Simon knew he was in a fuck-load of trouble the minute he walked in the room and realized Sage was in the shower.

He nearly turned and walked back out, but the sight of her small computer on the floor—out of sight of the camera, which, he noticed, was no longer blocked—gave him hesitation. And that was all it took, because as if she'd sensed his arrival, the bathroom door opened and there stood Sage: flushed and steamy, her hair and body each wrapped in a towel, slender arms and legs and shoulders . . . and feet . . . showing little droplets of water mingling with her freckles.

"I guess they found you," she said. Her smile was wry and a little shy.

"Yeah." He glanced at the dog picture in warning, and to get his eyes and mind off the fluffy white towels.

She stood there for a minute, then came into the room. Her uncertainty rolled off her in waves, mingling with his own tension. Which made the room feel tighter than the time Mancusi had crashed Paul Newman's after-Oscars party.

Simon gestured at the computer with his foot. "Anything?" He wondered if she'd responded to Theo's message. Or if she'd received any other ones.

"Yes." Sage looked meaningfully at him, and his curiosity was piqued by the excitement in her eyes. She had news. Then she pulled the towel from her hair, and it fell in bright, damp waves over her shoulders. "Let's get in bed."

His heart stopped.

Fuck, vato, *be a man. You've faced a lot worse.*

Simon sat at the opposite edge of the bed, fully, wholly, agonizingly aware of the camera watching every move they made, and pulled off his hiking boots and socks. Then his shirt. Followed by the worn jeans that were going to need a wash pretty soon.

The bed shifted behind him as she crawled under the covers. He hoped like hell she had something on underneath that damn towel. Simon stood and went over to pull the heavy curtains closed, blocking out much of the sun.

Then, taking a deep breath, wishing he could be anywhere but here, Simon lifted the covers and slid beneath them.

He rolled toward the center of the bed and found Sage lying there on her side, facing him. Her wet hair trailed over her pillow and down into the crevice next to his.

"Everything okay?" she asked. Her breath was soft and minty and Simon found himself hypnotized by that lovely little freckle, now crushed into a crease in her lips because she lay on her side.

"Yes. What's up?" he asked, low. This was good . . . they would look as if they were having a little pillow talk, maybe even a bit of foreplay, and she could bring him up to speed.

Damn. She smelled good too. Same shampoo and soap he used, but it smelled so much better on her.

"Someone gave me this today. Do you know what it is?"

Beneath the covers, she reached toward him. He moved swiftly to connect with her hand, and took the object she offered. It felt like a stiff credit card, but when he glanced down at it he recognized as an employee ID. For Remington Truth, when he was at the National Security Administration.

"Where did you get this?"

Sage explained about the woman who'd shown it to her, and how a younger woman and man had visited Falling Creek four years earlier and left it behind. In turn, he told her what the object was, adding, "This is a very personal object that had to have belonged to him. Which means that the woman and man must have gotten it from Remington Truth—either voluntarily or involuntarily."

"So this is our best clue so far?" she said, eyes wide and beautiful.

"I'd say. It's like part of his personal effects, something that either he or someone close to him would have kept."

"I sent a message to Lou about Redlow, to see if he and Theo knew anything about it. Maybe we can go there next and try to find this woman."

"But you don't know anything about what she looks like except her hair color and age."

"And that she was reading *The Count of Monte Cristo*," Sage added, her crinkled lips smiling. "It's the best we have for now."

He nodded, realizing that through this entire conversation they'd moved closer to each other. And now he felt the warmth of her newly showered skin beneath the blankets and realized he still didn't know if she was wearing anything. Or not.

He looked up from the employee ID he'd been examining—hell, to be honest, he'd been hiding by looking at it—and found himself caught by Sage's gaze. As before, he was struck by the unusual color of her eyes. More aqua than sapphire, almost a sea green–blue. With long dark-brown lashes tipped in blond and not a swipe of eyeliner or glitter of eye shadow in sight.

"Did you hear from Theo?" he said, forcing the words out, using them as a much-needed barrier. His heart had begun to pound erratically.

Sage's eyelids fluttered and he felt her subtle drawback. "No."

"He's in love with you, Sage," he forced himself to say in a voice low and dark. Build that barrier. Set her back. Make Dragon Boy the elephant in the room. Or, better yet, the elephant in the *bed*. Right the hell between them.

Again her lids fluttered, and he swore her mouth tightened a bit. "I know. But I—"

"Sage, let's get this over with," he said quickly, forcing the words out. "Okay?"

And before she could respond, he did what he did yesterday—he lifted himself quickly, but very gingerly, and straddled her slender body beneath the sheets.

Settling himself over her, careful not to touch any skin, definitely not to let her feel the erection straining his briefs . . . fighting to ignore the warmth emanating from beneath him . . . oh so close . . . Simon tucked his head into the pillow next to her and began to move. Counting. Praying. Imagining a gun barrel pressed to the back of his skull.

But this time . . . this time, his face was buried in damp, sweet-scented hair, next to warm skin. And this time, he knew how those lips just beyond his jaw tasted. And how smooth was the cheek against his hair. And the blood pounded through his body, and she was so damn close . . . Simon squeezed his eyes closed, buried his face in a pillow that fucking *smelled* like her, and kept his mind blank.

And then, as he was just about ready to pull away, she arched her torso up beneath him, meeting one of his false thrusts. The contact with skin and warmth shocked him, and he faltered, realizing that, thank God, there was cotton at least, between them . . . but he was all too aware of the swell of her breasts against his bare chest and the movement of her hands, her body, sliding against his rigid one.

The next thing he knew, she was kissing his neck and jaw, tugging at him, pulling him closer until his trembling arms gave out and he collapsed to the side.

Taking her with him.

She found his mouth, or he found hers—he wasn't certain which—and their lips melded, fitting together fiercely. Then he couldn't stop, couldn't keep the soft groan of surrender from the back of his throat as her mouth opened beneath his.

Sweet, slick and hot and deep . . . she tasted like mint and warmth and comfort, and he felt her body, now

aligned next to his, her leg sliding along his thigh, one
hand on his shoulder, smoothing along his arm. Her hair
plastered to his face and the hand that had reached up
to brush it away, and she gave a quiet little moan as his
tongue thrust deep and long.

Thank God she still wore something—a tank top and
panties from what he could tell—but it provided little barrier and Simon couldn't keep his hands from sliding up
beneath that stretchy top, over warm, taut skin and curling around her slender rib cage. Her breasts pressed into
his chest, and he held on to her sides, trying to focus, to
keep some semblance of control, knowing that this had to
stop . . . *soon.*

But, just a little longer. Just . . . a little . . .

Her fingers combed into his hair, pulling it loose. "I've
been wanting to do that," she whispered against his jaw,
her warm mouth nibbling there and to his ear. "You have
such beautiful hair." Her small hands moved over his
head, warm and confident, sliding through his loosened
queue and down over his shoulders.

"Sage," he murmured. "We . . . this isn't . . ." But the
words evaporated when she lifted her face to kiss him
again, and he took her mouth, and swiping long and deep,
she smoothed her hands down over his shoulders to flat-
ten them over his chest.

Their noses bumped and lips and tongues slid as he
bent forward again, no longer able to fathom stopping,
sooner or later. He filled his hands with her—her hips, her
rear, her slender shoulders, and down to those beautiful
breasts . . . now bare as he pulled her tank up and snapped
it to the floor.

Heaven help me.

He bent beneath the sheets, somehow having the

wherewithal to keep them in place and hide her from the camera even as he kissed one pretty pink nipple. Dusky with freckles, giving her skin a peachy glow, she was lush and curvy and when he drew the sensitive point into his mouth, gently, tenderly, she tightened and shivered beneath him.

He tasted her, using his tongue to flick lazily over her, she sighed and shifted and he felt a greater surge of desire, wanting to make her cry out and writhe with pleasure even more. Her eyes had closed and Simon watched her face, chin lifted, full, puffy lips parted as she sighed and shifted beneath his mouth.

"Simon," she breathed blindly at the ceiling, her hips twitching next to him as if she didn't know what she wanted.

He was out of breath himself, painfully hard and ready, yet unable to stop from kissing and touching, stroking and coaxing. He took his time, languorous and thorough, knowing in the recesses of his mind that this was an anomaly, that she wasn't ready for this and that there'd be a time when he'd have to stop . . . but not yet.

Not until . . . *ah.* She arched toward him, her hand sliding down his belly. His skin leapt and jumped beneath her fingers—fingers that seemed to know exactly where they were going, what they wanted . . . and unaware that they weren't about to get there.

Simon moved sleekly, shifting a bit so that he pressed her back into the bed, bending over her torso with his to cover her mouth once more, keeping his own straining equipment out of reach. *No, my dear.* And as he rose up over her, face angled above face, propped on an elbow, he slipped his other hand down, down over her belly, over the sensitive, trembling skin, beneath a bit of cotton,

down to the warm nestle of the place he wanted to be . . .
the current center of his world . . . and found what he was
looking for.

Sage's eyes flew open when he slipped into her moist
warmth, his fingers gentle and instantly slick. "Oh," she
gasped, and he smiled against her luscious mouth, concentrating on the wonder in her eyes and the taste of her.

His fingers stroked and slid, slipped and entered and
fluttered and tickled against her until she writhed and
gasped beneath them. He watched the pleasure settle
across her face, as her cheeks flushed and her body tightened and stretched and he felt her orgasm begin, rise . . .
and then crest with a low erotic moan that nearly set him
over the edge.

Overwhelmed with her scent, sounds, taste, warmth,
Simon gritted his teeth, closed his eyes as she shuddered
and trembled beneath him. He rested his forehead against
hers, feeling the brush of her fluttering lashes and the
warm puff of breath against his face.

His body pounded so hard, and before she even opened
her eyes, he fell back from where he'd hovered over her,
flat on his back, breathing as if he'd run a marathon. He
was in pain, pulsating pain, but at the same time, rampant
with exhilaration and deep pleasure. His fingers trembled
and his mouth felt full and hot, and he could still taste her
on his lips . . . but it was over.

"Simon."

The breath of his name had him turning to look at her.
Once again, there she was . . . close, too close, temptation and heaven rolled into one package of blue eyes and
creamy skin, tousled peachy hair and lush red mouth. But
this time, her lips were swollen and crinkled, and her eyes
were lidded heavily—filled with knowledge and awareness. And something else he dared not try to define.

"Yes?" he managed to say without sounding like he was dying.

"Is that . . . I mean," she closed her eyes, swallowed, caught her breath, and, reopening them, said, "Wow. Simon . . . I . . . my God, Simon . . ." It all came out on low, husky breaths.

She was babbling and if he hadn't been in so much discomfort, so intent on keeping himself rigid and separate, he might have chuckled. Sage never babbled. But he didn't allow himself even a smile, for that little bit of softening could lead to more.

"Thank you," she managed. And then she moved, reaching for him and he had to react quickly to grab her wrist before she could touch him. *No. No, we don't need that.*

Her eyes darkened in confusion, and he squeezed her wrist. "It's fine. Just . . . that's enough."

"But . . ."

He shook his head sharply, knowing that the expression on his face was bordering on forbidding, but what else could he do?

"Don't you need to—well, it has to look like we, uh—"

He couldn't hold back a short laugh—half in frustration, half in amusement. "I think that what they saw will suffice just fine," he said in his low, strained voice. "Now, please. Remember there is a man back in Envy who loves you, Sage."

This time, he hardened his tone, keeping it quiet, but looking at her straight in the eyes. "Theo is waiting for you. And I promised him I'd bring you back. Whole. And safe." There was that wall again.

Where the hell had it been five minutes ago?

She stared at him, and he saw a myriad of emotions flash through her eyes. Her mouth tightened, her chin, even on its side, lifted in stubbornness. "That's fine. I love being treated like a damn doll that has to be protected and accounted for," she said in a louder voice than she should have. It sounded as if it were about to crack. "Don't think I haven't noticed that you keep bringing him up like some sort of damn talisman." She blinked rapidly.

"Sage—" What the hell could he say? He sure as fuck couldn't tell her that if he had his way, he'd tell her to forget about Dragon Boy and run off with him . . . even though he already knew he couldn't run off with anyone. Even Sage.

Then suddenly, she flung the covers back with a great, chilly *whoosh*, leaving him half covered. Simon gaped as she stalked across the room to the bathroom, completely naked, in all peachy-skinned, curvaceous glory, bouncing and swaying and with a toss of her hair.

She didn't slam the door, but she might as well have.

The short, sharp click said it all.

It was just as well that Sage didn't see Simon for the rest of the day.

As it was, by the time she sat down next to him at dinner, she'd worked herself into a ball of nerves. After what had happened in their room, beneath those hot sheets, she took care not to do as much as brush against him. For fear she might send him scuttling off in terror.

Because she'd finally realized what it was that shone in his eyes when he looked at her. Fear. Bald-faced, flat-out fear.

And she didn't quite understand why.

"When will the Strangers arrive?" he asked, leaning toward her, bringing with him what had become a familiar feeling . . . his warmth, proximity, and subtle masculine scent, all wrapped up in one package. He'd pulled his hair back into its short club, sleek and dark—but that didn't keep her from remembering how thick and heavy and sexy it had looked, falling in his face and over her hands.

"Any time," she replied coolly. She didn't look at him, for fear he'd see what was in *her* eyes.

"Everything go all right today?" he asked.

Was he trying to drive her crazy?

"I'm just a little tired," she replied, noticing that Dawn, one of Sharon's friends, seemed to be fascinated by their low-toned conversation. "Maybe your sperm's already in action," she added, loudly enough for the other woman to hear. He flashed her a look that would have been amusing in its acute discomfort if she hadn't been so annoyed with him.

Even though all she could think about was twining her body with his, and kissing him, touching him . . . at the same time, she wanted to string him up by his toes and swat the hell out of him.

Or hide in a corner and cry from shame and frustration.

For the time, she opted to feel annoyed rather than rejected and hurt, because it was easier. But sooner or later, she was going to have to examine those feelings and figure out what it was.

Instead of looking at Simon, she engaged herself in conversation with Dawn, and Sharon, who'd arrived late. She tried not to notice every time he bumped against her thigh—which wasn't often—and attempted to block out the deep timbre of his voice as he chatted or laughed with the others at their table. Why, though she was angry with him, did the mere sound of it make her want to cuddle in next to him?

The meal was interminable, yet the expectations were

palpable. As Sage looked around the large community, the entire settlement—not a portion of it—that had gathered here in the dining area filled with tables and spilling outside through the open walls, and she remembered other times with the same sort of feel to them.

The whispers, the watching, the anticipation. The joviality that nevertheless seemed a bit forced. Beneath the revelry, Sage sensed something else. Fear? Trepidation? As if the people of Falling Creek knew the arrival of the Strangers would be exciting, yet horrifying.

Or was she simply making all of this up?

Sage had never credited herself with an overly active imagination, but now as she thought about it, she realized she'd been wrong. After all, someone who researched and investigated information the way she did, in a cobbled-together Internet, had to be creative to find ways to do it.

Then finally, it happened. The wave of whispers rose followed by the sounds—unfamiliar to the residents of Falling Creek—of a vehicle's engine approach, heralding the arrival of the Strangers.

Sage found herself sitting up expectantly, her heart thumping in her chest. She might have seen them before, years ago when she lived here as a girl—her memory was foggy—but she hadn't seen one of the immortals since then. She knew they looked like any other human, except for the powerful crystals they wore embedded in their skin.

And now that Quent had identified one of the Stranger leaders as his father, Parris Fielding, they had all come to the conclusion that the Strangers were humans who had lived before the Change, and had taken on the crystals of immortality. And, according to Lou and Theo, had somehow caused—or at least enabled—the Change.

Because of their relation to the Cult of Atlantis, and the

fact that crystals were widely believed to be part of the Atlantean legend—along with the fact that a continental-sized landmass had appeared in the Pacific Ocean, possibly risen from the depths—the Strangers were thought to have some connection to Atlantis. Either they were looking for the lost continent, or had somehow found it, and its powerful, life-force crystals.

The Strangers were greeted by the two eldest Corrigan men, and brought to the front of the room, not far from where Sage and Simon were sitting. She watched, waiting for a wave of recognition to sweep over her—but when she saw the two men and one woman, Sage wasn't prepared for the shock of that identification.

"Oh my God," she breathed, reaching automatically for Simon's arm. "That woman . . . that's Tatiana. The actress! Isn't it?"

His arm was solid and taut beneath her fingers, and she felt waves of tension rolling from him. Instead of watching the Strangers and gaping at them as the rest of the room was doing, he was looking slightly down and off into the distance.

"Do you see her?" she whispered, looking at the woman.

"Shh," Simon growled behind a tight jaw, and Sage tried to relax, even as she stared at the three immortals.

The woman seemed to be in charge, and Sage definitely remembered seeing her before, when she was younger. But at that time, she had not recognized her as the actress famous for her real-life rags-to-riches story, and the sharp, seductive roles she played in films. Perhaps the leaders of Falling Creek had made certain there were no Tatiana movies available in the settlement.

Tatiana stood at the front, speaking with the community leaders. Her two companions, the very faint glow of crystals showing through their shirts, stood deferentially behind her. While Sage vaguely remembered seeing them as well from the Strangers' previous visits, she didn't recognize them. She memorized their faces now, though, so she could search through the list of Cult of Atlantis members and try to identify them when she returned to Envy.

Tatiana, of course, as an immortal, had not changed since her films. She wasn't tall, but she had a commanding presence and what Lou would call a killer body. Ink black hair cascaded down in a straight waterfall around her shoulders, nearly to her hips, causing Sage to wonder if the hair and nails grew on Strangers. And if they could bear children.

Maybe that was why they liked to take young women from Falling Creek . . . to use them for procreation purposes?

Sage shook her head to clear the morbid thoughts. Simon was going to help keep them from taking any young women this time, if that was indeed what they'd come for. She found herself reaching automatically toward him, wanting desperately to touch him—for stability, strength, and comfort . . .

Certainly she wouldn't be a candidate for the Strangers to take—she was too old, and was presumably already married—and even if she were, she knew Simon would never let it happen.

But something unsettled her, and that feeling of trepidation grew as Tatiana spoke congenially with the leaders, who fairly slathered over her hands, they were so reverent. The room had fallen completely silent except for the low hum of their voices. As she conversed with her hosts, Tatiana scanned the room, and even from where she was sitting, Sage could feel the chill of her gaze. She knew from the films that the actress's eyes were brown, but they'd been warm and sparkling in movies like *The*

Girl Can't Go Home and *Stand Down or Die*. Now, she recognized flat chilliness that made her distinctly uncomfortable.

Tatiana finished her conversation abruptly, and the settlement leaders seemed to be surprised, for she was walking away from them, and coming down into the rows of tables.

Sage didn't remember that happening before, and from the expressions on the faces of her fellow diners, neither could they. The settlement leaders appeared confused as well.

Every eye was on the woman as she walked through the room, moving with a purpose, her long hair shining and shifting, her eyes focused . . . on Sage? No, not on her. But . . .

Sage felt Simon's entire body tighten next to her, the tension pouring from him, yet he didn't move.

Tatiana came to a stop right in front of their table, and now Sage could see the brilliant glow of a pale blue crystal from beneath the woman's sheer white shirt. Heart slamming in her chest, palms damp, she looked up into those eyes, and found them trained not on her, but on the man next to her.

Tatiana's voice was low and throaty when she spoke. "Well, well . . . Simon Japp. It *is* you. And you haven't changed a bit in fifty years."

_____

March 29
Nine months later.

I still can't believe this. About three weeks ago, Thad Marck blew up at a city council meeting and they got into a big fight.

I guess they were done with him, because the entire council, along with a bunch of other men kicked Thad and the rest of us out of Envy!

Well, they didn't kick me out, really, but I decided to go with Kevin. He believes in what Marck wants to do—which is to organize the repopulation of the world, and really focus on making it happen efficiently instead of haphazardly.

I think his basic ideas are all right, I just think he went about it a little too harshly. But anyway, I had the choice to go with Kevin or not, and I just didn't want to lose another man I love. I mean, it's been so hard.

So I decided to go with them, and Kevin and I have gotten married. Is that wrong?

There were about twelve of us who left that night, and they gave us food and water and didn't even wait till sunrise to make us leave. I heard people saying that Thad had gotten violent in the meeting that night, that he and Kevin and Robert had knives and bombs??? That someone almost got killed . . . but I don't believe it. It's just not like them.

I think they just wanted him out of Envy because Mayor Rowe didn't support his ideas. Whatever.

Anyway, we've found a place to live. It's called Falling Creek, and it's a much nicer place than Envy will ever be.

—from Adventures in Juliedom, the blog of Julie Davis Beecher Corrigan

CHAPTER 11

"Hello, Florita," Simon replied, keeping his voice cool and even.

He felt Sage's shock and confusion emanating from her rigid body, but dared not take his eyes from the woman in front of him. The moment she and her companions had appeared, he'd recognized her.

He'd gone cold and blank, and a wave of memories rushed over him, bringing him back to the nightmare, the lost, suffocating nightmare of his other life. It had paralyzed him for a moment, swathing him in darkness and loathing, until he pulled himself beyond the night, and his strength and purpose came roaring back.

He was not that same person. He'd been given another chance.

Now, Florita Tatiane—now known by her stage name Tatiana—looked down at him with the same dark eyes filled with fascination and lust that she'd trained on him more than fifty years ago. Almost fifty-seven, if one were counting.

She looked the same as she had on the poster of her final movie and the cover of her last magazine shoot—thanks to Hollywood, more physically perfect than she had been when he knew her as his boss's mistress. The only difference was the small blue crystal. The collar of her tight white scoop-neck shirt had shifted as she bent toward him (old habits died hard, apparently), giving him a clear view of her impressive cleavage and the glowing, faceted gem embedded in the soft part of her skin, just below her collarbone. The power that kept her preserved at the height of her youth and beauty.

A jewel for which the rest of the world had paid an incredible price. Loathing burned through him as he looked up at the woman he'd known as Florita.

"What a small, small world," she said.

Interesting. Even through his horror and discomfort, Simon was able to pare through his reactions to recognize both shock and confusion in the layers of her voice. After all, he'd known her very well when he was working with her. Not as well as she would have liked, but well enough.

She was just as surprised at their reunion as he, and she wasn't certain what to do about it. Simon knew that was to his advantage, and he'd play it more carefully than he'd ever bet on a hand of life-or-death poker.

Starting by keeping his feelings for Sage obscured. Which meant he should get the hell away from her before Tatiana made the connection. If she even sensed the possibility of a rival . . .

"The world's become a lot smaller in the last fifty years," he replied, still cool, still flat. "Thanks to you and your cult friends." He had no reason to hide his revulsion for her and the other Strangers. Now, more than ever, he was prepared to do what it took to bring these survivors to their knees. His last, most important, job.

Florita's full lips had tightened at his comment. Her eyes narrowed, then relaxed, and roamed over him, as if checking to see if he was still the specimen she'd tramped after half a century ago. "Indeed it has. I think we have very much to catch up on, Simon," she said in an unmistakable purr.

Over my fucking dead body.

"Where's Mancusi?" Simon asked.

Now her eyes widened in honest surprise. "Why, dead, I presume. Unless by some *other* miracle," she encompassed his youthful appearance and survival with a single gesture, "he survived."

That, at least, was a positive.

"Well," Simon said, standing. He looked down at her, at her glossy black hair and unbelievable body. He expression was flat and forbidding. *Don't fuck with me, Rita. You know better.* "Pardon me if I say I'm not terribly interested in catching up. If you'll excuse me, it's been a tiring day." He gave her a brief, polite nod and turned to walk away.

Would she let him? Was she sufficiently off her game to allow it?

But after all, she couldn't stop him. She might have strength and immortality, and even her cabana boys with their own crystals, but Simon could disintegrate into nothing.

Catch me if you fucking can.

He dared not look at Sage as he left, dared not acknowledge her in any way, for once Florita had her competitor—real or imagined—in her sights, she became worse than a Medusa.

"Simon."

Her voice came from directly behind him—Florita's, not, thank God, Sage's. He paused, knowing he had to play this out, despite the fact that every hair on his body had risen, every cell of his being screamed for him to ignore her, keep going, *keep going. Get out, get Sage out, dis-a-fucking-pear!*

She'd come around the table and met him at the end, near the wall at the edge of the room, and now her fingers, cool and strong, bit into his arm. Simon turned on her a steady, derisive look, and she dropped her hand. Yet, the expression in her eyes burned with cunning and determination.

"I don't think so, Simon," she told him.

He stepped back from her, and saw her two male counterparts leaving the front of the room to move swiftly in their direction. Adrenaline spiked through him, and that familiar cold confidence. *Just fucking try it.* Making a swift decision, he grabbed Florita's arm and pulled her through a door next to him.

They were in a back hallway that led to the kitchen, but it was deserted. Everyone, it seemed, had come to see the Strangers.

"Ah, Simon," she said, leaning into him, hands plastered against his chest, trying to push him against the wall. "I knew you—"

"Don't try it, Rita," he said, setting her back from him. "You have no idea what I'm capable of . . . especially now. I'd hate to embarrass you in front of your admirers."

She edged back a bit, eyes shifting up and over him as if scanning to look for a crystal or some other verification of his threat, some sign of his power. But he merely looked back at her, knowing that simply his appearance, his unaged body sans the life-force crystal was enough proof that she no longer knew him.

"Come on, Simon," she said, reaching for him again. She was damned strong, surprising him as she curled her long-nailed fingers into his shoulders. Apparently the crystals gave strength too. "There's no reason to be coy anymore. Leonide is long gone. And I could use a man like you. In more ways than one." She brushed herself, her torso and hips, against him. "I could keep you very, very busy."

Simon, filled with revulsion, was at first unable to move. The last thing he wanted was to get into a tangle with her, struggling and groping against him. He'd been there and knew how the claws would come out, the clothes would come off . . . she leaned into him, her breasts flattening against his chest.

"Do you know how many men I've been with? How many who were lusted after, and wanted by women all over the world? There was George, and Brad and Hugh and countless others—"

"Is this supposed to surprise me, Rita?" he said, keeping his voice steady with effort. Was it more effective to shove her away or to appear completely unmoved? "That you slept your way through Hollywood like you did East Los?"

"Do you know why?" she said, skimming her nails over his chin, leaving behind the slightest bit of a prick as she jabbed his jaw with one slender tip. "Because there was one man I couldn't have. Because he was too goddamned honorable. Simon." She lifted her face and managed to capture his mouth for a moment, brushing her full, hot lips against his, bringing another whiff of that unusual scent. He turned his face aside.

"It wasn't Mancusi that kept me away," he said, resisting the urge to wipe his mouth.

"I don't believe you, Simon," she purred. "I had the proof in the palm of my hand." As if to punctuate her words, as if he could misunderstand what she meant, she slid her hand over the front of his jeans, cupping over his damned cock like she owned it.

Now he shoved her away, not hard enough for her to stumble, but hard enough. "I warned you, Rita. You have no idea what you're dealing with."

"And neither do you, Simon," she said. "Things have changed more than you can imagine, and so have I. You saw where I was and what I became. How I made myself."

He laughed humorlessly and made no attempt to hide the disdain in his voice. "I certainly have. And I've no interest in it. In anything you have to offer." Now he turned to walk away, but she grabbed at him one more time with those strong fingers.

Her eyes had turned hot and determined and she stroked along his bare arm a second time. This time, the caress, the promise, was unmistakable. She leaned closer, bringing a rush of some odd scent with her, and added, "You escaped me once, but not this time. Things are much different now."

Simon extricated his arm, the sensation of an army of tiny creatures crawling over his skin filling him with disgust. "You don't have a chance, Rita. You didn't then, you don't now. Good night, and good-bye."

He felt the drill of her eyes into the back of his skull as he walked away and back through the door leading into the dining area, threading his path among the tables, the back of his neck prickling as his movements remained easy and arrogant. The rumble of buzzing conversation dipped to a hush when he made his way through the room and felt, more than heard, Florita come through the door after him.

How many times had he turned his back on an adversary, calling their bluff? Colleagues and foes alike had talked about his cold, emotionless reaction.

The one time he'd guessed wrong, Simon's prickling spine caused him to spin in just enough time to aim his own weapon and pop the guy in the head. Rita, as a matter of fact, had been there to see it.

Because the guy had been her other lover, the one she'd been two-timing Mancusi with. The one she'd set up to kill Simon in retaliation for his rebuff of her.

Now, as he walked away, shoulders broad and back unprotected, Simon felt that same surge of power, strength . . . and a niggling bit of the black fear that had driven him before. The fear that had allowed him to be so cold, so purposeful and so damned efficient. The fear that Mancusi had nourished in his manipulative way, then leeched from Simon for his own use.

The return of these emotions, this state of mind, scared the fuck out of him. But he kept walking, focused on the dining room exit. Ignoring the return of the pinching nausea.

He had to get Sage out of there next. And then they were getting the hell out of this place.

Simon knew Tatiana?

And from the crackling, snapping of tension between them, he'd known her quite well. Sage hadn't missed the possessive, hungry look in the woman's eyes, and the crafty way she leaned in toward him.

But Simon had been emotionless, showing no surprise. Had he somehow known she was the Stranger? Or was he just that good at hiding his feelings?

Sage didn't speak. When Simon got up abruptly, walking away without a backward glance or even the brush of a comforting hand against her, she did nothing but watch him go. Had he ignored her purposely, or was he so agitated that he'd forgotten her presence?

"Oh my God," Sharon was saying, reaching across the table and grabbing Sage's arm. "What's going on?"

Sage didn't even look at her, or Dawn, or any of the other people around her who gawked between her and the scene going on across the room. Instead, she stared as Tatiana went after Simon and watched with even more fascination as their conversation continued at the edge of the room. From the body language, Sage recognized Simon's complete aversion to the woman, and the actress's just as strong attraction to him.

"She knows your husband?" whispered next to her. "How?"

Sage ignored the voice behind her, still watching Simon. Suddenly, he opened a door next to him, and he and Tatiana disappeared, leaving a billow of whispers that surged almost immediately into a full-blown buzz. Moments later, Simon reappeared and stalked from the room without a backward glance. Tatiana emerged from behind the door as well, and Sage could feel her anger rolling in waves from across the room.

As Tatiana scanned the room with her furious gaze, Sage turned back around in her seat, heart pounding, kind of looking down—just, she realized, as Simon had been doing when the Strangers were up on the stage. He must have recognized Tatiana long before she saw him.

"Sage," Sharon said, bumping into her with her elbow. "What just happened?"

"I don't know," Sage was forced to reply.

"Where did he go?" asked someone else.

Then the barrage of questions came—who is he? How does he know her? Why is she angry?

Sage could do nothing but shrug, even as the same

questions blasted through her mind. Something told her to be unobtrusive and quiet—to keep out of the way of the Strangers and to stay beneath their awareness. Especially Tatiana's. So she settled back onto her chair and tried to join the low buzz of conversation around her without drawing attention. Camouflaging herself by joining the fray.

Tatiana had returned to the front of the dining area, talking quietly with her two cohorts. Her black hair shifted and shone with every jerky movement, and although the woman was shorter and smaller than either of the two male Strangers, it was obvious that she was in charge. And even more obvious that she was barely controlling her fury.

Simon, Simon . . . what is going on here?

Then, suddenly, Sage felt a little shove. She started, turning to look behind her, but no one was there but the back of the woman sitting at the next table. But then she felt it again, even more insistent, and then she realized with a flush of annoyance at her stupidity that it was Simon. Invisible Simon. He nudged her again, as if trying to get her to move.

She nodded, muttering "Okay" from between her lips.

But now what? Did he want her to get up and leave? Everyone had fallen into their own conversations, and no one seemed to notice her. But, with a glance at the front, where Tatiana was now speaking intensely with the community leaders, Sage feared that she would be noticed if she stood and left.

The nudge came again, even more urgent and Sage half rose to her feet. Feeling very self-conscious, she whispered to Sharon, "Do you think anyone will care if I leave to pee?" At least she could set up her "cover" for leaving.

Sharon shook her head. "I don't know if anyone would

care if you danced on the table, after that last bit of entertainment. Are you going to go look for him?" Her eyes were wide and sparkling with fascination. Obviously, such gossip-worthy events were few and far between in Falling Creek.

Sage shrugged in answer, and crouched low as she slipped out along the long table, sensing that if she stood upright, she'd attract much more notice.

She didn't know where Simon was, and once she stood, he'd ceased nudging her. So she followed the path he had earlier when he left, which was also the way out of the dining room and in the direction of their bedroom.

Once out of sight, Sage hurried along the hallway and then suddenly he was there.

"Sorry," he said briefly, and she wasn't certain whether he was apologizing for shoving her, for the scene with Tatiana, or for rushing her out of the room, but she didn't care. By now she knew Simon well enough to be aware that he wasn't mean or rude unless the situation required it. "We have to get the hell out of here."

"All right." She started toward their room.

He caught up with her, and gave her a quick look. "You don't have any questions?"

Sage shrugged. "Now's not the time for that. You can fill me in later."

He shook his head, then as they reached the door to their room, he paused, grabbing her arm. "As soon as you get in there, get the computer and email Theo to come, stat, to where he dropped us off." She nodded and grabbed the door handle, but he stopped her again. "I'm going to apologize in advance for what's going to happen in there." He nodded toward the room.

"Simon. I trust you." Sage reached up and gave him a kiss on the mouth. His tense lips softened beneath hers, and for a moment, she felt that wave of pleasure and heat filter through her . . . felt the momentary sag of his body flush against her. But then it was over too quickly and they pulled away. She knew they couldn't stand there and kiss like a couple on the run in a thriller.

There simply wasn't time for that sort of thing in real life, adrenaline rush or no.

So when Simon opened the door, Sage allowed him to go in first, and she ducked beneath the camera's all-seeing eye to scuttle along the floor to the dresser where she'd put her pack and the computers. Sitting out of reach of the camera, she logged on quickly, praying that the network was still functional, and sent an urgent message to Theo and Lou, telling them that they were in trouble (but not why) and that they should meet them at the drop-off point as soon as they could get there.

When she finished, Simon glanced down at her out of the corner of his eye, and, with his back to the camera, gestured covertly to the door. She understood, of course, that now she had to pretend to come in . . . so she did.

The expression he wore when she first saw him after her "entrance" nearly stopped her cold. She'd never seen him look like that—at her, anyway. But he had worn that same flat anger and barely contained violence the night he nearly strangled the man who'd attacked her.

Cold, lethal, and absolutely terrifying, he looked at her as they stood directly in front of the camera. "What the hell took you so long?"

She wasn't sure if she was supposed to reply, but when he covered her arm with his fingers and gave her a little jerk, she said, "I'm sorry. I didn't know if you were—"

"Get in bed," he ordered. "Now. Don't make me wait any fucking longer." And then he rattled off a bunch of words in a different language. They didn't sound very nice.

Sage's heart thumped madly, and she stumbled over her own feet as she hurried to do his bidding. She knew he was performing for the camera, but did he have to be so convincing?

Seated on the bed, she looked at him, knowing her eyes were wide, and making them wider with what she hoped was fear. Then he turned off the light, and she felt him come toward the bed, felt the shift as he climbed under the covers. Then, in the darkness, he moved roughly toward her, and she knew that the camera would see little but shifting shadows and no detail to speak of.

And so he moved toward her as he had before—*don't think about this afternoon*—and shook and rocked the bed, harder and more sharply than before. The mimicry was over in moments, and he lay next to her. His breath came evenly and smoothly, as if he were more in control than he had been in the past.

Sage waited, stiff and unwilling to move, until he reached for her hand stealthily beneath the sheets. He squeezed her in what she knew was another apology, his hand so warm and solid, then withdrew back to his side. She waited in silence, unmoving, ridiculously aware of the man next to her—despite the fact that he was still certainly more fully clothed than he had been on any other occasion under the sheets. But . . . holy crap, as Jade would say . . . what had happened this afternoon, here beneath these sheets . . . *Whew.*

Despite the uncertainty of her current situation, Sage couldn't hold back the memory of those moments.

Thankful for the darkness, she rubbed her hot cheek into a cool portion of the pillow, reliving the feel of those oh, so skilled fingers sliding in and around and against her . . . and the warm moist lips on her breast, tugging and sucking just enough to make her sigh and moan. And want more.

Her breathing rose a bit and she closed her eyes tightly, wondering how she would ever get him to touch her again when he kept dangling Theo between them.

She'd come to realize, during her hours of yanking weeds (pretending she was pulling out all of his lovely, long hair) that it definitely wasn't that he found her revolting. He found her attractive. And he cared about her. And that was why he kept bringing up Theo. For some reason, he thought . . . well, she wasn't sure what he thought.

That Theo had *dibs* on her, like she was the biggest piece of cake on the plate or something?

For a smart man, he certainly could be an idiot.

Then, after a while, maybe fifteen minutes of lying still and quiet in the near darkness, he stirred. Simon moved around energetically, rising and shifting, and she felt pillows and the blankets pile up in rough bundles around and next to her. What in the world . . . ?

And then there was a gentle dip and shift as he got off the bed . . . but she didn't see his shadow or silhouette. He'd turned invisible.

It took a few minutes, and she swore she heard the faintest slide of a drawer opening and the bare rustle of the canvas packs, but she dare not lift up to see. Then he came over to her side of the bed with a gentle bump against the mattress, and he curled his fingers over her wrist. Simon's grip shifted as he took a deep breath, and then, she felt that shimmery, lovely feeling sweep over her . . . and she disappeared.

He tugged her and she followed him from the bed, realizing with a blast of delight that the camera couldn't see her—no one could see her! What a freeing, heady . . . yet sobering realization.

Wow.

The sparkly feeling stuck with her as they moved silently across the room and then Simon stopped. She felt his invisible body, still warm and solid despite its visual transparency, crouch to the floor and pull her down next to him. As they sank, low and beneath the camera, he began to rematerialize and so did she. The silvery, soft prickling sensation eased and she felt Simon breathing heavily next to her, as if he'd been running or working hard.

"Need a minute," he muttered into her ear. "Then we leave."

She didn't know how much effort it took for him to turn invisible, and then to turn herself that way, but it was obviously something he couldn't maintain for an unlimited amount of time. And, she wondered for the first time, how he'd figured out he had that sort of ability. It wasn't an inherent skill, to turn transparent . . . how did one learn to do it?

They crouched there, knees angled up, thighs and shoulders brushing against the other, down against the wall, out of sight of the camera. Her computer pack lay where she'd left it, right within reach, and when Sage looked up at the bed, she saw the lumps of pillows and blankets and realized what he'd done to make it look as if they still lay sleeping.

He was so smart. And strong. And capable. And he made her feel . . . she shivered, deep in her belly. Oh, he made her *feel*.

Sage turned to look at him, bumping against his shoulder, her heart swelling in her chest. Their faces were so close as they huddled together that her hair mingled with his. His breathing had settled and slowed. Their eyes met, barely discernable in the low light, and he murmured something in that other language he used, something she couldn't understand . . . but it didn't matter because he was leaning toward her.

The kiss was gentle, and yet filled with meaning. Apology, sensuality, an edge of desperation. She shifted closer, wanting more of those sexy lips, a deeper slide of his tongue, hot and strong in her mouth. Her hand settled over his chest, feeling the mad pounding of his heart and the rise, again, of his breath.

"Simon," she mouthed against his lips. His hand moved into her hair, caught on a tangle, then gently smoothed on down as he pulled away. The soft sound of her lips releasing his settled on the silence, and then they both stiffened at the same time.

For they heard it, the sounds of heavy footsteps and loud voices, coming rapidly.

Simon swore low, and they scrambled to their feet. He squeezed her hand, and as the footsteps came closer, he bent down and swung up the pack over a shoulder that already carried two others, and gestured for her to press back against the wall next to the door.

The knocks on the door were perfunctory and sharp, and the intruders didn't wait for anyone to answer. A key moved in the lock and suddenly the door flew open with a gust of air, but by that time, the shimmery sparkling feeling had settled over Sage and she and Simon were transparent.

The men rushed in, four of them, and hardly had they breeched the door than Simon was running out, tugging her after him as they slipped right past them.

Down the hall they ran, the packs bumping and clunking against his back. He dodged into a different hallway.

and they found a room where he could rest for a minute and release the hold on their opacity.

Sage shimmered back to herself and looked at Simon. He seemed all right—a little out of breath, but not exhausted. Smart to take a rest when he could, for who knew what lay around the next corner.

The sounds of shouting reached their ears in the distance. Their ruse had been discovered—although their pursuers could have no way of knowing how they escaped.

"Come on," he said, grabbing her hand without turning them invisible again. They ran through the Community House, heading toward back of the kitchen. Apparently Simon had learned his way around the back ways from his shifts helping to cook.

Moments later, they were outside, and now instead of running, they were dodging from shadow to shadow. "You okay?" he asked once when they settled against the ivy-covered wall of a nearby mansion.

"Fine."

The night was dark, thank goodness, darker than last night, for the moon was a bit smaller and cloaked in heavy clouds. Shadows melded into shadows, giving them good cover, but then Sage noticed a blast of light.

"Look," she said, but Simon had already seen it.

"The gate. *Pinche*," he muttered.

The great wave of illumination shone like a raging fire from the area of the front gate, illuminating the entire space. They might have been able to sneak over there and through, using Simon's invisibility . . . but not now. Between the vast light that likely drove into every corner, it was also presumable that the gate was completely locked and closed. Sure, they could turn invisible, but they couldn't pass through walls.

"Wait, Simon . . ." Sage felt a rush of prickles over her. "There's another way out of here." She remembered what she'd been reading in the diary.

He looked at her, eyes dark and intense. "Where?"

"Not sure; we need a place to hide so I can figure it out. It's on that computer that I found." She shook her head sharply, snapping to silence as the sound of voices came nearer. Strident, angry voices.

Simon didn't waste any time. He pushed her up against the ivy and covered her with his body, and his protective invisibility.

Oh God. All thoughts of secret exits and computers disintegrated as his hard body pressed into her—her legs and arms and chest, warm and comforting . . . Sage buried her face in his shoulder and breathed deeply of him, her arms curling around his neck, her face resting against his jaw.

As soon as the voices were past, she felt the tension leave him and the shimmery feeling fade and they were back again.

"Come on," he said. "I know where we can go."

They ducked and dashed, Simon directing her to a familiar route. She realized they were on their way back to the house where they'd secreted the NAP. Good thinking. No one would look there for them.

Lights shone in the distance behind them, moving about as the group of pursuers grew to encompass more members. Shouts and calls filled the night air.

Why were they after them, anyway? What had Simon done to Tatiana?

Only once did they have to resort to the invisibility trick, when they nearly ran into a group of three men who were coming quickly around a corner. Simon yanked

Sage into the darkness and they were not quite transparent when the men came into view.

She felt him tense next to her as one of the trio stopped, peering closely into the shadows that they had become part of.

"I swore I saw something . . ." he said, coming closer.

If he took two more steps, he'd walk right into them . . . Sage felt Simon go even more rigid, felt the faint tension in his body, a low tremble as he fought to keep them clear even as he held his breath. Automatically, they edged ever so slightly to the left, out of his path, as he stepped closer.

Sage could feel his presence and she tightened herself even closer to Simon, holding her breath.

"I know I saw something," the man said. And he moved closer. Close enough to touch them.

April 15
Almost ten months later.

I'm pregnant! I'm due in late October, we think.

Kevin is so happy, and everyone is celebrating. There are five of us here at Falling Creek who are expecting, and that's almost half of the females here.

Our number has grown from the original twelve that left Envy. A few people were already living here in FC, and we've gotten to know them. We're up to seventeen now.

Many more women than men, which is good for the idea of repopulating the human race. But we need more men to even things out.

A big river runs nearby and they've figured out a way to get electricity here from its energy. There's talk about solar panels and also a windmill, too. We're all living in one big mansion right now—the houses here are ridiculous. But Kevin and Robert and the others are rebuilding another one so we can spread out when the babies come.

It makes me a nervous to think about having a baby here, without a doctor and without medication or drugs or anything. I always pictured being in a hospital, with Drew holding my hand, and Donna videotaping the event, all safe and sterile in case something goes wrong . . . But I have to do my part, and women have been having babies for millennia. It won't be that bad.

Interesting. I just noticed the date. Tax
Day. But not anymore. Not ever again.
— from *Adventures in Juliedom*, the
blog of Julie Davis Beecher Corrigan

CHAPTER 12

Sage held her breath, clutching tightly to Simon.

But at last the man turned and ambled back to his friends. "Guess not. I musta seen an animal or something."

No sooner had they gone out of sight than Simon released, and they both returned to their normal state. Now he was breathing heavily, and even in the dimness, she could see the lines in his handsome face. He was becoming exhausted from the constant changing, and, likely, the additional effort of changing her as well.

At last, they approached the house, but this time, Simon didn't leave Sage in the shadows while he went in. Three men stood in front of the house, talking. No one could approach without being seen—which was good for the two of them.

No one would suspect or even consider that they were in the house, and they could walk right past the men on guard.

And that was what they did . . . silently, carefully, but as quickly as possible—Sage being conscious of Simon's limitations. The door was closed, but the men were facing the opposite direction. Simon stopped, and of course she couldn't see him, but she knew why he paused.

It was a risk to open the door and go in, but it was a risk they had to take. They wouldn't be seen, of course, but they might be heard.

But just then, the door opened of its own volition—or, actually, because someone inside was coming out.

Simon moved quickly, and Sage had to take care not to trip or bump into anything as she was yanked along. He caught the door with his foot so that it didn't close behind the man who'd just stepped out, and whisked Sage through before the other guy knew what happened, leaving the door swinging in their wake.

The sound of it slamming shut followed them as Simon dashed up the stairs, pulling Sage along faster than she could go. Watching for things to step or trip on, she couldn't even see where her feet were. It was a strange sensation, and slowed her down.

The sparkly feeling began to ebb as they reached the top, and she felt Simon breathing heavily against her. They both filtered back into solidness and stood on the landing of the grand, sweeping staircase.

Five minutes later, they'd reached the attic safely and soundlessly. Sage settled on the floor in a corner, out of sight of the door. Simon joined her, sitting on the floor with the three packs he'd carried the whole way. He pulled out the hand-crank flashlight and set in on the floor, where it would glow too low to be seen beyond the four-story-high dirty windows, but enough to light the area for them.

"Wow," she said in quiet voice.

"Wow?"

"That was pretty amazing."

She couldn't really see his face, but from the way he tilted his head, she thought he might even have lifted an eyebrow in question. Then he turned to pull a blanket from one of the packs, and gestured for her to sit on it.

"That escape," she said. "You were . . . amazing. Thank you. For saving me."

He gave a short, derisive laugh. "I haven't saved you yet."

"You will. We'll get out of here." She looked at him and felt her heart swell again. She opened her mouth to say something . . . to tell him how she was feeling, but he looked away. And she chickened out.

So, instead of saying what she really wanted to, Sage asked, "How did you figure out you could turn invisible?"

That got his attention, and he looked back at her. "Trust you to ask that question." His lips twitched in a bit of a smile.

She had to call him on it; he was always so sober and serious. "Did you just . . . smile? Well, not really, but almost?"

Now his mouth lifted again and . . . *holy cow* . . . he *did* smile. Briefly, but it was there, in the glow of the flashlight. *Whoa*. What that did to her belly. And what thoughts it put in her mind . . . the mobility of those lips. Those perfect, perfect lips.

Whew.

"I mean . . . it's not like someone just figures out they can turn invisible. Unless you were born that way and your mom taught you or something?"

His eyes had widened, then narrowed with humor, then sobered again. "I didn't know my mother. And no, I wasn't born this way. If I had been . . ." His voice trailed off and he glanced out into the distance, as if looking beyond the walls of the attic. "If I had been, things would have been a lot different."

"So . . . ?" she prompted.

"Aren't you supposed to be looking up something on the computer?" he asked, straightening the blanket beneath them, as if he needed something to do with himself.

"I will, but I can still listen." She obediently pulled out Julie Davis Beecher Corrigan's heavy, clunky laptop. She could look for a plug in the attic, but it would be easier and faster to use the hand-cranked power bloc that Lou had created for such emergencies, so she plugged the old laptop into it.

"It was an accident that I figured it out," he said. As often happened when he spoke low and easy, that exotic accent flavored his words. She wanted to ask him about that.

Suddenly, she wanted to ask him about *everything*.

She opened the computer and waited for it to boot up, listening to the whirr and crank that made it sound like it was on its last legs. It probably was, for it had been a miracle it had survived fifty years or more. Sage wasn't sure she believed in guardian angels, but if this computer belonging to her grandmother ended up having information that helped them escape; she would definitely become a believer.

"It was weird . . . I happened to be in a place . . . this was after all of us—Wyatt, Quent, Elliott, Fence, and his partner, Lenny, and I—came out of the cave in Sedona. Lenny's dead," he added as she drew in her breath to ask. "He died about a month after we got out. An infection. That's how we know that though we're . . . different . . . we're not immortal. Like the Strangers."

"Is that bad?" she asked, not quite sure how she felt about it. Living forever while everyone else around you died would be sad and eventually boring, but at the same time, she wasn't all that fond of dying in the first place.

He shrugged. "It doesn't matter. It's not an option. Anyway, I happened to be in a room by myself in an old building . . . just needed to be alone for a few minutes. Wyatt and Quent walked in, and they thought they were alone, and they started talking about something very personal. I didn't want to be there, but couldn't leave . . . and didn't want them to know I was there, witnessing this very . . . emotional conversation."

Sage nodded and glanced down at the computer to click into the document "Juliedom," now that it had finally cranked alive.

"And so I sort of held my breath and tried to . . . well, disappear. It sounds odd, but I've . . . needed to do that in the past . . . to not be noticed, and it's an ability I . . . had. Sort of. Not like this. But to be unnoticed, kind of melt into the shadows."

It occurred to Sage that she'd never heard Simon put so many sentences together at one time. She dared not speak and break the spell.

"And then I felt this weird prickling, almost sparkling feeling as I concentrated, trying to be unnoticeable, and . . . my hands *disappeared*. And my feet. And I realized what I had done." He shrugged again, those solid broad shoulders moving smoothly, silhouetted by the very faint cast of moonlight from the window behind him. "It fucking blew my mind."

"I can only imagine."

"Yeah." His voice remained low.

Silence but for the faint tapping of her fingers on the page-down key as she scrolled through the diary. She'd seen something somewhere about another exit . . . a rear door, an escape route . . . for the Corrigans.

"Ah . . ." She paused scrolling and began to skim. This was it. "Blah blah . . . near the Wall . . . capitalized," she looked up. "Wall's capitalized, so she must mean Hell's Wall . . . blah . . . blah . . . okay, here, she says, 'An opening in the enclosing wall, camouflaged by a pile of debris. They piled it there, garbage, but Kevin showed me how there was a tunnel hidden in it.'" She looked up at Simon and the expression on his face sent her stomach dropping.

How could he look at her like that and then mention Theo?

Although, in his defense . . . he hadn't done that for a while.

"Okay," he said, nodding. "Does it say anything else?" His voice . . . it was so smooth and low, it seemed to caress her. "How to find the entrance?"

"Um . . ." She looked back down and skimmed some more. "By the old Lexus." She looked up. "That's what it says. I don't know what that means."

"A Lexus is—was—a kind of car. So now we know what we're looking for." He nodded, and seemed to relax a bit, leaning against the wall. "Do you want to check your computer and see if there's a response from Theo?"

Well, so much for him not bringing up Theo again.

Sage mentally shook her head and did as he suggested. There was indeed an email from Theo, indicating that he would be on his way, and that his estimated arrival time would be about six A.M.

"That's five hours from now," Simon said, glancing at the cloud-swathed moon. "Once we're out beyond the gates, it'll be only an hour on foot to get there." He didn't ask the question, but she read it in his eyes.

"There might be *gangas* out there," she said. "Do you think it's safe to stay here awhile, then try to leave? By the time we go, the sun will be close to coming up."

Simon seemed to hesitate, then his shoulders sagged as if in acquiescence. "If that's what you want, all right. But I don't think we ought to wait more than an hour to try and find the way out. In case it takes some time."

"Besides, we could both use some rest," she added, thinking of how hard he'd worked tonight to keep them safe and invisible.

He gestured to the blanket as if to say, *Have at it.* Then he got up and silently moved across the attic space, taking care to keep away from any revealing window. She watched in trepidation, afraid he was going to leave her while he did something manly like check on things, especially when he headed toward the small door through which they'd come.

But instead, he moved a large armoire easily and then a trunk in front of the door without making a sound. "So we won't be surprised," he said over his shoulder, then opened the chest. "More blankets here—a quilt. And this is a tight trunk, so it's in good shape." He pulled it out and brought the blanket as he returned to their corner.

Sage closed up her computers, putting them away, and settled against the wall perpendicular to his. With her feet curled up to her body, half sitting on her side, she leaned toward the corner next to Simon. "What's that language you speak sometimes? Is it Spanish?"

"It's called *caló*, which is a sort of slang spoken by Chicanos. Mexican–Americans. It's derived from Mexican Spanish, and L.A. street talk and other influences." He sort of grimaced. "Most of the words you have heard me say aren't very polite."

She gave a little laugh and looked at his swarthy skin, dark hair, and perfect, chiseled face. Dark hooded eyes, angular jaw and cheekbones. "All right. So you're . . . what is it? Chicanos?"

"Chicano. I'm a little bit of a lot of things," he said, leaning his head back against the wall. She could see the outline of his profile, thanks to the flashlight glowing below . . . his straight, elegant nose, his perfect lips, square chin, and even a hint of long lashes. He closed his eyes, those lashes sweeping down onto his high cheekbones. "A little Puerto Rican, a little Italian, a little Korean, and God only knows what else." Without opening his eyes, he added, "At least you know where you come from."

"You said you didn't know your mother." Sage figured she sounded like she was grilling him, but, well . . . he knew a whole lot about her, and she didn't know anything about him. About this man who'd really begun to affect her. This man that she needed to know better. Sage the analyst, the researcher, the curious, needed some answers.

"She died when I was young."

Apparently, that was all he was going to say about that.

"Are you going to tell me what's going on with Tatiana?"

That got him to open his eyes and lift his head. "I wondered when you would ask. I'm amazed it's taken so long."

She smiled at him, feeling the corners of her tired eyes crinkling. "I had other things to cover first."

"Like my pedigree?"

She wasn't sure what he meant by that, so Sage merely shook her head and waited.

"I used to know her," at last he said simply, resting his skull back against the wall. "A long time ago."

Sage adjusted her position, which brought her bumping against his arm. "You don't expect me to be satisfied with that, do you? Especially since we're running for our lives all of a sudden after you and she had a little tête-à- tête in the back hall."

"I'd rather not talk about it." His voice sounded like a slap in the quiet.

"Okay, then." Sage lapsed into silence, leaning back

against her wall. What was a bit of dust and cobwebs that might be getting into her hair?

No sounds other than the distant howling of wolves, and the nearby scrabbling of rodents. Thankfully, off in the corners. Not that they bothered Sage, really—they offered no threat, and mice were pretty cute—but she didn't want to get up close and personal with the little critters.

"That's it? You aren't going to press?"

She turned to look at him, rolling her head along the wall and found that he had done the same, and their faces were close, nearly meeting where their respective walls intersected in a corner. "You said you didn't want to talk about it."

He looked at her, his eyes dark and shadowed despite the glow of the flashlight on the floor below them. "Sage . . . you are quite a woman. It's no wonder—"

"Don't say it," she interrupted sharply.

"What?"

"Theo. Don't you dare bring him up again." Her voice was hard.

Simon closed his eyes. His lips flattened and he rolled his head away, looking back out over the room. "Where I come from, there's a line of honor when it comes to a . . . colleague's . . . woman."

"Yeah? So? I'm not Theo's woman." Her voice rose.

"He wants you to be, and—look, it's a line I've never crossed, and, Sage," he said, his voice growing stronger, harder, "I have crossed a *lot* of damn lines in my life." And now, weariness. "A whole damn lot."

"He might want me to be his woman—which I find to be a derogatory term, by the way—but I'm not. I *don't love Theo*," she said as clearly and distinctly as she could. Maybe then it would sink in. "What the hell is wrong with you, always trying to push me toward him?"

"I—"

"Do you think I'm some sort of—I don't know—child? Rag doll? Toy? A damned *pet*? I can think for myself, you know. I don't have to have a damned man telling me who to be with or—or anything. And I know how I feel—and *don't* feel, Simon, and if you even *say* his name again, I'm going to scream." She was keeping her voice low with effort, and realized her words were coming out from between clenched teeth.

"Sage, I promised him—"

"What? That you'd keep me safe? Well, that's great. You've done that—with a little help from me, by the way. But I hope to *hell* you're not just fucking keeping me safe for *him*, Simon. That's—that's—" She was so pissed she hardly knew what she was saying. Other than the fact that she'd used the F-word.

But she didn't care. She knew what she was going to do . . . what she needed to do. Because here, and now, she knew Simon was the man she wanted. And since Simon had made it clear he wasn't going to cross the line, she was going to have to do it. Not that there was any line to cross, in her mind at least.

And now she was babbling nervously in her own thoughts.

Sage shoved them away, her thoughts, her nerves, her fears, and shifted up on her knees. Bracing herself—literally, with her palms on the soft blanket, and figuratively, with those worries pushed away—she levered toward him. He murmured in a sort of desperate way, meant to hold her off—but she covered his mouth with her gently parted lips, stifling any other argument or barrier he might try to build. The time for that was over.

His mouth remained rigid for only a moment, then softened as he moved all at once, his arms coming around her, quick and hard, pulling her close as if to make certain she wasn't going to change her mind and pull back.

She could have told him that wasn't going to happen . . . if she'd been thinking about anything other than the warmth buzzing through her, flushing over her face and body . . . about the strong shoulders beneath her hands and the slide of a powerful jean-covered thigh against hers.

The next thing she knew, Sage was on her side on the blanket, lying next to Simon in the same position they'd lain in the bed these last few nights. Only this time, there were no sheets and blankets to contain the heat . . . and this time, hands roamed and slid, caressed and undressed.

Oh, God, he was so strong and warm . . . and he felt so *good* . . . Sage lifted her face as he bent over her, kissing her deeply and thoroughly, sliding his fingers into her thick hair and brushing it back from her face by the handful so that he could kiss along her temples and the rise of her cheekbone. So soft, tender . . . almost reverent. Those lips, those amazing, perfect, angel-sculpted lips . . .

Sage arched up into him, her hips mashing against his and the rigid bulge behind the buttons of his jeans. Her belly surged and leapt as he gave a soft, deep sigh from the pressure, and she pulled him down on top of her, wanting to feel him . . . instinctively twisting and rubbing against him, grinding their hips together, pulling him onto her by his belt loops.

Her breathing rose, his became hotter and harsher over her skin as their lips fought and slipped and mashed. Somehow her shirt and bra came off, and then his, and they were skin to skin, sleek and warm, curved and muscled as he rose over her on the blanket.

He slid his hands to cup under her breasts, holding them and sweeping his thumbs over her nipples. Quickly, in short little strokes that sent darts of pleasure shooting down to her belly and beyond. When he bent to kiss one of them, so tight and sensitive, his mouth warm and his tongue sleek, she nearly cried aloud at the sensual feel of his lips and heat closing around her, sucking and tugging and drawing her into his mouth.

Since he'd walked out of the shower in a towel—no, since she'd seen him from behind as he stripped off his T-shirt—she had wanted to touch him, to really explore the sculpted muscle, the ridges of his belly, the slender line of dark, silky hair that led down to his waistband. Her hands flattened over the warmth of his skin as he lifted from her breasts and looked down at her. The heat in his eyes, the intensity as he gazed down at her for that moment made her stomach flip and flutter again. Then he scooped an arm around her waist to pull her up, flush, hard, against him, her breasts crushed against his hard chest as he nuzzled her neck . . . and slipped his hand beneath her cargo pants.

Oh . . . yes . . . His fingers found the right place, her warm, ready, slick place—and Sage gasped into his shoulder as he tore open her fly, yanked down her panties, to give him more room to move. The cool air over her belly and upper thighs contrasted with the heavy warmth of his palm, settling over her. Simon's breath heated her temple and she felt his lips moving against her cheek, speaking or maybe gasping soundlessly, as his skillful fingers slipped in and around her, teasing the tight, swollen core. The pleasure built, tightening through her body, and she shifted urgently, tasting the faint salt on his hot skin, her eyes closed, her body taut and ready . . .

"Simon," she said, shifting, trying to shift away from him, wanting to feel him over her, in her, one with her.

"Wait . . . wai-it . . ." she gasped as his fingers moved faster and more expertly, his mouth covering hers as if to drown out her arguments.

He murmured something unintelligible in her ear, low and rough and exotic, sending deeper shivers down into her core. His tongue slid out, curling into the deep, sensitive part of her ear and she shuddered, trembling against him, reaching for the waistband of his jeans. "No . . . Simon . . . wait . . ." she gasped, trying to ease away, trying to hold off on the rise of pleasure. She tugged at the edge of his fly and the top button popped open.

"Sage, no . . ." he said, lifting his mouth from where he'd been kissing the corner of her jaw. He stilled, pulling up and away, and rolling his body from her . . . though his hand remained there, over her, as though he couldn't bear to let her go.

His rough breathing filled the room, filled her ears, her body thrummed and hummed and she was full and throbbing. "No," he said again. And moved his fingers, gently and languorously, and nearly tipped her over the edge.

Sage stiffened, closing her eyes against his sensual argument. "No, Simon, don't pull away from me." Her words came out breathless, even more so when he found that right spot, the perfect spot, and did a long, slow stroke three fingers wide, down and over and up and back. "Mmmph," she groaned, but shifted sharply so that his hand fell away. "Please."

He pulled away and collapsed next to her on the blanket, head half tilted back against the wall, breathing rough and heavy. At last . . . they were getting somewhere. She was getting to him.

She reached for him again, her hands smoothing over his belly, noticing the way his dark skin shuddered and leapt at her touch. His hair had come mostly undone and fell in a sheen against his cheeks and curved at his jaw, brushing his shoulders. He appeared wild and erotic and, with his full lips half parted and his eyes closed as if to gather control, the very expression on his face made her belly shiver.

"Sage, really," he said in a low, desperate voice. "It's your first time . . . not here, not in this dusty place. Not now. Not with *me*."

"Yes, with *you*," she said, giving a tug at the flap of his jeans. Another button popped undone. His eyes flew open.

She met his gaze, unwavering and purposeful, and in the golden glow of the flashlight her mouth went dry at the heat . . . and anguish in his eyes. He ate her with them, but it was torture. She read it there.

"You don't *know* me," he said desperately. "You can't."

"I know enough," she said, leaning toward him, reaching for his jeans once more. The third button gave way with a dull snap, and she looked up at his face, her heart beating hard as she readied to pop the fourth button. "I know I can trust you, that you'll do the right thing, that you're smart and kind—"

His laugh, short and bitter, stopped her as his hand closed over hers, halting her fingers. His mouth twisted hard and angry, his eyes squeezed shut. "You don't fucking know me, Sage," he said in a dark, grating voice. "I'm none of those things. You'll be better off—"

"You are to me, Simon," she said, talking over what was surely going to be yet another reference to damned Theo Waxnicki. Did he have any idea how much that ticked her off? She yanked roughly at his jeans, dislodging his grip, and his hips jerked a bit as the fourth and fifth buttons popped.

"Sage," he groaned, heartfelt and agonized. From deep in his chest.

She stopped and looked down at him. He'd still not opened his eyes, and now he had the back of his arm resting over them . . . and, *holy cats,* was that a trickle of a tear gleaming down the side of his temple? From the corner of an eye? *Simon?*

Her anger faded. He wasn't just being an ass. He was frustrated.

His mouth still flat, his body rigid as if he dared not move . . . God . . . what did he think?

She paused, putting her hand square on the center of his chest, feeling the rise and fall of his breath and the rampant beating of his heart. "It's one damned thing if you don't want me," she managed to say, her anger leaking out a bit. Then Sage suddenly became dry-mouthed from fear that he *didn't* . . . that she'd been wrong, read him wrong, pushed herself on him. After all, she really didn't know anything about men. She hadn't even known Theo was in love with her. "But if you want me as much as I want you, Simon . . . please. I want you. I want you to be my first."

And my last.

But she dared not say that. Not . . . now.

His arm moved and his eyes opened, and she saw that they did glisten and her heart seized up again. But his gaze held her. "It's a mistake, Sage."

"Not for me."

"If you *knew*—"

"Simon, the only thing I know is that I want you, now, and if you don't, then you need to say something *right the hell now.* I'm not a damned child. I'm a *woman.* And I know what I want. And it's you. *Not* Theo." She bent forward and pressed a soft, light kiss against his lips. "If you really don't, then I'll leave you be," she breathed against his mouth.

He released his lungs with a *whoosh* and his hand went

around the back of her head, pulling her close as if he wanted to inhale her, to devour her. His tongue, stronger and harder and deeper than before, his hands tight and yet gentle. "Sage, I do . . . want you," he whispered over her lips, then something in *caló* that she didn't understand. Then, soft and desperate, "More than you . . . know. I do."

"Then stop being noble," she said, which for some reason garnered another laugh from him. Another humorless bark. "And make love to me." She reached for his jeans and yanked open the last button.

And slid her hands down into the heat there, finding the heavy length of him. He made another guttural sound, and then, as if surrendering, he sat up and pulled her to him for another kiss, holding the side of her face. She smelled the musk of herself on his fingers, there on her jaw, and the scent excited her even more.

In moments, he had his jeans off and they lay again, now completely skin to skin, legs twining, mouths busy, hands busy. She lifted, stroked, explored his heavy erection, noticing the way every movement caused him to react—to tense, to shift and shudder, to sigh and to stroke her more intimately, driving her desire higher and higher, her chest flushing and her body tensing. She sighed and writhed, her breasts tight, her core tighter and pulsing, and he stroked and teased, leaning forward to take her nipple in his mouth, flickering over it with his tongue as his fingers found her spot.

Her breath caught as she climbed, tightening, heat and pleasure rising, his mouth and fingers busy, coaxing, leading . . . and then she dragged in a last breath and jerked herself away. "No," she gasped. "I want it all, dammit, Simon. Give me all of you." She reached blindly and closed her fingers around him, feeling the dull throb of pulsing blood beneath her touch.

"Sage," he gasped, then dissolved again into that sensual language, breathing deeply, as if fighting himself. But then he opened his eyes.

Looking down, he searched her face again. A lock of his hair had caught in the trail of the tear at the side of his face, and his eyes, though hot and ready, examined her for a last minute change of heart. "I . . . are you sure?"

"Please, Simon, please," she said, and opened her legs, shifting beneath him.

Some of the tension eased from his face . . . at last, at *last* . . . as he held himself up over her. His mouth relaxed from that awful, rigid state and became sensual again. His eyes softened and even his jaw seemed to shift. His gaze burned over her, and she saw how much he really did want her. Right there, in his face, he could no longer hide it.

The very expression made her hot and shivery and ready.

He reached between them and guided himself to her. She felt him hesitate once more, and she squeezed the arm he used to hold himself up, and then . . . he moved. Slowly, carefully . . . she felt the stretching inside her . . . but it was a beautiful stretching and she wanted more of it. She shifted, moving up impatiently, wanting it over— and suddenly he filled her. There was a sharp pain and she winced, and he froze, and then she opened her eyes and looked up at his concerned face, his wide eyes and tense mouth and she smiled and said, "Beautiful."

She moved, because it was apparent that he was still worried for hurting her . . . and then his lips softened and he began to move himself . . . faster and longer, slowly at first, and then when her own eyes grew wide and her mouth parted in little, grasping sighs, his rhythm increased and she tried, clumsily, to meet his, and he laughed a little, but then they met it . . . synchronized . . . and it was, oh, so perfect . . . the slide and the deep strokes, his fingers there between them, to help her along, and when she gave that last sound of triumph . . . blasting over the top . . . he gave a hard groan and yanked himself away, twisting to the side, and matched her gasp with a deep one of his own.

And they lay there, damp and hot and twined, sprawled on a thin blanket and an old quilt that had a sudden wet spot, in the shadows of a dusty, gritty attic . . . while a whole city of people searched for them below.

When she came back to herself and realized all of this, however much time had passed later, Sage couldn't help but laugh a little.

"Something funny?" Simon asked, picking himself up and looking at her. His gaze was wary, as if he expected her to scramble away from him, as if he were a little rodent.

"Yeah," she said, reaching to touch his shoulder . . . that beautiful, square, powerful shoulder. He *was* gorgeous, all that rich, dark hair falling in his face, plastered to his neck and throat, and those sleek muscles everywhere. "After all those nights in the bedroom, sharing a bed, when we could have done this a little more comfortably . . . we had to pick a dusty attic while we're on the run for our lives." She laughed again.

But he didn't seem to find it funny. "Yeah."

"Simon," she said. "It was a joke. An irony."

"Sage, you deserved better than this to be your first time." *And it should have been someone better than me.* He didn't say the words, but she read it in his eyes.

"Well, I don't know how it could have been any better. Simon. Don't most people have a smile on their face afterward, instead of a grimace?" Her heart sank. Maybe he hadn't enjoyed it. Maybe it had been . . . what had Theo called it once, when they were watching a movie? A pity-fuck? *Oh God*.

His expression changed and that heat came back into his eyes. The one she recognized, the one that wasn't a lie. "It couldn't have been any better," he said. And she knew he meant it, and a rush of pleasure flowed back into her belly. "For me. For you . . . I'm not so sure." And he smiled, a sort of wavering smile that touched her heart.

What had damaged this man so deeply that he had to hold himself back like this? To be so resistant to happiness?

And why had he pulled away at the last minute? "You pulled out . . . of me," she said. "Before you . . . uh . . ."

"You're ovulating," he said, his voice flat again. "It was the best I could do to keep you from getting pregnant. And it might not work anyway." He turned away, rubbed his eyes. "I almost forgot. I almost didn't make it . . . I almost lost my mind, Sage. I've never done that."

She was ovulating. A sudden little flicker of . . . something . . . warm? Filtered over her. She could get pregnant.

"It's my body and I didn't even think of it," she said honestly. "I mean, who doesn't want a baby? Even people who don't live in Falling Creek. Babies are . . . miracles."

He looked at her, nodded slowly. "I know. But, where I come from, it's different. It was different. And responsible men from my time never had sex without trying to prevent pregnancy unless they've planned otherwise. With their partner."

"Preventing pregnancy?" Such a foreign idea.

This brought another smile from him. "I know it's odd . . . but that's the way it was."

She opened her mouth to speak again, but he raised an imperative hand suddenly. And tilted his head to listen, and then fairly leapt to his feet, naked and sleek and, oh my God, if she weren't so worried about what had prompted him to do so, she'd gawk at the beauty of him.

"Holy Mother of God," he whispered in such a voice that had her scrambling to her feet. She hurried over to the window. "Is that what I think it is?"

She looked out and saw Hell's Wall looming dark in the distance. There was a deep, low rumbling sound. An ugly one that sent shivers up her spine. "The wall . . . it's dark," she said. "The crystal lights—"

"Are gone." With a short, sharp curse in *caló*, he spun from the window and began to drag on his clothes. "Get dressed. We've got to get out of here. The Strangers—no, it's fucking Florita—are sending a message."

"What kind of message?" Sage asked, though she had a feeling, through her suddenly nauseated belly, that she might know. "Florita? You mean Tatiana?"

"An unpleasant one," he said, shoving their electronics into the packs. "For me."

"For you?"

"She's telling me to come out of hiding, or the wall's coming down."

"But . . . the whole city will be destroyed."

He stopped and looked at her. "I know. That's her message. She wants me . . . in exchange for the city."

May 11
Eleven months after.

I'm stunned. Hurt and angry and so, so, so shocked. I can't believe he would do this to me!

How long have they been planning this?

Kevin came to me today and told me that he's going to marry Britney. But he's already married to me!!! How can he do this? Marry both of us????

He told me that they (I guess he and Robert and Thad) realized that during the whole nine months I'm pregnant—and the other wives too—that the men are unable to do anything else to help rebuild our race. Their hands are tied, and they feel helpless and weak. So they decided that it would make sense if they had more than one wife!!

They could be more efficient in spreading their sperm around, for crying out loud.

Well, how the hell does this make me feel? Like crap, that's how. This is no way to treat a pregnant lady. No way to treat the woman he says he loves. I mean, I know we're focused on having babies, but I just thought we'd be trying every month. You know, all the time. And trying to get pregnant as soon as possible after every birth.

I wasn't planning on getting into some kind of polygamous arrangement.

And he claims to still love me. That Britney is purely for breeding purposes—yes, that's the word he used. But I'm not so sure. She's a little younger than me and she has bigger boobs.

Whatever. I hate this. I wish I'd never left Envy.

—from *Adventures in Juliedom, the blog of Julie Davis Beecher Corrigan*

CHAPTER 13

Fuck me fuck me fuck me.

I should have known. I shouldn't have underestimated the bitch.

Simon drew in a deep breath and gathered control of his blazing fury, his roaring fear. One thing at a time. *Think. Plan.*

She would give him time to show up, she knew he had to be in the settlement. She wasn't going to drop the wall immediately, because then she'd lose him too.

It was a warning. A potent one.

And he'd been too distracted by a copper-haired woman, his drive to keep her safe, his engulfing need that made him ignore his honor . . . too distracted by Sage to think about the repercussions of pissing off Florita.

He shouldn't have made such a mistake. Hell, the last time he'd shut her down, she'd tried to have him killed.

Apparently, this time, she wanted him badly enough to kill hundreds of innocent people instead.

All of these thoughts trammeled coolly through his mind even as he and Sage dashed through the darkness, making their way more haphazardly, more carelessly than before from tree to alcove to building.

The shadows were shortening, and a light gray burned

along the eastern horizon. Dawn was coming, the threat of *gangas* was fairly nil. Theo should be arriving any time—to the meeting place, which was still miles away.

Grasping Sage's hand, his body still humming, still damp and loose from being with her, Simon tore toward the massive pile of trash that he hoped . . . prayed . . . had the secret tunnel in it.

The massive wall rumbled in the distance like a mini version of Mordor, its crystal lights still dark. Simon glanced at it as it loomed ahead of them—the secret tunnel was on that side of the settlement—which in a way was good, because no one was coming in this direction searching for them if the wall was threatening to come down.

They reached the pile of junk and he darted around, looking for the old Lexus, knowing that after fifty years, it could be in any condition; it could even be gone. Using his flashlight—he didn't care at this point, he had to get her out of here, had to stop that wall from burying the settlement—he scanned it over the pile, knowing that the entrance to the passageway would be lower rather than higher up.

Then the light caught on a license plate, rusted and old, but it said LEXUS 2. *Thank you, God.* The plate was attached to a Lexus of indeterminable color, its silvery L-symbol gritty and dull, but still there in its recognizable oval.

Like the cars he and Sage had crawled through to get to the Beretta building back in Envy, this one had a door that opened. But this time, the other side of the car had been removed. And when they crawled in, there was plenty of room to stand once they moved across the split leather seats, long bereft of their stuffing.

He fairly shoved Sage in, acutely aware of how time

was ticking by and how the rumblings from the wall were becoming louder and more ominous. *Hell hath no fury . . .* The crash of a massive boulder bounding down the side of the cliff had him pushing and scrambling in after her.

Hurry, hurry, hurry . . . On the other side, the tunnel was tall enough for him to stand easily, and wide enough for three or four people to walk abreast. Simon considered whether there might be any booby traps or other surprises—like den-preferring creatures—or even *gangas*, and slipped ahead of Sage to clear the way.

Flashing the light ahead of them, he was gratified to see that the tunnel ran straight and empty. It couldn't be that long, less than a half mile by his estimation, if it were to dump them on the other side of the wall. But though he went quickly, his scanned the path ahead, watching for any sign of movement.

The pack clunked over his shoulder, and Sage's against her as they rushed along, the rumbling louder now that they were enclosed in a tunnel of metal and who knew what else. It was too dark to tell what was around them, and he didn't care to stop and examine it. Time was running out.

At last, they came to a wall—or what appeared to be a wall, but was, after a brief examination, determined to be a door. It took him only a moment to figure out how to open it—a little lever—and he peered around.

Light. Scrubby trees and tall grass appearing in various shades of gray. "Stay here," he said and slipped out, turning himself invisible as he did so.

Sure enough. There they were, outside of Falling Creek, only a short distance from the wall and on the opposite side of the main gate. Out of sight. No guards, no *gangas*, no glowing eyes of predators. In the distance, to the south, rose the trees from the forest through which he and Sage had come three days ago. Where Theo would, God willing, be waiting.

Simon slipped back inside with one last glance at the wall. Another large boulder tumbled down in raucous punctuation to the general warning, dragging three trees with it. It rolled to a halt only yards from the settlement wall, and he felt his belly tighten. He slipped back inside.

"Sage, get on the computer and try to get a message to Theo to come here. It's safer than trying to make a run for it to the forest. They'll be watching for us."

"But we can be invisible," she said, her eyes wide.

"Get on the computer," he said again, tension rising. He wished he'd never had to show her his ability. It had blinded her to reality. Made her think of him as infallible. "We don't have time. The wall's going to come down."

"But if it does, it'll bury us here," she said, yet she pulled out her computer and swiftly turned it on, her fingers clattering over the keys.

"No, that's not going to happen. I'm not going to let that happen. But we don't have time to run to the woods. Theo should be there already . . . it will only take him twenty minutes to get here and get you."

"Me?" She froze, her hands on the computer keys. "What about you?"

He shook his head. "I have to go to her and get her to stop. It's the only way. Otherwise, the whole city will be buried. People will die."

"I'll go with you and Theo can—"

"Are you *insane*?" His voice rose, cracked, and he gathered control of himself. "Do you know what she'd *do* to you?" He shook his head, aware that his fingers were hurting he was tensing them so tightly. "Just get on the damned computer and message Theo. *Now*, Sage." He knew he sounded like an asshole, but there was no other choice. She had to listen.

"But what about you?" Her tone was higher than he'd ever heard it, panicked and tight. And angry again.

"Sage, I told you. You don't know me. There are things you can't understand, things I've done . . ." His voice roughened, nearly broke, and he forced himself on, concentrated on a surge of anger at Florita to keep himself from getting weak and emotional. "I've got so much blood on my hands, I can't wash them clean. I thought I could . . . I thought this was my chance."

He drew in a breath, collected himself again. "You don't know me. You can't. So *get on the damned computer and contact Theo and have him come and get you.*"

She was staring at him with circular eyes, her beautiful lips parted in shock, her breath coming in hitches that he knew portended tears, fucking mother-fucking tears, dammit . . . why the hell did his last image of her have to be tears?

"Go with him and give the man a chance, Sage. He loves you, for God's sake, he's a good man, and he is a far sight *better* man than me. And he can give you everything you need."

"Simon," she said, her voice thin and thready. "I love you."

"No," he said, desperate now. "No, you can't. You don't know me." He had to go. He had to make her understand . . . and time was running out. "I'm not your damned superman."

And he disappeared.

Simon waited long enough to see that Sage did send the email to Theo—though she was trying not to cry while muttering death threats as if she knew he was still there—

and he actually looked over her shoulder and found that
Theo had already replied to confirm his arrival at the original meeting place. Thank God. He'd be there in twenty
minutes or less to get Sage, and now Simon wouldn't have
to worry about her.

Only about the other three hundred people here in Falling Creek.

He dashed back through the tunnel, silent, trying to
ignore the furious string of curses mingled with frustrated
tears echoing from Sage. He wasn't certain whether she
knew he was still there or not.

But regardless, he knew it was better this way. For all
of them.

Moments later, he was running to the front of the settlement, toward the light that still burned despite the rising
sun, aware of the increased number of boulders and even
chunks of cliff raining down on the expanse of ground
between Hell's Wall and the settlement. More than one
piece of debris had smashed into the protective wall, and
several had tumbled down so rapidly that they'd cleared
the wall and landed inside Falling Creek.

As he drew closer, he heard a shout, but otherwise,
no other noise except for the sounds of destruction
behind him.

When the crowd came into view—it seemed as if
every resident of Falling Creek had gathered at the gate,
which was tightly closed, effectively penning them in to
their death—Simon was struck by the silence. Clustered
there, staring at the dark cliff in the distance, they stood
as if waiting for the inevitable. Shocked, frightened, but
silent.

"I'm here," he shouted, slowing his death-speed run to
a fast trot. He wasn't out of breath, but his chest was tight
with black fury. The bitch. She would let them all die.

But why should this be any different than what she and her friends had done fifty years ago? This was a pittance compared to that.

"Tell Tatiana that I've come."

The crowd parted, their faces still slack with shock, but hope rising in a few eyes.

He walked up to the gate and bellowed, "Florita! You win. I'm here."

Silence, a bit of muttering and a wave of panicked gasps.

Simon waited. He knew she'd heard him. But she'd take her time.

The crowd began to murmur and he heard some soft crying as the rumbling in the distance became more ominous. A massive boulder, the size of a small house, barreled down the cliff and bolted over the settlement wall, smashing into one of the mansions on the west side. A little cry went up from the crowd, but then it settled into silence.

"Florita!" Simon shouted again. "Tatiana! Open up or I'll go and you'll lose."

A child began to cry, a young one from the sound of it, and then another and soon it caught like wildfire—infants' cries punctuated with the shushings of their frantic mothers.

When there was still no movement at the gate, Simon knew that he had to work fast to evacuate the settlement. If he could get them through the secret tunnel, at least they wouldn't be trapped inside the walls. But the tunnel was on the other side of the community . . . far away. On the side facing the wall.

He looked around for one of the community leaders, someone in charge, someone who could help him gather everyone together . . . but then, at last, there was the sound of a vehicular motor. A low rumble, and then the gate shifted, jerking slightly.

The Strangers had parked their Hummers up against the gate to keep it closed.

A little buzz of hope erupted from the crowd and there was a bit of shoving and pushing. "Stand back," Simon said, his voice clear and ringing.

They listened, settling back . . . although the panic and fear did not ebb. The gate opened a mere crack and Simon walked over. The people parted for him, but then curved back around, as if ready to follow him through the opening.

He looked through the space, which was wide enough for his arm and not much more. "Tatiana. Turn the crystal guard back on, or I'll leave."

Peering through, he saw the silver front grate and headlight of a humvee and one of the male Strangers, and then Florita. Their eyes met through the crack and he saw the delight and triumph there.

"Very well, then. I will put the protective guard back into place as soon as you come with me, Simon Japp." She smiled, a wicked, crafty one, and the gate began to open.

"No," he said, stepping back. "Not until the guard is back in place. You do it, or I'll stay here and die with the rest of them." Of course he wouldn't allow anyone to die, but she didn't know that. "When I see the glow of the crystals, I'll come out."

Florita swore in their common street language, but then, curling her full lips, she nodded. "Agreed."

Less than five minutes later, the blue glow of the crystal guard shone pale against the dark Hell's Wall. The rising sun made it difficult to see the light, but it was there.

And when a cheer went up from the crowd, Simon turned and found the gate open wide enough for him to walk through.

His gut tight, heart heavy, he stepped over the threshold—out of Falling Creek, and back into the life he thought he'd escaped.

"I always knew you had a soft heart," Florita said conversationally. "The way you'd come back and stick your head in the toilet after doing certain things for Leonide."

Simon raised his eyes and found them caught by her mocking dark ones. *Fuck you.*

"Oh, you didn't think I noticed, did you? Poor Simon. Always coming across as heartless and cold, and then there were those stray kittens. Remember them?"

He looked away. "What do you want?"

They'd driven in the humvee, leaving Falling Creek behind, and headed toward the north side of the settlement. To his surprise, they went up and around, behind Hell's Wall, for about three miles on a rough road that rose to the backside of the cliff. At the top, he saw that Falling Creek was in the valley below.

On the backside of the cliff rose a large structure built into the wall just above the ocean. As they drew nearer, he saw water running around and through it in narrow channels, and remembered the floating house that had belonged to Preston, the Stranger who'd abducted Jade last month. His home had had a similar design, with water flowing up through the center and down.

This house was more like a gothic castle set into a waterfall, with a lusty river surging over the top of it. Water cascaded down the backside of the cliff, funneled into the center of the structure, then trickled down and around in its channels, splashing from the base to the ocean twenty feet below. Was this how they generated electricity? For Falling Creek and for Florita's house?

Now, as they sat in an interior room of the castle, Florita smiled knowingly at Simon. "You should have just done like Al Capone and gone to confession, thrown some money in the alms box, and forgotten about it instead of burying your head in a bottle and cranking shit up your nose. It would have been a lot easier for you."

Simon didn't deign to reply. Instead, he looked around the room into which she'd brought him. Pale walls, tinged with blue, with a slender ditch of water running along one side. Florita had always liked feng shui . . . this waterfall shit was right up her alley. Too bad he didn't find it relaxing in the last. Bright and stark, the air humid and damp, the space was comfortably furnished with cushions and pillows scattered on short, sleek furnishings. He'd taken a seat in a low armchair—the only place he could sit without her next to him. But she'd settled languidly on a chaise adjacent to his seat.

"But what I really want to know," Florita said, settling a hand on his thigh, making his skin crawl, "is how you came to be here. Looking just the same as you did before. But . . . yet . . . different."

"I don't know," he told her simply. "It just happened."

She searched his face, and he did his best to keep the loathing he felt for her and her other crystal-wearing friends under control. It wouldn't do any good to antagonize her at this time. Not until he figured out what he was going to do.

Florita seemed to believe him, or at least decided it wasn't worth the energy to pursue. "Well, I'm not complaining." She smiled, her eyes dark and lusty. "I'm very glad to have found you again, Simon."

"Can't say the feeling is mutual."

Her fingers tightened on his leg. It didn't hurt, but, damn, they were strong. "We'll see how long it takes for you to change your mind." She settled back in her chair, withdrawing her grip. "So you and your . . . wife . . . was it? Your *wife*. You were visiting Falling Creek, and she was asking people a lot of questions about Remington Truth."

Simon kept his face impassive and his hands still. "I have no idea what she was doing," he said flatly. "Didn't really care."

"Oh. I see." Florita's smile became more feline. "So she's not one of your stray kittens?"

He looked at her, his face blank and a little bored. He shook his head, shrugging faintly as if she were hopeless, knowing that it was a fine line between protesting too much and not at all. Especially with the cunning Florita.

Dragon Boy better not have fucked this up. She'd better be far away and safe.

"You still haven't told me what you want from me," Simon said, partly in an effort to draw her attention from Sage, and partly to probe. The more he knew, the better plans he could devise.

"Simon, don't be foolish. You know exactly what I want from you—what I've always wanted. Your loyalty, your . . . shall we say, way with a weapon, and of course, *you*." Her eyes narrowed thoughtfully. "Wherever shall we start?"

"You won't get any of that from me, Florita. I'm here only because you threatened to kill an entire city on a whim, but you made a big mistake by bringing me here. I can see what will happen to your home, your castle here if you let Hell's Wall destroy Falling Creek. It will all collapse. So, no, I don't think you'll follow through on that even if I leave. Which," he added smoothly, standing, "I can do at any time."

She looked up at him, and he saw the flash of unease quickly masked. "Don't be an idiot. You wouldn't risk it."

"You can't stop me."

"Oh? I might need to argue that, Simon, darling. Wouldn't the safety of your wife be a good start in that direction."

He kept himself from tensing, from showing any reaction. "I'm not stupid, Florita."

"No, indeed," she purred. He didn't like the expression on her face, but he didn't sit. "But your wife . . . wouldn't you do anything to keep her safe?"

"Risk my life? You know me. I've never done that before—why would I do that now? You'll have to come up with something better than that."

"Bring her in," Florita called.

Simon couldn't keep himself from going rigid and cold all over.

The door opened and a Stranger came in, dragging, *dragging* Sage across the room by her bound wrists. Her long, lovely hair spilling over her face, just as it had fallen over his hands only hours ago. She was little more than a corpse-like sack of bones, head sagging and flopping with every movement. The man released her and she collapsed to the floor. Unmoving.

Simon saw blood streaking her filthy clothes and grime and dirt on her arms. He couldn't see if her eyes were open, certainly couldn't tell if she were breathing. But of course she wasn't dead. Yet.

With great effort, he looked away, though every muscle in his body screamed to go to her. But he remained passive. Uninterested.

He could become invisible right now, grab Sage, and bust the hell out of here . . . but something held him back. He didn't want to expose his ability to Florita unless he absolutely had to. Because once she knew about that, she'd never let him go . . . and she'd figure out a way to keep him.

"Is that the best you can do?" he said. Supremely bored. His fingers prickled, his vision threatened to glaze red . . . but he controlled it.

"You needn't pretend with me, Simon," said Florita. "I know you'd do anything for her."

He merely raised a brow. "I think I'll be leaving now," he said. "I've had enough of your clumsy attempts at blackmail. It didn't work before. What makes you think it would work now?"

Her smile growing wider and more delighted, she gestured with her long-nailed hand to a screen on the wall. Holding a remote, she turned it on and with a sharp, stark realization, Simon saw a view of the bedroom he'd shared with Sage.

Holy Mother of God . . .

Simon's knees felt weak as he watched himself pretending to fuck her, yesterday afternoon when the curtains had been drawn tightly. And then, in the middle of it, when she arched up into him and set him over the edge and it was no longer a pretense.

Now, he remained rigid and unmoving, watching the play of emotions on his face, blown up on the big screen. The desperation and anguish. His need. There for all to see.

"So," Florita's voice winnowed through his roaring ears. "Do you still want to leave?"

Simon's response was to move across the room to Sage. No sense in hiding it any longer, and at least he could see how badly she was hurt. Tell her she was going to be safe, that he'd get her out of here.

He crouched next to her, aware of Florita's eyes on

him, heavy and contemplative, burning with jealousy, and brushed the tangle of hair away from her face. And nearly fell back on his ass.

It wasn't Sage.

It wasn't Sage.

Did Florita know this? Was it another trick? Or was she mistaken?

Easy to do so—with all of the Corrigans. This was one of the younger ones, with hair almost the same color as Sage's . . . but it didn't quite have that pinkish tinge to the copper.

God. He should have noticed it right off, but he'd been too intent on showing disinterest. If he'd looked at her, really looked at her, he'd have noticed.

Regardless, she needed help, so he unbound her wrists—tearing the ropes with his bare hands—and rolling her onto her back to see if she was breathing.

Her eyes fluttered and she opened them, drawing in a ragged breath. Fear blasted through her face, but at least she was awake and aware, though her eyes were fogged with confusion and pain. "Who are *you*?" she cried breathlessly. "What do you want? Let me go!"

Pinche. Now Florita had to know her mistake. Simon pulled to his feet, walking back across the room.

But Florita had already swept over to the terrified young woman. The girl looked up, terror and confusion in her blue eyes, as Florita, in a swirl of angry hair, looked over at Simon. Measuring.

"The wrong woman," she said. "Then I guess you don't mind if I do this, then." And before he realized it, before he could stop her, she had a gleaming blade in her hand and lunged.

Simon leapt, grabbing Florita's arm and yanking her away so violently that she flew backward, stumbling across the room. But it was too late. Blood everywhere, spattering from her knife, seeping into the pale floor, coloring that bright thick hair, the girl's neck slit from side to side.

He turned to Florita, his gut churning, his hands raised to grab her and strangle her, but she had the knife raised like the street girl she used to be. Bold and angry, she faced him across the room.

"Touch me and I'll slice you, but I won't kill you," she said. "And I'll keep bringing those girls in here, one by one, until we find the right one. Because I'll know when we find the right one, Simon. And then I'll have you on your knees."

He stepped back, getting his fury under control. Letting her think she'd won . . . for the time being. Fucking *coño*. He was going to tear that fucking crystal out of her skin.

She lowered the blade, her eyes dark and wicked. "And until then, you'll have to follow my orders . . . or watch each of those stray kittens die."

June 10, 2011
It's one year later.

It's the anniversary of the Change, and several things happened today.

For the first time, I didn't throw up from morning sickness. I'm four months along now, so it's about time.

Kevin and Britney announced that she is pregnant. And that Kevin would be marrying a new woman who recently arrived here in Falling Creek. Her name is Margaret.

She seems nice enough.

Despite his decision to marry again . . . and again . . . Kevin still seems to care about me. He's deferent to me and always puts me first. Maybe he does really love me. Maybe he really is just doing this to help recreate the human race. I'd like to believe it. And I sort of do, because . . .

He showed me a secret today. A tunnel he and Robert made. Even Thad doesn't know about it. It's a hidden exit from the settlement, a way out of here besides the big gate. Deep under a pile of junk, through a Lexus. An opening in the enclosing wall, camouflaged by a pile of debris. They piled it there, garbage, but Kevin showed me how there was a tunnel hidden in it. I don't know why they felt it was necessary . . . maybe because of the other thing that happened last week.

A visit from those people . . . those Strangers with the glowing crystals in their skin. There's a woman, and she looks really familiar . . . but I don't know why she would. They're even creepier than they were back in Envy.

They met with Thad and Kevin and Robert, but Kev won't tell me anything about their meeting.

All I know is I don't trust them. And I'm glad I know how to get out of here in case something happens . . . like another earthquake. There's a big huge cliff right outside the settlement, and it would destroy us if it fell.

A year after my first wedding. I could never have imagined how this would turn out.

Today was a difficult day.

　　—from *Adventures in Juliedom*, the blog of Julie Davis Beecher Corrigan

CHAPTER 14

Sage's head hurt even before she opened her eyes, but when she finally managed to force them open, her skull really began to scream. Right in the back.

Ow.

It took her a moment to focus, and then someone moved into her view.

Theo. He'd made it!

She smiled up at him and he smiled back, a tender, warm one as he reached to touch her cheek. "You're back."

Then she remembered . . . something. She pulled herself upright. Her head pounded and panic leaped through her. The last thing she recalled was slipping out of the secret tunnel and, dodging the increasingly heavy rain of rubble from Hell's Wall, running toward Theo in the humvee. "What happened? Where am I?"

"Home," he said, and she realized that all she had to do was look around and see that, yes, she was indeed, in her room back in Envy. With Theo.

And without Simon.

"Where's Simon?" she asked, looking around even though she knew he wasn't there. Jade wasn't there. No one was there but her and Theo.

"I don't know," Theo told her. "You said he wanted to

stay, and then you tripped and got conked on the head by a good-sized rock. You were out cold."

"You took me away? You left him there?" She thought she might be shrieking, but she wasn't certain. One thing she knew, her head was pounding even harder now. And so was her heart. What had he said to her?

You don't know me.

I'm not your damned superman.

What the heck did that mean?

Theo's handsome face, rough with stubble, had been tender and happy. But now it tightened with confusion and anger. "What the hell was I supposed to do? You were *knocked out*, Sage. For all I knew, you could have a concussion or a brain injury, because you sure as hell didn't want to wake up. I brought you back here for Elliott to look at."

Well, put that way, she supposed she could sort of understand. "And do I?"

"What?" He was still frowning at her, and it made her heart sad. Because she knew he was going to be frowning even more.

"Have a concussion. Or brain injury."

He shook his head. "No. Just a good knot on the head and maybe a sore spot for a while." He sat on the edge of the bed, very near her. "And besides, your message had said you were in trouble and had to get out of there right away. What the hell was I supposed to do? Go looking for Simon, God knows where, especially after you said he wanted to stay?"

"He didn't want to stay, he *had* to stay," she said, trying to keep her voice steady. "The Strangers were going to destroy Falling Creek and he was the only one who could stop them."

"Really." Theo sounded supremely unconvinced. He

absently rubbed Scarlett, a sure sign that he was un-
happy.

"How long have we been gone?"

"We got back just a couple hours ago."

Sage closed her eyes because the pounding in her head
was becoming unbearable. "I wouldn't have left *you*, Theo,
even if you said you had to go in . . . I just can't believe we
left him." Even though that was what he wanted.

"You said he had to."

"We have to go back and get him, Theo," she said,
opening her eyes again. "We can't just leave him there."

"Yes, I know. We're going, first thing in the morning.
We were waiting to make sure you're okay, and to see
what you could tell us about what happened." His eyes
softened and he brushed her cheek. "I'm so glad you're
back, safe, and for the most part, sound."

She looked up at him, into his solemn dark eyes, familiar and warm, and waited. Nothing happened inside
her. Nothing.

He loves you. Give him a chance.

I don't want to give him a chance. I want you, Simon.

I'm not your damned superman.

She closed her eyes, surprised at the renewal of pain—
not from the bump on her head, but from the vicinity of
her heart.

"I'd better let you rest," Theo said, brushing the hair
from her forehead, then leaning forward to press a kiss
there. It was warm and soft, brotherly.

Good idea. Because as soon as he was gone, she was
getting the hell out of there and going down to the computer lab to Yahoogle what she could about Simon Japp
and Tatiana, or Florita . . . and someone named Mancusi.

You don't know me.

But I soon will, Simon Japp.

Theo rose reluctantly, perhaps because Sage made no protest nor suggestion for him to stay. She tried to look weary and in pain, but inside she was straining to get up and out of bed and back to work. There was no time to waste.

He moved slowly toward the door, and she watched him. He was a handsome man, just as well-built and strong as Simon, not quite as tall, but a little more buff. And he had his own special ability—that power-surge thing was kind of sexy. And he loved her. And he was kind and smart as hell and funny.

But he wasn't Simon.

"Theo," she said when his hand was on the doorknob. She had to do it now.

He turned, a flash of hope in his eyes. "Yeah?"

"About your email," she began.

But he held up a hand, his eyes hooding. "I meant to apologize for that. It was inappropriate . . . and not the best timing. I think we should just . . . talk about it later. When you're feeling better. Okay?"

Sage drew in a deep breath to go on, felt a pang in her head, and suddenly felt too tired to press the matter. Even though she probably should. "All right, Theo. Thank you for bringing me back safely. I'm sorry if I sounded like a shrew."

"I would never let anything happen to you," he said, his eyes serious and dark—completely negating his implication a moment ago that they shouldn't talk about their feelings for each other. "Sage, you know I wouldn't."

"I know," she said, and closed her eyes. Feeling like crap inside. He was a good man. She could see the love for her in his eyes . . . and she just didn't feel the same.

Could that change?

If Simon didn't—or wouldn't—come back? Should she do what he suggested and try?

Her instinct, deep in the core of her belly, said no. *There's no contest.*

No contest at all.

Simon had no intention of staying with Florita or letting her slice up any more Sage look-alikes, but he was also smart enough not to go blazing out of there. Although he was heartsick at the death of the young woman, he knew there was nothing he could have done to prevent it.

As soon as she'd been brought into Florita's custody, she was as good as dead. Perhaps it had been better that she was murdered in a fit of pique rather than tortured to death. At least it had been over quickly.

Simon was well aware how long a death could be drawn out.

He wasn't a prisoner in his bedroom, or any room. Florita had made it clear that he could move about as he wanted. "You aren't a prisoner, darling," she'd told him when she got her anger under control. "But if you leave, I'll have those kittens brought to me and start slicing them up, one by one. So know that your freedom will mean their deaths. You may not hear them scream, but you'll know it's happening."

So Simon would bide his time for a day. Maybe two. Pretend to play her game. And save a few more girls from certain death.

Being inside the private residence of a Stranger would give him the opportunity to find out more about them, information that could prove useful, and might lead to more clues about Remington Truth.

And the Cult of Atlantis.

Whatever he found, he'd somehow get the information to them in Envy—even if he never went back there. Which, at this point, was likely. He'd finish up here—he was going to have to kill Florita, he knew it already, and although the thought settled like a knot in his belly, he knew it was the only way. Either she was going to have to die, or *he* was—and although there'd been a time he opted for the latter, that time was long past.

He'd finish up here and get on the road and do his Good Samaritan thing.

And Theo and Sage could be together.

No, he was definitely not going back to Envy.

He prowled around the three-level house, the sound of rushing water following him wherever he went. Every room seemed to have a channel running through it, sometimes a narrow ditch at the edge, sometimes a wider one, and in Florita's bedroom, the water splashed down a wall and was caught in a narrow pool before rushing out of the room through a small aqueduct to the right.

"Come in, my dear Simon," she greeted him as he stood on the threshold.

"You called for me?" he asked. Of course she had.

"Join me," she replied, and he noticed that her eyes glittered brighter than usual. "For dinner, and perhaps a little . . . dessert."

Reluctantly, he came into the room. This was part of the game, for a few more hours. He'd wandered around the place, checking to see what sort of security and guards she had. A few seemed to be normal humans and they would be of no concern to Simon. He found no locked rooms that might contain more prisoners or victims of torture. *Good.* She hadn't replenished her supply from FC yet.

The other two Strangers had been in the lower level,

playing football on Xbox as more ditches of water rushed and gurgled around them.

A ridiculously low-key environment. Mancusi's house had had twice as much security, even when he wasn't there.

Was it because as Strangers, hidden away here behind Hell's Wall, they didn't fear the normal humans? Because they held so much power—and immortality? Or was it because Florita was certain she had Simon under control, due to her threats?

Either way, he kept himself on the alert for any other changes and sat down on the long, flat, low-backed sofa. Upholstered in white with pale pink flowers, and full pink throw pillows, it was the only piece of furniture in the room other than the massive bed. Florita sat at one end, and when he settled, she moved down so she was next to him, close enough that the long flowing blue dress she wore brushed his leg.

She did look lovely, Simon couldn't deny that. Her glossy black hair had been pulled up into a loose, messy sort of bundle, with strands falling randomly. She had a perfect, oval face, with full red lips, gentle cheekbones, and thick, dark lashes—a face that completely belied her manipulative, violent self. The neckline of the gown cut into a deep vee, and her breasts were pushed up enticingly, mounding over the top. Narrow shoulder straps revealed her shoulders, and the immortalizing crystal burning in her skin.

He looked at it, fascinated and repelled at the same time. "So that's what you destroyed the world for," he said, gesturing to her shoulder.

The multifaceted crystal was pale blue, barely tinted, and had been embedded into her skin just below the collarbone, in that tender area of skin near the shoulder.

The stone was about the size of a quarter, larger than his thumbnail, and it glowed brightly enough to shine through thin clothing.

"Isn't it lovely?" she purred, stroking the gem, which was not flush to her skin, but rose in a small dome, perhaps a centimeter high. "Immortality and eternal youth, Simon." She looked at him, her lashes heavy and thick over those shining dark eyes. "I can offer you the same. Just say the word." Her eyes narrowed thoughtfully. "Unless you've already got something else. Simon, how did you manage to be here? You look exactly the same, and not a crystal in sight."

"Talk about a fucking blood diamond," he said, unable and unwilling to hide the disgust in his voice. He had to keep himself from really thinking about what this selfish, violent woman had helped to do, or he would snap her neck right now. But it was too soon. *Patience.*

"It's not a diamond," she said. "It's so much better than that. There's nothing like it on this earth." She stroked his arm and the light scrape of her long nails made him want to shove her away.

"Where did you get it?" he asked. "Where does it come from?"

"Below the earth, deep in the depths." She brought her hand into her lap, spreading it open, palm up, and traced each of his fingers, then down over his wrist to his leather band. "I could get you one," she said again.

Simon forced himself not to snatch his hand away, and to suffer her touch, even though his pulse leapt and jumped and revolted at her proximity. *Soon.*

"How did you do it?" he asked. "Tell me how the Cult of Atlantis destroyed the world."

Now she seemed surprised. Her fingers tightened a bit

over his hand as she held him there in her lap. "How do you know about that? The cult?"

"I told you not to underestimate me."

"Simon, I've never underestimated you. That's why I'm so delighted that you found me. I mean, George was one thing . . . he was such a naughty man . . . but it's always been you that floated me. Ever since we were young."

Hell, she made it sound like they'd grown up together. He hadn't met her till he was twenty-three, and well corrupted. "How did you get to join such an elite group? I understood it was only the cream of the crop, Florita. Why did they let you in?"

Her grip jerked and he saw a flash of annoyance in her eyes. "You forget, Simon, that after I left Mancusi, I became one of the most sought-after, highly paid, and bankable actresses in the world. With Reese and Julia and even Kate." She said their names with loathing. "And look at me now. They're all dead, and here I am, just as beautiful and young fifty years later."

She reached to the long low table in front of them and lifted a shallow black dish among the plates of food and glasses. The dish was empty except for a thin layer of sugar or salt on the bottom and a tiny spoon. "How did you learn about the cult?" she asked again, scooping up a bit of the sugar into her hand.

It glittered in her palm unlike any sugar he'd ever seen. It almost looked like fine diamonds or ground crystals.

"We've learned a lot in the last six months. Where's Parris Fielding? Where do the rest of your . . . kind . . . live?"

"So many, many questions." She curled her fingers tightly around his hand and with the other, carefully dumped the sugar onto the tender skin of his wrist. "Just like I had, when I first joined them. I didn't know what they had in mind, you know. I just knew the prize at the other end. And I was willing to pay anything for it."

"And you didn't give a fuck how you got there, did you?"

She'd begun to rub, gently, in slow motion, over the tendons and shallow blue veins, as if giving him a salt rub—something Simon had experienced exactly once in his life, when Mancusi took all of his "people" to a spa he was thinking about buying and made them test out the services.

But the gritty substance chafed the sensitive skin inside his wrist, and that's when Simon realized—too late—what she was doing. He yanked his hand away, but the coursing sensation of pleasure and heat was already streaming through his body.

"Crystal dust," he said, trying to brush it off his skin, but it did nothing to alleviate the sensations. In fact, the brushing only ground it in more deeply. God, it was *fast*. He felt dizzy and light-headed and . . . *fuck it* . . . instantly, violently aroused. He grabbed her arm and looked, and there was the telltale sign—the red rash on the same place on her arm. "What are you trying to do, Florita?"

"This is so much better than the stuff you used to use," she said. He realized belatedly that the gleam in her eyes was from an artificial high, not merely the triumph and excitement he'd assumed. "It makes everything so much . . . better."

Simon pushed away from her, settling back into his corner of the couch, fighting the sensations rushing through him, the coursing blood. *God, help me.* But he couldn't shake off the familiar edge, the lightness and energy, and the deep, insistent tug at his hormones. Everything became clearer, cleaner, sharper . . . more urgent and frenetic.

He knew a little about crystal dust, or grit, as it was also called—the drug of choice for post-apocalyptic users—but he hadn't known that it was rubbed into the skin, or she would never have gotten so close to him. *Dammit.*

Simon closed his eyes as his veins jumped and his heart rate climbed, and the next thing he knew, Florita was in his lap. Settling her perky ass there right on his shifting cock, her long fingers capturing his face and jaw as she bent forward for a long, deep kiss.

He opened his mouth, he couldn't stop it—she was insistent, and he'd fallen off the wagon so fucking hard he'd landed on his head and was still rolling. Her tongue was sleek and insistent, hungry, and yet, his stomach revolted. His skin crawled even as his fingers itched for something . . . to touch her.

Not her. Christ, not this woman.

Her hands slipped under his shirt, and Simon dragged his mouth away, placing his hands on her shoulders, holding her back. His thumb bumped her crystal. It felt rough and hot under the pad of his finger, and he focused on that for a moment, pushing away the sensations of her hands sliding over his chest, trying to forget that the last woman who'd touched him like that had been Sage.

Sage.

If she could see him now, hot and sweaty, fucked up and high—just the same as he'd always been. His thoughts whirled, his breathing kicked up, and he struggled to concentrate, to focus on something other than his frenetic mind. *Steady.*

Across the room was a window, and beyond it, darkening blue sky. It felt like he was flying, high above the ground . . . hell, he *was* flying.

How long does this shit last?

He counted his breaths, felt Florita's hands moving to the fly of his jeans, the familiar little jerking motions as each of the six buttons popped open. "Ahh," she sighed in his ear, her hands thrusting down into the heat concentrated there.

Simon closed his eyes, gathered his strength, fighting the pleasurable sensations and focusing on the revulsion, centering on the disgust and loathing . . . only that gave him the ability to wrap his fingers around her wrists and pull them out.

"No," he said, focusing as steady a look as he could muster into her glittery eyes. "Not until you tell me more about how you did this. I want to know . . . all about it."

He replaced her hands onto his thighs, and as a consolation prize, so to speak, he rubbed his hands up along her shoulders like a lover would. Trying to keep the loathing from his eyes, trying to appear as if he weren't ready to throw her across the room.

Or out the damned window. The only thing that kept him from doing that was the uncertainty as to whether it would actually kill her or not.

And because he hoped crystal dust made people chatty.

"About what?" she asked, her voice easing into a little purr, leaning toward him as he stroked her chilled arms. Her eyes had become more heavily lidded and her mouth open, glistening and full from the frantic kissing.

Simon rubbed her arms, stroking them gently, forcing himself not to think about what he was doing, how soft her skin was, how her odd scent seemed to curl into his nose . . . how her ass settled and shifted against his cock, now freed from its confines, and with a mind of its own. "This," he said, rubbing his thumb over her crystal.

Florita sighed and gave a little groan as he did so, arching toward him again. Fuck, was it an erogenous zone too?

"How did you do it? What did you do?" he asked again, pressing a reluctant kiss to her jaw.

"I don't know," she said on a little sigh. Her breasts had come out of the dress, and pressed against his shirt, naked and full, nipple-hard and hot. "They did it all, Fielding and Truth and the others. We just helped prepare."

"Prepare?" Hard enough for a guy to ignore breasts crushing against him, harder when they were naked and she was grinding her ass into his crotch and he was flying higher than he'd ever flown.

Sage. Think of Sage.

And her lovely, innocent face, freckled lip and all, slid into his mind . . . centered him. Her klutziness . . . her brilliant mind, with the secret pages in the back of that book, her trusting gaze. She'd *trusted* him.

He felt the spiking in his body calm, the tension ebb . . . and Simon accepted, at that moment, when the mere thought of Sage became his refuge, when she became his talisman . . . that there would never be anyone else for him.

"Money. Funds. Information." Florita pulled away, this time arching back so that he had a full view of the breasts half the world had seen on the big screen—she had a ring in one nipple; that was new. At least, from the last time she'd flashed them at him.

"Money?" He looked away from her offerings, a bitter taste in the back of his throat.

"The buy-in was fifty million American dollars," she bragged. "Just to get into the club. And it was only by invitation."

"And your goons, your other friends below? Did they have fifty mill each too?" he said.

Florita laughed. "Oh, no, no . . . they're my pets. I created them about thirty years ago. But I'd throw them both over for you, Simon."

She shifted on his lap and her fingers began to slip lower again, her lips coming closer. Simon tensed, the room spinning a bit and the colors in this pale chamber turning deeper and more vibrant as he tried to concentrate. *Fuck, is it getting stronger?*

"Who was the leader? Of the club?" he managed to say as she closed around him again. His breath caught and he felt a trickle of sweat run down his spine, and another one gathering at the back of his neck. "Truth? Fielding?"

"Oh, it was Truth . . . until he betrayed everyone." She covered his mouth with a sloppy kiss that helped distract him from what her hands were trying to do . . . and he pulled away from her lips, yanking her hands up once again.

"Florita," he said, half groaning, half warning.

"Stop calling me that," she ordered. "I'm Tatiana!"

"Truth betrayed everyone?" he asked, trying to get her back on track, trying to hold her off until the grit wore off . . . however long that would be. "What happened?"

"I dunno," she murmured, her voice thick and her hands tugging at his shirt. "I want to see you without this on, Simon. There's no need to be shy. Leonide is long gone. There's no one between us now."

There's never going to be anyone between us because there will never be an us.

"So you bought in with fifty million, and then what? Immortality after all hell breaks loose? Where did the crystals come from? Are they electronic?"

She laughed uproariously, as if he'd said the most amusing thing, tipping her head back to show a long, white throat that, instead of being sexually inviting made him want to snap it in payment for all her sins. But even now . . . he didn't. "Not electronic. They were payment to us, the cult. For helping."

"Helping what?" he pressed when she suddenly stopped.

Her gaze turned crafty. "I can't tell you that." She giggled. "Or I could, but I'd have to kill you if I did."

Her eyes had turned wild and dark, and she was panting by now. She'd become more sloppy and slappy in her movements than sleek and controlled.

"How about something to drink?" he suggested desperately. Anything to get her off his lap, to give him a chance to fight off the hold of the crystal grit.

"Old habits, hmm, Simon?" she said, staggering a bit as she pulled to her feet.

"Right," he agreed, drawing in a deep breath, trying to break his mind through the sparkly fog that had gripped him. *Get the fuck out of here.*

He looked around the room, seeking something he could use to slice the crystal out of her skin. No knives in sight. He wondered if she still wore the one she'd had on her body earlier, when she'd slit the Sage look-alike's throat.

But he couldn't. He couldn't do it. There had to be another way.

The clink of a bottle and glasses drew his attention, and he saw that she'd poured two short drinks of a rich golden color. To his horror, saliva sprang to his mouth and the desire flashed through him like a runaway train. His fingers trembled as he curled them into his lap.

He *needed* it. He needed that so badly . . . to take the edge off.

No . . . steady, Simon. You're already on the edge.

But when she brought the glasses over, and he smelled the Scotch, his heart began to slam in his chest and his mouth watered even more. Swallowing hard, he closed his eyes, lifting the glass to slam it down his throat, already relishing the heat, the golden feeling that would fill him . . .

He tightened his fingers around the glass and slowly dragged it away from the temptation of his nose and mouth, eyes opening and fastened on it as if they had the strength to bring it back. Somehow, somehow, he managed to set it on the table next to him. But he couldn't make his fingers relinquish the glass, the smooth, cool object that held his desire.

This was it. It was all he could take.

Still gripping the glass, he looked around the room, desperate for a weapon that could hold her off. He was done with her, done with the games. He had to get the hell out of here before she completely destroyed him.

Then she leaned forward, forcing a kiss once again, but this time, she tasted of ambrosia, of manna . . . of Scotch . . . dark and heavy and smooth . . . he tasted it, inhaled it, felt the wave of desire again, and pulled her close to get every bit of it from her mouth, her tongue . . . the room closed in on him and he lifted the glass in his hand, bringing it closer even as he knew nothing but the feel of his own breath, the measure of his own pulse.

And then, with a sharp, violent movement, he gave it up, slammed the glass back down on the table, hard enough to shatter it in his palm, sending shards digging into his skin and clattering onto the floor.

Out of breath, but in control, he opened his eyes and pulled away from Florita, and realized dimly that he held half the glass in his hand. Broken in half, edges jagged, the thick bottom cracked too . . . it was the weapon he'd been looking for.

He had it in his hand. All he had to do was bring it down, slam the curved, jagged edges into her skin and cut out the crystal . . .

All he had to do to end this . . . was to kill her. In cold blood. Right here. Now.

No remorse. No second thoughts. No regrets.

But *no. No.* That was no longer him.

Simon pulled away, shoving her off his lap. Stumbling to his feet, he banged against the table. Glasses clinked and crashed.

With a shriek of fury, she lunged after him, and he spun her from his side, pushed at those clawing hands. He dropped the broken glass and backed away. "Don't touch me," he growled, meeting her eyes, steadying himself. The pleasure still trammeled through his veins, and his heart beat erratically. The room tilted, shimmered.

Florita's face turned dark, her eyes still lit with false light from the grit. "You have no choice, Simon," she said. The purr was gone from her voice; it was as ragged as the glass that lay at his feet.

"Keep your murderous hands away from me."

"People who live in glass houses . . ." Florita replied, breathing heavily. She moved suddenly, whirling away toward the wall, and the next thing he knew, she had a blade in her hand again. Her eyes glowed brightly with possession and greed. She smiled. "If I can't have you, no one will."

Simon stood there, breathing heavily as she lunged toward him. He stumbled out of the way, still slow and unsteady, the room expanding and contracting at the edges of his vision. He felt the slice of the blade on his arm, the heat bursting over his skin.

Whirling, staggering he whipped his arm around, catching her off balance. But she was strong and somehow steadier, and the long blade scored the back of his shoulder. He roared in pain and anger and whipped around, hands grasping, closing over her throat in a heartbeat.

She looked up at him as he fought to catch his breath.

The point of the sword rested against his belly. "You can't kill me," Florita reminded him with that sly smile.

"I wouldn't be so certain of that," he replied, tightening his fingers and looking at her crystal.

She edged the point deeper against his shirt, through to his skin. A simple thrust, and it would be over. "Come now, Simon. You'll enjoy it. I promise. You and me." She reached up and stroked his damp cheek.

Simon closed his eyes, focusing on the metal pricking his belly, not on her poisonous touch. Over at last. Freedom. *Do it. Put me out of my fucking misery.*

Then . . . *Sage.* Her face blossomed in his mind, her sun-bright hair and gentle, freckled smile, pragmatic expression.

If there was a chance . . . any chance at all . . .

Galvanized, strengthened, he shoved Florita away with every bit of strength he had. She flew through the air, crashing against the wall, settling half onto the water trough like a broken doll.

He knew she wasn't dead, but he didn't wait, wasn't about to find out. Gathering every bit of his composure, pulling his strength and fighting off the high, he shimmered into nothing.

CHAPTER 15

You don't know me.

Well, she did now.

Sage settled back into her computer chair, the pounding in the back of her skull having shifted to the slamming of her heart. Her stomach felt tight and unpleasant, and bitterness settled in the back of her throat.

Simon Japp, the man who'd been so tender and kind and *good* to her had been a bodyguard for one of the most powerful and violent mobsters in Los Angeles. Bodyguard, she was pretty sure, being a euphemism for . . . well, hired gun. Thug.

Bottom line . . . he'd lived a life of violence. He was a killer.

That explained a lot of things. An awful lot of things. The way he'd acted when he dragged away the man who'd attacked her—murderous and lethal. His familiarity with knives—lecturing her on cleaning the blade after she sliced up the wolf. The way he handled himself in tense situations.

And, in general, the dark, dangerous undercurrents of his persona.

Those hands . . . those violent, capable, elegant hands that had caressed and stroked and loved her had taken lives. Had probably pulled triggers, or held knives, or even, maybe, killed all on their own.

She could hardly comprehend it, hardly mesh the Simon she knew with the man he'd been.

You don't know me.

That was what he meant. She understood now.

If only she could figure out what he meant about being her superman. Her hero?

The soft *ding* announcing a new arrival drew Sage's attention from her whirlwind of thoughts back to the computer screen. She clicked quickly away from a photo of Leonide Mancusi, his mistress—at that time known as Florita Tatiane—and the mobster's bodyguard . . . a fierce, dark, younger-looking Simon Japp.

Even in the photo, she could see the torment in his eyes.

"Sage," said Theo. "What are you doing down here? I thought you were going to stay in bed for a while."

Great. Theo. Just what she needed right now.

Give him a chance. He's a good man . . . a far better man than me.

"What's wrong?" he asked, obviously recognizing the trauma on her face. She hadn't been crying or anything, but he knew her. He loved her. He'd be able to read her . . . just as she'd begun to be able to read Simon.

"Nothing . . . just tired, and a little headachey," she said.

Give him a chance.

Should she? Now that Simon had made it clear where his loyalties lay? Obviously he'd known Tatiana. They'd had some sort of relationship . . . and she wanted him back, and he'd gone to her.

Hadn't he? It was all a blur, now, after her head injury. Had he been willing?

All she knew was that he hadn't stayed with her. And that he was with Tatiana.

Maybe the torment on his face in the photo was due to the fact that his boss had the woman he loved, and he had to look on in misery.

Maybe now that he'd found Tatiana again, he really was exultant and happy. A man who'd lived the violent life he had wouldn't be bothered by the fact that she was a Stranger . . . a person who'd helped create the Change.

Maybe Theo and Wyatt and Quent would find him happily ensconced with the gorgeous actress when they went after him in the morning.

Or maybe she was making up stories to ease her broken heart, to pump herself full of anger at him for sending her away.

"Sage?" Theo had come to stand next to her chair, and she spun to face him, jolted from her circular mental arguments. "Are you sure you're all right?"

She stood up. Maybe she should just forget about Simon. She had a man right here who loved her, whose past was clean and clear and admirable. After all, he and Lou had been the spearheads of rebuilding Envy and helping to create a new civilization.

"Theo, would you think it strange if I asked you to kiss me? Just . . . without anything else? Just a kiss?"

He let out his breath in a *whoosh* and dragged her up out of the chair, folding her against him. "Of course I wouldn't. I was so afraid that I'd scared you off, with that stupid email I sent . . ."

He closed his arms around her and bent his head to meet her upraised lips. Their mouths met, his gentle at first, then hungry and insistent . . . hers opening willingly, curiously . . . even desperately.

Desperate to taste him and erase the one who'd come

before, hopeful and willing . . . but in the end, defeated. Because it was a nice kiss.

A nice one that made her pleasantly warm—but not weak-kneed and light-headed or hot and trembly and breathless. It didn't make her feel comfort and safety, as if she'd come home, as if she was exactly where she needed . . . and wanted . . . to be.

Sage pulled gently away, her hand resting at the side of his face. "Theo," she said, aware that he was out of breath, that his eyes were hot and avid and that she was about to throw a bucket of cold water all over him, "I . . ." She sighed and stepped back, bumping into the computer chair and knocking it into the table with a little clunk. "I don't feel . . . the same way you do." She pushed out the last few words in a rush, watching the change in his face.

His eyes shuttered and turned empty, his face, which had been slack with desire, tightened and stilled. "Is it Simon?" Then he muttered something nasty under his breath, his eyes blazing.

"Theo, no. It was even before we left for Falling Creek. I didn't feel the way I sensed you felt. I didn't realize it at the time, I mean, how you felt, but I knew something was changing. And it made me . . . uncomfortable, sort of."

"I never meant to pressure you, or make you feel uncomfortable," he said. Misery laced his voice, his dark eyes remained blank. But the corner of his mouth had twisted into a deep crease and she knew he was hurting.

"You didn't pressure me. You didn't do anything wrong, Theo. I care about you very much. You're my oldest and best friend, but I don't feel the sort of emotion you feel for me. You're more like a brother than . . . a . . . a lover."

His hands fell away from where they'd slipped to her shoulders, as if they'd been trying to hold her close to him, knowing she was backing away. "Sage, I've loved you for years. I'd hoped for a long time that you might see me as more than an old man, more than a friend."

She felt as though he'd punched her in the stomach. *Years?*

"Won't you give this . . . us . . . a chance? I know the idea is new to you, but it might just be the newness of it that's got you confused." *And now that Simon is out of the picture . . .*

He didn't say it, but she knew he was thinking it . . . because she couldn't help but think it herself.

"Theo . . . I don't know. I don't want to hurt you. I just . . ."

"Shh." He put a finger to her lips, gently, and said, "Let's end this conversation here and . . . just let it go. Okay?"

She nodded, afraid to meet his eyes, but forcing herself to do so. Such deep pain there, such darkness.

"So," he said, stepping back, his face shifting into something that resembled normalcy even though his movements were stiff. "Redlow. I haven't had a chance to catch you up on things, you being out cold and all." He tried to smile, but she could see what it cost him.

"You found it?"

He nodded, but before he could continue, the quiet *ding* sounded, and the sounds of multiple voices and pairs of feet trooped down the circular staircase.

Sage couldn't help a mental sigh of relief that there was now a buffer between her and Theo.

Quent led the way, followed by Wyatt and Lou. The sight of the handsome blond man had Sage realizing with a start that she had something for him. But Theo had already begun to talk, explaining that they were just about to debrief on Redlow.

"Quent, do you want to check something for me?" she

asked, pulling the thing that Simon told her was an identification badge, the plastic thing with Remington Truth's
picture on it, out of her pocket. "Can you tell me if this
belonged to Remington Truth?"

He didn't hesitate, sitting down in her computer chair
and then reaching for the badge. She handed it to him and
he closed his eyes, frantic, ugly emotions running across
his face. He appeared to be in pain, and she glanced at
Wyatt, who seemed to be monitoring the situation.

Moments later, he opened his eyes, pitching the badge
onto the desk with effort, as if he couldn't wait to get rid
of it. His eyes were haunted, his face tight with pain.

He spoke rapidly, like gunfire. "It's his. And it also belonged to a woman. Dark hair. Blue eyes. Young. But it
was definitely his first. For a long time."

"What else?" Wyatt said.

Quent drew in a breath that shook audibly. "He was
a bloody fucked-up wank. Most of what I got was anger
and guilt and horror. Power. Desire. He was suicidal, I
think. A brilliant man, but suicidal. It was all a blur, a
horrible, horrifying fucked-up tornado of shite. He—or
at least that ID badge—lived through some fucked-up
times. I couldn't stay there long enough to peel it away, to
understand it. It's too . . . horrible."

"Thank you," Sage said, brushing Quent's shoulder
lightly with her hand. He trembled beneath her, and she
got a sense of intense loneliness from that simple touch,
and that he wasn't used to comfort. "I'm sorry, I didn't
realize it would be so difficult for you."

She looked up and found Theo eyeing her, and she gave
Quent's shoulder a little rub, then withdrew her hand. She
glanced at Lou, who was unusually quiet.

"No," Quent replied, "no. That's my . . . contribution to
this whole battle against these bastards. We have to find

them, and destroy them, right? It's not going to be easy, and I'll do whatever I have to do."

He swiped his honey blond hair off his forehead, and she saw a bit of the tension ease from his eyes. His voice became stronger, and she got the impression that he might have been a good orator . . . in his previous life. "We're here for a reason—me, Wyatt, Dred—and Simon and Fence too. None of us are the men we were when we went into those caves in Sedona. For whatever reason, the universe protected us, brought us here. Who knows, maybe we even traveled through time. Ever hear of string theory? It's possible. But here we are, larger than life, different . . . reborn in a way, I guess. And the way I see it," he said, sitting up straight, now his expression determined, "we have a responsibility to do what we can—to destroy the Strangers, and whoever else annihilated everything that we knew and loved." And there, his voice cracked, just a bit, at the very end.

Silence reigned for a moment, and Sage almost felt like she needed to clap. Instead, she glanced over at Wyatt, who'd turned away and was looking—glaring—at the floor. His broad shoulders were unmoving.

"Right, then," Quent said, a little more subdued after his outburst. "I think I can handle the mental assault of a few bad memories that I can discard at any time—let alone didn't have to live through. It's part of the deal." He smiled up at Sage and she blinked back a bit of dampness in her eyes. "But thank you for your concern."

And thank you for that little speech. I really needed to hear that.

"So," interrupted Theo. His voice sounded a little steely, drawing Sage's gaze, but he wasn't looking at her. "We're going after Simon, then should we follow up on this Redlow lead? They're in the same area. Since the ID badge definitely belonged to Truth, he may have given it to this dark-haired woman. She may have been the last person to see him—at least four years ago."

"We find Simon first. Then we go to Redlow," said Wyatt flatly. "I'm fucking tired of waiting around here scratching my ass. Let's get something done."

"I'm going too," Quent said. "I'll be able to identify the woman if she's there, or possibly determine whether she's been."

"In the morning, as planned," Lou reminded them, speaking up for the first time. Sage couldn't help but notice the way his attention had gone from her to his brother and back again, several times, during the course of the discussion. "It's getting late and it's been a long day."

"I'll go too," Sage said.

"Haven't you had enough adventures?" Theo asked. "What about your head?"

She ignored him to say, "I'm the only one who knows my way around FC."

"You said Simon went back voluntarily," Quent said.

"I'm not sure how voluntarily it was," Sage replied, acknowledging the truth. "It was more like he offered himself as a hostage. To save the city." She tried not to show her worry. She might be furious with him, but she— well, heck. She might as well admit why her heart was so broken. She loved him.

But Simon was able to take care of himself. Especially since the man could turn invisible. How could anyone catch him if he didn't want them to? He could do anything he wanted and never be caught.

Her stomach felt tight again. She hoped.

"We leave first thing in the morning," Wyatt said in a voice that brooked no argument. "Makes sense for Sage to come with us," he added, giving Theo a curt look.

"I'm going to go up and get some sleep," she said, suddenly needing to be alone . . . to think. She rubbed the back of her head for emphasis. "Don't leave without me." She looked at Quent when she said it, and then Lou, considering them the most sympathetic people in the room. They both nodded.

At the top of the circular stairs, she pushed the buttons that opened the old elevator doors and started the walk back to the flights of stairs that would take her to her room. She passed the Pub, briefly considering a stop in there—where Jade happened to be singing for the after-dinner crowd. She saw Elliott sitting in the front row, as always, and the mayor of Envy, Vaughn Rogan, who'd had a big thing for Jade before Elliott came along, sitting in the corner.

But she didn't want company.

Nor, Sage decided, was she quite ready to return to her room.

Instead, she went outside, glad to get into the relative quiet of the night. Low voices and the sounds of people walking along the old sidewalks and trimmed pathways reached her ears. The natural light was dim, for the moon waned and was now a mere quarter. Only a few nights ago, she and Simon had sneaked to the abandoned house to set up the NAP, under much brighter light.

Ah, Simon.

Was he with Tatiana now? Happy, reunited with and old friend . . . maybe a lover? She had to accept it was a possibility. It wasn't like she'd missed the tension between the two of them during their confrontation at dinner.

Yet . . . it just didn't fit. It didn't feel right to her . . . meshing with the Simon *she* knew. Not the Simon he'd *been*. Fifty years ago, in a completely different world.

None of us are the same men we were when we went into those caves in Sedona.

Even Simon.

Especially Simon. She had to believ—

Suddenly, a strong hand clamped around her mouth, and an arm around her waist, and Sage was being dragged back into the shadows. She kicked and fought, but he was too strong. Something heavy and dark whuffed over her head and she was wrapped up in it, bound and roped and completely stifled.

She couldn't breathe well through the heavy material, and the world around her grew murky as she was lifted and carried . . . and then she felt her consciousness slide away, leaving her in darkness.

No blood on his hands.

Not this time.

Simon's head ached from the high slamming down, his body hurt from being cranked out of his mind. But at least he had a clean conscience.

In the end, he hadn't needed to slice into Florita's skin, hacking the crystal out of her body, smashing its fiber-opticlike tendrils that snaked into her muscles and tendons, embedding it in place. The Xbox junkies had done it for him.

Florita had tried to pull to her feet, but she was out of it and in pain. Apparently Strangers could be slowed down, but not permanently eliminated without taking their crystal. Simon, still trying to clear his own mind, ignored her, invisible and *free*, and did a quick search.

He'd left the waterfall home in Rita's humvee, after hunting down the four humans and two Strangers left over. The SIG Sauer 229 he had in his hand, one he'd found after searching Florita's room, felt horribly familiar, comforting even, had set the mortals scuttling into the corners. He casually waved the gun, then left them to piss their pants.

And the other two Strangers . . . Florita's "pets"—Simon had spared the Xbox junkies too.

No wonder Florita had been bored with them. At one time, they might have been handsome, interesting young men, probably in the prime of early twenties when she crystaled them. But after thirty lazy years of Xbox, iPod, and an infinite collection of DVDs—after growing up in a post-Change world where those things didn't exist in such wealth—and knowing they had an infinite life of such monotony, they had become soft and slow.

Yet, they hadn't been part of the cult, and in his mind, they needed to take no responsibility for their actions. He warned them that the crystal guard must remain in place over Falling Creek and when they learned that Tatiana was incapacitated, and that they needed to fear nothing from Simon, they raced up to her.

As he left, Simon heard her screams for mercy and realized that Tatiana's pets had revolted. Too much Mortal Kombat, apparently.

His arm still burned and tingled from the grit, and his mouth watered for the heat of Scotch. He found himself rubbing his wrist, as if trying to score any last crystal dust into his skin.

Was he on his way back? Or could he wade through it?

Was he strong enough?

Simon started the truck and drove away, back down the cliff in the dark, checking to be certain that the crystal guard was still glowing blue. From what he'd learned from the Xbox junkies, the guard was more or less permanent—the earlier threat of it being removed had simply been a trick by Tatiana, and implemented by the junkies in order to catch Simon.

Probably the first time they'd done anything interesting for a decade. Besides kill their mistress.

So, Simon could believe that Falling Creek would be safe . . . although he was going to stop in and warn the settlement leaders to keep watch on the blue glow.

And then . . . what would he do?

Sage's face flashed into his mind once again, and he settled on it for a moment. Just a moment. His fingers tightened over the steering wheel. Then he pushed the thought away. Tempting, oh, so damned tempting. What would it be like to wake up next to her every morning?

To have a normal, solid life?

Simon shook his head. "No." He said it aloud, to himself. Though the Sedona cave had given him a new chance, he still couldn't erase his bloody past. He could make amends for it, but he couldn't eradicate it. How could someone like Sage be with someone who'd done the things he'd done?

Never.

And he'd have to tell her. To show her, so she'd understand who he was. He could imagine the expression, the crumpled expression on her face, the shock and fear that would come into her eyes. The blank look on her face.

No. Not a fucking chance.

Simon sat in the vehicle, the engine rumbling low and sleek, its headlights cutting into the darkness. Not a sign of orange *ganga* eyes anywhere, although he had seen the golden glitter of some feral predator slinking into the dark. Falling Creek lay ahead, glowing in its warm, comfortable lights. Creepy and unsettling though the place was, he couldn't and wouldn't judge its residents.

Because he, of all people, wouldn't stand up to anyone's judgment.

Yet, as he looked at the small village, he couldn't quite ignore the large house that sat, dark and empty, at the north side of the settlement. Where he and Sage had been together.

He gritted his teeth. No sense reliving that.

No sense wondering what she was doing now . . . if she and Theo were back in Envy, or if they'd stopped for the night somewhere.

And that, he definitely didn't want to think about.

So he considered his other options . . . and tried to sleep.

Quent knew it was too soon, but he walked outside anyway. They were leaving for Redlow in the morning, and would be gone who knew how long.

And, just in case . . . well, *fuck*. He didn't know when he'd be back.

The night air still carried a bit of the day's humidity, and, as was his habit . . . as he'd learned to do . . . he walked away from the well-traveled paths most people took. Sticking to the shadows, he tried not to spend all his time looking up for slender shadows that moved about with great daring and agility. And that had quivers of arrows that slid and clunked over their shoulders.

But he did.

Bugger it, he was one fucked-up knobber.

He walked for maybe fifteen minutes, concentrating on keeping his mind blank from those horrible memories belonging to Remington Truth. One could almost feel sorry for the man.

If he hadn't been the architect of the Change.

And that was one thing that Quent had sensed from the memories. That the man they sought—the one the Strangers and the *gangas* and now he and his friends were moving mountains to find—that man had been instrumental in the catastrophic events.

Something whooshed silently in front of him and Quent froze, his heard pounding. He didn't look up; instead, he followed the sound, and found an arrow embedded in the ground just in front of him. From its angle it looked as if it hadn't come from too high . . . maybe one story above. Possibly two, at the outside.

"Watch it," he said up into the darkness. "You almost shot me."

Her snort wafted down. "If I wanted to shoot you, I fucking would have."

He smiled, his heart suddenly considerably lighter. "Why don't you come down here and retrieve your arrow." He put a whole lot of meaning into that suggestion.

There was a faint shift above, barely audible, and something like a pebble or clump of dirt dropped from wherever she was sitting. "I thought you'd want to know . . . the woman. The Corrigan woman. Someone took her."

Quent peered up, squinting in the darkness, all thoughts—well, most thoughts—of coaxing her down here evaporating. "What?"

"I saw it. I was too far away to get there in time. He was fast, and he's got her. I'm pretty sure they left Envy, in one of those machines."

"Machine?"

"You know, those damn driving things."

"Which direction? Any idea where they were going?"

"Northeast."

"What did he look like? The man who took her?"

"I recognized him. It was Ian Marck."

The son of a bitch.

"How do you know Ian Marck?" he asked, wishing like hell she would step into what little bit of moonlight there was. So he could see her.

"I know who he is." A pause. "And his father."

Then it hit him. "Was that who you wanted to talk to the other night, at the party? The reason you disappeared?"

"Nosy bastard, aren't you?"

"Zoë . . ." His neck was hurting from craning back so hard. "Come down here."

Her raspy little laugh trickled down. "You've got work to do." More sounds of movement above, and another little tumble of dirt. Then, "Make damn sure you wear a bandanna when you go after her. Don't need any fucking *gangas* grabbing you, 'cause I won't be around to rescue your ass this time."

Quent couldn't help but smile. "You could come with me."

"Get the hell out of here."

"Thank you for telling me about Sage."

"You can thank me later."

"Is that a promise?"

She snorted again, but it sounded farther away. "Can't you come up with any original lines?"

"The sound of your voice makes me crazy. How's that?"

Nothing. He smiled again, though, because he heard a little choked sound that might have been a surprised gasp. In a good way.

Just wait till he got his hands on her again. And it would happen soon . . . because she'd be coming after her arrow again.

He knew it for a fact. "Just so you know," he called up into the darkness, "I'm taking the arrow *with* me. So you'll have to wait till I get back to get it."

"Wear a fucking bandanna."

CHAPTER 16

At last, the darkness lifted and Sage dragged her eyes open amid renewed pounding in her head.

About that time, she realized her arms were bound in front of her. And that she was half slumped, half sitting on a seat that rumbled beneath her.

In a vehicle? Yes. The terrain whizzed by beyond the window. Her cheek rested on the edge of the door, jolting with every little—or big—bump.

It was daylight and she closed her eyes, head throbbing and body bouncing in its seat. *Oh, God, I hope I'm not going to be sick.*

When she was brave enough to open her eyes again, she looked to the left and saw the man who'd talked to her the night of the festival—Ian Marck. He glanced over at her briefly, then he turned his attention back to his driving.

"I need to stop," she said, her stomach pitching violently. Between the knock on the head, the motion sickness, and her fear, she wasn't going to make it much farther. "Or I'm going to make a mess."

He looked back at her and must have seen the alarm in her face, for he stopped the truck quickly—and the jerking halt was almost as bad as if he'd kept going. Sage closed her eyes, gulping air, trying to regain control of herself. She did not want to puke in front of this guy. That would sort of ruin her whole idea of being strong and fearless.

When she opened her eyes again, she found herself looking into the barrel of a gun. Her stomach dropped and her mouth dried, and, amazingly, all of her nausea evaporated.

"This is as good a place as any," he said.

"For what?"

"What did you find out in Falling Creek? About Remington Truth?"

She opened her mouth, then closed it. Falling Creek. He knew she'd gone there . . . because he'd sent her there. Conveniently gave her the clue. And used her Corrigan blood. Jerk.

Although "jerk" was a pretty weak word for a guy who had a gun on her. And who looked ready to use it. Asshole.

"You think you and your friends are the only people looking for Truth?" he said, his blue-gray eyes cold. "Do you know how long I've been waiting to find a way into Falling Creek? Now tell me what the hell you found out."

"Are you going to kill me?" she asked, her heart beating so fast she could hardly form the words. She might have thoughts filled with bravado, but she wasn't brave enough to talk that way. *I need to find Simon first, asshole.*

He didn't reply, just brandished the gun a little more threateningly. Closer to her face. She swore she could smell the cold metal. "I'm not a very patient man. What did you find out?"

"Truth's not there," she said. "Is that where you're taking me? To Falling Creek?"

Once again, he said nothing, but she suspected that a trip to FC had been his plan. "What else? I know there's something there. Tell me what you know." He wasn't asking nicely.

"There's nothing else."

A loud click sounded. Ominous. And though she'd never been around a real gun before, Sage had seen enough movies to know what that noise portended.

"I have no patience for lies," he told her. "I'm going to count to three. And then I'm going to lose my patience. One . . ."

"Someone who knew Remington Truth was going to a place called Redlow."

His chilly eyes scraped over her. The man might be considered handsome if those eyes weren't so empty and cold. And he weren't holding a gun in his hand. "What do you know about this someone?"

She shook her head. "A woman. With dark hair. That's it. That's all I know."

"It seems like every time you say 'that's all' there's something more," he said in an unfriendly tone. "I know where Redlow is. You can come with me. That way you'll be able to help find this woman. Or . . . not."

Sage swallowed hard, feeling the motion sickness return with full force. The "or . . . not" part was very clear: she had to help him find the woman, or she was going to be hurting.

Probably even dead.

Asshole.

Simon might have laughed when he reached the settlement of Redlow and realized how it had gotten its name . . . if he weren't so weary and sick at heart.

As it was, when he saw the familiar letters still hanging from a building that had once said RED LOBSTER, complete with the iconic red creature, he couldn't contain a brief roll of the eyes. RED LO was all that was left.

He'd awakened this morning cramped in the front seat of the humvee, sun streaming down, magnified by the window glass so that he was hot and sweaty by the time he awoke. He'd left the windows closed and doors locked overnight in case of curious *gangas*.

Simon had had a quick wash-up in the river that flowed near Falling Creek and gave it much of its electrical power. He figured it was probably the particular geographic formation that had given its name to this neighborhood once upon a time. Or perhaps the neighborhood had been built first, and the falling creek created to go along with it.

And while he was in the water, which felt so cool and cleansing after the stuffy night in the humvee and the even more stifling day with Florita, Simon decided he needed to follow up on Sage's lead about the woman who'd had Truth's ID badge.

When he stopped in Falling Creek to let the community leaders, whose names he never really knew and easily forgot, know about the crystal guard, he also got directions to Redlow.

And here he was.

What had obviously once been a parking lot for the large store and the restaurant was a familiar sight—overgrown with trees and bushes, grass sprouting up from the wide cracks in the old concrete. But here, in a row, was lined up about a half dozen semi-truck trailers, and perpendicular to the former parking lot was a single row of about six townhouses. Still intact and looking fairly well kept. A small little settlement that had probably sprung up some time after the Change, built around the scavengeable items in the grocery store and even in the restaurant.

There was no protective fence around this village—either to keep the *gangas* out or the people in, and he wondered about that. Maybe they took other precautions, like locking their doors and not going out at night, living on the second floor, where *gangas* couldn't get to.

He was glad he'd parked the truck he'd taken from Rita out of sight of the settlement, behind a cluster of trees. Since most people equated vehicles with the Strangers, he hadn't wanted to jeopardize his chances of getting information.

A dog barked, deep and low, in the distance, and a small group of children played on a pile of salvaged semi-truck tires. Just another day on Main Street USA—or the closest thing to it now. A few people walked about, going about their business, looking at him curiously as he approached from the distance. But he was a single man, hardly a threat and more of a curiosity, he supposed.

His lips curled humorlessly. What were the chances they'd find this woman, who *might* have been coming here four years ago, and who *might* have known Remington Truth? It was such a slim lead, he wondered why he was wasting his time.

But he knew why. And it had less to do with finding Remington Truth than . . . other things.

Just then, as he walked closer to the small settlement, he noticed another humvee, parked behind a sag-roofed garage with full bushes sprouting from roof and windows. His instincts went on high alert, and he detoured over to the vehicle. The windows were tinted, so he couldn't see whether it was occupied, so he approached cautiously.

Right away he knew it wasn't the truck used by the Resistance, which had been his first thought. Hope. That they might already be here, following up on the same lead. But this one didn't sport the dent in the passenger side, nor the scratch along the back.

It was in much better shape.

Simon sneaked up to the truck from behind, wondering if there were Strangers inside, and wondered what would happen if he put a bullet into their crystals. Would that kill them? He gripped the SIG, crouching as he came up to the passenger door, readied himself, and flung it open, gun pointing in instantly.

The vehicle was empty and Simon climbed in, shutting the door behind him, figuring he'd take a look around. A few water bottles in the back, a pack of food, some clothes . . . someone was on the road.

He found a box of pistol magazines under the driver's seat. Fucker had a gun, and since it wasn't in the truck, it had to be with him. On the floor were some ropes that looked like they'd been cut off something. His mind humming, Simon searched further . . . then suddenly a faint glint, very faint, hardly noticeable, stopped him. Hair on the dash, caught in the sun . . . a few very long, curly, reddish-golden-pink hairs that made him go cold.

No. There were lots of Corrigans nearby; Falling Creek was only a couple hours away. It didn't have to be Sage's—unlikely to be Sage's. But it could be.

Simon backed out of the truck and closed the door, adrenaline pumping. No one was about, and he adjusted the SIG in the back of his waistband, making sure it was easily reached, and hidden by his untucked shirt.

He did not like the feel of this.

He swiped the keys that had been hidden under the

driver's side mat and pocketed them, hurrying off toward
the settlement. As he approached, he controlled his expression, one that he knew could be frightening when he
was on alert as he was now, and made certain to exude
calm and casualness when he asked if anyone had seen a
woman with long reddish hair.

A young man pointed him in the direction of the semi-
truck trailers, then went back to weeding a small patch of
carrots and green beans. At least, that's what he thought
they were . . . Simon hadn't spent much time in a garden.

Keeping his movements casual, he nevertheless hurried toward the semi-trucks and asked a few more people
on the way. The truck trailers had been outfitted with
windows, or their doors were wide open, for it was much
too hot and stuffy to be closed up.

Simon shimmered into invisibility and sidled up to one
of the vehicles, looking inside. Just an old woman sitting
on a bed while two young children played in front of her.

The next one was empty of people, but obviously was
used as a home. But the third one . . . Simon stood at the
end of the truck, looking in through the wide opening
and stared in shock. Then cold, black fury washed over
him, nearly shaking his invisibility with its force. But he
held on.

And he reached for his SIG.

It was fucking Ian Marck . . . and *Sage*. Marck had his
gun jammed into the soft part of her neck, and he had a
grip on her arm that, even from where he stood, Simon
could see the white marks emanating from around his
fingers.

"I'm tired of playing games," Marck said, and Sage
gave a soft little grunt as he shoved the gun harder. They
were alone in the truck, which appeared to have been

abandoned some time ago. Furnishings and debris cluttered the area as if no one had lived there for a while. "Tell me who this woman is, and quit leading me around in circles."

Simon had already moved into the truck. It was almost too easy, too ridiculously easy, after everything he'd been through . . . but there he was, gun to the back of Marck's head before he even realized it.

But when Simon kissed the back of Marck's skull with the nose of his SIG, the man froze. "Give me one good reason why I shouldn't drop you right here," Simon said, shimmering back into visibility.

"What the *fuck*?" Marck said. "Where the hell did you come from?"

"Let her go and drop the gun. I won't say it twice."

"Simon," Sage squeaked. He wasn't sure if it was surprise, delight, or horror.

Marck didn't move, and Simon pushed the barrel harder. "You got a death wish, *chavala*?"

"You have no fucking idea," Marck said wearily. And he released Sage, raising his hands.

"Drop the weapon," Simon told him. *Fuckhead.* "Slowly. To the floor." Hell, he sounded like a damned cop.

He trained his weapon on Marck as the other man crouched to drop the gun, then lifted it slowly with him, and only then did he move around into the other man's view. He'd cast a quick glance at Sage, confirmed the absence of blood and bruises, but otherwise, spared her not a look. He dared not.

"You," Marck said, recognizing him from the Pub.

Simon ignored him. "Did he hurt you?" he asked Sage, without taking his eyes from the man in his sight. The SIG was looking Ian Marck in the eye, steadily.

"No," she said. And then he chanced a look at her again, saw the expression on her face . . . and that's when he knew. *She* knew. All about him.

His body turned cold, not with the fury that had consumed him, but with some other emotion he dared not define. He swallowed and tore his eyes from her, back to Ian Marck. The son of a bitch deserved to die. There was no reason not to pull the trigger.

This world was no man's land, every man for himself. Hadn't Marck helped to abduct Jade a month ago? And now he'd kidnapped Sage. Put his hands on her, tied her up . . . Simon noticed the red on her wrists, which was around them and definitely not from crystal grit.

"So you going to do it or what?" *Asshole.*

Simon jerked himself from the pit of his dark thoughts and his finger tightened on the trigger. He'd relish it. He looked at Sage, knowing his eyes were dark and wild, and said curtly, "Get out of here. You don't want to see this."

Her mouth rounded and she moved, as if to reach for him . . . but Simon, intent on proving to her that he was, indeed, not her fucking superman, not her goddamned hero, but exactly the man she thought he was . . . that she now *knew* he was . . . gave her a black look that brooked no disobedience. No tolerance. No tenderness.

She recoiled as if he'd slapped her—and he supposed he fairly well had, with his expression, and it was all right because it was necessary—and she ran out of the truck trailer.

Leaving him with the gun pressing into Ian Marck's jaw.

"On your knees," Simon ordered.

The man actually hesitated. "What, you don't want to get blood on you, asshole?"

Simon drew in a long, easy breath and smiled his death-smile. The SIG had a nice, long trigger . . . and he started to pull on it. "On your knees. Hands on your head."

Marck didn't move; instead, glared at him eye to eye, boldly and angrily. "Fuck you. I don't mind the mess. I won't be around to care."

His finger tightened a little more, he felt it slip into the second half, and he said, "Good-bye, Ian Marck."

CHAPTER 17

Sage heard the sharp report of a gunshot. It echoed inside the huge metal space she'd just left.

Simon . . . no.

Oh, God.

She brushed away the tears and realized her fingers were trembling. It wasn't for her. It was for him. Damn it.

When she'd first sensed Simon's presence, when he moved into the room, invisible, she'd had a surge of hope. But then she'd seen his face. The gun. The way he carried it, as if it were an extension of him.

Then, all of a sudden, Simon was here again, next to her. She looked up, searching his face, but it was just as empty and cold as it had been inside the room. She couldn't help it, she glanced behind him, looking, hoping for Marck to follow him.

"He's not coming out," Simon said. Flat and hard. His eyes locked on hers, so dark and angry that she nearly took a step back. "He deserved it for putting his hands on you. Are you hurt anywhere?"

"No," she said. She wanted to reach for him, to touch him, to see if she could find her Simon beneath this cold, statue of a man.

"What happened?" he asked. And she saw him adjust

the weapon in the waistband of his jeans, there just behind his left hip. "How'd he get you? Where's Theo?"

"Back in Envy, as far as I know," she retorted, allowing the anger into her voice. Damn him and the Theo game.

"He never came to pick you up?" Simon said, his voice showing the first bit of emotion—surprise—since she'd seen him.

"He got me, and we went back to Envy. I hit my head and blacked out when I was coming out of the tunnel, and he took me back so Elliott could look at me. Otherwise, we would have come into Falling Creek to look for you." She measured him boldly, trying to hide her confusion and sorrow. "Obviously, you weren't in need of our help."

"Florita is dead," he told her.

She nodded, her heart filling her throat. Another one dead. But at least she'd been a Stranger. And obviously not his lover.

And she'd meant to kill an entire city, just so she could have Simon. For a moment, Sage empathized with her.

"After she slit the throat of a girl she thought was you," Simon added. "In front of me." He moved his shoulders fluidly. "I don't take kindly to seeing women mistreated."

"Simon, why—"

"So you've done your research, I see." His beautiful mouth narrowed in a humorless smile. "Now you know who I am. So don't bother to ask why."

"But, Simon . . . that's not you."

It was his turn to step back. He looked like a fierce gang member—heck, he had been one, a long time ago—with his dark hair pulled back and the black T-shirt, black jeans he wore. And the gleaming handle of his pistol sticking out of his waistband. "It is me, Sage. You just didn't understand it until now. And now you do, and now you can put away those happy thoughts of me and get on with things."

He turned and started to walk away, then paused after a few steps. "Come on. Let's see if we can find that woman, and then we'll get you out of here. I've got things to do."

She followed, dazed and lost. Weary and slow. But she noticed the way his shoulders sagged, as though drawn down, and she thought again . . . *Simon, Simon . . . why? You didn't have to fall back into it. You didn't have to.*

He slowed so she could catch up to him, but he didn't look at her. She had to walk fast to keep up with his long strides, and she struggled to find something to say, to break through that barrier and find the man she loved and drag him back out.

Definitely. The man she loved. Not a surprise to her, that the word had definitely settled in her mind.

I think I've known since he asked me if I wanted to go into the Beretta building with him . . . instead of leaving me behind.

"Have you asked people about her?" he said, pausing and turning to look at her. No, not at her . . . over her head.

"There's a dark-haired woman who lives over there," she said, pointing to the row of townhouses. "And we checked out two already who lived in those old metal things, and one over in that little house over there. But this last one, she's been here about the right amount of time. So I'm sort of hopeful this is the one." She looked over at him, hopeful in another way. But there was nothing.

"All right," he said.

Sage led the way and knocked on the door of the building that had been pointed out to her. It took a moment, and there was a loud, gruff barking from inside, but finally the barking stopped and a woman opened the door enough to peek out. "Yes? Who are you?" she asked. "Are you here to see my work?"

She had long dark hair pulled back into a low tail, and she looked as if she were in her late twenties. Maybe thirty. Sage was struck by how strikingly pretty she was, and she couldn't help but glance at Simon to see his reaction. He seemed uninterested, his face immobile, waiting for her to talk.

"Um . . . I know this is going to sound odd, but we're looking for someone who might know Remington Truth. Or knew him. And we were told that a woman of your description was here, and had known him. Would that be you?"

The woman shook her head slowly. She had lovely blue-violet eyes with a black ring around the irises. "No, that name doesn't sound familiar to me. I'm sorry I can't help you."

She started to close the door, and Sage dug in her pocket, pulling out the ID badge. "This is a picture of him. Are you sure it doesn't look familiar?"

The woman glanced at the picture briefly and shook her head. "No, I'm sorry." She started to close the door again, but Simon stuck his foot in the way. "Pardon me?" she said, her voice sharpening.

The dog inside must have heard the change in his mistress's voice, because he started barking again. Loud and in warning.

"Did you say you had some work that we might look at?" Simon said. His voice sounded . . . normal now. Not that flinty cold tone he'd been using.

The woman's eyes narrowed at him. "What kind of work are you looking for?" The dog kept barking, sounding more and more agitated, and the woman turned to look back into the house. "Dantès! Enough!"

Sage's eyes widened and she looked at Simon, who, being much better at hiding his feelings—no kidding—merely gave her a brief nod of agreement.

When the woman turned back to them, Sage said, "Dantès. That's a character from one of my favorite books."

For the first time, the woman smiled. "Yes, *The Count of Monte Cristo*?" She shook her head. "I started reading that book a long time ago, and I never . . . well, I never finished it. So I named him"—she gestured inside, at the now-silent dog that was out of sight—"after Edmond Dantès from the book because I always wondered if he managed to get out of prison."

Sage nodded, smiling, knowing they'd found the right woman now. "He did. And he went on to become quite an amazing character. You ought to finish it some time."

"I would certainly like to," the woman said.

"And we'd like to see your work," Simon said. Pushing his foot a little more firmly through the door.

"What are you doing?" she asked, the rapport gone from her face.

"We know you knew Remington Truth," Simon said pleasantly. "Because we found that picture of him in your copy of *The Count of Monte Cristo* that you left in Falling Creek a few years ago."

The woman drew back and tried to close the door, but Simon's foot, and now his calf, had wedged in the way.

"What do you want?" she said. She didn't sound frightened, simply annoyed.

"We just want some information, we're not here to cause trouble. But I think it would be best to have this conversation inside the house." And he shifted so that the gun on his hip was obvious.

The woman's eyes widened, then lowered in acceptance. "Very well, then. Come in."

She opened the door and the two stepped into her small little home.

The type of work she did was immediately evident to Sage by the smell lingering within, and the items stacked around the room. "Pottery?" she asked, trying to be kind and to rebuild the rapport they'd had a moment earlier.

The woman nodded, but her face was still set angrily. Dantès, who was a very large, ferocious-looking dog on the other side of a small gate, barked again, sharply—as if to assess the situation. She turned to him with a sharp movement and he settled. "I don't allow him in here because he's more than a bit clumsy," she said, gesturing to the stacks of pots and plates and mugs.

"Now, what do you want from me?" she asked again.

"We just want to ask you a few questions, that's all," Sage told her. "But, first, let me introduce myself. I'm Sage, and this is Simon. And . . . you are?"

The woman sighed, her gaze sweeping over Sage. Reluctance oozing from her body, she shrugged and shifted her shoulders. "I'm Remington Truth."

CHAPTER 18

"You can't be Remington Truth," Sage said. "We're looking for an older white-haired man."

But Remington—if that was really her name—didn't answer. Instead, she walked over to one of the many shelves that held stacks of bowls, and vases and pitchers lined up. All of them were in dark purple, violet or indigo colors, slashed with black and speckled with pale blue.

If Sage were in the market for plates or a vase, she'd be happy with one of them.

When Remington turned, she held a gun in her hand. Pointing it at Simon, she said, "Put yours on the floor, there, Simon, if you please." Remington held the gun like she meant it, and her voice was cool and calm.

Insolence blaring from his every move, Simon withdrew the weapon from his jeans, and dropped it on the floor. Then, he kicked it toward their hostess, who reached to pick it up without her own weapon wavering.

Sage, who'd never seen a gun in her life before today, but had now seen three in the space of a couple hours, could hardly assimilate the situation. Was she living in some Jason Bourne movie?

Dantès, for his part, had remained silent and watchful

from his side of the gate, other than a brief little whine when Sage had exclaimed her disbelief at the woman's announcement.

"Why are you looking for Remington Truth? And yes, that's my real name," she added. "He was my grandfather. I was named for him."

Before Simon or Sage could answer, there was a knock at the door. A hard, impertinent pounding that prompted another warning yip from Dantès, followed by a deep-throated growl.

Remington glanced at them, and at the door, and seemed to make a decision to do nothing. "Sit, please," she said, gesturing to a sofa that might hold three people. If they squished.

Sage, unused to having a gun trained on her, sat, immediately. But Simon measured the woman, taking his time . . . although he did, at last, sit. Far enough away that they weren't touching, but close enough that he could grab her if he needed to.

The knocking on the door sounded again, and it was accompanied by a shout. "Simon! Sage! We know you're in there. Let us in, or we'll come in."

That sounded like Wyatt. *Wyatt?*

Remington frowned at the door, then, lips pursed, she walked closer to Sage and, pointing the gun at her forehead, said to Simon, "You answer the door. Let them in. No funny stuff, or she's got scrambled brains."

Simon glanced at Sage as if to assure her he wasn't about to let anything happen to her, and she noticed that that fierce, wild look had gone from his eyes. He looked like Simon again.

Her Simon.

He opened the door, slowly, and Sage heard him say,

"Hello, guys. We've got a bit of a situation in here, if you want to join us, you may. Though I don't recommend it, but if you must, just come in slowly."

The door opened and in filed Wyatt, Quent, and Theo. *Why the heck had he let them in?*

"You're *safe*," Theo said, looking at Sage. Then he snapped to a halt, frozen as he comprehended the tableau before him. She saw his eyes go from her to the woman holding the gun, and back again. The others did likewise and for a moment, the room was silent. "Uh, guess not?" Theo amended.

Remington had shifted slightly away from Sage to face the door, but the barrel was aimed at her. Their hostess was still vibrating with vigilance.

"How did you find me?" Sage asked, looking at Theo. How had they known where Ian Marck had taken her?

"Show me your hands," Remington ordered impatiently.

Wyatt, Quent, and Theo did as they were told, lifting their hands away from their bodies. Sage noticed that Simon had shifted to stand behind them, sort of out of the way . . . and she wondered if he had some plan in mind. Maybe he was going to turn invisible, hoping to do it without Remington noticing. *That could be why he let them in. Camouflage?*

Either that, or they wouldn't listen and stay outside, and . . . that could be a problem. For me.

Remington was in full control of the situation. "Now sit down, and keep your hands where I can see them. The first person who moves, I pull the trigger. And I'm a perfect shot."

Wyatt shifted and Remington snapped a look at him. "You don't believe me?" She moved suddenly, and there was a sudden sharp *ping*. Pottery smashed and clattered, tumbling from a shelf just behind Wyatt's shoulder, spilling down and over him and onto the floor.

"Holy fucking *shit*," Wyatt said, brushing at the shards on him. The bullet had nearly grazed the top of his shoulder and might even have trimmed off a bit of his hair. His face was slack with shock . . . then it faded to anger. "What the *hell*? I *breathed*!"

"I warned you." Remington looked around the room as if to say, *Who's next?*

Sage glanced over at Simon, desperate to warn him not to try anything, but he wasn't looking at her. *Simon! Don't be stupid.*

Theo sat down next to Sage, and Quent settled next to him, and that was all that could fit on that couch. Sage noticed that Quent had kept his hands in his lap, obviously unwilling to touch anything that could send him falling into memories . . . and Simon had continued to edge back, into a corner, without appearing to do so.

"Now, who are you and what are you doing here, ruining my day? Do you know how long I've been here, living happily, where no one's been able to find me? And now here you are, a whole parade of you forcing your way in here and screwing everything up."

Sage kept her mouth closed because she sensed the woman didn't really want an answer. She was just furious for being found.

But the more Sage looked at her, the more she believed that she was, really, Remington Truth—the granddaughter of the real one. Her eyes, for one, were the same. And she'd seen enough pictures of the man to recognize the set of her chin and the shape of her nose. Smaller and more feminine on the woman, but the resemblance was there.

Remington kept the gun trained on Sage, obviously aware that she was the weak point for a group of men, but she was backing away at the same time. "So, if you'll excuse me, I'll be on my way. Sorry I can't stay and be a better hostess. And I'm really pissed that I'm going to have to leave all my work behind!"

By this time, she'd reached the gate that confined Dantès, and, still keeping the gun trained on the group of them, she reached behind her and unlocked the gate.

The dog . . . no, good grief, now that he was in full light, Sage saw that he was a *wolf* . . . trotted out. The dog had to be well over a hundred twenty pounds of lean muscle. His head reached Remington's elbow, and his girth was as wide as Simon's shoulders.

Holy crap. Sage dared not even breathe.

"Dantès, guard," Remington said, and the hound moved to the center of the room and sat down.

He fairly quivered with attention, his ears straight up, his eyes bright and sharp. Wyatt drew in a deep breath, and Dantès swiveled to him, lifting his lip to show *huge* canines.

"Some dog," Theo breathed. And the wolf turned to fix him with his eyes, this time baring his teeth.

"Sorry I can't stay and visit any longer. I'm sure you have a great story to tell me, but now that you've ruined my life, I've got to get on the road again." Remington walked past the gate through which the dog had just come, obviously heading for a rear exit. She paused and added, "Don't worry. I'll send someone over to release Dantès in a few hours. But by then, I'll be long gone."

"You're going to leave him behind?" Wyatt asked, accusation in his voice. "Nice."

Remington turned and fixed her blue-violet eyes on him with loathing. "Don't worry about Dantès. He always finds me."

And then she was gone.

And there they sat, guarded by a wolfhound. Sage
turned to Theo, trying not to move enough to catch their
guard's attention, and trying not to think about the fact
that it had been a while since she'd peed. She didn't think
Dantès would understand if she asked to go. "How did
you know where to find me?" she said to Theo.

"Well, a friend of Quent's saw Marck abduct you, and
it really wasn't difficult to put two and two together once
we thought about it. Obviously, he gave us the clue that
sent you to Falling Creek, and it wasn't out of the goodness of his heart. We figured he wanted to know what
you'd found out, and it made sense that you were either
here or at Falling Creek. We came here first, on a hunch
. . . and we saw you and Simon knocking on this door."

Suddenly, Quent said, "Where the hell is Simon?"

Sage looked over to where he'd been, and, sure enough,
he was gone. He'd turned invisible and he'd begun to carefully ease the door open . . . ready to sneak out.

Dantès noticed, and the hackles rose at the back of his
neck. He growled and Sage gasped, "Simon, be careful!"

"Where is he?" Theo asked.

"Bugger me blind, is he *invisible*?" Quent said, noticing the door opening.

"Simon, I think he can *see* you!" cried Sage, as the dog
got up on all fours, showing all of his many teeth.

But then the door closed, and Simon was gone.

She swiveled back to look at Dantès, who'd sat back
down, but still glared at the door. With her movement, the
dog fixed his glittering eyes on Sage and she tried to sit
very still. And not look directly at him, in case he thought
she was challenging him.

Moments later, there was a sound from the back of the
house, and Dantès gave a low growl, but he didn't move.

The gate swung closed by an invisible hand, and then

Simon shimmered back into invisibility, on the other side of the gate.

"She's gone," Simon said. "By the time I got around the building, she was gone."

"Simon, be careful. He might be able to jump over the gate," Sage said.

"I'd expect he could if he wanted to," Wyatt agreed. "That is one fucking bad-ass dog. Simon, go see if you can find someone to release him. She said she would send someone."

"And you believed her?" Quent didn't move any muscle but his lips.

"She didn't lie about pulling the trigger," Wyatt replied.

Sage couldn't help a choked giggle. Not funny, but in a way . . . it was. And heck, if a girl was going to be in a standoff, a hostage, these were the men she'd want to be fellow captives with. Especially Simon, who didn't seem to be able to stop looking at her.

When she wasn't looking at him.

Theo looked at Dantès and said, "Dantès, *release*."

The wolf merely looked at him, curling his lip to show a very sharp, very lethal fang.

"Dantès, *leave it*," Theo tried again. "*Out?* Drop it?"

Wyatt shifted his stance in impatience, and the dog glared at him. "If it were that easy, he wouldn't make a very good guard. Usually, they have a keyword, like a password, that tells the dog to listen to someone not his or her master."

Sage didn't know much about dogs, but this gave her an idea. "Dantès," she said, and the dog's attention shifted to her. "Mercédès."

The ferocious expression on the wolf's face eased and she saw a light of recognition in his eyes. He wiggled in his seat. "Dantès," she said, her heart pounding, "release!"

And to her amazement . . . and the amazement of the others, the big dog rose to his feet and ambled over to her, butting her with his head. He seemed to be smiling! "Good dog," she said, patting him, but still more than a little leery about his size and ferocity.

"How did you know that?" Wyatt asked. When the dog looked at him, he added, "Dantès, Mercédès . . . come."

Sage had to admit, she was relieved when the beast moved away from her and went over to be petted by Wyatt. "Well, it's sort of obvious. He's named after Edmond Dantès in *The Count of Monte Cristo*, and Mercédès is the woman he loves. They go together."

Then, the first time since she'd released the dog, Sage looked up beyond the gate.

But Simon was gone.

Shimmering quietly, Simon watched as his friends filed out of the little townhouse. The rough trunk of a tree scraped the back of his arm, and the cool shadow felt good after the warm sun.

Where the hell had Remington Truth gone? Yeah, it had taken him a few minutes to get out of the house, and then because it was a long building, he had to run all the way around the back . . . but still.

She had to be very fast, or very clever.

Speaking of clever . . .

His eyes were pulled to Sage as she stepped out of the townhouse, down the well-kept stairs. Theo hovered over her, which just made Simon get all tight and black inside.

Someone had to have seen the woman go. Simon would take his time to speak with everyone in this little town, then set off to find her. And let Sage and Theo head back to Envy.

But they'd moved off to the side, and Simon, still shimmering invisibly, found himself drawn toward them. He hated himself for doing it . . . he knew it was an invasion, he knew it was repulsive, like looking in the panty drawer of a friend's sister . . . but something compelled him.

Silent, he eased nearer as Theo and Sage stopped beneath a large oak.

As he came closer, he heard Sage explaining what had happened with Ian Marck—some of the details even he hadn't heard.

"Where's Marck now?" Theo asked.

Sage looked down. "Simon took care of him. He's dead." Simon watched her face, but he couldn't see her expression.

"Bastard."

Sage looked back up. "Don't say that," she said, her voice sharp, her eyes steely. "He's a good man. Just a little . . . lost." Now her words turned sad. Simon's heart stopped and he nearly lost his concentration, grabbing it back just before he turned opaque again. She still cared about him?

How could she?

"How can you defend the man? He kidnapped Jade, he kidnapped you—"

"Oh. I thought you were talking about Simon." Sage gave a little laugh.

Theo shook his head, and though Simon couldn't see his face, he recognized the sag of his shoulders. "It's not going to work, is it? You and me?"

No. Simon shook his head, silently, invisibly. *Don't give up on her,* vato.

But Sage was shaking her head, now looking up at Theo. "It's Simon. He's the one. I'm sorry, Theo, I'm so sorry, but I think I've known it . . . well, for a long time. Since before FC."

Before FC? Before she knew about my ability?

Theo shifted on his feet, clearly uncomfortable. "I'd like to take a few shots at the guy, you need to know that, Sage. But I'm not going to stand in your way, though . . . I don't even know where he went."

Sage nodded slowly. "I think he's gone."

Theo moved to pull her into his arms, but Sage stepped back. "I need a few minutes, okay? Then . . . we can head back to Envy. And I'll figure out what to do then."

Reluctance in every movement, Theo turned and started back toward Wyatt and Quent, who'd been talking to other members of the settlement. Simon recognized the expression on Theo's face—the agony and pain, trying to be subdued . . . but when it was that deep, it's fucking hard.

Then, suddenly, Sage was there, right next to him. "Don't you ever do that again," she was saying, pointing and shaking her finger at him. Sort of.

She was off by about a foot, aiming toward the tree, but in the general vicinity of the height of his face. "Dammit, Simon, show yourself. Right now."

He couldn't hold it any longer, and shimmered back into himself. "Sage," he began, trying to think of a way to excuse his horrible invasion, "I—"

"Just be quiet." She glared up at him, tears sparkling in her aqua blue eyes.

That did it. The tears. He couldn't stop himself and the next thing he knew, she was in his arms, and he was kissing that beautiful, freckled mouth that had driven him crazy since he first saw her.

She wrapped her arms around him, kissing him back

just as breathlessly, just as hungrily. "Simon, please . . . don't leave," she said, pulling away just long enough for that entreaty.

"I can't believe you want me to stay . . . after all . . . after everything," he said, searching her eyes. The tears had gone, and what he saw there gave him hope. Warmth and love.

"You heard what I told Theo," she said, a bit of that accusation back again. "It's you. It's only going to be you." She stroked his hair. "I think I fell in love with you when you asked me to go into the Beretta with you. Because you trusted me and you gave me credit for . . ."

"For your brains. You're a damn smart woman, Sage. Not to mention the most gorgeous woman I've ever met." He closed his eyes for a minute, resting his forehead against hers. "I've done a lot of things I'm not proud of," he said quietly, and felt her tense, ready to reply. "Let me finish," he said quickly. "You'll never know half of it. But . . . the fact that you trust me and believe in me, even though you know about my past . . . I couldn't ask for any better blessing."

"Simon." She said his name so sweetly it hurt. "I know the man you are—trustworthy, brave, fierce, and honest. That's who you are to me."

He shook his head in amazement. "I love you."

She smiled. "I know that. I just didn't understand why you felt the need to hide it. Did you not think I could follow my own heart?"

"Maybe I was being a little too rigid," he said.

"Rigid? How about ridiculous?" She smiled up at him, with such love in her eyes that he wondered how he could ever have been so stupid as to think he could live without her.

Joy and delight overwhelmed him and he tugged her

close for another kiss, just to feel the warmth and softness of her body . . . for real. Without the guilt. Without being watched.

But then, they were.

"Hey. Yo." Wyatt's sharp call interrupted whatever might have happened next. "Guess what."

Simon, feeling a little awkward as his arm slipped around Sage's waist, nevertheless sucked it up, and they turned to face the other men. He met Theo's eyes head-on in masculine understanding. "Yeah?"

"Truth's gone. Someone saw her get into a truck with a man. Big guy, blondish hair."

"Fuck." *Should have hit the* chavala *harder, dammit.* "Was he forcing her?"

Wyatt shook his head. "No, as a matter of fact, according to the witness, she was the one in control. Apparently, she had a gun and was pointing it at him, forcing him into the vehicle . . . because she didn't know how to drive it. And apparently he did."

Simon almost laughed. Almost. "The guy?"

Wyatt nodded. "Yeah, he was moving a little slowly—had a big bump on the side of his head, blood on his shirt. Someone saw him come out of one of those trailers over there, sort of staggering a bit, and the woman must have found him by the truck. The witness didn't get too close, of course, but said Truth was ordering him into the vehicle. Then they drove off."

Now Simon couldn't hold back a chuckle. "Serve him right, being stuck with her."

"Who? What are you talking about?" Sage asked, but there was suspicion in her eyes. She turned on him. "You didn't really kill Ian Marck, did you?"

What could he say? He shook his head. "Couldn't do it. That part of my life is over," he replied, fully aware that everyone could hear. But he didn't care that they heard, that they knew, that his past was exposed.

Because she loved him . . . had loved him even when she thought the worst of him. And that was all he needed.

Wyatt was still chuckling. "So Remington Truth kidnapped Ian Marck at gunpoint?"

"Yeah, but I'm still wondering where they got the truck," Simon said. "I've got my keys, and Marck's keys."

Theo looked at Quent, who looked at Wyatt, who patted his jeans pocket. Then his other, and then the back pockets.

"Fuck," was all he said.

EPILOGUE

"So," Sage said, sitting up as Simon came into the room. She patted the bed next to her and watched as he stripped off his T-shirt and jeans. She never tired of watching him, eyeing those fluid muscles and sleek movements.

"So . . . what?" he asked, standing next to the bed.

"Sorry," she said. "Lost my train of thought for a minute there." She smiled and the look he gave her was enough to melt her into a puddle of butter. "You and Theo . . . talk? Everything okay?"

He shrugged. "It's not going to be pretty for a while, but he's a reasonable guy. He'll get used to things."

"Did you talk?"

He frowned at her. "Talk? Men don't talk. We went a few rounds—"

"A few *rounds*?" Sage gaped, her eyes wide. "You *fought*?"

"Not like that. We played basketball. Shot some hoops. Not very politely, but at least no one got hurt. Well, much."

"What?"

He shook his head. "Don't worry about it. He needed to get it out of his system, and I know how to take care of myself. Both of us are still walking. Now . . . what was it you said about being distracted?" He slid onto the bed, leaning forward to kiss her.

Sage kissed him back, long and thoroughly, glad at last to have a bed without a camera tracing their every move.

"God, you taste so good," he said, his hand moving to slide down her arm and around to pull her closer.

"Any news about Remington Truth and Ian Marck?" she asked, pulling back just a bit. Her hand traced the muscles of his pecs, smooth and warm and solid. They shifted beneath her fingers as he tilted back a bit to look at her.

"Not yet. Quent is studying some things from her house, slowly, you know, because of the memories, and Wyatt's keeping an eye on the dog for the time being. When and if Dantès goes after his mistress, he'll have company. But for now," he said, "I'm really not interested in anything but this . . . right . . . here."

She sighed and arched into him, the warmth of his mouth on her, sleek and tender, licking, nibbling, sucking . . .

"Simon," she said, shivering deep inside. "I'm curious . . . Will you try something out for me?"

"Does it involve our two naked bodies?" he murmured into her breast, his voice vibrating against her nipple.

"Most definitely," she sighed.

"Then, yes." He looked up at her, hot and curious.

"You know that shivery feeling you get—or at least, I get it—when we turn invisible?" she said, smoothing her hand down his bicep, a little shy about asking . . . but too curious not to. "Well, I was thinking . . . what would it feel like if you did that . . . while we were kissing. And stuff."

His eyes widened with delight and lust. "Let's find out." He bent forward, and as his mouth covered hers, she felt the wave of warmth and desire she always felt . . . and then the little sparkly, shimmery sensation on top of it.

The blast of sensation took her by surprise, and suddenly Simon reappeared in front of her. He too looked wide-eyed and shocked, but then a very naughty smile curved his beautiful lips. "Let's try that again . . . I don't know how long I'll be able to concentrate, because you blow my mind . . . but I'm all for it."

"It'll be great discipline for you," she suggested impishly. And leaned up to kiss him, and reached down to curl her fingers around him.

The beautiful feeling settled over her, shivery and sparkly, and they slipped off into a hot maelstrom of love, and passion . . . and invisible shimmers.

AVON

978-0-06-172880-8

978-0-06-172783-2

978-0-06-112404-4

978-0-06-157826-7

978-0-06-185337-1

978-0-06-154781-2

At Avon Books, we know your passion for romance—once you finish one of our novels, you find yourself wanting more.

May we tempt you with . . .

- **Excerpts** from our upcoming releases.
- Entertaining **extras**, including authors' personal photo albums and book lists.
- Behind-the-scenes **scoop** on your favorite characters and series.
- **Sweepstakes** for the chance to win free books, romantic getaways, and other fun prizes.
- Writing **tips** from our authors and editors.
- **Blog** with our authors and find out why they love to write romance.
- **Exclusive content** that's not contained within the pages of our novels.

Join us at
www.avonbooks.com

AVON

An Imprint of HarperCollins*Publishers*
www.avonromance.com

Available wherever books are sold or please call 1-800-331-3761 to order.